Undertaker's Resurrection

Book 1 Dark Patriots

by Ciara St James

Copyright

Copyright 2022 Property of Ciara St James LLC. All rights reserved, as this is the property of Ciara St James LLC.

The characters and events portrayed in this book are fictitious. Any similarity to real persons, living or dead, is coincidental and not intended by the author.

No part of this book may be reproduced, or stored in a retrieval system, or transmitted in any form or by any means, electronic, mechanical, Photocopying, recording, or otherwise, without express written permission of the publisher, Ciara St James LLC

ISBN: 978-1-955751-33-9

Printed in the United States of America
Editing by Mary Kern @ Ms. K Edits
Book cover by Tracie Douglas @ Dark Waters Covers

Blurb

Five long years, Undertaker has been gone. He has been presumed dead. In reality, he's been risking his life to take down scum. In the beginning, he loses his memory and doesn't know who he is. However, once he regains it, he sticks to his course. Finally, the day has come, and he's free to go home to his family and friends. Only he knows there will be hell to pay when he gets there for his deception.

Feelings are hurt and the road to forgiveness is hard, but he's not giving up. All he wants to do now is settle back at home and run his business with his friends. Only, his past reputation as Undertaker, doesn't let him go so easily. When an old friend comes asking for his help, he can't say no. Not to a fellow SEAL. He's willing to go back into hell to bring his friend and his wife peace of mind.

He thought he would be providing guidance, only to find he needed to go back undercover. Except this time, he won't be going alone.

Sloan is a tough former Marine who loves her job. She's used to danger and is willing to jump into anything. When faced with a resurrected boss she never met, she's left breathless. Luckily, he feels the same. Only can they make this work, especially when it looks like her past will make her the ideal one to partner with Undertaker on his new mission? He says no. She insists. In the end, they put both their lives on the line to save lives, help a friend, and to make the world a better place. Come see how Undertaker's Resurrection leads to a life neither he nor Sloan ever imagined.

Warning

This book is intended for adult readers. It contains foul language, adult situations, discusses events such as stalkers, assault, torture and murder that may trigger some readers. Sexual situations are graphic. There is no cheating, no cliffhangers, and it has a HEA.

Dedication

This book is dedicated to the men and women who sacrifice their lives every day to ensure the world is a safer place for all of us. I know we never know all that you do or can say thank you enough. Know that your sacrifices are appreciated. Thank you.

Dark Patriots Members/ Ladies

Mark O'Rourke (Undertaker) w/ Sloan
Sean Walterson w/ Cassidy
Gabe Pagett w/ TBD
Griffin Voss w/ TBD

Reading Order

For Dublin Falls Archangel's Warriors MC (DFAW), Hunters Creek Archangel's Warriors MC (HCAW), Iron Punishers MC (IPMC), Dark Patriots (DP)

Terror's Temptress DFAW 1
Savage's Princess DFAW 2
Steel & Hammer's Hellcat DFAW 3
Menace's Siren DFAW 4
Ranger's Enchantress DFAW 5
Ghost's Beauty DFAW 6
Viking's Venus DFAW 6.5 (free novella)
Viper's Vixen DFAW 7
Devil Dog's Precious DFAW 8
Blaze's Spitfire DFAW 9
Smoke's Tigress DFAW 10
Hawk's Huntress DFAW 11
Bull's Duchess HCAW 1
Storm's Flame DFAW 12
Rebel's Firecracker HCAW 2
Ajax's Nymph HCAW 3
Razor's Wildcat DFAW 13
Capone's Wild Thing DFAW 14
Falcon's She Devil DFAW 15
Demon's Hellion HCAW 4
Torch's Tornado DFAW 16
Voodoo's Sorceress DFAW 17
Reaper's Banshee IPMC 1

Bear's Beloved HCAW 5
Outlaw's Jewel HVAW 6
Undertaker's Resurrection DP 1

Reading order for Ares Infidels MC

Sin's Enticement AIMC 1
Executioner's Enthrallment AIMC 2
Pitbull's Enslavement AIMC 3
Omen's Entrapment AIMC 4
Cuffs' Enchainment AIMC 5
Rampage's Enchantment AIMC 6
Wrecker's Ensnarement AIMC 7
Trident's Enjoyment AIMC 8

Please follow Ciara on Facebook, For information on new releases & to catch up with Ciara, go to www.ciara-st-james.com or www.facebook.com/ciara.stjames.1 or www.facebook.com/groups/tenilloguardians

Mark: Prologue – 5 Years Ago

I hated to leave Cassidy alone like this. I knew that Sean, Griffin, and Gabe would look out for her while I was gone on this assignment. It should be a simple extraction of a high-value target and then a quick plane ride back to the States, with delivery into the hands of those who would ensure the informant testified. Sean had volunteered to make the trip, but he'd gone the last three times when it was my turn.

None of them complained, but I was letting them carry more of the load when it came to assignments that took us away from Virginia. They were all understanding and said that I needed to be close in case Cassidy needed me. The last few years have been tough. We lost our dad, who'd been a big part of the company and our sole parent for many years. I was the only family she had left. Even if she wasn't a kid, she still needed her big brother to make sure she was safe and cared for. She might technically be an adult, but to me, she would always be my kid sister. I didn't want her involved in this particular assignment. Something about it didn't feel right to me.

I blamed Dad for the reason she took such an interest in our company, Dark Patriots. She wasn't satisfied to be an analyst or do research and back us up from the safety of the office. She wanted to be out on missions. I couldn't keep her out of all of them, though I tried to keep her away from the worst ones. She'd asked to be part of it when she turned eighteen and I had stupidly said yes, thinking she'd help in the office. She was smart, and I knew she'd pick up on anything we asked her to do. The only way to get her away from it would be to fire her and if I did that, I'd probably lose her all together. I wasn't willing to risk it.

I couldn't use the excuse that she had no skills because she did. My dad, me, Sean, Gabe, and Griffin, all saw to it that she could handle her own shit and then some. She was a sharpshooter with any gun you gave her and her knife work was almost as good. She had hand-to-hand combat training. It just wasn't what I wanted her to be doing with her life. I wanted her at home, married to some normal guy, baking cookies, and raising a family, living the American Dream. She was vocal when she told me if I thought that was the dream, I should settle down and bake some cookies and stay at home. It was an ongoing argument.

I didn't want to argue with her this time about the assignment. She'd want to come, and I didn't want her anywhere near the man I was bringing back. He was in bed with a one-percenter motorcycle club that was nothing but bad news and they'd found he was cheating them. He had run and now he had to live to testify if he wanted any chance of surviving. She was young, beautiful and everything a man would want. I wanted her far away from the likes of him. No need to expose her to that kind of man or the life he had lived.

Which was why I boarded this plane without

telling her I was leaving, when I'd be back, or even who I was going after. I'd wait to get my ass chewed when I got back home. I didn't care. I took one last look to be sure we hadn't been followed, then closed the door to the small plane. Luis Latoya was huddled in one of the seats. Three other guards, hired to be the muscle by Uncle Sam, were scattered around the plane.

The government thought Latoya would be their way into the Tres Locos MC and if they could get inside, they could take them down from within. I hated to tell them no one would believe the clean-cut boys they sent along on this trip would fool anyone. I'd heard they were thinking of sending these men undercover. Every damn one of them would be coming home in a body bag before the first day was done.

There were too many intricacies in an MC you had to know to navigate, on top of looking and acting the part. Slapping on a few tats wouldn't do the trick. Hell, I looked more like a biker with my tattoos, long hair and dangerous vibe. That's what eight years as a Navy SEAL got you. My dad had taught me a lot about the MC life growing up—how to act, what to look for and how to play the games. He'd learned it as a young man in a one-percenter club in the seventies. He'd gotten out of that life when I came along and then, years later, he and Mom had Cassidy. He made his final break for his family. He didn't want us living that life. However, he taught us about it, so we'd know how it was, just in case we ever met up with one.

I sat down to read the Locos' file one more time and then maybe nap for a bit. We had a five-hour flight to Virginia from California, our layover spot. I'd read through the file we had on Luis and the Tres Locos and then I'd get an hour or two nap if I was lucky. I wanted to know the material inside and out about this club and this man. Why? Because he had my gut screaming that there was something we didn't know. I needed to find out what it was.

An hour later, as I closed my eyes, I could picture everything that MC was doing and how I'd handle the takedown if I was the one doing it. As I dreamed, something started to nag at the back of my mind. I jerked awake to find the others all in a panic. They were running around the plane. Latoya was staring out his window, looking terrified.

"What the fuck is going on?" I growled as I sat back up.

"The plane is going down. Something is wrong with the engine. The pilot says we're not going to make it to an airport," one of the men hurriedly explained as he sat down to buckle himself in. Another one was frantically talking on the plane's phone.

The third one added more. "It had to be sabotaged. Someone knew we were transporting this fucker and now we're all going to die." He spit at Latoya, who was sitting frozen. I unhooked my belt and made my way to the cockpit. The pilot and copilot were frantically working on the various dials, levers, and buttons.

I didn't waste their time. "Are we crashing, and how soon?"

The copilot gave me a grim look. "We are and we'll try for a flat, open area if we can. All you can do is buckle in and pray we can find a safe spot to land. We've lost the left engine almost completely. Some kind of explosion."

I didn't argue. I went back to the others and told them, "Take your damn seats, buckle your asses in, and stay there. Curl your head down and put your hands behind your neck when they tell you to brace for impact."

I took a seat next to Latoya and made sure not only to buckle my seatbelt, but to cuff myself to him. He gave me a weird look, but I didn't care. My luck, he'd survive without a scratch and run. If I died, he'd have to drag my corpse to get away or saw off my fucking arm. He wasn't getting out of this.

It was a blur of announcements, and my heart raced as I prayed. *Don't let this be the end. Don't let me never see Cassidy or my friends again. Lord, if you get me out of this, I'll never leave without talking to her again. Don't let me die because of Tres Locos and Luis Latoya.*

Mark: Prologue- 4 Years Ago

I checked the darkness to make sure I was really alone. I had to be sure, before I made this meeting, that no one had followed me. If they did, I was dead and so were the men I was meeting. Seeing no one or any movement, I walked toward the abandoned building. I made sure to walk in the deep shadows, going slowly and to keep scanning. As I got close to the door, I gave a three-toned whistle and listened to hear if it was repeated. It was. Here goes everything. I took a deep breath and stepped inside.

It took my eyes a moment to adjust, and I knew I was the most vulnerable then. I kept to the wall and low, as I slowly scanned the building and then my eyes landed on three men who I'd know anywhere. I heard Sean swear, "Son of a bitch, it sure looks like him."

"Of course it's me, you mangy cur. I told you when I called it was me," I growled back, feeling a little impatient, which wasn't fair. It had been a year. They cautiously came toward me. I saw they didn't put down their guns, and neither did I. When we all met in the middle, I could see the strain on their faces and the hope. I lowered my gun and held out my hand.

Sean broke first, lowered his gun, and grabbed my

hand. Then he pulled me in for a hug. I was passed around like a pack of smokes in prison. When they finally had squeezed me enough to prove I was real, I stepped back. "Damn, it's good to see you guys. How's it going?"

"How's it going? Is that all you have to say after letting us think you were dead for a year? What the fuck, Mark? You gutted us and Cassidy, and that's how you're going to play this?" Sean snapped.

I felt myself flush with anger. Did they think I'd been on a fucking vacation? I'd literally been treading water to stay the fuck alive. I shouldn't even be talking to them. Should I go and tell them to forget about me? There was no way I could walk away from what I was doing now. "I'm not playing shit, Sean. I didn't mean to gut anyone, especially Cassidy. How is she?"

"We know you wouldn't have done this without a good reason. Cassidy is alright. She takes things one day at a time like the rest of us. She misses you and still wants you to walk through the door, so she'll be pissed rather than thrilled to see you," Gabe answered.

"I can't let her see me and you can't tell her that I'm alive. I can't come back yet."

"Why the hell not?" Griffin exploded and yelled.

"Why're we here if not to bring you home? Tell us what's happening. Where have you been? What have you been doing?" Gabe demanded.

"Take a seat. This'll take a while." We all sat down on some old equipment. "Okay, remember I was on the plane bringing Latoya back?" They all nodded yes. "I was studying his file and everything Tres Locos when I fell asleep. I woke up to find the plane was having issues due to a blown engine and they were going to crash land, which we did. The agents onboard thought it had been sabotaged. The pilot said there was an explosion."

"We know about the plane. We saw what was left of it. We went to look for you and there was no sign of you or Latoya. They said your bodies had to have been ejected and thrown God knows where. We searched miles of that damn mountainside. Nothing. We searched on and off for over a month," Sean snarled.

"Will you listen and let me finish, then I'll answer your questions?" They all sat back silently and watched me. "You're right, we went down hard in the mountains. I can't even describe the sounds or feel. I must have blacked out after hitting my head. When I came to, I was miles from the plane wreckage, but I was still with Latoya. I'd handcuffed his ass to me when the plane started to go down. We'd been ejected together. He was in bad shape and I wasn't a whole lot better, though not delirious like he was." I paused to take a moment before I hit them with the next part. "The reason I didn't stick around the crash site was I didn't want to get caught."

"Get caught for what?" Griffin asked.

"Caught by the feds. Guys, all I could remember was the Tres Locos and that they wanted Latoya. I think my mind focused on that and not on what had happened. I couldn't remember my name other than Undertaker." They hissed in surprise. That was my old Navy SEAL nickname.

"Something kept pushing me to go to the Tres

Locos and deliver Latoya to them. I knew that I had to do it, but not why. Anyway, I found them despite Latoya trying to get away every step of the way and mumbling nonsense. By the time we made it to them, which took a few days, Latoya was more or less on death's door. He had injuries that I couldn't do more than field dress. He was delirious with fever."

"How did you get in or approach them? Weren't they suspicious?" Sean asked with a note of disbelief in his voice.

"I walked up to their compound and knocked on the damn door. When they answered, I told them I had something of theirs and threw Latoya at them. They were suspicious, of course, and they were less than welcoming for a few days as they questioned me. But nothing they did compared to our old training. In the end, they couldn't break me or get me to change my story. Believe me, they tried."

"What story did you tell them?" Gabe asked, sitting forward to get closer. I could see the interest on his face.

"Since I couldn't remember more than who they were, that I needed to get to them for some reason, and that I'd been on the plane with Latoya, they assumed I was a prisoner they were transporting on the same flight. I ran with it. I told them how the plane went down and that they had the two of us chained together. We were the only survivors, and I knew Latoya was important to them.

"All he did was yap about it as we were transporting him, so it was easy to sell that. He was in no condition to tell them I was working for the feds to help bring him to trial. I'm tattooed with long hair and I can fight, cuss and anything else you'd expect a biker to do. I pretended to be a nomad biker. I played it cool, like I needed to get back to the open road after I figured out what the feds did with my bike. They held me for a month and it was no picnic, but in the end, I'd fed them enough bullshit, they believed it. For all I knew, I was a biker of some kind. I knew all about the life. Latoya never got better and eventually died, so that ended that. They eventually asked me if I wanted to prospect for them and I said yes."

"So, you're telling us you had amnesia and joined a fucking one-percenter MC that's on the feds' top-ten most-wanted list and you've been with them for a year?" Sean almost screamed. He was pacing and running his hands through his hair.

"That's exactly what I'm telling you. It wasn't until a month ago that I started having dreams. It was bits and pieces of you guys, Cass, and my life. I didn't know what it all meant until finally it was like a light switch flipped all the way on and everything came back to me. I realized I knew so much about the MC life from what Dad taught me growing up. That, along with what was in that file and what Latoya spilled, is how I was able to fool them for the past year. I knew I needed to get in touch, so I worked out a way to do it without them knowing."

"Jesus, that's incredible. Come on, let's get out of here and someplace nicer so we can chat more, get you cleaned up and get Cassidy. She's going to lose it when she sees you, bro," Gabe said with a big smile on his face.

"I can't go back with you and you can't tell Cassidy or anyone else that I'm alive. I told you that."

Their stunned and disbelieving looks made my gut clench. I hated to do it, but I knew it was the only way. They had no idea the shit the Tres Locos were dealing in.

"Are you smoking crack? Like hell we're not telling Cassidy. You're coming with us, even if we have to carry you," Sean growled.

"Listen, I'm in now and they trust me. I'm a fully patched member and though I'm entry level, I'm starting to see a lot of shit they do. I know the goal was to take them down. The agents they were going to send in wouldn't have lasted a day. I've seen them kill a couple of guys they thought were feds. I'm in. I can do what the government has been trying to do for years—help bring down the Locos. But in order to do it, I have to maintain deep cover. That means no contact with anyone. Even though they trust me, I could be dead at the drop of a hat. I can't risk exposing you and her to them. They wouldn't hesitate to use you all against me, especially Cassidy. The way they treat women is disgusting."

"You want us to keep the fact you're alive a secret from even your sister? That's fucking so wrong, Mark," Gabe said as he frowned.

"I know it is, but it's to keep her safe. Let's face it, what I'm doing is dangerous as hell. I could get killed. She's already through the bulk of her mourning. I don't want to chance it happening again. Besides, with the way they are, I should be able to take them down in less than a year. I won't risk them coming after me and finding her. Come on, give me time. Help me, but do it from afar," I pleaded.

I knew I had to do this no matter what, because the shit I'd already seen this club do made my skin crawl. I felt dirty just being near them. However, under deep cover, you had to assume the skin and get dirty. I was there, and I wasn't going to back out. Those bastards were going to go down if it was the last thing I did.

They all stood silent for several minutes. I waited rather impatiently. The clock was ticking, and I needed to get back before they missed me or got suspicious. Finally, after what felt like forever, Sean nodded reluctantly. "Okay, let's set up a way to communicate. You have to have that at least. It'll remain between us. We won't tell her, but you know she's going to be royally pissed in a few months when you appear and tell her what you were doing. Be prepared."

"I know it and I will be. Thanks, guys. I really need to do this. So, here's what I was thinking…"

Undertaker: Prologue- Spring 2011- Two Years Ago

Two years, I couldn't fucking believe it. I rolled out of bed after pushing the woman half lying on top of me away. I looked at her. I didn't even remember her name—just some woman I picked up in a bar who thought it would be fun to sleep with a biker. I smacked her naked ass lightly. She jolted awake and looked at me. In the light of day, she was looking worse for wear with her hair messed up and mascara smeared around her eyes.

"You need to get dressed. It's morning and I have work to do." I grabbed my pants and tugged them on as she lay there watching me. She had what I guess she thought was a sexy smile on her face. One I vaguely remembered from last night. In my alcohol-soaked brain, it looked sexy. Now, it was just sad.

"Why don't we have a proper good morning, then we can have breakfast?" she asked coyly, as she ran her hands down her naked body. A naked body that wasn't even making my cock twitch. It was always this way after I gave in to my need for sex. Afterward, I felt dirty and wanted nothing to do with the woman again. It usually pissed them off, but I was clear before we ever got naked that it was a one-time deal. In the life I was living, you didn't get serious with a woman and certainly not a barfly or one of the club girls. Most of them caused trouble by just breathing.

"Nope, I've got shit to do. I need you to get up. You can use the shower if you want, just don't take all day. I need to shower, too." I'd be a gentleman and let her go first.

"We can shower together and save water," she said as she got up and shimmied her hips as she passed me. She stopped at the doorway to the bathroom and looked back at me with her brows raised. She had a pout on her face. I shook my head.

"No thanks, hurry up. I don't want to be late for work." Her expression got dark and pissed. She stomped into the bathroom and slammed the door. I sighed in relief. I sat down on the edge of the motel bed. I never took anyone to the compound. Even if I didn't plan to see the women again, I tried to protect them from the club. They treated women like interchangeable socks and they shared them whether they wanted it or not. I might be a dick at times, but I never forced a woman or called her names like they did. I laid out the rules before we ever went to a motel or her place.

As I waited for her to get done, I thought back over the last two years. Two fucking more years had passed with me being stuck with Tres Locos. They'd been harder to take down than I imagined and then, as I found more and more, we didn't want to take them down without getting all their pipelines. They were into so much illegal shit, it made my head spin—drugs, smuggling, gun dealing, prostitution, arson, extortion, and muscle for hire. You name it, they did it. They were the lowest form of humans on the planet and I wanted to exterminate all of them, including the ones who helped them or profited from what they did. We consisted of me, my Dark Patriot brothers and the feds. Sean, Gabe, and Griffin found a way to work with them as their black ops team that infiltrated the club. The guys wouldn't share anything about who they might have inside, but the information I did get, I secretly fed to our company, and they passed it along.

I looked at the clock. Today was the day. Cassidy was going undercover to help take down a human trafficking ring in the Middle East. I hated she was doing that kind of work and so were the guys, especially Sean. However, she was the only female operative that fit the bill. What killed me even more was they were working with another MC to do it! I never imagined after experiencing the Locos that an MC could actually be a decent one, but apparently, this one was. The guys had worked with them a little before and said they were a legit club. I knew they wouldn't be helping them or letting Cassidy near them if they weren't the real deal. Apparently, their hacker worked with Anderson. That said enough. He'd been in the government for ages and everyone knew his name. If he trusted this Smoke guy, then so would I. I'd take all the help we could get.

I took a moment to pray.

Dear Lord, look out for my little sister and keep her, the other woman going in with her and the team safe. Bring them all home. And Lord, if you get a chance, help me to get this wrapped up so I can go home, too. I don't know how much longer I can take this. I'm starting to feel like this will never end. Amen.

Undertaker: Prologue - Present Day

I breathed in the cold crisp late December air. It always smelled so clean this time of year in Virginia. The trees were bare. The plants might be dead and brown, but the hint of snow always made it smell fresh. I'd missed my home in Hampton. Though it was only a five-and-a-half-hour ride from Princeton, West Virginia, home base of the Tres Locos, to here, it had seemed like another planet. I'd only made the drive twice in five years, not wanting to risk exposing myself or my family.

I took several moments to soak in the view. I was looking at what had been my house all my life. The guys had kept it up, and even after Cassidy moved out and in with Sean, they refused to sell it. I was still trying to come to grips that my little sister was all grown up and married to my best friend, Sean, and they had a little baby, a son, Noah Mark Walterson. He was over a month old.

I shook off the memories of when Sean told me he was in love with her, that they were living together, and he wanted to marry her. I could think of those later. First, I had to stop procrastinating and get my ass in the house. They were waiting on me. Sean didn't want to tell Cassidy anything in advance. I was afraid it would be too much of a shock, but he felt it would be better to do it all at once. If they told her I was alive, she'd insist on seeing me immediately.

Since I didn't have a key anymore, I walked up to the front door and rang the doorbell. My palms were sweating even in the cold. A minute later, the door opened and there stood Gabe. He gave me a man hug and stepped back so I could come inside. "She's in the kitchen," he whispered.

"Who is it, Gabe? Why in the world would anyone ring the doorbell here? Don't they know it's empty?" I could hear an underlying tone of pain in her voice. My knees weakened, hearing her voice after all this time. I was frozen. Gabe pushed me forward a few steps, then shut the door.

"Shit, maybe this isn't such a good idea, Gabe. She just had a baby and the shock of seeing me might be too much. We need to think this through and come up with another plan," I hissed to him. He frowned and shook his head.

Before I could turn and leave, I heard her voice getting closer as she said, "Sean, I swear, leave me alone. I want to see who's at the door. It's taking Gabe too long."

"Sorry, Cass, I'm coming. Stay there," Gabe yelled back. I'd taken one step backward when she popped around the corner that separated the kitchen from the living room slash entry. Sean was right behind her. She stopped dead in her tracks. Her mouth dropped open. I saw disbelief, fear, pain, and then maybe a tiny glimmer of hope in her eyes. I stood my ground and tried to smile.

"Hi, Cassie."

Her hand came up to cover her mouth. Tears formed in her eyes and rolled down her cheeks. "M-Mark, is that really you?" She sobbed. I could see she was shaking.

"Yeah, it's really me, little sister."

She took off running across the room and flung herself into my waiting arms. I hugged her tight and closed my eyes so I could savor her smell. She always smelled like strawberries, which was her favorite shampoo and bodywash, for as long as I could remember. She felt a little different. Her body was softer, but then again, she did just have a baby.

When I was done hugging her, I pushed her back a little so I could look at her. Her eyes were red and wet, but she was smiling. "Oh my God, I can't believe this. How is it possible? Where? How? When? I have so much to tell you," she said in one long breath. I laughed. That was her when she got excited.

Sean had come up behind her. He took her gently by the shoulders. "Let's let him take a seat and then he can explain, babe." He led her to the sofa.

She never took her eyes off me. They sat down and I took one of the chairs. Griffin had followed them out of the kitchen and he sat in the other chair. Gabe sat on the arm of the couch beside Cassidy. As they all looked at me, I didn't know where to begin.

You'd think after all these years I would have

had a speech prepared. I did, and it flew right out the window as soon as I saw her. The guys must have seen my struggle, and Griffin came to the rescue. "Why don't you start with what happened on the plane?"

"Okay, so I assume you now know I was on an assignment and was helping to bring back an informant when the plane we were on crashed?" She narrowed her eyes a little, but all she did was nod her head yes. "When the crash happened, I hit my head. When I woke up, all I could remember was the guy I was cuffed to was associated with a motorcycle club. I had all the information on them in my head and that was what I could remember. Though I could also remember things about MC life and stuff. Anyway, he was mostly out of it from his injuries and I was able somehow to get us to the compound of the motorcycle club."

"Wait, you mean you had amnesia?" she asked.

"Yeah, I did. I won't go into details on the club, but suffice to say, they were dirty as hell and didn't trust anyone. They tried to get information out of me, but I didn't recall any I could tell them. I told them my name was Undertaker. It was all I could remember. I knew enough about myself to realize I wouldn't want a club like that existing. I just didn't know why I was on that plane or cuffed to the guy. So, I decided to see if they'd let me in and I'd figure out how to take them apart from the inside.

"And you've been with them, not knowing who you are for five years. Are they still out there? Are you staying undercover longer? This doesn't make sense, Mark," Cassidy cried out. Sean was holding her hand and rubbing her tense shoulders. Here comes the hard

29

part.

"I had no idea who I was and they let me prospect. Around a year into it, they finally patched me in. You remember Dad's stories of his time in an MC. This one made his old one look like preschoolers, Cass. The shit they did. The people they hurt. I couldn't let them get away with it."

I paused to take a deep breath and the plunge. "Around that one-year mark, I started to have dreams. I now know they were about all of you and my real life. One day, it all came back crystal clear, and I remembered everything that led up to the crash."

She sat forward. "You knew four years ago, and you never told any of us! We thought you were dead. We put up a headstone and held a funeral without a body, Mark. How could you do that?" she shouted.

I looked at Sean for guidance. I didn't want to get him in trouble, but there was no way to tell her everything without outing the guys' part in it. He gave me a chin lift. I looked at the others and they did the same. I sighed.

"I didn't keep it a secret. I reached out and made contact, to tell someone where I'd been and what I was doing. I had to have someone who knew there was a man on the inside of the club. Once that contact was made, the feds were brought in, and I started feeding them information indirectly through my contacts."

"Tell me the name of your contacts," she said quietly. I could see she was about to blow and that she knew it was Sean and the guys.

"I told them and not you, because I had to make sure nothing could lead to you. If I saw you, it could compromise both of us."

"Tell me," she ground out softly. She was at her most pissed when she was talking softly like that.

"Babe, it was me, Griff, and Gabe. I swear we all talked about telling you, but what was happening in that club was so damn dark, no way we'd endanger you like that. In our defense, we thought it would only be a matter of months and he'd be home. He was afraid that if he did tell you and then something happened to him, you'd have to mourn all over again," Sean told her in a rush.

She came bounding up off the couch, despite his hands on her shoulders, and she whipped around to stare at him. She pointed at him with a shaking finger. "You knew for almost four years that my brother was alive and you lied and hid it from me. You fucking let me cry over him and you comforted me, all of you!" she screamed. Her whole body trembled with how mad she was.

I got up and went to her. She shoved me away. "Don't try to hug me. That shit worked when I was little and skinned my knees. It's not for when you've been lied to and betrayed by your family."

"Baby, please, we didn't betray you. We were protecting you. None of us could stand the idea of something happening to you," Sean pleaded. He was within arm's reach of her.

She glared at him then looked over at me. "Why

are you telling me now? Did your assignment finally end?"

"Yeah, the case ended. You probably heard it in the news. The Tres Locos MC went down a week ago in a huge fed raid. They shut the whole operation down."

"A week ago... you finished a week ago and it took you this long to come see me," she cried out louder.

I could hear the pain in her voice. "Honey, I had days of debriefing. They just finished with me late last night. I wanted to tell you in person, not over the phone. The guys agreed, and that's why they got you here this morning. I've been dying to see and talk to you since the day I left."

"Bullshit! You've been off playing war like you love to do. And they helped you do it while you all lied to me. I can't stand to look at any of you. You make me sick."

Sean tried to wrap his arms around her, but she rounded on him too fast and she punched him in the gut. I heard the air leave him as he hunched over. "Keep your hands off me. I'm leaving and if you know what's good for you, you won't follow me. I need to think." She headed for the door.

"Cassie, please don't leave. I know you're upset and you have every right to be, but we need to talk this out. You shouldn't drive when you're upset," I begged.

She looked at me like she was looking at a stranger. "You're damn right I have the right to be upset. I'm so fucking mad right now. If I don't leave, it's going to be more than a punch to the gut. It gutted me when I thought you were dead, Mark. I cried for weeks and then on and off for months. I have a son, Noah Mark, that I named for his dead uncle. I'm already telling him stories about what a great guy his namesake was and you pull this. I'm glad you're alive, but I can't deal with this right now. Sean." She looked at him. He was standing up straight again. "I suggest you stay away from the house today."

He didn't argue. We knew when she got like this to stay clear and let her calm down, even though everything in me shouted to not let her go and to make her sit and talk to me. He nodded and as she went out the door, he shouted, "I love you." She just slammed the door.

We all slumped in our seats. "That went well," Sean said with a groan.

"Did you expect it to go better? I mean, come on. Imagine yourself in her shoes. I'd be pissed at us too. We need to give her time to calm down and then talk to her again. I think you should stay away from the house, Sean. She might shoot you," Gabe said with a shake of his head.

"What the hell? He's the one who decided not to tell her, but she hit me," Sean complained as he pointed to me.

"I can't help that you were dumb enough to actually touch her when she was that pissed. You know she has a temper. It might be hard to trigger but when you do, look out. I only acted like I was going to hug her. I'm sorry that she took it out on you, but she probably feels doubly betrayed. You're her husband and you hid this. God, I hope she doesn't stay pissed for long. I want to see my nephew and spend time with her. She looks so different now."

"She grew up while you were gone. You remember her as this fresh-faced twenty-something. She's twenty-seven now and a mother and wife. She works with us still, though she stopped doing undercover once she got pregnant. She's done a lot of stuff in those five years. You're going to have to learn about the new Cassidy and we'll have to learn the new you," Griffin said quietly.

"The new me?"

"Yeah, you went through five years of hell. You're not the same guy who left one day and didn't come back. You look different," Griffin said. Sean and Gabe nodded.

I knew what they meant. I had more lines on my face and I was harder looking. My tats had multiplied and my muscle mass had increased. You couldn't be living my life and not be hypervigilant all the time. When I wasn't doing what I had to, to keep my place in the club and to gather intelligence to bring them down, I worked out. It was the best way to blow off steam besides sex, and that had gotten old. Strange women all the time held no appeal for me.

After seeing how the Locos treated women, even the ones they called old ladies or daughters, it made me hate being a man at times. The look in their eyes made me want to throw shit and beat the hell out of the men, which I couldn't do.

"Since we're in the doghouse, mind filling us in. Where do you stand in all this? When you called to let us know it was over, all you said was you were coming home and to get her here. We saw the news. It was a huge bust and all over the TV. Did they blow your cover in front of any of them?" Sean asked. He knew how the government could inadvertently put targets on your back.

I shook my head. "No, they told me when they were coming and we arranged for me to be a few towns over. I got drunk and then arrested, only I didn't go to jail. If anyone checks, I spent the whole night locked up for being drunk and disorderly. It was just bad luck that they didn't catch me. The only reason they had warrants on the others is because of me. If anyone was left to ask, I'd tell them I wasn't high enough in the pecking order for the feds to worry about me getting away. I enforced for them but stayed out of what I could without them suspecting me."

"So, your cover is still intact. Shit, I hope it stays that way and that no one associates Mark O'Rourke for the Undertaker of the Tres Locos," Gabe added.

"I used an alias, Rex Reed, as you know. There shouldn't be anyone from that life running into me. What do you say to a beer? I'll fill you in and we can wait for Cassidy to cool off before we go try to talk to her later."

"Sounds good, and I prepared for it. I came early and put some in your fridge." Griffin jumped up and went to the kitchen. He came back with four beers. As we opened them, he held his up. "To Mark. We're so damn glad you're home, brother. So damn glad. Cheers." All of us clinked our bottles together and took a big drink. God, it felt amazing to be home. As soon as

Cassidy was sitting with us, it would be complete and perfect.

Mark: Chapter 1

It had been two days since I told my sister I was still alive. I hadn't seen her since she stormed out of my house and neither had Gabe nor Griffin. When Sean went home that night, the babysitter met him at the door. She handed him a note from Cassidy before she left. Basically, she told Sean he could spend time with Noah that night and then he needed to find a place to sleep, and it wasn't with her.

They'd spent two uncomfortable days and nights not talking, despite his attempts to talk to her. She'd shut down and wasn't communicating with any of us, other than in a few texts. They communicated the need-to-know information. Only one had been about me and she'd told Sean to tell me she did love me and was happy I was alive, but she was too mad to talk to me right now. I didn't blame her.

She'd lived five damn years, thinking I was gone. I hated that I'd taken that route, but even if I had to do it again, I think I would do it again. It had been dangerous enough communicating rarely through the guys, let alone if I had tried to do it with her. She would have wanted to try and meet and there was no way I could have ever risked that. The chance of blowing my cover or getting one or all of them killed would have been higher. It was a risk I couldn't take.

I wasn't ready yet to go to the Dark Patriot offices and see everyone. For now, they were told I was alive, and we were taking time as a family. The explanations would come later. I figured there would be some pissed employees too. Some of them had started with the company as our first employees and some we'd known from our military days.

The guys were keeping the business side of things away from me. I wasn't ready to jump into anything that required me to think. I wanted to decompress and worry about nothing for a little while. Sean was with me this afternoon, since he said he couldn't stand to be at work or at the house with a stone-faced Cassidy. We were at my house, having a beer in the backyard.

I'd looked around yesterday and found they'd kept up the house and the yard as if someone still lived there. They told me they knew I'd be back, and they wanted it to be as good as it was when I left. "How did you sell Cassie to upkeep this place?" I asked Sean.

He shrugged. "It wasn't hard. This was her house growing up and after you supposedly died, she couldn't step inside often, but she still thought of it as home. Even when she got rid of her apartment and moved in with me, she never suggested we get rid of it. I think deep down she hoped it was all a big misunderstanding, and you'd show up one day."

"Well, she got that right. But I need you to go back to the moving in together part. Speaking of that, I have a bone to pick with you. You go and seduce my little sister and then marry her and knock her up while I'm off trying to make our country a better place." I fought not to grin and to continue to glare at him. Hell, I knew years ago he felt more than brotherly toward her, even if he wouldn't admit it.

"Come on, Mark, you know it wasn't like that. I've been in love with Cassidy since she was too damn young to be in love with. Don't beat my ass for saying that. I tried to keep pretending she was just my little sister but then she did the mission with the Warriors. I hated having her involved in that, but she was the only one that could do it. When we were preparing, I tried to push her away for good and it almost backfired on me."

"What do you mean it almost backfired?" I was curious now. Gabe and Griffin had told me once that Sean had a wake-up call and finally pulled his head out of his ass. They didn't tell me what that call was.

"I was trying to piss her off by letting her see me with the bunnies." He quickly held up his hands. "Nothing happened, I swear, but I let her think it did. There's a Warrior, his name is Falcon. She started to hang with him and spend her evenings in his goddamn room. I wanted to kill that fucker," he growled.

"Did they—" I stopped. I didn't want to know. She was my kid sister. It was hard enough knowing she sleeps with Sean.

He shook his head. "No, they didn't, but they sure had me thinking it. I went after him, and Gabe and Griffin stopped me. Said if I didn't want her, someone else would. In the end, I found out she was going to move to Florida to get away from us, well, from me. I also found out she'd never slept with Falcon. He was doing it to make me jealous and to force me to man up."

"Is that what finally did it? Him doing that?"

"That and having to watch her be taken and then sent across the world to be sold in a damn auction. We had it covered, but there was no damn way we could guarantee that they wouldn't be raped or hurt. I was so damn sick, I couldn't stand it. Smoke was in the same boat with his old lady, Everly. When we took them down and I saw she was alright, though shaken, I couldn't do it anymore. I had to tell her how I felt. Luckily, she forgave me and we worked on it from there."

"I told you when you said she was doing that mission it was too dangerous, but it was already in motion. I want to pick her brain on what that was like and how she felt doing things like that. I never imagined her doing that kind of work."

"We didn't want it, but you made her the owner of your shares. She had as much right as we did and we had no one else who fit the description. It was like they picked her specifically, she matched so damn well. Everly taught her everything she needed to know and do. Everly's a computer geek like her old man, Smoke, but she's a deadly badass too. They make a great couple."

"Do you think she's going to forgive you for lying to her? Because I'm starting to wonder. It's been two days, and she hasn't even called to scream at me. Usually, she totally blows up and it's over by now. She might not forgive me for making you guys go along with this." I told him one of my biggest fears.

He laughed. "She'll forgive you. She'll make us all pay for it for a long time to come and in inventive ways, but she'll forgive. You didn't see her when she found out you were supposedly dead or the way she would get quiet later and we knew she was thinking of you. That was a killer for the three of us. We debated about telling her more than once, but we knew the risk might be too much."

"I debated having her know too, but God, the way I saw them treat people, especially women, was sick. They were less than human to them. Their sole value was what they could do for the club. That was selling products and running errands, selling themselves or both. Even their kids and old ladies were treated like shit. The boys were treated a little better when they got older and they became soldiers for them. The women and girls never got treated any better."

"That sucks, man, and it's totally different from how the clubs we've become friends with act. Their kids and old ladies are treated like gold. Don't mess with them or you're dead. And their women aren't weaklings or pushovers either. All of them are strong in various ways. They stand with their men. They've done a lot to deal with various things like what you ran into with Tres Locos, especially human trafficking, and such. You're going to get along with them when you meet them."

"I'm looking forward to it. Right now, I can't imagine any club being anything other than what I saw with Locos and their friends." I finished the last of my beer. "What would you say to us taking a ride to your place and seeing if we can get her to talk to us? I need to just look at her, even if she doesn't want to talk to me." I was desperate to be close to her.

Sean stood up, taking our empty beer bottles. "Let's go. You need to see and hold your nephew. She can't stop that. She's letting me near him, so that means you can too. Come on, let's go face the dragon."

He smirked as he said it and I stood up laughing. A quick trip to the bathroom to freshen up and I was ready. I went to the garage and opened the door. Inside was the beautiful bike I'd been riding for most of the last five years. It was the one thing I hadn't been able to leave behind. It was a black and dark red Fat Boy with blacked-out chrome all over. Sean came over to look at it.

"It's a beauty. You always did want to get one. All those years riding rice burners and now you're a Harley man," he teased. He knew that I rode the others for years because they were cheaper but having a Harley had always been my goal.

"Yeah, she's a beauty. I got lucky and found a guy selling her with very little miles. He was too sick to ride. I promised to treat her like a lady, so he sold it to me. I've had it for just over four years." I started the engine and let it purr. I saw the urge to get on it in his eyes. He'd driven over his truck. "You get me into the house and I'll let you ride it. Deal?" I shouted. He nodded over the roar of the engine.

Closing the garage door, I waited until he was in his truck and ready to roll, then we took off. It was cool out, but it helped to clear my crowded head. I wanted to think of Cassidy only. The shit with the Locos needed to go away, especially at night. I was lucky if I got a total of four hours of sleep a night.

We pulled up to what was his house, twenty minutes later. My palms were sweaty because I was nervous that she'd slam the door in my face. We killed our engines and got off and out of our vehicles. He went up the long sidewalk ahead of me. The fucker was humming the funeral dirge. I punched him in the back of the shoulder. He laughed. When we got to the door, he used his key to unlock it. As we stepped inside, he turned off the alarm and waited.

A minute later, Cassidy came tearing into the living room entry. She wasn't unprotected. She had a gun in her hand and a determined look on her face. She saw us and I noticed her shoulders sag a tiny bit. She lowered the gun but didn't lay it down. "Sean, do you want to get killed? Why the hell didn't you knock or ring the doorbell?" she snapped at him.

"Because the last time I looked, I still live here too, Cassie, unless you've decided I don't," he snapped back. Whoa, I didn't want them to break up over something this stupid.

"It's my fault. I insisted we come see you. I want to talk if you do and I want to see Noah. Please, Cassie, this is killing me. We didn't know if you'd answer or not. I know you're still royally pissed at us, especially me. I don't know what to do to fix it. I can't change it. Yes, I told them and not you, but you're my little sister. It's ingrained in me to protect you, just like it's ingrained in you to protect Noah, right? That's why you had the gun," I said to her on the fly.

She laid it on the end table. "Yes, I was protecting my son and myself. He's all I seem to have." I saw tears in her eyes. I fought the urge to go over and hug her.

Sean walked over to her but he didn't touch her. "Baby, you're not alone. I know it feels like it, but you're not. You have me, Gabe, Griffin, not to mention that jackass brother of yours." He smirked at me when he said it. I flipped him off, and that got a tiny laugh out of her.

"I'll have you know I'm not a jackass. If anything, I should be protecting her from you. Evil sister-stealing fucking gnome is what he is." I pretended to growl.

He laughed as she shook her head. "You can stay for a little while. It's time for Noah to get up for a feeding and you can see him. I'm not over being pissed and until I am, I can't talk about what has been happening the past five years. Sean, if you're here to stay, I'll cancel the babysitter and you can stay with Noah this afternoon."

"I can stay but where are you going?"

"I have some things at the office I want to take care of. Some stuff to get ready for my return in two weeks."

"Babe, you don't have to go back yet. Take more time with the baby."

"I can't. I need to work. There's so much going on. I have a meeting set for three. I should be back by six. Until then—" she was interrupted by the baby crying. She smiled and looked at me. "Ready to meet your nephew?"

I eagerly nodded and followed the two of them down the hall and into what I knew was Sean's room.

He'd had this house before I left. It looked different with new paint on the walls, different decor, but it fit both of them. Beside their bed was a crib. Cassidy bent down and lifted a tiny baby. Looking at him as she changed his diaper put me in awe.

They had created a whole new life. One that was a part of them both. When she was done changing him, she walked over to me, holding him in her arms. He'd calmed down.

"Say hi to your uncle Mark, Noah. You're named after him. Remember, I told you stories about him," she whispered softly. Tears gathered in my eyes as I watched her mothering her child. When she looked up at me, she saw it all. She gestured with her chin. "Have a seat and you can hold him. I'll get his bottle ready."

I let her lead me to the rocker in the corner and I sat down. As soon as my ass was in the chair, she started to instruct me on how to hold him. I was about to ask her to run through them again when she plopped him down, looked for a moment, nodded, then hurried out of the room. I looked at Sean in a panic. "What do I do?" I whispered urgently. Noah was starting to squirm.

"First, ease up. You don't need to hold him that tight. Just rock and hold him like that. You're doing fine. You should have seen me the first time I held him, changed a diaper, or fed him. When he puked it up, I had to then learn how to bathe him. It was not a pretty picture. I can promise you that."

"Oh my God, you're one hundred percent responsible to make sure he doesn't grow up to be a worthless being who becomes a serial killer," I said in awe as the whole thing hit me. And to my surprise, as much as it terrified me, there was a sliver of me that was jealous Sean had found this before I did. Whoa, talk about a mindfuck thought. I wasn't looking for a woman, let alone a kid.

"Yep, that's our job. It boggles our minds, more mine than hers. She was more than ready for this. Hasn't missed a step and I fumble along trying to do it right," Sean said just as she came back. She held a bottle. Good, she's taking him back. He looked too small to me. I was shocked when she handed me a cloth and the bottle.

"Cassie, I don't know how to do this. You or Sean should feed him."

"Nope, you came to see him, right? Well, that means hands get dirty. Tuck the cloth under his chin and tilt his head up like this." She showed me how. Once I had his head up, she put the bottle in my hand. I hesitated then touched it to his mouth. He automatically opened and latched on. Over the next few minutes, he drank and grunted like a little piglet. I had to laugh.

"God, he sounds just like a pig, Cassie."

She smiled and nodded. "Yes, he does. He's had enough to need a burp before he eats the rest. He sucks in too much air when he feeds. Here, let me show you." She showed me how to put him on my shoulder and then pat his back to make him burp. When he did, we all laughed. He rivaled a man. I then cuddled him in my arms again and fed him the rest.

We all quietly watched him. I glanced up at

Cassidy. She was watching us. She saw me looking at her. "I knew I was going to have a boy. I just knew it, so I started telling him stories in the womb about his uncle Mark. I used to cry when I'd tell him. I tried to do it when I was alone, but Sean caught me sometimes and would comfort me."

She looked at him. "I can't let go of the anger right now, Sean, at any of you, even though I'm so happy Mark is okay. You lied about this. All I can think of is you lying about other stuff that might affect me. Assignments at work, where you're at when you're gone, or if you're having an affair."

"J-Jesus, you know I would never cheat on you, Cass," Sean sputtered.

"I thought I could read you too, and that's been proven wrong. I need to find a way to deal with all this, whatever that might look like."

He got up off the edge of the bed and hurried over to her. She held up her hands to ward him off. He ignored them and tugged her hard against his chest. I felt like I should leave the room, but I had Noah. I saw the raw love on my friend's face.

"It's not going to look like us not being together. I love you and our son. I'm not going anywhere. I regret more than you know not telling you. So does your brother and the others. We did it for the right reason.

"He told me just a tad of how they treated their kids and women. No way I'd let you suffer that. I already told Mark, no more secrets. If an assignment comes up that requires undercover work, we'll make sure you're in the loop the whole way. Just realize, depending on what it is, the person doing it might not be able to communicate with us."

"All of you communicated with him," she said angrily.

"They only did it in code and only if I initiated contact via an encrypted online account. We didn't talk to each other or see each other. It was too risky, but I had to have some help to take them down. By the time I realized who I was, I knew why I was there. Tres Locos needed to be taken out, and I was the man who could do it. I regret losing five years with you guys, but not for doing what I did."

"Intellectually, I think I get it, but emotionally, I'm all over the place. I need time. Speaking of time, I need to head into the office. I'll leave Noah with you and if you need to leave before I get back just call Maggie. Mark, we'll talk again later. Bye."

She got loose from her husband's arms. At least she gave him a kiss on the cheek. She kissed Noah, and I waited. She hesitated then gave me a quick kiss on the cheek too and then hurried out of the room. I looked over at Sean.

"I swear, I'll find a way to fix this. You won't lose her. We won't allow it."

"I know. I just hate that she's in the same house with me, moving around like a ghost. If I try to sleep in here, she goes to the couch. She needs rest, so I've been sleeping on the couch. She at least lets me help with Noah and spend time with him, but none with her. I feel like I'm living with a damn roommate."

"I don't know how or when, but I'll make sure she comes around." All he did was nod and take Noah. As I watched him change his diaper and take care of his son, I thought of ways to get Cassidy into forgiveness mode sooner.

Mark: Chapter 2:

I was back to work or at least back to the office. They'd expanded since I'd been there. I saw numerous faces that I had no idea who they were. Maybe I was rushing it but sitting at home on my ass wasn't doing it for me. I needed to be doing something, or I'd go nuts. I passed the front desk, headed for the elevator that would take me to the top floor where the executives had offices. The guys had told me about them. Gabe jokingly called it the lair of the dragons.

I was almost to the elevator when a man in a guard uniform stepped in front of me. I could see the woman at the desk staring at us, but she wasn't doing anything. I glanced at my watch. Fifteen to twenty seconds from the point I cleared the front door, bypassed the receptionist's desk for the guard to get to the elevator. I waited for the guard to say or do something.

"Sir, you can't go upstairs. Those are restricted access. Go have a seat and give the receptionist your name and who you're here to see."

"I'm here to see Sean Walterson, Gabe Pagett, and Griffin Voss. They're on the top floor. I don't need help finding them. They're expecting me," I told him gruffly.

It wasn't a total lie. I did tell them I was planning to stop by this week. I just never said when or gave anyone a warning that I was coming today.

I knew I was being a dick, but I wanted to test out the new staff, to see if they were up to snuff. I watched as the guard checked me out. I knew all he was seeing was a guy dressed in jeans, boots and a t-shirt, who looked like a biker. So far, he had no idea I was carrying a gun, two knives and a garotte. I stepped to the side to go around him. He moved with me. Good. He was staying between me and my goal, but he was still too relaxed.

"Sir, take a seat and we'll call them to see if one of them is available. What's your name?"

"Mark. They're expecting me," I told him again.

"Well, Mark, they're very busy men and they usually don't let people up to the top floor for regular meetings. They only see VIPs up there. There's a conference room right over here."

He pointed to a room behind the receptionist desk. I didn't say anything. I let him lead me toward the room. It was where they kept anyone unruly or unsavory. I knew because I designed one like it in the old offices. As we passed the receptionist, I heard him hiss to her, "Call for more security." He didn't bother to tell her to call and see if anyone was expecting me. I wasn't impressed with him. The guy was barely looking at me.

I didn't sit down when we got in the conference room. I stayed up on my feet and paced the room. The guard leaned against the wall by the door and watched me. He still hadn't checked me for weapons. I mumbled under my breath, as I held up my watch to my mouth.

In reality, I had my phone in my hand. I'd just tapped it to call Sean's number. He didn't pick up, but I told his voicemail where I was.

"What are you doing?" the guard asked. I mumbled more and walked off. He didn't come to investigate. About five minutes or so later, two more guards came sauntering in like they didn't have a care in the world. They greeted the first one and then stared at me.

I'd had enough. I had shit to do. They'd shown me what I needed to know. I headed for the door. The one closest to me grabbed my arm. I twisted around on him and had him on his ass and disarmed in two… maybe three seconds. The other two rushed me and similar things happened to them. All three were on the ground, looking pissed and scared, as I stood there with all three of their guns.

"What're you gonna do, shoot us?" the first guard yelled.

"I could. See how unprepared you were. You never let someone get to the elevator and you never handle them alone in a room. You didn't bother to search me. You assumed a lot of things."

"Who are you?" the third one asked. Before I could tell them, the door to the room opened and in came Sean with Gabe and Griff. All three were trying not to laugh at the scene in front of them. I saw them fighting to keep smiles off their faces.

"I see you've all met. I would guess from your looks, not formally. Gentlemen, standing before you is Mark O'Rourke. He's the fourth founding partner of

Dark Patriots and your boss. He's been out of town undercover for a long time as you probably heard."

Looks of shock then stunned disbelief raced across all three of their faces. "This can't be O'Rourke, look at him! I saw him ride up on that bike. He passed me and the reception desk like we didn't exist. Why would he do that?" guard one asked, looking pissed.

"I did it to see how security was around here. Security was my department when I was here. It's lax and that's going to change. Don't assume what a person can and will do based on how they look. What's your name?" I asked the first guard.

"It's Morris, Thad Morris. All you told me was that your name was Mark," he said begrudgingly.

"Yes, and you didn't ask any more questions. What about you?" I pointed to guard three.

"Nat Yost, sir."

"I'm Danny Frost," the second one volunteered.

"Why didn't one of you search me?"

They looked at each other and shrugged. Frost said, "I assumed Thad already did."

"See, right there, never assume. I'm sorry if this is harsh, but it could save your life one day. Morris, you turned your back on me at times and didn't keep enough distance between us. On top of it, you didn't search me." I laid down their three guns then I took out my weapons. I watched them pale.

"I don't need any of these to kill you. We do dangerous work here at times. This building has to be secure at all times and everyone must know what to do when someone comes strolling in like I did, no matter if they're dressed in jeans and a t-shirt, or a suit."

I looked at Sean, Griffin, and Gabe, who were watching with stern faces. "I want to start working through protocols with everyone. I think they've gotten lazy with you guys being so busy. Right now, I'm available, so why not use me for that?"

"Let's go upstairs and we'll talk about it. Guys, get your stuff and then get back to your duty stations," Griff growled. They scrambled to get their guns and get the hell out of the room. I saw the looks they gave me. Besides being pissed off, they looked a little scared.

"Jesus, way to stir up the troops on your first day. Let's go up to the offices and get you better acclimated. No wonder they thought you were bad news. You look like a rough-ass biker," Gabe teased.

"I am one and I'll always be one. Things have changed. Let's get going. I feel the need to start introductions to the new people and to reconnect with the old, if we still have any."

"Oh, we still have some old ones and lots of new ones. We'll call a meeting, though a few are gone on assignments and you'll have to meet them later."

"Works for me. No need to do a huge-ass meeting, a quick intro is fine and then I'll kind of wander around and meet people on my own, if you don't mind."

"Whatever you feel the most comfortable with, Mark. You know you can take more time if you need it," Griffin said with a tiny frown.

"I know you're worried I'm jumping back into work too soon, but I'm not. It's been almost three weeks since the whole Locos thing happened. I can't sit at home, rehashing it in my head. I need to be active and get things working. If I can do stuff here, then I need to do it. Going from being on alert and working basically twenty-four seven to zero will kill me faster than doing a little work and re-acclimating to the office and staff. They need to get used to having me here. Some for the first time."

The ride to the sixth floor was a quick one. They had told me that they had taken over the rest of the building two years ago and now the whole thing was Dark Patriots. When we started it almost eight years ago, it was in my garage, then we moved to a small office space here and then the first floor. There was no lack of jobs for us. We did contractor work and had the clearance to help the government. It was based on our prior military service. One of those big reasons was Anderson. He'd liked what we did when we served and wanted to be able to still tap into it when he needed to. Not everything we did was fully "on the books" and we knew the risk. It was the same as being disavowed when we'd been in the SEALs, doing clandestine work in places the military said we weren't.

I looked around in awe at the top floor. There were five offices which were all open to a central hub where two women sat typing. I recognized one of them. She still wore her hair up in a gray bun on the top of her head with her glasses perched on the end of her nose. While our dress code was rather relaxed, business casual, she dressed in a three piece suit every day.

The other woman was much younger. I'd say late twenties maybe early thirties. She was dressed much more casually. Neither looked up from their computers when we got off the elevator. I walked quietly up behind the older one and gave a whistle. She jumped and whipped around in her chair. I smiled at her.

"Well, if it isn't still the best-looking librarian I've ever seen. Still giving little boys heart attacks with those shoes and skirts." I'd always teased her about her librarian look and that her heels and skirts would give little boys ideas. She'd blush and pooh me, but I knew she loved it when I told her that.

Her mouth gaped as she looked me up and down. I knew she was seeing a lot more than what was on the outside. I swore Margie McCoy could read a man's soul. Probably why her husband still thought she was the center of his world. I held out my arms. "Don't you have a hug for me, Margie? After all, I know I still have to be your favorite."

She slowly stood and then she was rushing into my arms. I hugged her tight as she silently wept. I knew she'd hate having anyone see her cry, so I kept her turned with her back to the others. I kissed her cheek and whispered, "I missed you."

"Oh, Mark, it's really you. I thought they had to be nuts when they said you were back, even though the boys and Cassidy said you were alive. Oh, it's so good to have you back." For such a little thing, she could give a fierce hug. Once she calmed down, I let her step back. As we smiled at each other, a throat being cleared brought my attention to Gabe.

He had a big smile on his face. "Now that you're done disrupting poor Margie's whole day, let me introduce you to Abigail Willis. Abigail, this is Mark O'Rourke, the other owner of the company. He's recently come back from a very long assignment as you probably heard."

Abigail gave me a big friendly smile and held out her hand. "Hello, Mr. O'Rourke, it's great to meet you. I heard you've been gone for a long time. I know your family and friends must be so relieved to have you back. I know the company is."

I automatically liked her. She had something that reminded me of what a younger Margie would have been like. I shook her hand. "Thank you, Abigail. Please call me Mark. If you call me Mr. O'Rourke, I'll be looking for my dad. Glad to see they got Margie some help. I'm gonna need both of you to keep me straight. Everything is so big and there's so many new faces."

"I already have the files ready for all the new staff. I knew you'd want to review them once you came back," Margie said with a tiny sniff. She was blotting her eyes with a tissue.

"I will, you're right. However, first, I need a space to work in and then I'll do the rounds and meet as many people as I can before I read anything about them."

"Right here is your office, Mark. We kept one for you, even though people assumed it was symbolic only," Sean told me as he pointed to one of the five offices. I saw the names on the doors. There was one for all of us and then one for Cassidy. I looked at the guys.

"Damn, you didn't forget about me after all. Thanks. Do Margie and Abigail work for certain ones of us or is it a division of duties or all hands as needed?"

"Margie handles anything outgoing and deals with a lot of the older accounts. Abigail works new contracts and incoming business. They float and mix as needed. They know their division, but we just come and ask and see who answers or does it."

I laughed, thinking that it didn't surprise me at all. "Well, since I'm here and I have that great office, why don't I start with you, Abigail? When you get a moment, come see me. I'd like to get to know all the new staff and I plan to talk to all the old staff too. There's so much I need to pick your brains about. It might take me months to get it all down, so be patient with me."

"Oh, don't buy that, Abigail, he'll have it all down, including names and everything else within a week. The man has a photographic memory. If he reads or hears it once, he'll remember. It's very frustrating for the rest of us, who are mere mortals." Margie pretended to complain.

I blew her a kiss. "You can't tell all my secrets, Margie. How's Chuck doing?" I asked her about her husband.

"The same contrary man I married forty years ago. He insists he won't ever retire, so I won't either. He still works in the armory here every day. I can't take the Army out of him."

Chuck was an old Army armorer. We'd snapped him up and then found Margie and snapped her up right behind him. I couldn't wait to see him and have a good long chat.

I decided to let the ladies work, and I'd settle into my office while I waited for Abigail. If she was too busy, I'd go check out some of the other offices and people. It already felt good to be back, even if it felt like my skin didn't fit like it used to. I had to keep reminding myself I wasn't the same man, so the company wouldn't be the same old hat either.

✝✝✝✝✝

I spent the afternoon on the top floor. After I checked out my new office, which was beautiful, set up a new username and password with help from IT and Margie, I spent time talking to Margie and then Abigail.

With Margie, it was catching up on her, Chuck and the family. They had three grown children and now, I found, seven grandkids. A lot had happened while I'd been gone. When I left, only their oldest two were married and they had four grandkids.

It was nice to sit with an old friend and talk. She didn't push me to talk about what happened with Tres Locos which had me relaxing. I knew a lot of people would be curious and I wasn't up to telling them about it. I'd shared a little with the guys and Cassidy when she finally started talking to me, but even with them, I didn't think they'd totally get it. If you hadn't been in that life, you had no way of making a true connection to understand it.

When I talked to Abigail, I learned she'd been there two years, and she came from a military family, even if she hadn't served. She didn't like to be called

Abby, and she was very serious about her work. Like I said, a younger Margie. They could laugh and have some fun, but at the end of the day, it was about the job.

The ladies were packing to go for the day when Sean walked into my office. He had Gabe and Griffin on his heels. "What's up?" I asked.

"We got a text from Cassidy. She said for all of us, you included, to be at their house by seven. Not sure if it's to talk or kill us. She said she didn't have your phone number, so we were to pass along the message."

"Shit, I forgot to give it to you guys, damn. Here it is." I rattled off my new number. "I got a brand-new phone. I don't want anyone who knows me from that life to be calling me."

"What did you do with Rex Reed's phone?" Griffin asked curiously.

"I have it turned off at home. I was going to toss it, but if the feds need it for some reason, I'll have it."

"Are they bugging the hell out of you still?"

We were slowly making our way to the elevators. Margie and Abigail told us goodnight, and we did the same. As we rode down the elevator, I answered him. "Yeah, I get at least a couple of calls or more every day, asking me questions, trying to get me to come back, so they can question me again. I told them I'm done seeing their faces until the trials. I'll testify if I need to, but with what I gave them, they shouldn't need me. They just want to beat it to death as usual. It's stuff I already answered."

"They're nervous. I get it. You just handed them

the biggest MC bust ever, it sounds like. They don't want to screw it up," Sean suggested.

"It is and you're right. The only way they miss out on this one is if they mishandle the information. I hope to God they're smarter than that. A couple of the guys I talked to made me wonder how in the hell they ever made it into the feds. With all the other stuff, with guns and drugs, it's an alphabet soup over there. FBI, DEA, ATF, ICE, you name it, and they're involved. All were jockeying for the lead on the case when I spent that glorious week with them."

"Jesus, I can't even imagine. Makes me glad that we rarely deal with them. Dealing with the various military departments and leaders is enough. That's why I love dealing with Anderson."

"Anderson will be here long after us. The man eats, sleeps, and pisses the job," I joked. Though it was only half a joke. He was always working as far as I knew.

"Oh shit, you don't know. There's more to him than we knew. Old Anderson apparently has a niece, who's a doctor," Sean added.

"Really? I thought he was family-less. How did you find that out?"

"It was because of the Archangel's Warriors over in Hunters Creek. One of their guys got involved with a doctor and shit went down with the cartels in Mexico. She was taken and then targeted after her rescue. That's how they found out Anderson has a niece. Old Demon has him as his uncle-in-law, the poor bastard. Though, he isn't hating life with Zara. She's a beautiful, strong woman who is perfect for him and his club. Anderson has even more reason to support them and their allies when they need help. He wasn't a happy camper when the cartel took his niece hostage," Griffin explained.

"I bet he was hell on wheels with them. I don't blame him." By now, we were at our vehicles. They were driving SUVs and my bike stood out like a sore thumb. But unless it got too cold or icy, I wasn't going back to my old truck, which was sitting in my garage at home. They'd held onto it too. We looked at each other, then our watches.

"Are you ready to face whatever she has in store for us?" Sean asked.

"Are you ready to see if you have to sleep on the couch again or maybe a hotel?" I asked back.

He shrugged. "I'll sleep on the couch as long as it takes to get her to forgive me. She's actually talked to me a couple of times about things other than Noah. She's coming around. She's more hurt now, I think. We all knew and she didn't. It stings."

"I know and I hate that it does, but you all know why. I told her why."

"Maybe what you need to do is really give her a scenario of what you saw that made you so determined not to involve her in any way. You've told us they treat their women and kids like shit. Tell us how," Gabe suggested with an expectant look on his face.

I sighed. "I don't want that in your heads or hers, but I can see I might need to give her at least one example. Let's go before I change my mind. Be on alert. She might be using this as her way to take all of us out in one fell swoop," I warned them as I got on my bike and fired it up. The startled looks on their faces were comical. They hadn't thought of that.

By the time we got through traffic, we were all pulling up to Sean and Cassidy's house around six forty. I was the first to park since my bike was faster in traffic. I waited on the others to get there then we all headed for the door. Sean unlocked the door for us. As the alarm alerted like last time, and he put in the code, we were on alert for my sister to come running with her gun. Only this time when she came around the corner, she wasn't carrying a gun, just Noah.

She nodded at all of us and handed Noah to Sean. I could see the love all over his face when he looked at her and their son. She didn't smile but I could see her face soften. Cassidy could hold onto a grudge sometimes. I was hoping she was almost over this one. She turned to the rest of us.

"Make sure to take off your shoes and dinner will be ready in fifteen minutes. Wash up and there's wine or beer in the fridge. Help yourself. We're going to have a nice quiet family dinner, play with Noah, and then when he goes to sleep, we're going to talk. Anyone not open to that plan, leave now."

None of us said a word. She nodded and then turned to head for the kitchen. I heard breaths being released. We quickly took off our shoes or in my case, boots, and then went to wash our hands in the hall bathroom. Noah was passed from person to person. All he did was look around and seemed content. I was still leery of holding him in case I held him wrong, but I was the last to get him. Sean made sure I was seated when he handed him off. I looked down at his sweet face. He looked a lot like Sean, but I could see parts of Cassie peeking out.

"Hey, big guy, Uncle Mark has a request. See if you can work some of your baby charms on your mommy. She's mad at me, Daddy and your uncles Gabe and Griffin. We did something I thought would protect her, but it hurt her. I never wanted that. It's killing me to see her so mad and upset. Can you talk to her for me?" I felt a little silly talking to a baby like that, but if he could talk, I'd take all the help I could get.

I heard a deep sigh from behind me. I looked over my shoulder and there stood Cassidy. She was shaking her head. "I know it's killing you, just like it's killing me. We'll talk later. Sorry, but Noah is neutral territory in this. Consider him Switzerland. He's the one thing we can all agree is safe and cuddleable during this. Let me take him and you head to the dining room. Dinner is ready." I didn't argue. I handed him off and went to the dining room.

Dinner was delicious, and we all kept up the small talk while we ate. Mainly the guys talked about their day at work, so Cassidy was staying caught up. I told her about the run-in with the guards and then meeting Margie and Abigail. She rolled her eyes at the guards' part and laughed about me teasing Margie about her librarian look.

When dinner was over, we cleared the table and cleaned up while she fed Noah and then gave him a bath. I went to watch her bathe him when I was done. I'd never been around babies and I was fascinated by all the things they needed and what they did. He seemed to really like the water. When he was all dried and dressed again, she took me to the nursery. It was beside their room. I saw they had put the crib and rocker from their room in there.

"Sit in the rocker. You can rock him to sleep. I usually read him a story. Tonight, I'll read and you rock." I didn't argue. He was so warm and soft in my arms. I snuggled him close. I saw the guys in the doorway watching. I stared at his little face as I rocked and she read. His eyes started to get droopy almost immediately. It wasn't long before he was out.

She stopped reading when I whispered, "He's asleep." She got up off the floor at my feet and took him to his bed. Sean joined her and they both kissed him before they put him in his crib. I stood up and stretched. As soon as he was situated, they turned on a monitor and closed the door. Cassidy turned to face us. Her face was serious now.

"Time to talk. I'll meet you in the living room in a minute. Sean, pour me a glass of wine, please. I think I'm going to need it." She left to go back into their bedroom. The rest of us looked at each other and ambled back to the living room. Time to pay the piper.

Cassidy: Chapter 3

I took a couple of minutes to take deep breaths and try to calm down. I was still mad and hurt at how they had all lied to me and let me think for five years Mark was dead. I couldn't even explain how badly that felt, losing my brother. Sean thought he knew, but he didn't. He was an only child and had never had a connection like I did with Mark.

While he was nine years older than me, Mark had been everything a big brother and friend should be to me. He gave me encouragement, love, and protection if I needed it. He was always in my corner no matter what. If I had a problem and needed to talk, he was there. He gave me sound advice and made me think things through before I did them.

When he died in that plane crash, or at least I thought he had, my world had almost come to an end. I didn't know which way was up. Now, to know that I went through that for nothing infuriated me. I needed to make them see that while at the same time, I had to try and let go of some of this pain and anger. It was eating me alive.

Pushing down those thoughts for the moment, I took a deep breath, held it then let it out, and hurried down the hall. The guys were all seated in the living room, holding beers. A glass of wine was on the coffee table in front of an open spot beside Sean.

I took my seat. I hated to be at odds with him. I was tired of not having him beside me at night, but they had to realize that what they did could never happen again. I didn't care how much they thought they were protecting me.

"Cassie, I'm sorry I—" Mark started to say, but I cut him off by raising my hand.

"I need to say something first, okay? Then you can apologize and explain. When you decided not to let me know you were alive, you have no idea how badly I was struggling. I hadn't lost just my big brother. I had lost my best friend and protector. All of that was gone in one fell swoop. You hadn't even told me you were going on an assignment, Mark, so I never even got to say goodbye or to hug you. That hurt me even more when they said the plane had gone down.

"I lived in hope for months when they said they never found your body. I just knew you were going to come walking in one day. I lived with that hope for a year. At that point, I knew it was a lie. Only in reality, I was right all along. You did come back, only not to me. You only told the guys, not me."

"Cassie, I know I messed up, I—"

"Shush, it's still my turn. At that point, things got worse for me. I was so low, I didn't know how to get out of it. At one point, I thought about committing suicide." All four gasped. I saw looks of horror on their faces. I hadn't even told Sean this. He was staring at me in total shock.

"Work kept me going, though the guys started letting me do less and less in the field. They said you would have wanted it that way. That they were honoring a promise to you to protect me. I thought it was a promise from way back, but it wasn't. It was one you asked of them after the crash, didn't you?"

I looked at my brother. He slowly nodded his head.

"I thought so. You wanted me kept hidden in case somehow that MC found out about you and me. I thought it was because they didn't think I could do the job. I needed someone so much and at that point, Sean was running as fast as he could from me. It was like I had the plague. They kept an eye on me but avoided me too."

I saw Sean's mouth opening. I shook my head. I had to get it all out before I started bawling. "When the job came along to help the Warriors, I was relieved. I'd get to do something meaningful. Sean kept protesting me doing the job, and he did his best to make sure I knew that I meant nothing to him, which later I found out was a lie. But at the time I believed it and I made plans with Everly to live in her house in Florida. I needed to be away from everyone and everything that reminded me of you."

I could see the pain and stress on their faces, especially Mark and Sean's. I hurried to finish. "After the mission, Sean told me how he felt and I started to heal and was able to cope better. I still missed you, but I could get through the day. Eventually, we got married although I cried my eyes out when you weren't there to walk me down the aisle and when Noah was born. All that pain and it could have been avoided, if you'd told me about the mission. I would have wanted to communicate, but I could have been like the others and only doing what you deemed safe. Yes, you could have been killed and I'd have to go through the pain all over again, but I would have had them going through it with me. You don't know how much it hurts to know they knew."

I stopped. I couldn't go on. The tears were getting ready to fall. I didn't want to cry in front of them. Mark came over and kneeled on the floor in front of me. He took both of my hands in his and squeezed.

"I know that I fucked up, Cassie. I did it, thinking I was protecting you. I can see that all I did was make it worse, and it hurt you more than if I'd told you. I won't tell you that I wouldn't still want to keep you clear of any threat to you from Tres Locos, because I would. I'll explain why in a minute. Going back to not telling you I was going on a mission, I did it thinking you'd worry or want to help. I didn't want you mixed up with Latoya. He was running from the Locos. We think they paid someone to sabotage the plane, only it didn't kill us.

"I told you when I woke up, I didn't know who I was other than Undertaker and the information about Tres Locos and Latoya. I think it was stuck in my mind because I read their file right before the crash. I was asleep when the engine blew. After I came to, and found we were the only ones alive, all I remembered was them and that they wanted this guy. In my mind, I knew taking Latoya into the feds wouldn't get them what they needed, but I could, even if I didn't know who or why I knew what I did.

"They had no idea who I was and spent days questioning me, trying to get me to break. It wasn't pretty, but my story was solid enough that they eventually believed me. They watched Latoya die and made me watch, so I knew what traitors got. Once that was over, they asked if I wanted to prospect with them. I'd seen a little and knew that they needed to be taken out even more than before, so I said yes. I spent a year working my ass off, doing what I had to in order to get in. They didn't let the prospects do the dirty work, but we saw it. It was right after they patched me in, that I had the dreams and remembered the rest of it. I made contact with the guys and we met. We only ever met in person that one time, and afterward, we only had contact through encrypted messaging online. They set up the feds on this end and I fed them what I got in batches. None of them had any other way to contact me and we wanted to keep it that way. I told the guys to make it clear to the feds that you were to be kept out of it, or I wouldn't be safe or able to carry out the assignment. For once, they listened."

"Did you ever want to tell me later or was it just a done thing for you?" I asked him.

"God, I wanted to change my mind and talk to you every damn day, and that's no lie. I told the guys I wish I could talk to you. But, Cassie, I wouldn't change it if I did it again because when you see what I saw, you never want your family in the sights of scum like that."

"Tell me what you saw that makes you so adamant."

"It wasn't the torture or killing, though that was bad. It was how they used and treated their women and kids. They meant nothing to them, but what they could get from them to benefit the club or their standing in the club. It was dog eat dog. They would have them run drugs and guns, deal shit on the streets. If they thought it would help a deal or their standing in the Locos, they gave their women and kids to other members or people to seal deals. Being an old lady or a kid to a member meant nothing. The guys told me how the Warriors are and that's not anything close to the Locos."

"Why did it take so long to take them down?"

"Because they were cunning enough not to let the lower members know what happened at the top or who their contacts were. We could have taken down the lower guys and shut it down for a little while, but we needed to have the whole thing, including the heads outside the Locos. It wasn't until a year ago when I became an enforcer, that they let me gradually know more about what was happening. I gathered up all the names and information I could and gave it over to the guys. It was only a month ago the feds decided that with me and what I had given them, they could take down the entire operation. To keep me free, I went to a bar a few towns over that night and got drunk, or so I acted, and picked a fight. They hauled me off to jail, and I supposedly spent the night in jail while they were all being rounded up."

"What if they get off or have someone on the outside and they come looking for you?" I asked, suddenly feeling scared.

"They won't. No one knows me as Mark O'Rourke. They know me only as Rex Reed or Undertaker. When I went on the flight to pick up Latoya, I'd set up the Rex Reed backstory, just in case. I was glad that I did when it came time to face the Locos. I had a backstory they couldn't shake and luckily, I recalled that story when I came to. It was funny what things I could recall or knew on instinct and what I couldn't remember that first year."

"Why did they call you Undertaker if they didn't know your name? That's what they called you in the SEALs," I asked, not understanding how some truth was mixed with the lies.

"I told them I wanted that name when I was patched. Said I'd heard it somewhere and I liked it. They didn't know I was a former SEAL. I never tattooed the SEAL trident emblem on my skin or the word Navy. My tattoos never gave me away. Rex Reed had a background of petty shit with drugs and guns that worked right into what they mainly dealt. Anything in the prostitution area they kept away from me for the most part."

"Why did they keep that away from you?" Gabe asked.

"Because I broke one guy's arm when he beat the shit out of one of the prostitutes. I couldn't do the same for their families which sucked, but for the women they had selling themselves on the street, I could get more violent. It was bad for business if a john hurt one of the women and I got involved. But it also helped to keep them safer."

"Were the women there because they wanted to

be?" I dreaded asking him.

He shook his head and sighed. "Some were and others were forced by Locos to do it. I'm most happy that part of the operation got shut down. They can find a life again. I made sure Anderson and the others would help them relocate if they wanted to get out of the life."

"God, those poor people. I get it, Mark. I saw what those few women I was taken with were facing. When they sold us and our owners came for us, they saw us as nothing but meat."

"They didn't do anything to you, did they?" he asked as he glared at Sean.

I hurried to reassure him. "No, Sean and the Warriors got to us before they could do any lasting harm. But I'll never forget what that was like for those few days. Not knowing if they were really going to be able to rescue us and take down that scum weighed on us. Thank God I had Everly and then eventually Bryony there. We kept each other sane and confident."

"Who's Bryony? I thought there were only two of you who went in on that mission," Mark asked with a frown on his face.

"There were just the two of us, but there were other women captured. Bryony was one of them and she was a fighter. At first, she didn't know we were undercover until we told her. She was determined to get out of there one way or another. In the end, when we were rescued, she ended up going back with the Warriors for a while. Eventually, she got married to one of their guys, Storm, and they seem very happy. At least he hasn't been killed by her five brothers." All of us laughed as Mark shook his head in astonishment.

"You'll get to meet all of them soon along with their various friends. We now associate with bikers too, only the good kind. There are the Warriors in Tennessee, North Carolina and Kentucky. The Iron Punishers are here in Virginia. The Pagan Souls are in North Carolina and Georgia. The Ruthless Marauders are in Tennessee and the newest to join is a club in Florida called the Horsemen of Wrath. Their president, Diablo, is connected to the Warriors because his daughter, Brooklyn, is married to Torch. So you see, you won't miss that part of the MC life, because we seem to be seeing one or the other all the time," I told him.

"I really want to meet all your new friends and to see what it's like in a different kind of club. I won't lie. I loved the freedom of riding and being responsible to yourself and a club. I was just in the wrong club."

I asked him a question I wasn't sure I wanted to know the answer to. His description of the club life he lived made me see more why he didn't want to chance me being involved. Though it still hurts to know they didn't tell me. "Do you think you want to join a club and leave us?"

He didn't answer immediately, which made my heart race. What if he did? How could I stand to lose him when I just got him back? He finally sighed and then cleared his throat. "I wouldn't mind finding a riding group that I could sometimes go out and spend time with, going on rides and stuff, but I don't think I'd want to be in the MC life twenty-four seven. I missed the company and what we do a lot. I want to get back to work and see what we can accomplish."

I couldn't hold back. I'd resisted this long enough. I leaned down and wrapped my arms around him. He pulled me off the couch and onto his lap and held me tight. Just like he used to when I was a kid and upset. I let the tears I'd been holding in, out. He rocked me as I cried and he whispered to me. He told me how sorry he was, how much he missed me and loved me. How he would never do that again.

As we held on to each other, I saw the tears on his cheek. I wiped them away. "If you promise, then I promise to work to get over my anger at all of you. I can't promise it's gone. It's still there and you might be on the receiving end of some backlash from time to time until I work it all out," I warned all of them, but I looked at Mark and Sean the longest. My husband and I would be talking about this more. Sean nodded his head when I stared at him. He knew. The others along with Mark all nodded and murmured they understood.

It was a while before I got off my brother's lap and back on the couch. From there, we spent time talking about what had been happening with us and the company, getting him caught up on people and things he might recall. It was close to eleven when they said it was time to let us get some sleep.

Sean and I followed them to the door and saw them off. When the door closed, he looked at me. "Are we going to talk, or do you want to wait until tomorrow? I'd say I can wait until whenever, but that would be a lie. It's killing me that you and I are at odds, Cassie. I want my wife back and I don't know what to do to get you back."

"It's not something you do really, other than give me time to process and to understand. It kills me that I feel like I can't trust you now, Sean. If you kept something as big as my brother being alive from me, then what is to keep you from keeping other stuff, either things to do with him, the company or God forbid, another woman. If you did, it would kill us and probably destroy me," I confessed.

Horror, shock, and pain crossed Sean's face. "Baby, I would never cheat on you and I've told you that. If the impossible happened and I met someone else, I would tell you before that went anywhere. I would never disrespect you or our children like that, but I know that isn't going to happen. The love I have for you is forever and I know it. As for keeping something about Mark or the company from you, no way. I learned my lesson. That shit is never for the best. Please, please let me back in my family. I feel like a ghost floating around, watching as you and Noah live without me."

I hugged him and gave him a kiss. It was the first kiss since I found out that Mark was alive and everything came out about them hiding it. He eagerly returned it. When I broke away, he looked disappointed, but then he perked up when I told him, "Let's continue this in the bedroom." He held my hand as I led him to our room. It was time to let some more of my anger and hurt go. What better way than in my husband's arms? I needed comfort in more than one way.

Mark: Chapter 4

I'd been back to work for a week and I had met almost all the employees and talked to them. Those who were gone on assignments, I waited to talk to them before I reviewed their files. I liked to form my own opinions of people. The guys were slowly getting me up to speed on the various assignments the company was handling, but they were hiding something, I could tell. They were having meetings when I was otherwise busy. Ones that they didn't talk about or invite me to sit in on. It was mainly Sean, Gabe, and Griffin, though I thought I saw Cassidy a couple of times coming out of one of them.

I didn't like being on the outside and today I was going to call them on their shit. I wanted to know what they were hiding and why. I told them I had a lunch meeting and I would be gone the rest of the afternoon. No one asked what I was doing, which I found suspicious too. I left at noon and waited an hour to let them get situated, then I returned. When I walked off the elevator, I could tell by Margie and Abigail's startled and worried looks, that they were having one of those secret meetings.

The door was closed to Sean's office. I didn't slow down or say a word. I stomped right over and jerked open the door. All four of them were in there and they jumped when I came through the door. I saw Gabe reaching for the phone and I heard a voice in the background talking. I held up my hand.

"Don't stop on my account. Please go ahead and keep having your meeting or call or whatever it is. I would love to hear what we have going on."

The voice on the phone went dead quiet.

Gabe looked at the others. He looked worried, the same as the other three. What the hell was going on?

"Would anyone like to tell me what the hell has been going on here?" I asked with a touch of anger in my voice. They wanted me not to keep secrets, but it seemed like they were.

Sean was the one to say something. "We'll talk later, man. Thanks for the update. We've got to go," he said before he clicked off the intercom to the phone. He sat back in his chair and sighed. "Don't look at us that way. We were only trying to protect you. You've had enough shit to last a lifetime, Mark. We didn't want to drag you into this."

"Drag me into what? Protect me from what?" I growled. I felt a flush of anger go through my body.

"We're being asked to do another job. One that we've been ducking and they're not taking no for an answer," Griffin added.

I waited for them to tell me more. They could tell by the look on my face that I wasn't going to let this drop. It was Cassidy who finally folded.

"Jesus, this must have been what you felt like

when no one would tell me about you. We don't want to do this job, but we especially don't want to do it if it involves you. We have the feds wanting our help with another MC club. This one they want to take out is taking over other clubs. They love the success you had with Tres Locos and want to capitalize on it."

My heart pounded a little. Another five years of my life? I couldn't do that, could I? Of course, nothing said it would be that long or not longer. "Who's asking specifically? Did Anderson ask us?" I was curious to see if they had used their ace in the hole. I found it impossible in the past to say no to him. He was one of the few who understood what we did and what we sacrificed to do it.

Sean shook his head. "No, nothing from Anderson. They're just being persistent right now. Though we got asked today to think about helping, from someone else. It was hard to say no to him, but we're not sure who we could send in to do the job. You're the only one we think that could totally pull it off."

"Who asked you today? Why was it harder to tell him no?" I asked. I was curious to know who would hold that much influence.

"It was Reaper. He's the president of the Iron Punishers. You remember Reaper from the team. He and his club are friends with us and the Warriors. It was through them that the information on this other club came to light. Reaper's club had a run-in with some members of an outlaw club. They were after his old lady, Cheyenne. Apparently, she grew up in that club and her mom found a way to get her free. They knew we had someone undercover in an MC and they wanted to know if that person was available. We haven't told them about you yet. How you're back and it was you who was undercover. We told them we'd have to see if we could help," Sean explained.

"What are they wanting to do to this outlaw club?" I asked. I didn't want to be curious, but deep down, I was. Not enough to go undercover again for five years, but I could at least give them advice.

Sean shifted in his seat. "They want to find a way into the good clubs the outlaw one took over in the last few years and see if they can shut down the bad guys and free anyone left who doesn't want to be there. According to Reaper, they figure some legit members have been threatened to stay. They're using those clubs' good names to cover what they now have happening in the dark. All the illegal shit those clubs were never a part of in the past."

"So, this outlaw club is infiltrating these legit clubs and then taking over so they have to do the illegal stuff too." All of them nodded their heads yes. "How do they get in the door to begin with? I don't see clubs automatically letting them join. You have to prospect in every club I've ever heard of."

"They don't do it that way. They act like members of a real club that has supposedly disbanded and they pretend to contact other like-minded clubs to see if they're willing to have some members join. They have a well-thought-out speech they give and if they can get the club to believe it, they get three to five guys to come on as prospects. As soon as they get that foot in the door, it opens the way for more to show later and they work up to a patched member. In some cases, the prospect period is shortened, since the new club knows they've been patched before. We don't have all the details on how it works, only that it has and they've been taking over good clubs and hiding behind their good reputations while they do dirty and illegal things like Tres Locos did," Gabe explained.

I could almost picture what that might look like. Depending on the size of the club to start with, they could easily take over when the time was right. "I'm willing to talk to them and give them advice on what they might be able to do," I volunteered as soon as my mouth opened.

"We figured you would, we just didn't want to have you doing that. You just got out of being in this kind of hell for five years, Mark. No need to throw you right back into it, even as an advisor, if we don't need to do it," Griffin said with a shake of his head.

"Advising isn't a big deal. I can do that all day long. The problem is going to be getting someone into one of these clubs, to see what's really happening. What's the set up? Who are the main backers of the illegal operations? What is his dynamic with the others? Is there unrest and if so, how much? Can it be used to turn on the bad element with the right person and help? Will the whole club have to be dismantled to stop the illegal shit or can something of the old club be saved?"

The questions just flowed through my head. I could think of a million more, but without answers, they were just a lot of questions. Questions that I could feel a tiny burning need to know the answers to starting to flicker. I looked at the tense faces across from me. I could see worry there as well as some fear and dare I say, hope.

They didn't want me to take this assignment, but they needed me. No one we had that I'd talked to had anything they could compare an outlaw MC to in their repertoire. Some days I wished I didn't either. The dreams at night were killer. Always wondering if your cover was blown made you a very light sleeper and not a trusting person.

However, the man that my father raised was one who did the right thing and helped others when they were in need. Taking down a club like they had just described was essential. "Next time they call, tell them you have a guy who can help. I'll look over what they have and give them advice. If they have someone they're sending in, then I want to meet that person so I can prep them. It takes more than knowledge of the MC life to do that. It would help if they did work like ours or similar in the past. Working alone is nerve-racking work."

Cassidy got up and came over to kneel beside the chair I'd taken. She grabbed my hand. "Mark, no one expects you to do this. We appreciate any advice offered, but even that I feel is too much. You've tried to dive back into work after barely getting done with an assignment most would need a year or more to recover from. Don't you think you're pushing it?" I could hear the worry in her voice and see it all over her face.

I gently touched her cheek. "Cassie, you're right. I'm not recovered, but I may never be. As much as I try to explain it, unless you've lived that life, you can't know. Reaper's old lady is probably the closest we have to knowing what I had to do and see. She grew up watching it happen. Luckily, she got out. I have no idea how soon, so she might have been protected from a lot of it."

"She was a teenager, so she saw a lot of it. It wasn't pretty and her mom was killed for helping her escape. She was to be given to the son of one of the officers, Slither, so her dad, Ogre, could gain favor. The Iron Punishers took out the man she'd essentially been sold to," Griffin answered.

My heart ached for this woman I didn't know. I'd seen so many of the women and children used by their families in the Tres Locos. They were like the living dead in a lot of instances. They merely existed to serve.

"Let me guess, the rest of the club is still out there causing issues and carrying out their evil plans," I said.

"Yeah, it seems like they are. We know the name of at least one club they did this to in Ohio. They're called the Legion of Renegades. The disbanded club they pretended to be a part of was out of that general Ohio and Pennsylvania area called the Steel Falcons. They were a real club that we think the Soldiers of Corruption destroyed, so it had the cover of a legit disbanded club. If anyone was left alive, they would have threatened their lives if they claimed anything other than disbanding," Gabe added.

I hadn't heard of the Soldiers of Corruption, but if they were smaller and upcoming and doing it quietly, that wouldn't be unusual. However, I bet they knew of the Tres Locos before even the bust. They had the reputation of being outlaws and a one-percenter club.

Cassidy had taken a seat next to me. She was

holding my hand. I saw the worry on her face. "Wipe that look off your face. I'm fine. I'd like to be able to help Reaper and get this club back if I can." She jerked. I tightened my hand in hers. "That doesn't mean I go undercover without contact for five years, Cassidy. I don't plan to do that. I can give them advice, maybe work with whoever they find to go undercover, that sort of thing."

"I couldn't stand to lose you again, Mark. It almost killed me last time. Even knowing you were alive would worry me to death. These kinds of clubs are dangerous and anything can happen, even if they don't figure out what you're doing. I want you here to see Noah grow up. We're going to eventually have more babies. And I want to see you have children of your own," Cassie said as she sniffed. I knew she was holding back tears.

"Well, sis, that last one requires a woman who can stand me. Not sure I'll ever find one who can put up with me and my many quirks. They've only gotten worse over the last few years," I told her. I wasn't kidding. I had several quirks most women wouldn't be comfortable with.

"Bullshit, I know there's a perfect woman out there for you. You just have to wait to find her and not be closed minded to the possibility. I don't doubt you have quirks. I know some of them, but they don't make you unlovable, just a little overbearing at times. I'll teach her how to get what she wants," Cassidy teased.

"That's all I need, my little sister and my woman ganging up on me. Sean, you're in charge of making sure that doesn't happen. Keep her happy and busy."

He grinned as he wiggled his eyebrows at her. I groaned. "None of that shit. I don't need to see that. It's traumatizing enough when I have to watch you kiss her. I go away and the whole world goes insane."

"You knew I had more than brotherly feelings for her. You admitted you did. Me loving her should make your day. I accept her quirks." He winked at her when he said it.

"Just like I accept yours, Sean. Mark will find that one day too along with you other two." She looked at Gabe and Griffin. Both held up their hands and shook their heads.

"Don't be hexing us, witch," Gabe said.

"Yeah, no putting that out in the universe. Shit happens if you do that," Griffin added.

Cassidy just smiled at us. She had a gleam that told me my sister was already plotting to find us women. *Dear God, please no.* I had no idea what kind of woman she'd think was perfect for me. If there was one out there, I wanted to be the one to find her, even if I secretly didn't think one existed.

"Okay, enough of this. Is there anything else we need to do today for this secret meeting?" I asked. They all shook their heads no. "Good, I have a couple of security guards I'm meeting with to go over protocols. When we're done, let's all go have dinner. Cassie, can you get Noah? He should join the family."

"Would you mind if we met at our house and I cooked? I'd love to do it again like we did before. That way we can all relax."

"Are you sure? Isn't that too much? Or we could bring in dinner if you'd like. We haven't had your favorite Chinese or Mexican yet." She loved both and luckily all of us were of the same mind. I didn't want her to have to cook after working most of the day.

"Let's get Mexican if you want. That sounds good to me if it's alright with the rest of you," she said with an eager smile. All of us nodded.

After that was settled, we ended the meeting and got back to work. As I left the office, I saw Abigail and Margie with relieved looks on their faces. They must have been worrying about what would happen when I found out about the secret request. I gave both of them a wave before I went into my office. I closed the door and sat down for a moment to think over what they'd just shared. There were so many things floating through my mind, I didn't know what to think.

On the one hand, a part of me wanted to run as fast as I could in the other direction from anything to do with an MC. However, the other part was thinking of all the things that might need to be done to infiltrate and bring down such an operation.

When you thought about it, it was rather ingenious. Someone had put time and thought into doing it. No one would question a club which had a good reputation, as suddenly being behind surges in things like drugs, prostitution, guns or a whole lot more. People would think of outsiders before they would their neighbors. That would be true if the club had an excellent reputation in its community like the Warriors and their allies seemed to have.

I'd learned a lot about them from the guys and Cassidy over the past several weeks. Everything I heard had made me wish there were only those types of clubs. I loved to ride and the companionship of fellow riders couldn't be beat. Maybe one day I'd find that with a riding club. If not, I'd continue to ride alone. Nothing was like being on my bike with the wind in my face and watching the scenery flow by.

A knock at the door pulled me from my musings. In the doorway stood Thad, Nat, and Danny, the three guards I'd met on my first day back. So far, I haven't sat down with them to discuss protocols. I'd worked through the others and kept them for last. I wanted to give them time to see what they had done wrong and to settle their hurt feelings.

They were all stiff and standing at attention. I didn't want to be their enemy. I smiled and waved at them. "Come on in and have a seat. Let's get to know each other better. I know we talked a little already, but that was all business. I want to learn more about you." They came in and took seats at the table in my office. Right behind them came Abigail with bottles of water. She sat them in the middle of the table and left.

For the next hour I chatted with them. They were stiff in answering at first, but after twenty minutes or so, they started to relax. I think they were waiting for me to attack them for that first day. Once I knew more about them, we'd discuss that later. They had some experience, it just needed to be honed better and to our kind of business.

I was happy with the progress we'd made by

the time they left my office over an hour and a half later. I'd shared with them a little of my background. They'd been fascinated with my SEAL experience but more so with my brief explanation of my undercover assignment.

At five o'clock, we all wrapped up for the day and said goodbye to Abigail and Margie. I leaned over and told Margie, "Don't be much longer or that man of yours will be up here looking for you."

She laughed. "You're right, he will. I won't be long. We're almost done. Chuck and I have plans to go to the movies and dinner tonight. What about you?"

"We're all going over to Sean and Cassidy's. We're going to bring in Mexican food and relax. You two enjoy yourselves. Abigail, you have a good night too," I added.

She smiled and nodded. "I will. Thanks, Mark. I'm meeting friends for drinks. See you tomorrow."

The five of us headed out together. I followed the others back to my sister's house. I was ready to relax and just be in the moment with my family.

Mark: Chapter 5

Dinner had been awesome. I'd missed several of the restaurants we used to get food from while I was gone. We were all stuffed and sitting around the living room. I was holding Noah while Cassidy and Sean sat cuddled up on the couch. It was still strange for me to see them together, though I hadn't been surprised when Sean told me about them.

I knew Cassie had a crush on Sean since she was like fifteen or sixteen. I figured she'd grow out of it, only she didn't. Instead, she only moved from crush to love. Sean had been slower or maybe more reluctant to move out of the friend slash older brother role. I wasn't sure if he had worried about my reaction or not.

To be honest, having her with one of my three best friends made me very happy. I knew he'd do everything in his power to keep her and their children safe and happy. Just like I knew Griffin and Gabe would do the same. They saw her as their little sister. Everyone wanted to make sure Cassidy was safe and happy.

"What are you smiling at?" she asked me with a smile on her face.

"I was thinking about the two of you. I knew when you were a teenager you had a crush on Sean. I never imagined it would grow into this. I'm happy to see you happy."

They exchanged smiles. "It took him long enough to come around. I'd given up hope and then he declared himself after that trafficking assignment. I thought I was dreaming when he did," she admitted.

"I had to. There were men coming out of the woodwork and you were running off with Falcon all the time. Even as I tried to deny it, I hated anyone being close to you," Sean said.

"You sure wanted to kill Falcon, but we were never more than friends. He knew how I felt about you and kept telling me you felt the same."

"I know that now and that's why I don't try to kill him when we go see them. He did me a favor."

"Is he still single?" I asked. I was curious to know.

"Not anymore. He met his old lady, Soleil, about a year ago. She's his perfect match. They had a little girl a month or so after Noah was born. We haven't gotten a chance to see her yet. They haven't seen Noah either," Cassie told me.

"Damn, babies seem to be the theme," I joked.

All four of them laughed. "You wait until you meet them and the Hunters Creek chapter. They have babies coming out of the woodwork. Those guys claim a woman and they start immediately on having a family," Gabe said as he grinned. The others all nodded in agreement.

"I look forward to meeting them. Though I don't think any of them can compare to this little guy," I said, as I held a sleeping Noah up. His face scrunched up, and he yawned without ever opening his eyes. That got all of us laughing.

"Yeah, look at how impressed he is with his uncle's claim. He knows he's the shit when it comes to this group, so he's not worried," Griffin teased.

After the laughter abated, Cassidy got a serious look on her face. "I know we're trying to relax and I don't want to discuss it tonight, but we do need to discuss in the next few days the request from Reaper. I can say no to the feds, but it's hard not to give the Iron Punishers help. They're always there for us and their other friends."

All of us sobered. It had been nagging at the back of my mind ever since I walked in on their call.

"We will, but not tonight, babe. Tonight, we're going to enjoy having all of us here together. I promise we'll find a way to help Reaper," Sean told her as he hugged her closer and gently kissed her. I left it alone. I needed to think about what I knew so far.

✝✝✝✝✝

It took me three days before I couldn't hold back asking again about the Soldiers of Corruption and their infiltration into the Legion of Renegades. I couldn't stop thinking about them. I wondered if they were as bad as Tres Locos. Just the thought had me wanting to put a fist through something or someone.

Cassidy, the guys, and I were all sitting down to discuss it today. I'd kind of insisted we do it. I knew they wanted to put it off indefinitely, but with things like this, they would only get worse. We met in our personal conference room on the top floor. I leaned back in my chair.

"Okay, we know the drill. The ATF is the one who is calling asking for help. They heard what you did for the DEA and they want you to help do the same. Honestly, I think all the alphabet soup agencies want it, but they're letting ATF ask. Reaper says they run not only drugs but women and guns. Not sure which is the biggest money maker for them." Sean got the ball rolling.

"In most cases, they might be close across the board. They could be into more. I did some digging, and it seems the Legion of Renegades have solid reps in their area of Cleveland. They've been there for years and are seen as community leaders. Or they were until about two years ago. That's when they began to participate less in their community. Not enough to be suspicious, just for it to be noted," I told them.

"How did you find that out?" Griff asked.

"When you know where to go and who to ask, you can find out all kinds of things. Don't worry, it was with a contact who knows nothing of my true identity. As far as he knows, Undertaker is looking for a new home and he's heard things. He was quick to let me know that if I was interested, he was sure the club would be willing to talk to me."

"I thought you were staying low so no one from that life could trace anything back to you?" Cassie asked with a look of fear on her face.

"I was very careful. He got a call from me. I told

him I'd heard some rumors about this Legion MC and wanted to know what the skinny was. He confirmed they'd welcome me without coming out to say the club was dirty. He knows what to say and not say."

"Didn't he want to know where you've been and why you're not in prison with the others?" Gabe asked.

"He did, and I told him my cover story and how they had no idea they had a Tres Locos in jail until it was too late. I'd already posted bail and left. That's when I heard about what happened to Tres Locos and I was in the wind. However, it's been over a month and I need to consider getting back into a club and the game. Being a Ronin is too dangerous these days. He bought it."

"Are you sure?" Sean asked with a frown on his face.

"Yeah, I am. Lizard is hardly the mastermind of any group. He's low level in another outlaw club that the Locos knew. Small time shit, but he keeps his ears open. It's how he supplements his income and stays useful to his club and others. As long as he keeps their business quiet, they don't care," I assured them.

"Lizard? Really, who in the world would want to be called that? Makes me think of a slimy person," Cassie said as she shuddered.

"He is slimy in what he does, so he earned his name. I wouldn't trust him with some stuff but knowing what is happening in a five-state area close to him, oh yeah."

"Well, now that you know this, what do you want to do?" Gabe asked me. I could tell by the expression on his face, he knew what I wanted to do.

"I want to talk to Reaper. Do you think you could arrange that? We can do it over the phone or if he prefers, we can do it in person. I know they're in an MC, but this is a different animal than what they're used to. That's why he reached out to you for help. They need someone versed in the ugly side and God knows I'm that."

"Mark, are you sure you want to do this? We can find a way to help without having to involve you in this. You've barely gotten out from under it. You should be resting and enjoying life, not worrying about another club that needs to be infiltrated," Cassie pleaded.

I reached over and took her hand. "I know I just got home. I don't plan to leave for the next five years, but I think I can help. The battle to keep these outlaw clubs from taking over gets harder every day. I want this to be a good world that Noah grows up in. If I can help make that happen, then I will. Just set up a call or meeting with Reaper. I'd like to get his impressions. The more information I have the better."

They were quiet for a minute then they all sighed and nodded. Sean was the one to say something. "I'll get a hold of Reaper today and we'll get something arranged. I know he's anxious to go after the rest of the Soldiers of Corruption. As long as they're still out there, there's a threat to his old lady, Cheyenne, and his club. I'll let you know what I find out."

"Sounds like a plan. In the meantime, what would you think of us all hanging out this weekend, if you don't already have plans? We can go to dinner and anything else you want. If you have plans, I understand," I told them.

All of them shook their heads no. I was finding that I wanted to spend as much time as I could with them. Going home to an empty house was lonely and left me with way too much time to think. At night, my sleep was constantly interrupted by dreams of being with the Locos or alerting to every little sound the house made. Of course, I didn't want to tell them that. They'd worry. I just needed to find a way to get back into a normal routine.

"Sounds like a plan. There are some new places around town we would love to show you. Several restaurants and even shopping," Cassidy said with a grin. She knew I hated to shop.

"If you want to shop, I'll hang with Noah and the guys. We can grab lunch, but there's no need for me to go into any of those stores you like," I told her.

"Yes, there is. You need some new clothes. The ones you have are ancient and even if you're going to wear jeans to work, they need to be nice along with the shirts. Don't worry, I won't try to get you into dress clothes or anything. A couple of places are baby stores. I need to get a few things for Noah. He's growing so fast," she said as she gave me her best pleading look. She knew I wouldn't be able to resist. Besides, I owed her for the last five years of no shopping torture.

I sighed. "Fine, we'll check out one or two for me, but Noah is the priority. I'm behind on my nephew's gifts. I'd like to see what those places have."

We ribbed each other as the guys watched and

laughed for several minutes then we got back to work. Me and the guys had a meeting with a prospective new client. Cassidy was due to head home for the day. She was not back to working full time, and I knew Sean preferred that. Noah was tiny and needed his momma as much as he could get her. I understood her need for work while I loved that our business would allow her to be home as much as she wanted with him and their future kids.

After our meeting, I went to my office to work on some new ideas for the security department. I wanted to make some changes in how they ran things and the training schedule. While Sean, Gabe, Griffin and I all served together and understood security and training, it had always been kind of my specialty. They hadn't let things necessarily go, but they hadn't stuck one hundred percent to what I did. I understood why when I saw the amount of business we were doing.

A lot of it was civilian work for companies wanting help with their security or other problems. Many of them had offices overseas and needed advice on how to set up and run those based on where they were. Besides electronic and surveillance security, we did physical security work too. It could be for multi-millionaires, business leaders or even politicians or other dignitaries. Our work for the government could cover the gamut, but most of it dealt with helping do undercover work of various kinds.

When it was time to leave for the day, I was tired. A knock at my office door had me looking up. It was Sean. I waved him inside and pointed to a chair. He came in and dropped down with a big sigh.

"What's up? Something wrong?" I asked.

"No, just tired. Can't wait for the weekend. I wanted to let you know, I called Reaper. He's excited to talk to you. I wanted to see if you can see him Monday. He'll come over and meet with us. The rest have four o'clock open if you do. That way we can take him to dinner and have him stay the night. It's a six-hour ride from Bristol to us."

I looked at my schedule and made a note. "Sure, we can do four. Would he rather do it as a conference call? I hate for him to ride all the way here and back."

"I offered it, but he wants to meet in person. He said he might bring Cheyenne, which I know Cassidy will love. We haven't met her yet. We weren't able to go to their wedding."

"Then this will be ideal for all of us to meet. Hey, if you're tired, we don't need to hang out this weekend."

"Oh no, that's happening. Not only would Cassie kill me, but I'll also enjoy it myself. As long as it's with my family, it'll be great. I can't tell you how damn much we missed you, Mark. It was like this giant hole we all tried to avoid talking about. Even though me and the guys knew eventually you were alive, it didn't make it any better. We constantly worried about you and what was happening. I can't ever remember praying as much as I did then."

"I know brother, I had a hole inside of me. The only thing that kept me going some days was knowing what the outcome was that I was working toward. Every time I saw those men and how they treated others, especially their families, I wanted to take them down even more. I wondered all the time what you were doing, how everyone was, what Cassie was up to. I'll be honest, I was starting to think it would never end," I confessed.

He frowned. "That's why we were trying not to bring you into this case. We can only try and imagine what it was like for you in that damn club. We've been fortunate enough to see up close what happens in good clubs. We've helped with a few bad ones, but not on the scale that you did. After a while, you have to wonder who you are."

"You can and I did. I had to do shit that made me cringe, but at least I never did anything to directly kill someone innocent. It killed me to sit back and not intercede every time they did something that would ultimately end up hurting people. The drugs and extortion were bad but watching the prostitution was worse in some ways. Some of the women wouldn't have gotten out even if I gave them a way. They'd been in that life too long. Others were forced into it by people or circumstances. Those are the ones the feds were going to help get out of the life. Others I know went right back to it."

"We've seen what trafficking has done to several women. Hell, some of the Warriors old ladies were abused like that and in other ways. They survived thankfully and are living such better lives. We were able to help with a few of those, like the one Cassidy did. Our friend, Brielle, was one of the women rescued."

"I want us to be able to do more shit like that. And if helping with these Soldiers of Corruption makes that happen, then I'll gladly give all the support I can. Now, enough of this, you need to get home. I'll see you tomorrow morning. Give Noah and Cassie a kiss for me," I told him as I stood up. He met me coming around the desk and gave me a fist bump.

"Later, Mark. Hope you have a good evening. Maybe get out and see what there's to see." He wiggled his eyebrows. I knew he meant women, but since I'd returned, I hadn't felt the urge to be with a woman. It was like that part of my body was disconnected from my brain. I didn't even think I'd woken up hard.

"We'll see," was all I said. After he left, I sank back in my chair. I would just finish up a few more things before I headed home. There was no rush to get to an empty house or my crazy thoughts and dreams.

Mark: Chapter 6

Shopping had never been this fun in the past. Maybe it was because I watched as people came up and lost their minds looking at my sweet nephew. Maybe it was because Cassidy had such a big smile on her face and was so excited as she dragged us from store to store.

She'd kept her threat, and I'd walked out with some new clothes. They were still my jeans and shirts, but at least they were new, so she couldn't complain. The most fun was when we were shopping for Noah. I couldn't believe all the stuff they pointed out that babies needed. That didn't include the millions of things there were for what someone might want for a baby.

Despite their protests, I spent money buying Noah not only clothes but other things that caught my eye and interest. Cassidy said he wouldn't be able to use them for months but I didn't care. It was fun to shop for him. When we got tired, we'd had a late lunch at a new Lebanese place they'd found a couple of years ago. The food was amazing. I'd definitely be going back there again.

Remembering the weekend put a smile on my face and had me not paying attention as I hurried back to the office on Monday afternoon. I didn't want to be late for the meeting with Reaper. Since I was daydreaming, I didn't see the woman until I ran into her and she started to fall.

On instinct I reached out and grabbed her by the shoulders. I immediately noted how delicate she was. As I kept her from hitting the ground and she went oomph, I took a moment to check her out. She was young, maybe Cassidy's age. She was average height. Her long blonde hair was pulled back in a ponytail and her startled violet eyes met mine as she grabbed my biceps.

"Sorry, love, I wasn't watching where I was going," I told her as she regained her footing. She pulled away from me, which I found I didn't want. I wanted to hold on to her longer. She looked me up and down before she said anything.

"If you take off those shades, you might be able to see better. It looks like we're going to the same place. A bit of advice, if you're here for a job interview, you might want to dress up a bit. They're casual about the dress code but security has to wear a uniform."

I wanted to laugh at her assumption I was here for a job. I decided not to tell her who I was. I was curious to see who she was and why she was here. "Thanks for the advice. Do you work here?"

She was silent for a moment then she shook her head. "No, just visiting, but I've been here before. Good luck on your interview," she said as she opened the door and sashayed into the building. I let her go. I'd find out who she was from the receptionist. Right now, I have to get moving.

As I headed to the elevators, I thought about the woman I'd run into. I hated to admit it, but she was the first woman I'd had a physical reaction to in months. Even before the assignment was over, I hadn't touched anyone. All it did was fill me with disgust. They all thought I was a damn Tres Locos and it messed with my head.

The gorgeous blonde had everything on the surface I loved in a woman. She had to be shorter than me. I loved long hair and meat on their bones. Skinny did nothing for me. She was curvy and made me ache to feel all that pressed up against me. I felt myself getting hard just thinking about her.

Down boy, this isn't the time. We'll find out who she is later. She was in this building. Someone knows who she is. I stepped off the elevator fighting my erection.

Margie greeted me from her desk. "Hello, Mark, they're just getting settled in the conference room. Can I get you anything? There's water, coffee, and iced tea in the meeting."

I couldn't help but smile. "What, no Coke?" I teased. She knew that was my drink of choice.

"I took the liberty of hiding a few in the fridge in the conference room," she said as she smiled.

I went over and gave her a kiss on the cheek. "I'm telling you, if I didn't think Chuck would kill me, I'd steal you, Margie."

She laughed and patted my arm. "If I didn't love that old coot to death, I'd run off with you. You wait, one of these days, you'll find someone and forget all about little old me. She'd better be perfect for you or I'll have to get ugly," she warned.

"Well, if that ever happens, I'll be sure to get your stamp of approval first. Okay, I guess I'd better get in there. See you later." I quickly rounded her desk and went to the conference room. After a brief knock, I opened the door.

I immediately noted Reaper. It had been a long time since I'd seen him, not since our time together as SEALs. He stood when I entered the room. I saw a smaller beauty sitting next to him. That must be Cheyenne. He came around the table with his hand out. When I took it, he pulled me into his arms and gave me a hard man hug.

"Goddamn, it's good to see you, Mark. When Sean told me who had been undercover in that club for all that time, I almost died. Shit, that had to be hell. I can't tell you how good it is to know you're still alive and kicking."

I hugged him and chuckled. "Well, I thought some days I'd never make it back, but it's good to be home. It's good to see you, too, though I never thought I'd see you with a woman. What the hell does she see in you?" I ribbed him.

He pulled away and laughed as he turned to the woman. I could see love shining in his eyes as he looked at her. He gestured, and she got up and came over to us. He took her hand. "Cheyenne, baby, I'd like you to meet Mark aka Undertaker. I told you about him and the guys. Mark, this is my wife, Cheyenne."

"It's a pleasure to meet you, Cheyenne," I told her as I took her offered hand and kissed it.

She blushed then smiled. "It's nice to meet you too, Mark. Reaper has told me about all of you and what you did. That's truly an amazing thing. I hate that we have to ask for help with another one, but we didn't know who else to ask."

I led her back to her seat. As they took them, I sat down in an empty one. I nodded at Gabe, Griffin, Sean, and Cassidy, who were very quiet.

"Thank you, Cheyenne. I admit, I didn't know I was getting into what I did when it first happened. Amnesia is a bitch. Once I realized who I was, there was no way I could walk away. I understand you've had experience with this club, the Soldiers of Corruption."

"I do, unfortunately. It was purely by accident Reaper and his guys found out what they were doing. They lied and told him a different story."

"Why don't you fill me in on what that story was and then we can discuss what you need. First though, does anyone need anything to drink?" They all shook their heads and indicated the glasses or cups in front of them. Cassidy turned, opened the little fridge, pulled out a Coke, and pushed it toward me. I winked at her. She laughed.

"I think Cheyenne should start and then we'll talk about what they were doing," Reaper suggested.

Cheyenne cleared her throat. "Okay, so to start, I grew up in an outlaw club called the Soldiers of Corruption. They were involved in just about anything you can think of, drugs, stealing, guns, prostitution, arson, extortion, you name it. They didn't care who they had to hurt to make a profit, which included their own families. In that club, being someone's kid or old lady just meant they owned you."

She paused then continued. I could tell it was hard for her to tell her story. "My dad was a regular member, but he wanted to move up and get an officer's position. I had no idea at the time, he saw me as his way to do it. He used me to do things like deliver drugs and other things, but he didn't pimp me out. He did that to my mom, if the situation was one he wanted to gain favor. I saw every despicable act you could think of growing up.

"When I turned ten, I had gained the attention of one of the officer's son's, Serpent. He was eleven years older, so you can imagine how creepy it was. He constantly watched me whenever I was at the clubhouse. Early on that wasn't often, since my mom would do everything she could to not have me there. My dad, Ogre, went along with it for the most part.

"I thought it might be because he cared even if he didn't seem to care about my mom. When I was fifteen, I discovered he had another reason. I overheard my parents fighting. Dad had bartered for an officer position in the club. All he had to do was give me to Serpent, which he was going to do in a month. I think that was when the vote was supposed to happen. Mom begged him not to do it, but he just beat her and told her to shut up."

She paused to take a large drink of the water she held tightly in her hand. Reaper was rubbing her back and whispering in her ear. I saw her relax a little. "Sorry, this is hard for me."

"Take your time, Cheyenne. We know this is hard," Cassidy told her as she took her hand. She was sitting on the other side of her with me and the guys across the table.

"After she found out, my mom contacted her aunt. She was someone my dad had no idea existed. For some reason, my mom had kept her secret all those years. She made arrangements for this aunt to take me. Aunt Candace arranged to meet us in town one day when we pretended to be shopping. My dad wasn't very trusting, so he had a couple of guys go with us. They were prospects. Anyway, we went into a store and Mom sent me to the back to try on clothes. What the guys didn't know was there was a back door and Aunt Candace was waiting for me. She snuck me out the back and into a car."

"What about your mom?" I asked.

Her face got sad and she looked like she wanted to cry. "She'd told me that if we both went in the back, the prospects would follow us, so it could only be me. She said she had another way to get away and she'd join us as soon as it was safe. I didn't want to leave her, but she insisted. Her joining us never happened."

"You don't need to say more, Cheyenne, I don't mean to upset you," I told her gently.

"No, you need to know the kind of people you might be going up against. She didn't join us because a week later, on the news, I heard of a body they pulled out of a river. The sketch they showed was my mom.

I know deep down that my dad knew she helped me escape, and he killed her. I figure he tortured her to find out where I went and when she wouldn't tell, he killed her."

"So, your dad never got his position in the club. Is he still with them?"

"I'm not sure what happened but I do know he's the enforcer. Serpent became the VP and his dad, Slither, is now the president. Dad called me a few months ago, telling me I had to hold up the bargain and give myself to Serpent. Of course with Serpent dead, they'd have replaced him. We have no idea who might have moved into his spot."

I looked at Reaper. He looked like he wanted to punch something. I switched over to him. "What can you tell us about the Soldiers and their plans? I assume Serpent disappearing was your work." He nodded. "What did you learn? Anything could be helpful."

"I took care of him and the three guys with him, plus there was a dirty cop helping them. We questioned them and they were able to tell us some stuff. The names of the clubs they've infiltrated being one of those. They had a great ruse going. They pretend to be part of a legit disbanded club from Pittsburgh called the Steel Falcons. They find other successful legit clubs that they want a piece of and they send in some men to pretend to be looking for a new home. Serpent showed up with Tires, Chubbs, and Loon. They gave us false names. Not sure if they ever had anyone do a background check on them or not. We would have, but before we could, Cheyenne saw Serpent and the whole truth came out.

"There have been five clubs they've done this to. They only go after ones that have a single chapter. They claimed the Falcons disbanded since it was mainly old guys. The younger ones didn't want the hassle of running a club. And they want to be in a club with a good reputation, not a one-percenter one. Once they get in the door as prospects, they learn the routine and then start working things. Eventually, they get patched and they bring in more prospects that they can recommend. By the time the club figures out what happened, they have the bad guys inside. Some up and quit but others stay. All of them have threats against their families if they tell."

"How did they find out about you down here?"

"They claimed it was someone named Chains at a rally. They didn't recall which club he was with because they were drunk. We've done a lot more digging into the Soldiers. The Legion of Renegades is the largest one they overtook, and it's also the first one. It's in Cleveland, Ohio and the Soldiers also are based or were based out of the Blue Creek area of Ohio. Serpent had some notebooks and a laptop. It gave us information on who was in each club and what kind of illegal activities they had going on. Not every club has the exact same things. I think it's based on the area and how long they've had to infiltrate."

When he finished, I sat there thinking about what they said. It was definitely something I think I can help them with. The question was what would be the best form of help. Advice on who to send in and help prep them or go there and do some snooping of my own. I knew none of them would like the second option, but it might be the best one.

Sean spoke for the first time. "We're so damn sorry about all this. I know it's hanging over you guys with them still out there. Mark will have to think on this, I think. Before he does, tell us how you're doing, Cheyenne? Has there been any more contact from your dad or anyone else associated with the Soldiers?"

"No official contact although we saw bikes in town one day. They ended up having stolen plates. We think that had to be some of them checking on what happened to Serpent and his friends. I'm trying not to worry, but it's hard," Cheyenne said softly.

"I don't let her go anywhere alone. Unfortunately, with this happening, she and her friend, Alisse, haven't gone back to work. They both work for a doctor in town, who surprisingly knows about clubs and she's been very understanding. I hate that she's so stressed. It's not good for her or the baby," Reaper said as he placed his hand on her stomach. When he did, I could see a tiny swell.

"A baby? Damn, no one told me that. Congrats, you two. When are you due?" I was excited for my old friend.

"The baby is due on July twenty-first. We're waiting to find out in five to seven weeks what we're having. If the baby cooperates with the sonogram," Cheyenne said with a smile.

I laughed. "If this baby is like its daddy, good luck. Reaper has always been contrary, Cheyenne."

This got the guys laughing as Reaper tried to

protest. After we finished laughing, I got back to business. We'd have time tonight to hang with them. They were staying the night.

"I know time is urgent, but I need a few days to go over everything. Did you bring copies of what was on the laptop and in the notebooks?"

Reaper nodded and slid a USB across the table to me. "Everything we know is on there. Thanks, Mark. We know it's asking a lot, but when I heard who had been undercover all those years, I knew I'd asked the right people for help. Anything you can do would be great. I know the feds are asking for your help on this. Not sure how they got wind of it, but if they can send in someone like what you did, that would be great too. I don't expect you to give up your life here to do something like this. However, your unique experience would help guide others. I know all about being part of a legit MC. It's all the nuances of being in an illegal one like this that I don't know about. From what Cheyenne said, they don't stick to what I consider basic rules. For example, to protect your brothers, and families no matter what."

"I get it. It's a different world and all of them are a little different. There are even one-percenter clubs that honor their families and would die for them. It makes it hard when you can't even count on that."

He nodded. We spent a few more minutes just chatting and then we ended the meeting. I wanted to start immediately, but we still needed to entertain. Cassidy brought up going back to their house.

"Are you ready to get out of here? You have to be tired from that drive, Cheyenne. We're going to relax at the house and we have a room ready for you."

"Oh, thanks, we didn't plan to stay all night with you. We're getting a room in town with the guys," Reaper answered.

"The guys?" Sean asked.

"Yeah, I drove in the truck with Chey, but a few of the guys came along as an escort. With the Soldiers out there, we can't be too careful. Lash and Mayhem came with us. I had a hard time not having the whole bunch come. Mayhem argued as our enforcer he had to come and Lash is medically trained. Or at least those were their excuses. They're going to come escort us to the hotel when we're done."

"Hell, we can't have you staying in a hotel. We can figure this out," Sean said.

I jumped in, "If they don't mind staying with me, I have extra bedrooms no one is using. They're more than welcome. I only live a few miles from Sean and Cassie. You two could stay with them and let the ladies get to know each other better. This will let me get to know a couple of your guys since it seems the others know them."

Reaper and Cheyenne looked at each other. A silent thing happened between them, then they nodded. "Thanks, that would be great. Let me call them and have them get here. They were going to patrol the area. We hadn't checked in anywhere yet."

While he was on the phone with one of them, I watched as the ladies chatted. I could tell that my sister really liked Cheyenne. Thinking of the fact that Reaper was now a husband and soon to be father, had me longing for someone in my life. As I thought of that, the image of the woman from outside the lobby door popped into my head. I wondered who she was and what business she had here? Had she been here meeting her boyfriend or husband? That idea didn't sit well with me. I made a mental note to ask tomorrow who she was.

Two hours later, we were settled at Sean and Cassie's with Reaper, Cheyenne, Lash and Mayhem. I instantly liked the two men when I met them. We'd just finished dinner that we'd brought in and were relaxing in the living room. Noah was awake and getting lots of attention. I was surprised to see Reaper so comfortable handling a baby. I had to make a remark on it.

"Hey, Reap, since when did you become such an expert with babies? I'm terrified every time I hold Noah that I'll break him."

He laughed as he held Noah up and patted his back gently. "Remember my little sister, Harper?" I nodded. He'd talked about her all the time and we'd met a few times.

"Well, she's married to one of the Archangel's Warriors down in Dublin Falls, Tennessee. They have a little boy, Cayden, who is two and a half. Plus, the Warriors have babies constantly. You can't be friends and not get exposed to babies and children. I learned from them, which I'm thankful for. It'll be good practice for our baby. You should take advantage guys, so when you find someone, you know what to do," he told the single ones of us in the room. There was some good-natured grumbling, but I saw that even Lash and Mayhem had held Noah.

We sat and talked until almost ten. I saw Cheyenne yawn and Cassidy looked like she was tired. I stood up. "I think it's time we went back to my place. Everyone has to be tired and work comes early in the morning. Will I see you before you leave in the morning?" I asked.

"We can stop by the office first thing and then we'll be on our way. I'd like to get back before dark," Reaper said.

"No, I don't want to stop you. Why don't we say goodbye tonight, so you can get on the road earlier? I have a meeting first thing outside the office anyway. Cheyenne, it was wonderful to meet you." I went over and gave her a hug which Reaper growled about. I shot him a smirk. After a man hug and a few words with Reaper, I said my goodbyes to my sister, Sean, Gabe, and Griffin. Lash and Mayhem I'd say goodbye to at my place. They followed me out to my bike and we took off. It was a quick ride. After I got them settled for the night, I started to think about what I could do to help with the Soldiers of Corruption. My mind was already whirling.

Sloan: Chapter 7

If I never did another protection detail, it would be too soon. This last one had taxed my last nerve. Wayne Wallace was a grade-A pain in the ass. Just because he was worth millions, he thought that entitled him to anything he wanted, which in this case, had been me.

I should have known when he came to set up security for a European trip he was taking, that he chose me for a reason. There had been several of the guys available, but he insisted that a woman was fine with him. I should have run, but I didn't.

For a whole month, I'd done nothing but dodge his advances and tell him in every way possible that I wasn't interested or available. I'd gone as far as hinting I was involved with someone. He'd asked the guy's name, and I had lied and said I couldn't talk about personal things on the job. It was against company policy.

The only thing that kept me sane was the talks and emails I exchanged with my friend, Cassidy. She might run the company with her husband and a couple of his friends, but she was real people. Heck, all of them were. It was a great company to work for despite the Wayne's of the world.

As I entered the building for the second time in two days, I paused at the lobby door. I was remembering the hot-ass man I'd seen there yesterday afternoon. He'd almost sent me crashing to the ground, but his quick reflexes had saved me from a fall. His bulging arm muscles had saved me. I drank in the tats I could see on his arms. When I looked up, I saw a guy with longer dark hair. His eyes were covered by sunglasses, but what I could see of his face told me he was a very handsome guy. His face had just a couple days' worth of hair on his jaw.

He was deeply tanned and dressed in jeans, t-shirt and boots. He looked like a typical biker. I had no idea what he was doing here unless he was interviewing for a security job. If so, he certainly had the physique for it.

Thinking of him being a biker made me shiver. Bikers could be bad news. I knew that better than anyone, but he struck a chord with me. Something most guys had a hard time doing. I had a type and I tried to avoid it, because I knew those men were usually nothing but bad news.

As I opened the door, I wondered if I'd run into him again. I laughed at my fanciful thinking. Instead of being greeted by a hot tattooed biker man, I was greeted by Thad, the security guard. He had a huge grin on his face. I held in the groan. Here it comes.

"Hi, Sloan, long time no see. Missed your beautiful face around here." Yep, I was right. He was still trying to be a flirt. I'd shot him down several times and he just never seemed to take the hint. Maybe he was related to Wayne Wallace, only Thad was less irritating.

"Hi, Thad, it's been a while. I was off on an assignment. I see you helped keep things calm here. I'd love to stay and chat but I have a meeting upstairs with the bosses." Which wasn't a lie, but I had a few minutes.

He grew more serious. "Are you meeting with the one who just came back from the dead?"

"He wasn't dead. He was deep cover and they thought he was dead. Yeah, I think he'll be there. Why?"

He followed me to the elevators. As I got on, he held the door for a moment. "I don't trust him. There's something about him. You be careful, Sloan."

"I'm always careful. Don't worry, I can handle Mark O'Rourke. Now, really, I've got to go. See ya." He let go of the doors so they could close. I rode to the top floor and thought about what Thad had said. What was it that spooked him so much about Cassidy's brother?

As I got off the elevator, Abigail greeted me and got me seated. "They're just about done with their meeting, then they'll see you. Can I get you anything?"

"No, I'm fine, thanks." I took a seat and let my mind wander. Cassidy had told me about her brother returning and how upset she was that her husband and the other two bosses, Griffin and Gabe, knew he was alive. I would have been pissed too, though she was happy that he was alive. I looked at the closed conference room door and wondered what they had called me in for today. Hopefully not another protection detail. I'd already told Cassidy never again for Wayne Wallace. God, don't let it be someone worse.

I sat there contemplating for maybe fifteen

minutes when the door opened and out came Cassidy. She shut the door behind her and came over to me. I stood and gave her a hug. "It's so good to see you. I missed you yesterday. Thanks so much for coming in. We want to talk to you about helping with something," she said in a rush.

I walked with her toward the conference room. "As long as you're not sending me to babysit Wayne again or someone like him, I'm your gal. I'll do surveillance, take out an enemy, you name it, just not that."

She laughed. "No, it's not another Wayne assignment. Though I have to warn you, he has already called and wants to plan another trip in a few weeks. He wants you as his personal protection."

"God, what did you tell him? Please say you told him I died."

She kept laughing as she shook her head. "No, not dead, just on another assignment for the foreseeable future. Is he still bugging you?"

She opened the door as I answered, "Only sending flowers every damn morning. I throw them out or give them away. He can't take a hint."

"Who can't take a hint?" a deep gruff voice asked. I turned and looked up into the face of the sexy biker God from yesterday. Only today, he had no sunglasses on to cover his eyes. I fell into the darkest green eyes I'd ever seen. I stood there frozen. He looked from me to Cassidy then back.

"Cassie, I thought you went to get this Sloan guy.

Who's this and who isn't getting a hint?" he asked with a frown on his face.

"Mark, you're such a man. I never said Sloan was a man. This is Sloan Doyle, the operative we were telling you about. Sloan, I'd like you to meet my brother, Mark O'Rourke, recently resurrected from the dead." She said the last bit with a bite to her voice. He sighed.

He looked at me and I watched as he checked me out from head to toe. When he was done, he held out his hand. "Hello, Ms. Doyle. Nice to meet you."

His grip was firm and I made sure mine was as well. I shook his hand and gave him a smirk. "Hello, Mr. O'Rourke. Nice to meet you. I guess you weren't here for a security job yesterday. My bad."

He chuckled as he held onto my hand and led me to the table. As he pulled out a chair for me, I greeted the others. "Hi, Gabe, Sean, and Griffin. Good morning. You're all up early. It must be something important. What do you need?" Mark sat down beside me. He didn't say anything else. He just watched me speak to the others.

"Hey, Sloan, glad to see you're back. Yeah, we have something we want to talk to you about, but first, how was the Wallace assignment?" Gabe asked with a twinkle in his eye.

"Hell on earth. If you ever send me to protect him, send another guard to protect him from me. I almost killed him," I told him with a mock glare on my face.

He laughed. "So I heard. No worries, we'll tell him from now on you're not available."

"Thank you."

"Who's Wallace and why is she not doing any more of his assignments? What was the problem?" Mark asked. I was trying hard to act normal and not stare at him. He had my nerves humming as he sat next to me, almost touching me.

"Wallace is a multimillionaire who asked for a personal guard for a European trip. When he came to us, he picked Sloan to be his guard. We should have known he'd be trouble and said no, but we didn't. She just got back from a month with him and..." Sean explained then stopped.

"He was a raging asshole who spent most of his time on this oh-so-important trip, trying to get me in bed. Despite my refusals, he's still at it. Cassidy already said he asked for me for another trip. Thank God she said I was on another assignment. I'll kill him if he doesn't stop."

"He hasn't stopped harassing you?" Mark growled. His face got darker.

"Just flowers and a few calls. It's nothing I can't handle. I just don't want to be too ugly and have him bash the company. Dark Patriots has a stellar reputation. I could see him running his mouth," I explained.

"You let us worry about our reputation. No one who works for us, should have to put up with harassment. Let us know if you have any more calls or flowers," Griffin added.

"Okay, thank you, but let's forget about him. I'm

curious what it is you think I can help with."

They all paused and looked at each other before they looked back at me. I could see cautious hope on four faces and what looked like doubt on the other. For some reason, Mark O'Rourke didn't think I was going to be helpful. That only pushed me to know more and to prove him wrong. There wasn't anything I couldn't do. Bring it on!

Mark:

I sat there in my chair, trying not to stare at the woman next to me. Earlier, when we were talking more about Reaper's request and how we could help him, a name was brought up. Cassidy suggested we talk to someone named Sloan who worked for them. This Sloan had a unique background she thought would help. They wouldn't tell me what it was, only that this person would be a great resource.

Before I could get them to tell me more, Cassidy dropped the bomb that she had invited Sloan to join us and the call she'd gotten a few minutes earlier was to tell her that Sloan was here and waiting. I'd told her to go get who I thought was him. Imagine my shock when the beauty from yesterday came through the door, talking to my sister.

I had to admit, this second meeting hadn't lessened the impact she seemed to have on me. I still felt like I'd been hit with something. Her long blonde hair, violet eyes and perfect smile had me scrambling to think. Though I was able to think about the man she's just admitted was harassing her. That needed to stop immediately and if it didn't, he'd be getting a visit from me. I couldn't stand the thought of any woman being harassed or hurt, but she struck an even deeper need in me to be protective.

My wandering thoughts were brought back to the present when Sean cleared his throat and spoke. "Sloan, Cassidy seems to think you have a unique knowledge base that might be able to help us with an assignment. She didn't go into detail as to what that is, so we'd like to talk to you about it."

"Okay, I'm not sure which one she's referring to that you wouldn't know. I've been here three years. I think you know me pretty well and what I can do." She looked a little lost.

Cassidy leaned closer to her. "It's not your professional experience, Sloan. It's personal and it's about how you grew up," she told her softly. I watched as Sloan stiffened in her chair. I saw one of her hands clench before it relaxed.

"What about how I grew up?" she asked softly. She was staring hard at Cassie. What the hell?

"Why don't you fill my brother in on your background. He hasn't met you yet, so he hasn't read your file? Then we'll tell you what the assignment is and we can discuss how you grew up," Cassidy asked her kindly.

Sloan took a deep breath. "I spent seven years in the Marines before I came here. During that time, I got experience in the field as part of an artillery unit. I learned a lot of other things as well. When I got out, I heard about the Dark Patriots and decided to give it a try. The worst was they could say no. I had no idea if I had anything they were looking for. Imagine my surprise when they hired me. Since then, I've worked a huge number of assignments. Some have been personal protection to assisting in setting up artillery strikes and such. My file will tell you all of my assignments. That's really all there is to tell about my work background."

I was surprised to hear she had been a Marine. That was no slouch and working artillery couldn't have been a comfortable job. Most men didn't think women should be in combat situations. The Marines were some of the loudest in opposition to it, though not all.

"Sloan was an exemplary Marine and they were sad to lose her. But we're so happy we got her. She's been on a variety of assignments and has never failed to bring them to a satisfactory conclusion," Griffin added as he smiled at her. She smiled back. My gut tightened. I didn't like them smiling at each other.

"Thanks, Griff," she said.

I broke in before he could say anything else. "What does that have to do with our problem and what does her personal life have to do with it?" I was getting impatient. I wanted to go read her file and talk to her like I'd done the others.

"It shows she sees the assignment through once she commits to it. She has grit and determination. Now, tell them about your personal life before the Marines, Sloan," Cassidy told her.

I saw her steel herself and then she started talking. "What Cassidy is talking about is that until I went to the Marines, I grew up in a motorcycle club in New York State. My whole life was spent being part of that club. My dad has been a member since before I was born. I knew nothing but that life."

I stiffened as she admitted she'd been in an MC. Had it been a good one or one like the Tres Locos? Had she been abused like those women and children?

She continued not missing a beat. "I grew up knowing that the club came first and your family second. My mom was content with that life. I wasn't. She knew it and tried to make me understand why the men called all the shots. It didn't help. I was constantly getting into trouble. At one point, they sent me to live with an aunt who wasn't part of the club. That didn't help. It only showed me what life could be like on the other side. When I returned, it was worse than ever for me. I felt like I was suffocating. I knew that I couldn't stick around after high school and live like that. My mom figured out the same. She talked to my dad and they agreed. If I wanted to leave after I graduated, he wouldn't try to stop me."

"Did he keep his promise or did he try to get you to come back?" I asked.

"He had no choice. I made sure he couldn't make me come back. I joined the Marines and went off to boot camp within days of graduating. I stayed in long enough that he gave up on trying to convince me to be part of that life," she told me.

"Was it the whole life you hated or only certain things? How did they treat the women and kids?" I asked urgently. She looked surprised.

"I didn't hate the whole thing. I loved the closeness of so many families and the bikes. It was more the things they did that I didn't agree with. Illegal things like selling drugs. The club was always first no matter what, which I couldn't understand. Some of them were really mean to their women and kids, though I knew of others who never raised a hand to them. No one was free to do what they wanted. It had to always be done with the good of the club in mind."

"Was your dad abusive to you and your mom?" Sean asked with a calm look on his face. I knew he was asking things I wanted to know.

"He yelled a lot and she toed the line. I never saw him hit her, though he could have done it when they were alone. She seemed to be a little scared of him. He never laid a hand on me other than to spank me when I was smaller. He yelled, but I wasn't as afraid as Mom. He threatened to lay hands on me, but it never happened. I think he might have been scared."

"Scared of what?" I asked.

"That I'd take the knife I always carried to his balls. I threatened him once with that when he got pissed and threatened to beat me." She laughed as she said it.

"I take it you haven't seen or spoken to them since you left?" Gabe asked.

"Oh, I have. Mom comes to visit me or I find a place for us to vacation together at least once a year. I've talked to Dad on the phone but he's too busy with the club to ever take time off. He still tries to convince me I should come back and rejoin the family as he calls it. He thinks if I do and meet one of their members, I'll settle down and stop being stubborn."

"He wants you to marry within the club. That's

how a lot of these clubs are. It's very cultish if you will," I added as I thought of the Tres Locos. They had been the same, only wanting their kids to marry within the club or into one that brought them some kind of benefit.

"Exactly, and that's why I could never do it. May I ask what this has to do with why you asked me here today? You said there was an assignment."

"Do you know what has been going on the past five years with Mark?" Griffin asked her.

She nodded. "I know that he was inside of a club trying to help bring them down. Cassidy told me that. She thought he was dead. He came back about a month ago. That's about all she told me. Why is there a problem with that club? I can't think of anything I would know that he doesn't."

"No, it's not the club he was dealing with that we're talking about now. We had an old friend ask for our help. Remember, anything we say here is confidential and not to be discussed outside of the six of us. You might not want to help but we still will need you to stay mum about it," Gabe cautioned her.

I wanted to shout that I didn't want her help with any of it. It wasn't because I thought she couldn't help. It was because I didn't want to drag her or anyone else into this mess, especially a woman. My thoughts flashed to the Locos and how they were and then to the Soldiers of Corruption and what Cheyenne had told us about how they acted.

"I understand. Tell me," she said softly though with some steel behind it.

I decided to lay it all out to her. "There's a club in Ohio that has been overtaken by a one-percenter club also in Ohio. The takeover was covert and the regular community has no idea. The bad club has done this now to five clubs, and they tried with our friend's club, but his old lady knew them. They want help to find a way to get inside that infiltrated club and liberate it from the bad seeds. Before all this, they were a good club and did a lot of good in their community."

"How did they infiltrate? How many men do they have on the inside? Are there enough old members to help?" She rattled off one question after the other. I was impressed already.

We spent the next twenty minutes or so filling her in on what we knew about the Soldiers and the Steel Falcons. She asked several more questions. When we were done, all of us sat quietly around the table. Finally, the silence was broken by Sloan.

"When do I start and what do you want me to do?"

"Don't be so hasty. We're not sure what it might take, but Mark has agreed to study it and come up with a game plan. We didn't want him to do it alone, though he could. I thought you might be a sounding board for him and could help him figure out how to best do this. I don't want to see him sucked back into that and be all on his own again. However, we can't understand the intricacies like the two of you," Cassidy said as she stared hard at Sloan.

"If you haven't experienced it firsthand, it is hard to understand. We work hard to be seen as equals and it doesn't always work. But in a club like you described, they're less than second class. They have little to no self-worth and think they have to stay in order to have some meaning. My dad's club isn't that bad, but they don't like to see anything come before the club, not even their old ladies and kids."

She did understand. I could hear it in her voice and see it on her face. She would be able to see all the nuances we'd have to consider in examining this club to take out the trash. Could I work with her on this and keep it professional?

The reaction I was having was saying probably not. But I wanted her to work with me on this. It would give me an excuse to get closer to her and learn all I could about the very complex Sloan Doyle. The glimpse yesterday got my attention, but the conversation today solidified my interest.

"Why don't we give her a day or two to think about it? We have no idea how long this will take or where it might take us. If they find out we're doing this, we'll be in danger. You need to consider all these things and more. If we have to go undercover for example, it can take time. Will your boyfriend be alright with that and you being undercover with a man?" I had no intention of taking it to undercover work, but I wanted to find out if she was seeing anyone. I saw the guys look at each other and get tiny smirks on their faces. Cassie was staring at me like she was trying to figure something out. I kept my face blank.

Sloan shook her head. "I've done undercover work before. I know it can go long and tedious. I don't have a boyfriend, but if I did, he'd have to understand this is my job. Whether I was doing it with a man or woman makes no difference. I don't need a day or two to think about it. I'm in. I think I can be a help and I'd love the opportunity. I don't know of anyone else in the company with my background."

"There isn't as far as any of us know. Your background check and Cassidy's friendship with you is what told us about you. If you're sure, then I say we get you set up to help Mark starting immediately. You can decide where it makes the most sense and how to do it. I'll let Reaper know we're a go, if that's alright with you, Mark?" Sean asked as he stared at me.

I thought over all that I'd learned and what she'd said. Though a huge part of me said not to bring a woman into this, the rest was saying to do it. I didn't know why, but I was going to go with my gut and ignore what my head was telling me.

"Sounds like a plan to me. How about we get back together at eight tomorrow morning? That'll give me time to set up. I think until we know what we're doing, we should stick together. Here's my address. Be there in the morning. We won't be interrupted there like we would here. I'll let Abigail and Margie know not to disturb us unless it's an emergency."

"S-sure, I can do that. Anything I should bring?" she asked.

"Clothes. You'll be staying at my house as we work on this. I don't want to have to break the flow for you to go home or anything. I tend to work odd hours and it makes more sense to have you there whenever the mood strikes. I have plenty of rooms for you to choose from."

"You want me to stay at your house?"

"Yes, is that a problem? You said you had no one at home." I waited to see if she'd do it or not. I know it was over the top. Though it was true. I did work and sleep at odd hours. I could update her the next day.

She was quiet for a moment or two then she shrugged. "Nope, it's not a problem. Besides, it might help."

"Help what?" I asked.

"Get Wayne Wallace to stop sending me flowers. I blocked his calls already. This way the flowers can accumulate and he can watch them die on my porch. I think when he met me here, he saw a box I had on the desk that had been sent to my home. It had my address on it. That's the only way we can figure he got it. I watched him stop his car and then speed off when he saw his dead flowers on my porch." She laughed. This got a chuckle out of the others. As for me, it made me more determined to get her away from her place and over to mine. I had a lot to learn about Ms. Sloan Doyle. Let the research begin.

Sloan: Chapter 8

I was sitting on my couch at my apartment, trying to decide if I'd lost my mind or not. Had I really agreed to spend twenty-four seven with the hottest man on the planet? Yes, yes, I had. I needed to get myself under some kind of control. Sitting in that room, it was all I could do not to stare at him. It was more than his looks, though he had rugged looks I knew most women would find handsome and very attractive. It was the sense of power and command he gave off. It made you feel safe even if you were like me and didn't need someone to take care of you.

He'd been dressed in what I was now thinking was his everyday wear of boots, a shirt, and jeans. All he lacked was a cut, and he looked just like any biker you saw in an MC. In fact, he kind of looked odd without one. The tats on his arms made me want to trace every single one and see if he had more. I'd bet he had them on his chest and back, maybe even his legs.

My dad was almost covered in them the last time I saw him, which meant he probably was fully covered now. I'd resisted getting any because I didn't want to have that associated in my mind with his club. However, I was drawn to them and looked at designs all the time. Who knows, maybe after this assignment, I might go get one.

I pushed away those thoughts and got back to the problem at hand. I had to pack for God knows how long of a stay. I knew I could come get more, but I wanted to make this as efficient as possible. I got the impression Mark would be taking up the majority of my time and thoughts.

I was just about to put my makeup in my bag when the doorbell rang. I looked at the clock. It wasn't really that late, only eight o'clock at night, but who in the world would be at my door? I didn't really have friends who would drop in unannounced except Cassidy. I hurried to the door. Maybe she had more news and wanted to see me about it in person.

I looked out the window as I turned on the porch light. I groaned. Standing there was Wayne Wallace. He was looking upset. I'd gotten his flowers this morning and had the florist take them back. I bet he was here about them. Time to face him once and for all. I opened the door and stepped out on my small porch.

"Hello, Mr. Wallace, what are you doing here?"

"I told you to call me Wayne, Sloan. May I come in?"

"No, I don't think that's a good idea. It's late, Mr. Wallace. Again, what are you doing here? If it's about your next trip, I believe you were told I'm not available. This should be done at the office."

"It's about you and why you keep refusing my flowers and calls. The florist said you returned the ones this morning and told them not to deliver any more to your house. Why?"

His petulance strummed my last nerve with him. I let him have it. "Because it's stalker behavior that I don't want. I told you for a month that your behavior wasn't appreciated. You ignored me. You kept trying, and I kept telling you that I wasn't interested. Now, we're home, and you're still doing it. If you keep this up, I'll have to go to the authorities."

He took a step back. He had a shocked look on his face, like he'd never had a woman not respond to his advances. "The authorities? For what, sending you flowers? No one will think that's inappropriate. I understood while you were doing your job, you didn't mix business with pleasure, but we're home now. That no longer applies, even if I do want you to go with me next month to Monaco."

"Well, you were wrong. I don't want to be in whatever this is with you now either. I'm not interested, period. Sorry if that's harsh, but it's true. As for your Monaco trip, I'm already on another assignment and it's going to last months. You'll have to take someone else."

"Can't they get someone else?"

The obtuseness of him was making me want to choke him. I hated what I was about to do, but if it got him to leave for good, it would be worth it. I hoped he would never find out.

"No, they can't, and besides, it's with my boyfriend. We're lucky enough to be on assignment together. I was just packing to leave in the morning."

"Boyfriend? You said that before. What's his

name?" he asked a little angrily. I could ignore it or tell him what he wanted to know. I was about to tell him it was none of his damn business when the roar of a bike coming down the street caught my attention. It pulled into my driveway and I saw Mark get off his bike. What was he doing here? He came strolling up to the porch.

When he reached me, he wrapped an arm around me and tugged me close. "Hi, babe, sorry I'm late. Work ran late. Who's this?" He let his eyes rest on Wayne. I saw Wayne swallow nervously as he took in the bulk that was Mark. At well over six feet, he was a solid slab of muscle.

I decided to play it for all it was worth. I'd explain later. "Hi, honey, that's okay. I was just packing for our assignment. This is Wayne Wallace, one of the company's clients. He was just about to leave."

"What the hell are you doing at her house and at this time of night? I know you. You're that asshole who kept harassing her while she was on your assignment and you've been doing it since she came back. I've been meaning to talk to you." Mark let go of me and took a step toward Wayne, who stumbled back to the steps.

"I-I-I don't know what you mean. I've asked her out on dates. I had no idea she was seeing someone. It's not harassment to send her flowers. And I'll have you know I'm an important client of the Dark Patriots. When I tell them how the two of you treated me, you'll be lucky to still have jobs," he said in a rush as he puffed out his conceited chest.

Mark laughed. "Really, you think so? Why don't we test that theory? By the way, I forgot to introduce myself. Such poor manners on my part. My name is Mark O'Rourke. You might have heard of me. I'm one of the owners of the Dark Patriots. I seriously doubt my brother-in-law, Sean, or sister, Cassidy, will side with you. And Griffin and Gabe are my best friends, so I know they won't. I think we're pretty safe with our jobs, babe," he told me as he smiled and threw me a wink.

"You're lying. There are only three owners. The fourth one died."

"That was an undercover thing. I'm alive and well as you can see." Mark reached into his back pocket and took out his wallet. He flipped it open. Inside was his work ID and driver's license. Both clearly showed his name and face. Wayne gulped and tried to backpedal.

"W-well, no one said you were back, or that she was your girlfriend."

"She shouldn't have to. I suggest you leave and forget you ever knew her or where she lived. As for the next time you need personal protection, we'll give you the names of a few others that can provide that. We can't provide what you want." Mark practically growled at him. Wayne quickly raced down the steps, never looking back. When he got in his fancy sport's car, he tore out of my driveway. I couldn't hold it in any longer. I burst out laughing. Mark chuckled as well.

When I caught my breath, I pointed to the door. "Do you wanna come in? I assume you came for some other reason than to scare the shit out of Wayne Wallace. Though it was fun as hell to watch."

He gestured for me to go ahead of him. As the door closed behind us, the nerves started jumping in my stomach. Had he come to talk about the assignment? Was he going to tell me they changed their mind about using me? I sure hope not. I led him to the living room and pointed to the couch. "Can I get you something to drink?"

"No, I'm fine. I actually should have waited until tomorrow, but when my mind starts working on something, it won't let me rest."

I sat down across from him. "Okay, what is your mind working on tonight?"

"Several things, one being to make sure you're really willing to do this. It wasn't a demand that you do this, Sloan. It is purely optional. Yes, you have experience that could be helpful, but I've done this alone before. I can do it again."

"I know it was optional, and I never thought my past MC experience would be of use. If it helps free some people from a dirty club, of course I'll do whatever I can," I assured him.

"It might get really dark. I'm hoping all we have to do is provide outside assistance on how to tackle this, but there could be a chance that I might have to go in and see if I can find out anything. If that happens, you won't have me to work with like we'll be starting to do tomorrow."

"If you have to go undercover, I can still help, Mark. I've done that kind of work, you know that."

"Yeah, I read your file. However, I don't want any woman exposed to what might be happening in that club. It could be way worse than what you saw in your dad's club."

"You mean, beating and raping and open dealing?" He nodded his head yes. "My dad's club might not have been that ugly, but they associated with a lot of clubs. Despite their best work, I saw shit I should have never seen. When that would start, Dad would get me and Mom out of there. Sometimes he had to bring us with him, and when that happened, he made sure we had a place all to ourselves to stay. He'd have Mom and I taken there and one of the prospects or club brothers would watch over us. A lot of them didn't like having it around their old ladies and kids either. My dad does have some good qualities and that is one of them. Plus, I saw stuff when I was in the Marines that showed me how others can treat each other. I'm not naïve. I can do this," I promised him.

"I hate that you saw any of that. Those are the things I don't want you to have to see. If I go undercover, I can't guarantee your protection."

"You can't guarantee I won't be hit by a car crossing the street tomorrow. I'm not asking for guarantees, just the chance to be a real help. Like you were tonight. Thank you for doing what you did, though I could have handled him." Maybe a change in subject would get him off trying to convince me not to do it.

"You're welcome. I assume he was here trying to convince you to go out with him."

"Yeah, or something. He didn't think it was harassment to send me flowers and call even though I told him more than once, that month I was his protection detail, that I wasn't interested. I even told him then I had a boyfriend hoping to deter him. You see how well that worked. I was about to lose it and probably go to jail when you showed up."

"I'm happy I could prevent you from having a night in lockup. Now you have the boyfriend to show him."

"God, I thought he was going to faint when you said that and stood there all imposing. Then when he threatened you with firing from the Patriots." I laughed. He laughed along with me.

"I admit it was fun to show him I wasn't lying. And I wasn't kidding. He can go somewhere else to get a protection detail. I'll have them warn any of our colleagues about his tendency to bother the female help. I guess he's never been told no by a woman."

"I guess not. Well, I'm glad you stopped by. I wasn't lying, I was packing and trying to make sure I took what I needed without bringing the whole house," I teased.

"Bring as much as you want. I have a four-bedroom house all to myself. There's plenty of room for you and your stuff. I have no idea how long we'll be at this, so I want you to be comfortable. I know it's inconvenient, but I find I'm up and working at night sometimes."

"Can I ask you a question? You can tell me it's none of my business if you want," I said I was curious to know if his nighttime working was because of bad dreams.

"Sure, ask away."

"Do you have nightmares about your time with the Tres Locos? I mean, you had to have seen a lot of horrible things and had to do some too. Is that why you're up at night and can't sleep?"

He sat quietly, saying nothing, but a look came over his face I couldn't describe. It was like he was remembering. I was about to tell him it was all right not to answer when he spoke softly.

"I do have nightmares. I can't get used to sleeping soundly. I was never able to relax while I was with them, in case they figured out who I was. Take that and then add to the shit they had us doing and what I saw, I haven't had a full night's sleep in years. When I start to dream, I wake myself up and then I can't fall back to sleep."

I got up and went over to sit next to him. I laid my hand on his arm. "I'm so sorry you have to live like that. It's miserable to not get enough sleep. Hopefully, with me in the house, you can relax a little and sleep. Sometimes having another person there that you know you can rely on is all it takes."

"Sounds like you might have experienced this yourself."

"When I was growing up, yeah, I did. My mom was the one who could always get me to sleep. I felt safe with her."

He took my hand in his. He looked at it and then at me. "There was another reason I wanted to talk to you tonight. It might change your mind about doing this, though I promise, if you say no, I would respect it."

"Say no to what?"

"Seeing if there could be something to this," he whispered, right before his mouth came down on mine. His lips were firm yet soft as they pressed and moved on mine. I didn't think. I just kissed him back. That's when I lost my last shred of resistance to the attraction that had been pulling at me for the last two days.

I slid my hand up into his hair and gripped him tighter as he deepened the kiss. His teeth were nipping at my bottom lip. I opened my mouth and his tongue slid inside to tease mine. His strong arms wrapped around me and he tugged me until I was plastered to him. His hands gripped my waist and he pulled until I was straddling his lap.

When we came up for air, he placed tiny kisses down my jaw and then neck. His teeth scraped my collar bone and then he started to talk. "I know I shouldn't be doing this. I swear I'm not like Wayne Wallace. If you say no, I'll back the hell off. I'd never force you into something, Sloan. But I have to tell you, I've been thinking about you since I ran into you yesterday. When I realized who you were, I was overjoyed to see you again and pissed that you worked for us. I don't want to affect our working relationship with physical stuff, but I don't know if I can stop it. Only you can. Tell me no and I won't mention it again and I won't lay a finger on you. I swear on the heads of my sister and nephew I'll keep it professional."

I knew I should tell him that we could only be colleagues, but my body and heart was telling me something else. They wanted me to say yes to him and see what came of it. I hadn't been with a man in two years and before that it had been a friends-with-benefits thing. I yearned to have a man inside of me again, only I was finding the only man I seemed to want was him.

"I wish I could tell you that, but I can't. I've been thinking about you too and I know you're nothing like Wayne. I don't know if this has a chance to be anything or not, but we're both adults. We have no attachments and I think we can go into this and see what happens. If it doesn't work out or we decide to end it, I think we're mature enough not to let it affect our work."

He growled as he pulled me closer and kissed me again. While he did, his hands kneaded both of my ass cheeks and then ran up under my top to trace my ribs. I shivered. He broke away panting.

"Thank you. I don't want to come in, like this is a wham bam and gone. So, as much as I want to lay you out on this couch and strip you bare and ravish you, I'm not. I just needed to know if you were of the same mind as me. Now, before I lose my good intentions, I'd better go. Walk me to the door." He eased me off his lap. I could see and feel the huge erection he was sporting, but he was calling it quits.

"You don't have to leave, Mark."

"Yes, I do. I want us to go into this clear headed. That means I leave and you think about it. If you still want us to do this, then you can tell me tomorrow when you come to the house. If you decide you don't want to do either, I'll know if you don't show. It won't affect your job either way, Sloan. I promise," he said as he slowly made his way to the door. I reluctantly got off the couch and followed him.

At the door, he paused and gave me a tiny peck on the mouth. "I have the feeling this could be something spectacular and I won't ruin it out of the gate. See you tomorrow." He opened the door and walked out the door. I stood there and watched him all the way to his bike. As he fired it up, he waved at me and I waved back. He waited until I closed the door before he took off. I locked it in a daze.

Had I just had the kiss of a lifetime and then let the guy walk out? Yes, I had. I knew deep down he was being a gentleman, but I hadn't wanted that. I wanted him to strip my clothes off and take me right on my couch and anywhere else he wanted. I knew that my answer wasn't going to change by tomorrow. I was going to throw all caution to the wind and see if there could be something between me and Mark O'Rourke. I knew already he affected me more than any guy I'd ever met.

An hour later, I was in bed and slowly drifting off to thoughts of him and what these next weeks and maybe months would be like. I fell asleep, remembering what his kiss had done to my body. Look out, Mark, you asked for it.

Mark: Chapter 9

I tossed and turned all night as I thought of Sloan and that kiss. Had I lost my mind in kissing her and practically declaring that I wanted to try and have a relationship with her? Then I'd done what I'd never done before, I left to let her think about it.

All the way home, I fought not to turn my bike around and go back to her place. That kiss had lit a fire that I couldn't put out. No matter how much I tried to ignore it, I couldn't. I'd had to relieve myself a couple times through the night. Suffice to say, my sleep had been disjointed, but that wasn't anything new. Only this time I had more pleasurable reasons for it than the usual nightmares.

I impatiently paced the house, waiting to see if she would show or not. Originally, we'd agreed on eight o'clock. It was going on seven and I was ready to scream. I decided to make coffee and go sit out back and try to relax.

As I enjoyed my coffee, I couldn't help but wonder if she would show. In case she did, I had the room closest to mine ready. Thank God the cleaning lady had come the day before yesterday. She always insisted on changing all the bed linens, sweeping and dusting even in the unused rooms. Though I was hoping Sloan wouldn't use that room and she'd share mine.

I'd never felt this much of a connection to a woman before. Sure, I had felt lust and had taken a woman home or went to a hotel for the night, but not like this. I was plotting ways to get her in my house and bed where I wanted her to stay for days, maybe weeks. It was an instant connection that I hadn't ever felt.

My phone rang. I looked at it reluctantly, afraid it was her calling to say she changed her mind and wasn't coming. I saw it was Sean. I picked it up. "What're you doing this morning?" I asked as soon as it connected.

"Seeing if you're ready for your houseguest. Did you call her and talk more last night? You said you were going to."

"No, I went to her place to talk to her."

"You did? How did it go?"

"It went fine except when I got there, Wayne Wallace was there, making a pest of himself. I ran him off but I don't want him to be one of our clients. He's harassing her and I have no idea how he found out where she lived to be honest. I'm not sure it was the box on her desk. I told him we could give him names for other companies. However, if we do, make sure they know what he's like before they say yes to him."

Sean swore, "Son of a bitch, I didn't think he'd be this bad. Okay, I'll make sure Margie gets to work on it. Maybe Sloan staying with you is a good thing. It'll get her away from her place and give us a chance to get him to move along. Anything else get discussed last night?"

Sean was my best friend, but I didn't want to discuss these odd feelings with him yet. He'd have something to say and right now, I wanted to savor them. "Nothing really more than what we did yesterday. I told her she could still change her mind, but she seemed committed. I'll know if she shows up today. How's Cassidy and my nephew? Did you guys get any sleep last night?"

He laughed. "We got a few hours before he'd wake up to eat and then go back to sleep. It's harder on her than me since she's breastfeeding. Though now that she's trying to pump her breast milk, I can get up in the night and feed him. I just have to get to him before he wakes her up, which is tough to do. She's a light sleeper."

"No kidding. When she was a kid, she would wake up at almost any little sound. Drove our parents nuts. On the other hand, I used to be the one to sleep like the dead."

"I guess the last five years changed that sleeping, didn't it?" he asked quietly. I could hear a sad note in his voice.

"Yeah, you could say that. Now, I'm like Cassidy and I hear every little thing. I know it'll take time to stop doing it, but I have to admit, it would be great to sleep one night without waking up."

"Shit, I'm so sorry, Mark. I know that assignment turned into shit in an epic way. None of us ever imagined when you got on that plane, it would turn into what it did. There were a thousand times Gabe, Griffin and I wished it had been one of us who took that plane that day instead of you."

"You can't think like that. Then you and Cassidy wouldn't be together right now and have my incredible nephew. The right person was on that plane, Sean. It wouldn't have worked any other way."

"Yeah, I guess you're right. Okay, well I just called to be sure everything was on track as planned. Let us know if anything changes, but I don't see Sloan backing out on us. She's too committed to her word. If she says she's going to do something, she does it."

His words helped to settle my stomach a little. We said our goodbyes and got off the phone. I finished my coffee and then went into the house. I took a final walk-through and made sure everything was in order.

The house was an older one and might not look as sparklingly new as some, but it had strong bones and had a great basis. My dad had chosen well all those years ago. Over the years I'd changed things and modernized the bathrooms and the kitchen. They had been top of the line when I left five years ago. With no one living here, you might think it would have broken down, but the guys had kept it in perfect working order.

It was later as I was wiping down the kitchen counters that I heard a knock at the front door. I looked at the clock and saw it was seven thirty. I hurried to the door, hoping it was her and not someone selling something. I opened the door and there she stood. She was dressed casually in jeans, a long-sleeved t-shirt and boots. Her hair was in what I now assumed was her go-to ponytail. She looked amazing.

As our eyes met, I saw the answer in hers. She hadn't changed her mind about the assignment or the two of us. I grabbed her and pulled her inside the house. As I slammed the door closed, I took her mouth in a deep kiss. It was one that would leave her in no doubt how I felt. She responded immediately and kissed me back. I don't know how long we kissed until we had to stop and breathe.

When we parted, her face was flushed and she was breathing hard. "Well, hello to you too, Mark. That's one helluva greeting. Is that how you greet everyone who comes to your door?"

I laughed and shook my head. "No, only the most beautiful woman I've been waiting to see all night and morning. Sorry, I couldn't control myself."

"Don't apologize. You can greet me like that any time you want. I'm sorry, I know I'm early but I couldn't seem to wait any longer." Hearing her confess she had been as eager to get here as I was for her to come made me warm inside. This was going to turn out to be good, I knew it.

"No need to be sorry, I've been waiting impatiently for you. I was hoping you wouldn't change your mind." I walked her into the living room. We sat down on the couch. I made sure she was right next to me. She looked up at me. Her hand touched my cheek.

"I told you last night I was going to do both things. Nothing made me change my mind. I might regret that decision or not. Time will tell. But I do want to let you know that if the personal ends up not working, we don't let that affect me helping you with the professional. I can compartmentalize very well when I have to."

"I can too, but I don't think we'll have to worry about that. I want you, Sloan, but I can keep it professional when we need to. This assignment is important for a lot of reasons, and one is our friend, Reaper. His old lady and club are in the crosshairs so to speak. We need to find the rest of these Soldiers of Corruption and get them out of the picture, so they can't come back on them or others."

"I totally get it."

"Good, so how about we get your stuff brought inside and you settle in, then we can get started. Did you have breakfast?"

"No, I was too nervous getting everything I thought I'd forgotten, and I was a little scared you might have changed your mind," she admitted.

"Baby, no way was I changing my mind. I was worried you would. Okay, after we get you settled then we'll go get breakfast and then get started." She nodded. I helped her to her feet, and we went out to her car. She surprised me. I was expecting her to have bag after bag of luggage. However, she had two large bags and a smaller one and that was it. It took no time to get them out of her car and inside.

I took her down the hall and to the guest room. She looked around. I pulled her into my arms. "I want you in my bed, but I know this is new and we need to take our time. So, this is your room. You can use it however you want. Mine is right next door. After breakfast, I'll give you the grand tour and then you can let me know if there's anything you need. I want you to be comfortable here."

"I appreciate you giving me my own space and I doubt there will be anything I'll need, but if I do, I'll let you know. Now, I don't know about you, but I'm starved. Let's go eat."

I led her downstairs and out to the garage. I looked at my bike and then my truck. I'd love to take her on my bike, but she didn't have a helmet. "We'll have to take the truck, but let's stop on our way back and get you a helmet. I assume you're not afraid to ride."

She laughed. "No, I'm not, though it's been a few years since I have. I'd love to ride again, but we don't need to get me a helmet. I have one at home if you wanna stop and get it. It's one I wore when I was a teenager. It should still fit."

"Okay, deal, we'll get it and anything else you might need to ride. Come on, I know the perfect place to go for breakfast." I opened her door and helped her inside. I pulled the seatbelt across her and snapped it. She leaned down and gave me a quick kiss on the lips. I wanted to groan in happiness.

When I was in and ready, we took off. I took her to Mamie's Diner. It was an older diner that had some of the best home cooking I'd ever had. They seated us as soon as we arrived. We were after the morning rush. I made sure to sit with her beside me but with my back to the wall. Old habits die hard. We were facing so I could see the door and she was on my left side.

As we looked at the menu, I explained to her my seating preferences. If she was going to be with me, she needed to know. It could save her life. "Sloan, I just wanted to let you know I picked this booth and which way we sat for a reason."

"You want a clear line of vision to the entrance and exit and your back is covered. You want me to sit on your left just like you had me walk on your left because you're right-handed and appendix carry on the right."

I gave her a stunned look. She grinned. "It works for me. I'm left-handed, so I can always get to my gun. I don't like to have my back to crowds or exits, though I bet you're way more aware of it than I am. If we have to sit where our backs are exposed, I know I'll be sitting across from you, not next to you. I'm all for being safe. I know that you have enemies if they find out who you are."

I grabbed her hand and kissed it. "Thank you. You're right, I do it for those reasons and to have you know that and agree with it, makes me very happy and more at ease. I know most of the employees carry and have to maintain qualifications. I'd love to go out to the range with you soon."

"Oh, you wanna see how good I am, do you?" she teased.

I shook my head. "Not really, I saw your qualification tests and you're an ace. I'd expect nothing less from an artillery person. I bet old Chuck loves you."

She laughed. "Chuck is so much fun. He cracks me up every time we chat. He and Margie are such a different couple, but they work. She keeps him on his toes and he loves her like crazy."

"Yeah, they are quite the team. We snapped them both up when we found them and I've never regretted it.

Margie and Abigail keep us on task." We chatted about people at the office until we ordered and then afterward. The conversation wasn't anything but mundane stuff, but I was having fun learning about her.

She had a sense of humor that could be a little dark. She loved animals and wanted to get a dog one day. She hated anything that had vinegar in it and refused to eat most condiments. She loved to paint and did it to relax.

I told her how I wanted to build my own bike one day and that I loved animals, especially dogs. There weren't any foods I could think of off the top of my head I hated. I didn't have any artistic abilities that I knew of.

After we finished an awesome loaded breakfast, we headed to her place. She had me come inside while she found her helmet and she dug out a leather jacket. She already had jeans and boots that would protect her on the bike. I wouldn't allow anyone on my bike who wasn't adequately clothed. People who were riding in shorts and open shoes were asking for trouble. You could be the most careful rider in the world and still go down. Helmets were a must in Virginia unlike some states.

We were done and back at the house around noon. We got down to work. In the room I used as an office, I'd set up a whiteboard. We'd use it as our main tracking board. We got to work on listing everything we knew about the Soldiers and the Legion of Renegades. Once that was listed, we started with our questions. She was sharp and asked all the right ones. For those we had no answer to, we started a list. We'd ask Reaper and Cheyenne these. If they didn't know, they would go into our to-be-determined bucket.

Before we knew it, It was going on six. I called things to a halt. "Okay, I think we have a great start and we can call and talk to Reaper and Cheyenne tomorrow to see if they can answer any of our questions. I don't know about you, but I'm starved. I'm not the best cook, but I can grill and I have some steaks in the fridge. Wanna do that for dinner?"

"Steak sounds great and if you handle the grill, which isn't my thing, I can see what I can come up with to go with those steaks. We should make a grocery list and get anything we think we need."

"I don't expect you to cook, Sloan."

"I know, but I like to and it's not often I can do it for more than me. I tend to prefer to eat in rather than out. And I like a lot of fruits and vegetables. If you're like most guys, the fridge and freezer is full of meat and not a lot else."

As she said it, she took off for the kitchen. I chased her just for the helluva it. She got to the fridge and opened it then the freezer. I admit, she was right. It wasn't that I didn't like other stuff, but meat was always easy to make. She shook her head and then went to the pantry. I heard her tsking. When she came back out, she held out her hand. "I need a pen and paper. We need to upgrade your supplies if I'm staying here."

I took her hand and pulled her in my arms. I kissed her like I'd been dying to do for the last several hours. When I was done, I lifted my head and grinned. "You're most definitely staying here. Try to run. I'll get whatever you want." I reached into a drawer and grabbed what she needed.

I sat back and watched as she took inventory and wrote a bunch of things down. I looked over her shoulder and was pleasantly surprised at what she was adding. If she knew how to use those and make them into something tasty, I was in for a treat. As soon as she had her list, she took out a bag of potatoes I had, cheese and a few other things. I watched as she quickly scrubbed the potatoes and then sliced them in an oven dish she found in the cabinets.

I took her direction and waited until she had hers started then I fired up the grill. When the steak was done, we sat down to steak, homemade au gratin potatoes and she'd found a head of fresh broccoli Cassidy had included in the shopping she'd done. She was always after me to eat more fresh fruits and vegetables. Sloan steamed it and seasoned it with a light coating of salt, pepper, and garlic.

The meal was simple but tasted like heaven. When we were done, I couldn't help but tell her how good it was. "Sweetheart, you can cook for me any time. It was great."

"Thank you. It was simple, I know, but once we go to the store, I'll have more things I can cook. Cooking was one of the things my mom and I did all the time. Dad liked his food and he was never much of a fast-food person. She taught me everything she knew and I've taken a few classes since then."

"When was the last time you talked to her or saw her?" I asked. I could hear the loneliness in her voice.

"I talked to her a month ago and it's been nine

months since I saw her."

"Why don't you call her while I clean up? It's only fair I clean since you did the cooking. Grilling isn't that hard."

"Are you sure? I can help and then I can call her. I'd love to talk to her. I didn't call while I was on Wallace's detail because I knew she'd be able to tell I was ready to hurt someone. I don't tell her specifics about work, since I don't want to violate confidentiality, but I know she'd get a kick out of you running him off last night."

"I'm positive. You go call and I'll be around when you get done. Take your time."

She got up from the table and came around it. She sat down on my lap and gave me a kiss. We were starting to get into it a little too much when she broke off and stood up. "I need to go make that call." She hurried out of the room. I sat there for a few minutes getting my erection under control. God, did I want to carry her off to bed, but this had to go at her pace, not mine. Otherwise, I'd have had her in bed this morning as soon as I opened the door. I groaned a little as I got up to clean up the dishes. I couldn't wait to see what the rest of the evening brought.

Sloan: Chapter 10

I walked out of my bedroom after my call with my mom. I was drying my tears. I always cried after I spoke to her. I missed her so much. I even missed my dad, though he and I didn't see eye to eye on most things. I ran into a hard chest. Arms came up around me and I was hugged close.

"Why are you crying, beautiful?" a deep voice asked. I looked up at Mark. He had a frown on his face.

"It's nothing. I just seem to do it every time I talk to my mom."

"Is everything alright with her? Your dad?"

"They're fine. I just miss them, especially Mom. Sorry I ran into you. I should have been watching where I was going."

"Well now, you can run into me any time you want, babe. It gives me an excuse to hold you," he said with a sexy smile. I wrapped my arms up around his shoulders. The tears were gone and my inner motor had started to purr again.

I'd been working hard all afternoon not to get distracted by him and it had been hard. I'd wanted to more than once tell him we needed to take a break and move off to the bedroom. Honestly, I wasn't a slut. I didn't just meet men and fall into bed with them. I had always in the past had to get to know them before we ever moved to sleeping together. However, Mark seemed to be the exception to the rule. I'd wanted him as soon as I laid eyes on him.

I pulled his head down so my lips could reach his. He kissed me before I could kiss him. It was another one full of nibbling and tongue. I felt my nipples harden and my panties dampen. His arms came around my hips and then grasped my ass. He tugged and my feet left the ground. I hastily wrapped my legs around his waist. We kept kissing as I felt him moving.

The next sensation I felt was softness at my back. I broke the kiss and looked around. He had me lying on his bed. I recognized it from the tour earlier. He was looking at me with a question in his eyes as he lifted away from me. "Baby, all we're doing is kissing, I promise. I just wanted it to be somewhere we could both be comfortable. If you want to stop or go somewhere else, just tell me."

He was trying so hard not to pressure me. I'd never had anyone be so concerned about my feelings and desires. I pulled him back down. "I think this is perfect right here. What isn't, is the fact you stopped kissing me."

He growled and got back to kissing me. When he kissed, he put his everything into it. His lips and teeth as well as his tongue were busy driving me insane with desire. I needed more. I ran my hands up under his t-shirt and felt all those muscles he had filling it out. I knew from his shirt that he was layered with muscle.

The kind you got from some serious working out. I ran my nails lightly across his nipples which were hard peaks. He hissed and threw back his head.

"Sloan, you have to stop that or I'm going to move this along faster than you probably want," he warned me.

I thought for a moment and then I answered him. I pushed so there was more space between us. I saw the disappointment quickly masked on his face. As he sat up, I reached down and grabbed the hem of my shirt. His eyes widened as I pulled it up and off. His breathing picked up as he took in my bra-covered breasts.

"Shit, are you sure, babe? We don't have to do this tonight."

"I know we don't, but I want to. This kissing is killing me, Mark. I need to be able to touch you," I pleaded. He didn't waste time or his breath. He had to have seen how serious I was. He yanked off his shirt and let it fall to the ground. I took a moment to look. I was right. His chest was tattooed like his arms. Muscles rippled down his chest and abdomen as he bent down and started to kiss his way down my chest.

His hand snaked underneath me and he undid my bra. He tugged it off and dropped it on the floor along with his shirt. I gasped as he took my left breast in his mouth and his other hand started to tease my right breast.

My body went instantly taut as he pleasured me over and over with his mouth. Teeth nibbling on my nipple had me shivering. He switched sides and gave the other the same treatment. His hands were firm but not too rough, just enough to increase my pleasure.

I didn't want him to be doing all the pleasuring. After a few minutes, I pushed him away. He gave me a concerned look, but I couldn't talk. All I could do was act. I pushed him over onto his back and straddled him. I put my mouth on his jaw and started to nibble my way down his neck. When I reached his chest, I stopped to trace his tats with my tongue then I took one of his nipples into my mouth and sucked. I felt him shiver. I teased the other with the tips of my fingers.

He groaned. "Damn, Sloan, that's amazing, but I'm dying. Why don't you give me that mouth again?" I lifted up and sealed my mouth to his and we went back to consuming each other. We kissed over and over for what felt like forever. I could feel my whole body going up in flames. My temperature was rising and my remaining clothes felt too hot and tight. I broke our kiss.

"I need these jeans off. Help me," I begged, as I tried to undo them with shaking hands. His flushed face and heated eyes brightened as he moved my hands out of the way and he undid the button and then my zipper. His big hands gripped the sides and slid down my jeans until he reached my feet, then he tugged them off along with my socks.

I lay there watching him take in my almost naked self. I wasn't perfect, but I knew my body wasn't the worst either. The look in his eyes told me he was more than appreciative of what he was seeing. He slowly kissed his way up my legs and paused when he got to my panty-covered pussy. He looked up at me.

"Can I take these off, babe?"

"Yeah, you can take them off," I said softly. He gently tugged them off like he had my jeans and then he slowly pushed my legs apart. I was soaking wet from the kissing.

He moaned when he saw my wet lips. "Fuck, that's a beautiful sight. I have to taste you, now, Sloan," he said, right before he lowered his head and flicked his tongue up and down my slit. I cried out and my hips came up off the bed. The electrical shock that he sent through me was unbelievable. I heard him growl softly then he was eating me with gusto. His lips, tongue and teeth were torturing me toward an orgasm almost as soon as he started. Along with his mouth, his fingers were touching and teasing. I shuddered when he thrust a finger inside of me. God, his finger felt thick and so good thrusting into me.

He paused in his teasing to slide another finger inside of me and look up at my face. He had a hungry look on his handsome face. "Come for me, Sloan. Come all on my face," he growled then he lowered his head again. He attacked me even more and it was only a matter of moments and I was there. I tightened around his invading fingers and gave a scream as I came. I spasmed over and over as I felt the intense wave of relief flow through my body. My whole body tingled.

I was close to recovering my wits when he sat up. He gave me a serious look. "Tell me now to stop, or I don't think I can. If this is all you want, tell me."

I shook my head. "No, I don't want you to stop. I need more, Mark. Please, don't stop," I pleaded. I knew if he stopped before I had him inside of me, I'd probably die. He stood up and tore open his jeans and shoved them down. When he stood up from removing them and his socks, I caught sight of his hard cock. It was large and angry looking. His hand stroked his cock a couple of times before he reached into his drawer and pulled out a condom.

He rolled it down his long length and crawled onto the bed with me. His hand slid under my ass and he lifted me up as he walked himself between my legs. He spread me wide. The head of his cock teased my slit, and I lifted up to impale myself on his hard cock. He chuckled and then I felt him pressing inside of me. I shook as he slowly slid inside taking his time to allow me a chance to get used to him. He was stretching me more than I ever recalled being stretched before.

When he was in to the hilt, he paused and blew out a deep breath. "Jesus, you're so damn snug. Tell me if it's too much." Before I could ask what he meant, he drew back his hips and pistoned back inside of me. I swear, I thought I saw stars. When I didn't say anything, he sped up his thrusts. As he pounded into me, his hands were busy teasing my nipples and my clit.

I lost track of time as he plowed into me over and over and the deep winding pleasure inside of me got tighter. I knew I was getting close to another release, and it was going to be spectacular. Both of us were panting and I couldn't help but tease his nipples and sink my short nails into his shoulders. He hissed and then sped up. Just as I was about to tell him, I was going to come, it hit and I couldn't do anything but moan as I clamped down on him and milked his cock with my pussy. He groaned and thrust a few more times then he froze and started to jerk. I could feel him filling the condom with his load.

When we both relaxed, he dropped down over me and helped himself from crushing me with his elbows. He nuzzled my ear as he whispered in a panting voice, "That was amazing, baby. I think you might have fried my brains."

I laughed softly. "Right back at you, stud. I can't think."

He chuckled and then slowly rolled off me. I vaguely watched him take care of the condom and drop it in the trash beside his bed before he was back next to me and he had me in his arms. He gave me a gentle kiss. His eyes were studying me.

"What?" I asked.

"No regrets?"

"No regrets, though I will admit, I've never gone to bed with a man this quickly in my life. You must have some strong voodoo, Mark. You completely made me lose myself."

"Baby, I've never felt like this for someone in my life, so I think that makes us even. I knew as soon as I saw you that first day, we'd be amazing together, I just didn't realize how amazing," he said as he rubbed soothingly up and down my arm. I leaned over and gave him a kiss. He took over and had my head whirling before he stopped again. I shoved at his chest.

"Let me up. I need to use the bathroom."

He reluctantly let me get up. In the bathroom, I

did my business as he stayed in the bedroom. I looked at myself in the mirror. I was still flushed and I saw whisker burns on my breasts. I touched one. Now that we'd seen what it was like, how would I ever be able to resist him? I could see that he could become like a drug. I'd never had a man make me feel what he just did.

Him stepping up behind me and wrapping his arms around me shook me out of my thoughts. His eyes met mine in the mirror. "Let's go to bed, babe." I let him lead me out to his bed and tuck me under the covers with him curled up around me. He turned out the lights and kissed me. "'Night, sweetheart."

"'Night, Mark," I said. He fell asleep before I did. I lay there thinking about what this would mean for me in the future, happiness or heartache? I prayed for happiness.

Mark:

I woke up to a still dark bedroom. The clock showed it was three in the morning. Sloan was curled up on her side with her bottom tucked into my groin. I felt myself getting hard just feeling her against me.

I lay there, trying not to react as I thought about our bout earlier. I couldn't call it sex because it was more than sex. I'd been honest when I said I'd never felt anything like that. She'd reached in and grabbed a hold of something inside of me and I wasn't sure she'd ever let it go. Nor did I know if I wanted her to let go.

Finding women to have sex with had never been a problem even before the whole biker thing, but I'd never been instantly enthralled by one. Not the way I was with her. Something deep inside told me to hold on to her with everything I had, because if I let her get away, I'd regret it for the rest of my life.

It was the same feeling that had kept me alive during my days in the Navy and during those years undercover. It had never failed me and I wasn't going to ignore it now, even if the idea of being with someone long term was scary. I didn't know if this was what loving someone started out like, but I was going to find out.

Her long hair was spread on the pillow and was teasing my face. I inhaled and took in her flowery shampoo. I ran a finger lightly down her arm. She shivered and edged closer. My erection grew harder. I needed to be back inside of her again. I eased my hand between her legs. The short hairs covering her mound were soft on my fingertips as I teased up and down her slit. She moaned and moved a little, but she didn't open her eyes.

I kept teasing her lightly, trying not to wake her yet. I wanted to see how prepared I could get her before she woke up. Within minutes, she was soaking my fingers with her creaminess. I couldn't wait any longer. I rolled until I could reach my drawer and I took out a condom. I got it on without too much of a fight then I curled behind her. I lifted her top leg. She jolted and turned her head to look at me sleepily. As I held her eyes, I slowly sank into her. She gasped then moaned as I filled her.

She stretched to let me inside her perfect warmth. I kissed her cheek. "I couldn't help it. You looked so damn good, I needed to be inside you again."

She pressed back into me. "Don't apologize. This is the perfect way to wake up. You can do this any time you want." Hearing her say that made me more desperate to take her. I pulled back and slammed into her. She whimpered.

"Is this too hard?" I asked. I didn't want to hurt her.

She shook her head and whispered, "No. More."

I thrust deeper. Soon she was pushing herself back to meet my thrusts. I wanted to go even deeper. I twisted until I was straddling her lower leg and had the upper one pushed up toward her chest. I snapped on the light so I could watch as my cock slid into her over and over. She was holding up her leg and watching us come together too. I felt her tighten. I leaned forward and kissed her.

The combination of all this and rubbing against her clit, sent her off. She yelled as she came. I growled as her contractions caused me to shoot my load. We both moaned as we came and came. It took a while for both of us to calm down enough to stop moving. I felt drained and I fell to the side. I grabbed to hold the condom. I took a moment to catch my breath then I removed it and threw it away.

For the first time in my life, I didn't want anything between me and a woman. I wanted to be able to let myself soften inside of her and move when I felt like it, not when the condom dictated. But I'd never been with a woman without one. That was something you only did when you were in a committed relationship. I'd never wanted to risk a woman getting ideas or giving me something.

I tugged her tight into my arms. "What would you think of us taking a bath in a nice hot tub of water?"

"I think that would be heaven. Let's do it," she said with a smile. I reluctantly let her roll out of my arms then I got up and followed her to the bathroom. She went in the toilet area while I started the water and then I got us towels and a washcloth. When there was enough water to start covering us, we both sank into the water. She sighed. I pulled her back to lie with her back on my chest.

I couldn't keep my hands from caressing her soft skin. My lips teased her neck and ear. She laughed. "That tickles with your whiskers, Mark."

"It's supposed to tickle. I love to hear you laugh. Tell me something about yourself that no one else knows."

She was quiet for a few moments as she thought. I wondered if I'd pushed for something too soon. Just because I was feeling like this was more than a fling, she might not feel the same, even if she confessed, she'd never gone to bed with a man this fast before.

"I've always been scared of commitment. I didn't want to end up like my mom. I think they love each other deep down, but I don't think she's very happy."

"You could be right about her not being happy, but that's no reason to be afraid of trying for yourself."

"What about you? Tell me something about you."

I decided to let her know what I was thinking. "I've never been in a committed relationship nor ever thought I'd want to be." She stiffened slightly. I hurried to continue. "However, with you, I seem to want to give this a real chance. It sounds crazy, but something is telling me if we don't, we'll regret it."

She looked over her shoulder at me. I saw the surprise on her face. "Is it that gut of yours or something else?"

"It's my gut and a whole lot more. I had the crazy

thought after we got done earlier that I didn't want to have to use condoms. I've never not used them, Sloan. I never wanted to risk it. With you, I wanted to say the hell with them."

She turned all the way around and faced me with her legs over my thighs. "Me too. I thought I must be nuts. I've always used them even though I'm on birth control. I never trusted a guy to be clean or stay that way."

"I can promise you, I know I'm clean and no way would I be with you and fool around with another woman. My dad didn't raise me to be like that. If I'm going to be in a relationship, then I'm loyal. My dad never cheated on our mom."

"But they were married. Most people don't see it that way. Some not even if they are married. We're not in that kind of relationship which makes thinking about that crazy."

"Call it crazy, but we're both thinking about it. I want to know what it's like to be bare inside of you. Nothing between us. However, if you're not sure, we'll wait until you are," I told her. I'd never make her do something she wasn't sure of.

She was quiet for a long minute. Finally, she looked at me again. "I need to be sure, Mark. I feel like I want to say yes and that's a little scary for me. Give me time to get used to us."

"Of course, I will. Just know, when you are, if you are, just tell me. I'll go get the test again if you want. Whatever it takes. Until then, we'll keep using condoms," I told her. She laid her head on my chest and

I held her tight. As we lay in the water and I rubbed up and down her back, I asked her another question.

"I know I got us off track earlier, but you said you cry every time you talk to your mom. Is everything alright?"

She shrugged. "It's as right as it ever is. Dad is still the one calling all the shots, and she does what he says even if she disagrees. Like I said, I think they love each other, but it's not what I'd want in a loving relationship. You know, growing up, I always wondered why they only had me. Now, as an adult, I'm glad they didn't have other kids. One of us growing up in that environment was enough."

"Abuse can be more than physical, you know that. Even if he never hit you, he has been mentally abusive to both of you."

"Yeah, I know and I still love him deep down. He's my dad. But I don't agree with him, and I won't change myself to make him happy, which is what he wanted. He's always wondered why I'm not more like Mom. In looks and some behaviors I am, but when it comes to taking what she does, no way. I guess that probably comes from him."

"I get it. I'm a lot like my dad. He was never mentally or physically abusive, but he had definite ideas. Our mom was never one to back down if she believed something he didn't. They'd argue once in a while, but it was still obvious they loved each other. That's why when she died, he was never the same. He lost the love of his life. Then he had to continue raising mainly Cassidy alone. It was tough on him. I think that's one of the reasons he put so much of himself into the company when me and the guys first formed it. It gave him something else to focus on."

"When did you lose him?"

"A little over a year after we formed Dark Patriots. He had an undiagnosed heart condition. One day he complained of chest pain and then a couple days later, he was gone. Losing him like that made me even more protective of Cassidy."

"Is that one of the reasons you never told her about the Latoya assignment?"

"Yeah, I knew she'd want to come with me. We both tried to look out for each other."

"Which was the same reason you hid the fact that you were still alive all that time. She's still mad about it, but she understands. She can't lie and say she might not have done the same to protect you."

"Probably," I told her. We grew silent and just relaxed. When the water began to get cool, I moved her. "Let's get out of here before you get cold." I stood and pulled the drain. I helped her out of the tub and dried her before I dried myself then I carried her back to bed. I cuddled her up in my arms.

"Let's try to get some more sleep. We have a lot to work on later today. I'm so damn glad you agreed to work on this with me."

"Me too," she told me sleepily. I watched her eyes close. I listened to her breathing until my own eyes grew heavy and I drifted off.

Mark: Chapter 11

Over two weeks had passed since Sloan had agreed to help on the case and she'd moved into my house. I couldn't believe two weeks was all the longer it had been. Besides the work we'd done on discovering what we could about the Soldiers of Corruption and the Legion of Renegades, our relationship had grown.

It felt like I'd known her for ages instead of less than a month. We worked well together though we did have our disagreements. Sometimes they could get a little heated, but we never stayed angry at each other. Or at least we hadn't until this latest one. She was insisting on something that I didn't think I could allow.

We'd determined all we could remotely. What was needed now was to get some feet on the ground and in the Legion's doors if possible. After talking to Reaper and the guys, I'd determined that we didn't necessarily have anyone else in our company who could do the job, other than me.

This had led to a big argument not only with Sloan, but with Cassie. Cassidy was adamant that I couldn't do another assignment. I knew she was afraid that I'd be sucked in for months if not years again. I was just as determined not to let that happen.

Sloan was just as adamant that if I had to do the footwork myself, I had to take someone with me. She was insisting she be the one to do it, which was why we were all gathered at my house tonight. I had to convince them that I could do this and get what we needed, which was a foot in the door, if they'd just let me do it alone.

"You can't do this, Mark! You gave up five years of your life already for a club like this. No way am I watching as you do it again. Let the feds find someone else they can put in the club to find out the ins-and-outs so they can take it down," Cassie yelled.

"You know they don't have someone like me, Cass. Not only have I done it, but I also have the Undertaker's reputation I can use. We know that they've heard of the Tres Locos. No way they'll turn down the chance to have one of them join their club or at least associate with them."

"Oh no, they won't ever suspect why you weren't arrested, will they?" she said hotly. She was standing with her hands on her hips. Sean and the guys were quiet. Sloan was sitting across from me with a determined look on her face. I knew she was going to argue with me for another reason.

"My backstory is a solid one. I told you, I can show proof that I was in jail and got out before anyone knew who I was. I was never arrested with the Tres Locos, so I didn't have a rap sheet like the others. The Soldiers only dream of being as big time as the Locos were. Even with their main chapter and the five they took over, they're scope isn't as wide or as deep. Besides, no one at the company has the experience to go into this and come out okay."

"Why can't they find someone else that has MC experience?"

"It would take too long to get them up to speed. We want to help Reaper and his guys now. As soon as we can start taking them down, we can help them get rid of Slither and Ogre. They're the biggest threats to them and Cheyenne."

"I know and I want to help, but not at the cost of losing you," she cried. I could see tears in her eyes. I went over and hugged her close.

"You won't lose me. I don't plan to stay like I did the last time. I'll get in and get what I need to start the process and then disappear."

"But you're planning to do it without backup. No one in there is guaranteed to be on your side. You won't know which of the guys are still good guys. Who can you trust to have your back?"

I was about to argue that I had all of them to back me up from afar when Sloan cleared her throat. I shook my head. I knew what she was about to say.

"Don't," I told her.

She narrowed her eyes on me. "Don't do what? Suggest a solution? Just because you're too damn stubborn to consider it, doesn't mean it's not a good idea."

"I told you no, Sloan. We're not doing that."

"Well, it's a good thing that you're not the only

one allowed to talk," she shot back.

"What's she talking about?" Cassidy asked as she looked between the two of us.

"Nothing," I said, trying to stop the inevitable conversation.

"Bullshit, it's nothing. Your brother is being a hard-ass and won't consider the one option that gives him backup, if he goes into the Legion's clubhouse."

"Who?" Cassidy asked hopefully.

"I said no, Sloan. Drop it," I growled. I hated fighting with her, but no way was I doing this.

"No, I won't drop it, Mark. You have me and I know what it's like to be in an outlaw club. I can go in as your backup. That way you have at least one person you know you can rely on. While you work the men for information, I can work the women."

I let go of Cassidy and handed her over to Sean. I saw the look of hope on my sister's face. I had to stop this now. I stormed over to Sloan and took her by the shoulders. I gently shook her. "It's not happening. I'm not taking you or any other woman into that kind of environment. Those clubs are hell for the women."

"I know they are."

"I can't guarantee your safety."

"I'm not asking you to. I've done assignments before where my safety isn't guaranteed. However, I know we can do this together."

I shut her up from saying more the only way I knew how—I kissed her. She kissed me back but I could tell she wasn't giving in. Everyone else just stared at us looking a little shocked.

I was about to argue my point more when Gabe spoke. "I get why you don't like the idea, Mark. No one wants to put Sloan or anyone else in danger, but she does have a point. Out of the ones we know, you two are the best situated to pull this off. You can approach the Legion with her at your side. Claiming her as your old lady will give her some protection, even if they aren't like the Iron Punishers and our other friends when it comes to family. She's right that an old lady or girlfriend is more likely to get a woman to talk than a man."

I gave him a pissed look. He shrugged. Sean was frowning. I looked at him. "Back me up here, Sean."

He sighed. "I'd like to, but it does make sense."

"So, you'd want Cassidy to do it, if the roles were reversed?" I asked him angrily.

"Hell no, I wouldn't want her to do it."

"So, it's fine as long as it's Sloan but not my sister?"

"That's not what I'm saying," he sputtered.

"It doesn't matter, I said no and that's it."

Sloan pulled away from me and started to pace. She was looking more pissed. "So that's it, you just refuse to discuss it and we all fall in line. That's not fair, Mark. You promised you'd never dictate like that."

"I promised we'd always talk it out when it came to us. This is work and the last I checked, you work for the Dark Patriots. We tell you your assignments, not the other way around."

I knew as soon as I said it, I'd overstepped. She went rigid and stared at me. I saw the shock and disappointment on her face. "Fine, if that's what you want, Mr. O'Rourke, I'm off this assignment. If you'll excuse me, I have something I need to do." She swung around me as she walked out of the room. She was headed for the stairs. Shit! I looked at the others.

"I need to continue this another time. I hate to cut your visit short, but I think I need to talk to her alone."

"Brother, you need to do more than talk. That is one pissed-off woman. We'll leave you to it. We'll talk more about this later. Come on, let's leave them in private," Griffin said as he headed for the door. Gabe was right behind him, nodding. Sean drew a reluctant Cassie behind him. At the door, they all said goodbye and she gave me a hug. I closed the door and took a deep breath. Time to face the mess I'd just made.

When I got upstairs, she wasn't in my room. I went next door to the room I'd given her that first day. Though she'd stayed with me in my room every night, she still had some of her stuff in it. I walked in to find her packing. I walked over and took the suitcase away.

"Don't do that. Talk to me," I said.

"Why should I? It's obvious you won't listen. You've made up your mind, so there's no reason for me to stay."

"Of course, there's a reason for you to stay! This has nothing to do with you and me, Sloan."

"Yes, it does. It has everything to do with

us. I thought we were building something here. A relationship that was built on respect and honesty, a partnership. I was wrong. All that stuff you told me was a lie. It's really like my parents. Things will be fine as long as I go along with what you want. I told you I never wanted that and that's why I never had a lasting relationship. You agreed with me. Now, you're backing out. I can't be in whatever this is turning into. You made that clear when you pulled the boss card. So, I'm getting my stuff and we'll keep things professional. I'll take the assignments I'm given and you won't need to worry about me pushing for more."

The bottom dropped out of my stomach. I never meant it like that. I'd let my fear of her getting hurt overload my mouth. I tried to take a hold of her, but she sidestepped me. She put the bed between us.

"Please, don't do this. I'm sorry. I know I should have never said the assignment thing."

"Then why did you?" she asked with her arms crossed. I could tell she was fighting not to cry.

"Because I can't let you do something I know is dangerous. It would destroy me if something happened to you because of me."

"And I wouldn't be destroyed if you go in there and something happens to you?"

I didn't know what to say. She came around the bed and sat down on the edge. I sat down beside her. She looked me deeply in the eyes and took my hand. "It would hurt as much if something happened to you as if something happened to me. My gut tells me we can do it together, but you alone, I'm afraid of what that could mean. I'm being selfish because I can't let you go for days, weeks or months. For this thing between us to work, we need to be together."

"This thing? It's not a thing. I know this is too soon and you're gonna think I'm nuts, but what we have is most definitely a relationship that I want to be a partnership," I told her.

"Well, I'm going to probably scare you into running with what I'm about to say, Mark. But I feel like I need to say it and let the chips fall where they may. I'm falling in love with you and it's crazy to say that this soon, but it's how I feel."

I sighed. "Thank God, because I'm feeling the same way about you. That's why the thought of you going with me is so damn hard. I never had to worry about someone like I would you. If they treat their women like the Locos or the Soldiers do, I'll lose it if they touch you, Sloan. I could put us and the whole assignment in jeopardy."

"You know that I can take care of myself. It's not like a defenseless woman going into this. I was brought up in the MC life and I was a Marine. I won't go in there unprepared. Just like you won't go in unprepared. However, it makes sense not to go alone. You've had the first few nights of actual full sleep in years. You told me that. It's because you know you can relax and I have your back."

She wasn't wrong. I had told her that I'd gotten the first full nights of sleep I've had in five years since she had been staying with me. The first night it happened, I was amazed. There was something about her that calmed my mind and body enough to actually sleep. One night, I came awake to noises and found her already awake and checking the windows with her gun in hand.

"I do relax, but we won't be able to do that there. Everything is pointing to making contact with them and seeing if I can get them to trust me. I don't have a clue what that will be like and taking you into that is not something I want to do."

"Well, I don't want you to go alone. So, we're at a standstill it seems. Are you going to order me to stay or let me come with you?"

I looked into her eyes. I knew if I made it an order, she'd do it but then I'd most likely lose her. I couldn't live with that option either. I was between a rock and a hard place. As I thought, she stayed quiet. I could see the unease and almost panic on her face. She had no idea what I would do. Finally, I came to a decision. I might live to regret it, but it was the one that I knew I could live with the most. I stood up and grabbed her suitcase.

"What're you doing, Mark?" she asked as she jumped to her feet. I grabbed the items in it and took them over to the dresser. I shoved them in a drawer.

"You're not leaving me, Sloan. Put this shit back. I may end up regretting this, but we'll do it together. Just don't think that the next time we argue that you can pull this on me again. We'll talk it out. Scream if you need to, but don't threaten to leave me. Understand?"

"Okay, I understand as long as you actually listen and don't pull rank on me for no real reason. I meant what I said. I won't become my parents," she said as she finished putting the clothes back. I pushed her suitcase to the floor with a clatter and grabbed her. I swung her around, carried her to my room and put her on the bed.

"Strip, I need to feel you around me. Show me that you're here and with me. If we're doing this, you need to get used to being a part of me at all times. I won't want you out of my sight for long. We'll be in constant contact even when we're in the same place."

I started to strip off her clothes. She hurried to help me. "How will that look? Won't they be suspicious?"

"I don't give a damn if they are. You'll be going in as my old lady. We're newly together and I can't get enough. I'll also be insanely jealous and no man will be allowed to talk to you let alone touch you. I'll make that clear from the beginning. They can think it's because I'm nuts, I don't care, as long as it keeps you safer. Now, enough talk, I need inside of you," I growled as I looked at her naked body and hurried to strip my clothes off.

As I finished undressing, I reached for my drawer that had the condoms. She grabbed my wrist. I gave her a puzzled look. Didn't she want to make love?

"You don't need that. I want you to go bare, like we talked about."

Her words shook me. We'd been using condoms, and I'd wondered if she'd ever want to get rid of them. I'd shown her my test results showing I was clean, and she'd assured me she had her old ones showing she was. She hadn't been with anyone in a couple of years, which made me damn happy to hear.

"Are you sure, baby?"

"I'm sure. I told you that I'm in love with you. I think this is a good time to throw those away. I'm protected and clean. You're clean. Let's do it."

I didn't argue. My excitement increased as I got her sprawled out on the bed. I teased her until she was ready to explode with my mouth and fingers on her sweet pussy. It didn't take me long to get her to that stage. However, instead of pushing her over like I usually did, I held back and placed myself at her entrance. She was panting as I held her gaze and slowly started to push inside.

Instantly, the heat was what I noticed. She was even hotter than usual. And she felt tighter which didn't seem to be possible. The sensation of her heat and tightness had me groaning as I pushed into her slowly. I wanted to savor this first time completely bare.

Once I'd gotten all the way in, I couldn't wait. I pulled back and slammed back inside. Streaks of fire seemed to race through me. Oh God, it felt so much better. I grabbed her hips and lifted them off the bed. She wrapped her legs around me. I pistoned in and out of her.

"Fuck, that feels perfect, Sloan. It's so much more. Do you feel it?"

She moaned and nodded as she pushed to meet my thrust. "Yes, oh God, Mark, I'm close already." She nipped my chest and more fire raced up my legs. I was close too.

I pulled out of her. She cried out, but I flipped

her over. "Get on your hands and knees." She nodded as she hurried to do it. As soon as she was in position, I pounded back inside of her. This position put me in place to go just a little deeper and I could go harder. I wanted to howl as my balls slapped off her pussy and she whimpered. She had her head buried in the pillow.

I used her hips as handles to be able to pull her back hard to meet each of my thrusts. The tingling was rushing up my legs. I was close and her pussy was starting to grip me tighter, which I knew signaled the start of her orgasm. I sped up and then felt the world explode as she cried out and clamped down on me, milking my aching cock and I let go of my own release. I could feel my warm cum filling her.

I slid in and out to prolong the pleasure even after I stopped coming and she'd relaxed her tight grip on me. I didn't want it to end. It had truly been the best sexual release of my life. Finally, I was too soft to do anything else but pull out. I flopped down on the bed and took her with me. I cuddled her tightly against me so I could kiss her.

When we stopped kissing, I told her, "That was out of this world, Sloan. I'm never wearing a condom again."

"If you do, I might have to kill you. That was truly unbelievable," she whispered. Her hands were gently rubbing up and down my chest. She placed scattered kisses across my chest and shoulders. I grew drowsy. Suddenly, she rolled away from me.

"Where are you going?"

"To clean myself up. This is a little messier than

with a condom. I'll be back."

I laughed and lay there. It might be messier, but it was far better. When she came back, she had a washcloth with her. She used it to clean me and then she tossed it in the hamper by the bed.

"Thank you, baby. Are you ready for some sleep? I'm tired."

"Yeah, me too," she said with a yawn. She snuggled into me and closed her eyes. I heard her breathing change right before my eyes got too heavy to keep open. My last thought was we'd talk about what we were going to do in the morning. It looked like I was going to have a partner this time.

Sloan: Chapter 12

It had taken a week, but we'd ironed out our plan for approaching the Legion of Renegades aka the Soldiers of Corruption. Mark still wasn't happy that I was going, but he agreed it would make sense to have backup with him and that there was no one he could use to do it besides me.

Gabe had suggested we use one of Reaper's men, however, Mark had shot that idea down. There was no way to know if their guys were known, since they were targeted by the Soldiers. This was why he didn't want to chance using one of the guys from the Warriors or one of their other friends. There was no way to know how much they'd dug up before approaching the Iron Punishers.

We set up our communication drop online with Sean and the rest of the Patriots' team. It would be like the encrypted site Mark used when he was undercover with the Locos. A code word was established that if used, they would know to immediately extract us. It would only be used in case of a true emergency.

Mark spent hours drilling me on what he wanted me to do and not do. He'd been serious. He wanted me with him every possible second he could.

Thankfully, I looked the part though nothing like him. I knew how to dress and talk. It would be a harder and sometimes cruder version of myself. I went to a secondhand store and bought more clothes that would be appropriate for my role as an old lady. They were tight and sexy, though not totally slutty. After all, I was going as his old lady, not a bunny or hang around.

We set up a room at a local hotel not far from the Legion's clubhouse. The night before we left, we had a get-together with Cassidy, Sean, Noah, Griffin and Gabe. They couldn't let us go without one. It had been hard to see the tears in Cassidy's eyes and how Mark held her. The guys had looked stressed. I couldn't blame them. Thank God I got to go with him or I would have been a mess.

Before we left the hotel to ride up to the Legion's clubhouse. Mark kissed me and asked, "Are you ready?"

I nodded. "I'm ready. Let's go see what we can find out. Be careful. I love you."

He smiled. "I love you too and you remember to be careful. Don't trust any of them, not even the women." He'd already told me this a million times. I nodded. We got on his bike and took off for the clubhouse. We'd scouted and knew it was an old run-down bar on the outskirts of town. They had put up a fence around the place. There had been a dozen bikes there last night. I wondered how many more would be there tonight with this being the start of the weekend.

I tried to settle the butterflies in my stomach as we roared up to the gate. I saw a young guy looking out through the chain link fence with a frown on his face. He had on a cut that had the word *Prospect* on it. We stopped at the gate and waited for him to approach. When he finally did, Mark, or Undertaker as I now had to remember to call him, turned off his loud bike. I'd been practicing all week, calling him only that.

"What do you want?" the prospect asked surly.

"I'm here to see your president, Dax. I understand this is the Legion of Renegades clubhouse." Mark had a confident air about him. He looked like he was almost bored.

"So, what if it is? Who're you?" the young man snapped back. Undertaker lowered his sunglasses and glared at him.

"I'm motherfucking Undertaker. I have some business to talk to your president about. I suggest you find me someone with a brain. I don't talk to the underlings. You've got five minutes and then I'm gone."

He turned just enough to act like he was whispering something to me. This flashed his cut. He'd decided to pull out his old Tres Locos cut. It was a chance he was taking if he was seen by the wrong people wearing it, but he knew they wouldn't have bought his story if he didn't have it. You'd have to be under a rock not to know who they were if you were in a club. The guy's eyes got big.

He stumbled back to the small shack by the gate and pulled out his phone. He was talking animatedly to someone and he had a frown on his face. When the five minutes had elapsed, Undertaker fired up his bike and started to back up. The kid ran to the fence. "Wait, someone will be coming."

Undertaker shook his head. "I said five minutes and that's come and gone. I guess they're not interested. I'm out of here. Too bad. It could have been good for you and your club." He backed up and took off. In his mirrors, I could see the guy running toward the clubhouse.

He took us back to the hotel in town. It was one that was along the main drag and he made sure to park his bike out front where it would be easy to see. It was all part of his plan. As soon as we got in the room, I started to laugh.

"Damn, Undertaker is such an impatient asshole. How soon do you think it'll be before they come to find you?"

"Not long. Once he tells them I left and didn't seem to give a shit, they'll be wondering what I wanted. You need to be ready for when they come. I'll do the talking and you look unapproachable as hell. Undertaker is a hard-ass and his woman needs to appear to be hard too."

"I know, I won't forget. I have to admit, when you put on that cut, your whole persona changed. I could see Undertaker."

"That's what kept me alive for all those years. Now, it's going to keep us alive. Why don't you relax while we wait? I'll let the guys know we made initial contact." He sat down and got on his laptop. It only took him a few minutes to get into the system and leave them the innocent looking message. *Met the first of the family. Seemed busy. Hope to see them later today.*

I worked hard to settle and not be nervous as we waited. He turned on the television and was watching some car show. I tried to read a book on my e-reader but it was hard to concentrate. Not quite an hour later, we heard what sounded like a large group of bikes pulling up outside the hotel. Undertaker went to the window and peeked out. I went to look too.

A group of half a dozen bikes were pulled up in front of the hotel. All the men getting off the bikes wore Legion of Renegades' cuts. They looked around and went over to Undertaker's bike. I felt him tense as they checked it out, but no one touched it. One of them broke away and went inside to the front desk. A couple of minutes later, he came out and pointed in the direction of our room. He must have gotten our room number from the clerk.

Undertaker eased us back away from the window. He pointed to the dark bathroom. I took up position there as he got behind the door. Both of us had our guns out. A moment later, there was a loud knock at the door. He yelled through it. "Who's there?"

"Open up. We heard you wanted to speak to us," came the reply.

"I want to speak to a lot of people. That doesn't tell me shit," he yelled back.

The guy banged on the door. "Listen, asshole, you came to our clubhouse, asking to speak to us. Open the hell up or we're coming in." He'd barely finished his threat when Undertaker whipped the door open and pointed his gun in the guy's face. I heard the others all curse.

The guy's eyes got round as he looked into the .45 pointed at his face. His face went white. "Are you Dax? If not, I don't wanna talk to you or any other cheesedick he has doing his work for him. I wanna talk to your pres or forget it. I have business to discuss," Undertaker growled. The other guys had all pulled their guns, and he didn't even blink. I could feel sweat building down my spine. If they started shooting, Mark was dead.

"And I don't like all these assholes pointing their guns at me. Half of them will shoot you before they ever hit me," he told the man in front of him. As they waited in an uneasy standoff, one of the guys in the back, pushed to the front. He took off his sunglasses and stared at Undertaker for a moment and then he spoke.

"I'm Dax. Who the hell are you and what business would we possibly have? My man said you had a Tres Locos cut on. Turn so I can see the back of your cut, Undertaker," he demanded as he read his name on the front. Undertaker twisted just enough to show the name on the back without turning his back on the guns aimed at him. A murmur went through them.

"Where the fuck did you get that?" Dax hissed as he read the name.

"Where the fuck I got it, is from the Tres Locos when I joined them almost five years ago. I'm Undertaker. I'm their enforcer."

"Well, Undertaker, in case you haven't heard, the Tres Locos have been taken down by the feds, which means you're full of shit. You stole it off the real Undertaker," Dax sneered.

"Alright, if that's what you think, head on home boys. I'll go take my business elsewhere. I heard that the Legion was now dealing in more lucrative things. I guess I heard wrong. I'm sure someone is interested in making more money than they ever did." He went to close the door, but Dax's hand shot out and stopped him.

"Who told you that the Legion would be interested in whatever you're talking about? For all we know, you're a cop trying to set us up."

"Well, your man, Serpent, didn't think so when I ran into him a few months back. He told me all about you and how the Soldiers of Corruption were taking over clubs and putting them on the right path. He seemed to think that was something the Locos and I would be interested in. Only thing is, before I could get my club to consider checking you out, they got hit by the goddamn feds. Fucked up everything."

"How did you get away from the feds?" a guy whose cut read *Roman, VP* on it, asked. You could hear the suspicion in his voice.

"I don't like to stand outside, telling my business. If you want to talk, I suggest we do it somewhere more private. There's an old, abandoned barn not far from your clubhouse. How about we meet there in half an hour? You bring a couple of your guys but no more," Undertaker told him. I knew he didn't want to be caught inside of their compound yet. We'd done this as a calculated risk when we first rode up to their gate. So far, none of them had seen me hiding in the doorway of the bathroom. I had my gun aimed at Roman.

"Who will you bring as your backup?" Dax asked with a smirk.

"I don't need backup, but I'll bring my woman along to watch the show. Hey, baby, why don't you come out here?" he yelled. This was also part of our plan. I put away my gun and came sashaying out like I didn't have a care in the world. I went up to him and gave him a kiss on the cheek, as I wrapped myself around his left side. I heard several of them murmur. I'd made sure I was dressed to the nines and looking extra sexy.

"Well, well, if you're bringing this tasty thing to the party, we might just have something to talk about," Dax said with an oily tone to his voice. Undertaker looked at him with death in his eyes.

"She's not on the menu. I don't share. However, she goes where I go. Do you wanna talk or not? If not, I have other places I can be. I heard of a club over in Virginia that might be interested in what I have to talk about."

I could see the greed and wariness in Dax and Roman's faces. The others looked like they were just there to follow the lead of their president and VP. It didn't look like there was much in the brains department. That didn't mean they were less dangerous, just more easily fooled, hopefully.

Greedy eyes were checking me out which made my skin crawl. I should be used to that feeling. There had been plenty of guys who had looked at me that way in my dad's club. Only they were too afraid of him to do anything. I smiled up at Undertaker like I didn't have a care in the world.

"If you want to meet, we'll do it at our clubhouse, not at some old barn. We can't party there like we can at the clubhouse. Why don't you and your bunny come tonight at eight and you can meet the rest of the club and we can talk?"

"Let's get this straight. I go to your clubhouse with no guarantee I get to leave, and you expect me to do that, while you have your whole club there. I'd like to talk to Serpent. He's the one I talked about this with first. I trust him. I don't know you."

They all exchanged nervous looks. We knew that they couldn't produce Serpent because Reaper had killed him. However, using his name gave us a possible in without it backfiring in our faces.

"Serpent isn't available right now. He's off on another assignment. When did you say you spoke to him? And where?"

"It was almost three months ago and it was down in Tennessee somewhere. We met one night. I was there with some of the guys. We were passing through on our way home from a rally. We got to drinking with him, Loon, Tires, and Chubbs. I told my club about it but they got taken down before we could make contact."

I saw a couple of them relax when he mentioned those four names. Undertaker was weaving enough of Reaper's story with his to make it sound believable.

"How did you escape the takedown?" Dax asked.

Undertaker smiled for the first time. "Because of this angel here and fucking timing. Listen, we'll meet you at eight. If you don't like what I have to offer, we'll say no hard feelings and we'll bounce. But I think if you give me a chance, you'll see it's a chance of a lifetime."

Dax thought about it and then nodded. "See you at eight. To make sure you don't need anything, I'll leave a couple of guys to escort you there. That way you don't have any trouble getting inside this time."

Undertaker nodded. We both knew we couldn't refuse. They wanted to be sure we didn't run or meet with someone. We could always call I guess, but that would only get us so far. Dax and the others backed away as Undertaker lowered his gun. As the door closed, we heard bikes roar to life. After they faded away, I peeked out the peephole on the door. There were two guys seated right outside our door on their bikes. The game was in play.

I sagged into his arms as he kissed me. I could feel his desperation. "Baby, I wish like hell this could be different. Pray like you've never prayed that they believe us and I can get us out of there tonight. They may try and get us to stay. If they do, we'll have to go with it. I want you to keep your knife and gun on you at all times if you can. They may take our weapons. If they do, stay near me, and stay alert. Fuck, I wish like hell there was an easier way to do this.

"I wish there was too, but it's the only way to get them to even consider what you have to say. None of them spotted me covering you, so they might not think of me as much of a threat."

"No, but you can be used as a threat against me. Jesus Christ, what was I thinking?" he growled.

"You were thinking of how to keep us both happy.

I still think we're safer together than apart. Plus, you figured out how to work me into the story. That has to help when the time comes. Now, why don't we do something to ease all that tension and stress I feel coursing through you?"

His face broke into a grin as he backed me up toward the bed. I knew from the hungry look on his face, I was in for the time of my life. Something that would make us both feel alive and remind us of what we were fighting for later tonight.

✟✟✟✟✟

At twenty to eight, there was a knock at the door. Undertaker opened the door to the two men who'd sat outside all afternoon watching us. They gave him a chin lift. "It's time to go."

Undertaker nodded and turned to me. "Let's go." I grabbed my cut and headed out the door. We'd had one made to match Undertaker's only mine said *Property of Undertaker*. On the front was my name. We'd decided not to deviate too much from my own name. Sloan might have been memorable, but Slo wasn't. Undertaker joked that it was for slow burn. I told him I was much faster than that.

He made sure to keep me behind him and to his left the whole way to his bike. When we got seated, he fired up the bike and the other two did the same. We took off with one of them in the lead and the other behind us. I felt like there was an itch between my shoulder blades. At least he could get a good look at my cut.

Fifteen minutes later, we were pulling into the gate of the Legion's compound. It didn't look much better in the dark than it did in the daylight. Lights lit up the old bar. The guy in front of us pointed to a parking spot. Undertaker stopped and backed into the spot. The two escorts parked down from us.

When we got off the bike, they came over and pointed to the door. One named *Sig*, according to his cut, opened the door. *Cage* was behind us. As we entered, the music got quieter, and we saw the men at the bar all turn and look at us. I quickly took in the room. Besides the men, I saw there were a few women in the room. A couple had on cuts and the rest didn't. Those would be the bunnies or hang arounds. I felt better at least knowing there were other old ladies. They would be the ones most likely to talk out of turn. Thankfully, there were no kids.

Dax got up and came over to us. He nodded at Undertaker. "Glad you came. Have a seat. Let's drink a beer while you tell us your story. She can go sit with the other women." He lifted his chin toward me.

Undertaker shook his head. "My old lady doesn't go anywhere unless I know who she's with. I don't know those women or you. She stays with me. Nothing I have to say is news to her. She knows the deal. If we get to the point of this becoming club business, then she can make herself scarce." He didn't lower his glaring eyes.

Dax chuckled. "If that's the way you want it, though I doubt she's gonna understand much. Women don't have a head for business, that's why they need us. Okay, come have a drink, both of you."

I followed them to the bar and took a seat next to Undertaker. Dax sat on the other side of him. After we were given a couple of beers, he dove right into it. "Tell me how you're out running the country when I heard all the Tres Locos were busted. Seems to me that's mighty suspicious."

"It does sound that way, doesn't it? I'll tell you the reason is all due to this woman right here. She's my lucky charm. If it wasn't for her, I'd be with the rest of them rotting in jail."

I saw them give me curious looks. I gave them a satisfied smile. Now for the story we'd come up with. "How is she the reason? She got connections or something?" Roman asked from the other side of Dax.

"Not connections, but she sure turned my damn head. Here's what happened... the night all the shit went down with my club, I was a few towns over. I'd decided I wanted to go check out what that town had to offer for female companionship. The same old thing was getting boring." A couple of the guys chuckled and nodded their heads.

"None of the others wanted to ride all the way over there, so I went on my own. Anyway, I was in this bar when I saw Slo here come in the door. Damn, did she get my attention along with every other guy's in that place. I gave it a bit to see the lay of the land and then I went to talk to her. Only I wasn't the only guy who wanted to talk to her. This other guy came busting in on our newly started conversation. He was trying to swipe her right out from under my nose."

He looked at the guys sitting around him. He

looked fierce as he said, "I don't let anyone get the jump on me. She was coming back to my place or else. The guy got shitty and started to run his mouth. When I got up to leave and take her with me, after warning him to leave it alone, he tried to jump me. We got into it and before I could get out of there after laying his ass out, the cops showed up. Someone had called them. They arrested me and I was off to jail."

"Why didn't you stay in jail after they caught you? They had to know who you were."

Undertaker laughed and shook his head. "No, they didn't. Since I was in another town alone, we were always told not to wear our colors into places without backup. There had been a few issues in the past. I didn't have my cut on and my name wasn't one they were looking for. Let's just say, I might have gotten caught in a few fights, but anything else, I kept my damn nose pretty clean. They kept me overnight and the next morning they let me leave when this little darling posted my bail. They had no idea that the man they had in jail was part of a big bust going down a few towns over.

"When I got out, we went back to her place. I wasn't about to miss out on a piece of this." He tugged me close. "Good thing I did, otherwise, I would have ridden right into the damn feds at my clubhouse. While I was at her place, I tried to call a few of the guys and got no answers. I was getting worried and planning to head home when she happened to turn on the damn television. Imagine my fucking surprise when I saw the news that the feds had raided the Tres Locos compound and placed the whole damn club under arrest."

He paused to take a swig of his beer. He shook his head. "That was twice that she saved me in less than twenty-four hours. I knew that she had to be good luck. I haven't let her out of my sight since. And she's not disappointed."

"Where have you been? It's been a couple of months since the Locos were arrested," Dax asked.

"I've been all over the place. I wanted to see if I could find any clubs that might be like my old one. Listen, I wore this cut today so you would hopefully recognize who I had been with. I don't ride around with it on, not if I want to stay out of prison. The Locos had a great thing going, but someone got sloppy and that let the feds get their foot in the door. I'm looking for a club where we can do some of the things I did with the Locos without bringing the whole damn thing down on our heads. I'm not finding that and I was about to give up and just go nomad, when I remembered what Serpent said."

"Serpent told you all this without knowing who you were?" Dax asked suspiciously.

"No, he didn't do it at first. We hung out for a couple of days. Then one night when we were all drinking and he was doing a little extra, he told me about the sweet thing you all had going. It's so damn devious, what's not to love. You take goody-two-shoes clubs that don't really get the whole biker life and you secretly turn them into what they supposedly hate the most. It's fucking brilliant."

"And what do you think you can bring to the table if we were really doing something like that?" Dax asked.

"I can bring you the lower-level production lines that were being fed to us as well as help set up something similar for you. The feds think they got our whole operation, but they didn't. They tend to only think of the big guys, not all the little ones that have a part in such a business."

You could see the interest along with the distrust on their faces. He'd at least snared them, now it was time to see if he could get them to believe it. If not, the two of us wouldn't be walking out of here. I inched closer and held my breath.

Undertaker: Chapter 13

I tried not to tense up as I waited to see what Dax would say to my offer. They could very well send us on our way or decide to kill us. I hated having Sloan here, though hopefully her presence would help sell my story.

Dax was quiet as he looked at me and took another drink of his beer. I made sure to project a relaxed air as I drank mine. Finally, he cleared his throat and spoke again.

"You have to understand that we have to be sure of you and what you're offering. We have all kinds of businesses. We'd hate to get into something that would lead us down the path of the Locos. Our brother, Grumble, needs to check out your story. In order to do that, we need to know more than your road name."

"I understand. My real name is Rex Reed. Have your guy do what he needs. I know I check out. How long do you think that's going to take? We weren't planning to hang around long if you're not interested. Like I said earlier, there's another likely club in Virginia." I read between the lines. They had to be sure I wasn't a cop. That's why he said the thing about not going the route of the Locos. However, he didn't realize his earlier comments would have confirmed they were less than a legit business kind of club.

Across the bar, the man, with *Grumble* on his cut, answered when Dax gave him a chin lift. "It'll take me maybe two days. Surely, you can give us that long."

I shrugged. "Two days and then we either sit down and talk business or we head out. Works for me. I'll come back on Sunday evening. Will that work for you?" I asked Dax.

"No need to come back. You two can stay here for the weekend. That'll give us a chance to get to know you. Hopefully, we can do some business together. I know the Tres Locos had a lot of shit going on. Were you involved in all of it or just certain parts?" Dax asked.

I glanced at Sloan and then back at him. I shook my head. "That's getting into specifics. She doesn't need to hear that and I don't wanna discuss it until we have something ironed out between us."

The men gave Sloan a head-to-toe look. I hated the desire I saw on their faces. I knew some of them probably had old ladies over in the huddle in the corner, but that didn't stop them from wanting my woman. I tugged her to me.

"Alright, we can do that. You're right. No need to discuss specifics in front of her. Why don't we just relax and later you can get your stuff and we'll show you where you can stay the night?" Dax added.

I didn't want to stay here, but I knew they might insist. I tried to get out of it, even though I thought it was futile.

"We don't want to impose. We have the room

booked in town for the next few days. I hate to pay for it and not even use it. Why don't we stay there but we can be here during the day if you want? We can get to know each other that way."

I could tell that didn't suit them, but they also didn't want to piss me off in case I was for real.

After a couple minutes of silence, Dax answered, "Fine, stay in town, but I think you'd like it here more. We have lots more entertainment than an old hotel." He grinned and then gave a whistle. The five women in the corner all stood up and trotted over. Two of them wore old lady cuts. One was *Jester's* old lady and the other said *Curly*. They went straight to their men.

One of the bunnies or hang arounds smiled at me and slid in close. "Hi, I'm Erica," she said with a sexy wink.

Sloan pulled away and came around to my other side and got between us. "In case you didn't notice, he's taken. Back off," she growled in a low, menacing voice. I smiled and looked at the Soldiers. They were watching with interest.

"I'd do as she says, ladies. Slo doesn't take kindly to anyone propositioning me," I told them with a wink.

I knew the Soldiers didn't care about things like their old ladies and kids, but I wasn't sure if all of them were that way. It was obvious that the bunnies didn't care if a guy was taken or not.

Jester's old lady frowned and snapped. "Erica, why don't you leave him the hell alone? You know he has an old lady. If he wanted your attention, he'd ask."

I could see the hate on her face. Ah, looks like there were some issues between them. The other two bunnies remained silent.

Roman laughed. "Erica, you better watch it. Slo sounds like she might mean business. Of course, if you wanna put on a show for us, feel free to catfight."

Sloan gave him a smile. "I don't catfight. I throw fists. Believe me, any of your female friends lay a hand on Undertaker, and I'll be beating her ass. I'm his old lady, right, honey?"

"That you are. My lucky charm isn't worth losing." I turned and gave her a kiss. I knew it was showing she was important to me, which could be used against me, but I didn't care. I wanted them to know I'd defend her, and I had no intention of sleeping with any of these bunnies. I preferred not to have them bothering me.

Even when I was with the Locos, I tended to steer clear of the bunnies. When I wanted sex, I'd go to a bar in town and find someone. It had been temporarily satisfying—nothing like being with Sloan.

Erica got a pissed look on her face, but she did back away from me. The other two didn't approach. "Whatever." She pouted.

"Damn, no fight. Okay, let's get the music going and have another drink. We need to get to know Undertaker and Slo."

For the next couple of hours, they tried to get both of us drunk. I knew they were trying to get us to talk more, but I knew how to make it look like I was drinking when I wasn't. I was nowhere close to being drunk and neither was Sloan. After the first hour, she went to sit with the two old ladies, who we'd found out were Jester's lady, Carla, and Curly's woman, Jane.

I was wondering if we'd be able to get away soon and how I would start the conversation when Sloan came up to me. She wrapped her arms around me as she leaned in to whisper, "Ready to get out of here. I have plans for us tonight."

I let the smile spread across my face. I saw Roman and Dax watching us. I turned to them. "I hate to leave, but me and Slo have some personal things needing attention." She nibbled on my ear. They got big leering looks on their faces.

"Don't let us stop you. Go right ahead, we don't mind watching," Roman said with a smirk.

"I don't know how you do it here, but I don't let others see my old lady naked. She's not a damn bunny," I growled back at him.

Roman put up his hands. "Hey, it was worth a try. Curly and Jester never give us a show. Thought maybe you and Slo were different."

"Not when it comes to that. I'm all for you guys enjoying yourself, but my old lady is for my eyes only. We're gonna head out. Does around eleven tomorrow sound alright to be back or do you want it to be later?"

Dax thought for a moment or two then nodded. "Yeah, that's fine. That way we can spend the day. Maybe talk some more and shit."

"Maybe. Okay, see you tomorrow. Thanks for the

invite."

They nodded and watched as I stood up and pulled Sloan close. I gave her a passionate kiss. When I was done, I made sure they could hear me. "Let's go, Lucky. I'm feeling a need."

She laughed and smiled. I threw up my hand in a half wave. We walked out with eyes boring into our backs. The whole way to my bike I was tense. Would they change their minds and try to force us to stay? Shoot us in the back?

I breathed a tiny sigh of relief when we made it not only on the bike but out the gate. The whole ride back, I thought of tonight's adventure. I knew my background would check out. Rex Reed had a deep cover that had been established years ago. The only thing they might hesitate on was the fact they thought I might be a cop, though I'd seen that had diminished a little as we sat there swapping stories. Finding out I had been with the Locos for five years had impressed them, especially to find out I'd advanced to enforcer for them in that time period.

At the hotel, I hustled Sloan inside. I locked the door and peeked out the window. As I watched, she sat quietly on the bed. About five minutes later, a truck pulled into the parking lot and parked where the driver and passenger could see our room. No one got out. Ah, just what I was expecting. I closed the curtain the rest of the way.

"They have two guys watching the room," I told her as I stripped off my cut and threw it over a chair. I hated wearing the damn thing. All it did was bring back bad memories.

"I figured they would send someone once you refused to stay. They won't let us out of their sight until they decide if we're telling the truth or not. If they decide we're not, we're going to pay hell to get out of here alive, Mark."

I went over and sat down beside her. I took off my boots and socks as she slipped hers off. "I know, baby, and I wish like hell you were back home. What the hell was I thinking, letting you talk me into this?"

She ran her hand down my face. "You were thinking it was smarter to have two of us here rather than be alone. Besides, I think I can get Jane and Carla to talk. When I was over with them, they started to talk a little about how the club had changed over the last couple of years. Their old men were part of the original Legion of Renegades from what I heard. Not sure if they like the new direction or not. They were rather reserved about it."

"Good, keep trying to befriend them. It's obvious that Dax and most of the others don't think talking in front of the women is an issue. Either they're that whipped or he just thinks they're stupid."

"My vibe says he thinks they're stupid and that they can be kept in line if they get ideas. I noticed he didn't ask for my real name. He doesn't see me as a threat."

I tugged her over onto my lap. I nuzzled her ear. "He's an idiot if he thinks that. I know it's hard but stick to our plan. I need you to make him think you're not a threat. Feel free to threaten the bunnies all day," I said with a grin.

She growled as she kissed my jaw. "I'll beat a bitch if they touch you. I wasn't kidding about throwing hands with them. You're mine and I don't share."

"I don't share either. Why don't you get out of those clothes so I can show you what you do to me?" My erection was pushing against the zipper of my jeans. It had been hours since I'd been inside of her. She laughed as she shimmied out of her jeans and panties. I watched as she took off her cut, top and then her bra.

I groaned to see all that perfection waiting for my touch. She walked over to me and tugged on my shirt. I let her take it off and then I tackled my jeans and underwear. In under a minute, I was naked and she could see how hard I was.

Her hand grasped me for a moment then she was on her knees sucking me into her mouth. I groaned as her tongue lashed all around the head and sides. I gripped the back of her ponytail and sank deeper. "That's it, babe," I hissed as she swallowed more of me.

I'd found that she could drive me insane with that mouth on my cock. My baby likes to give head and she did it like a champ. As she sucked, she made sure to work the base of my cock and tease my balls. All of it combined made me tighten. I could feel the cum boiling to be released.

I took a moment to decide if I wanted our first time tonight to be down her throat or in her tight pussy. It was a close call, but I decided it was going to be her pussy. I pulled out reluctantly. She pouted as she licked her swollen lips. I helped her to her feet and then laid back on the bed. I patted my hip. "Climb up here and ride your man, baby."

She smiled as she got on the bed and straddled me. I held my cock steady, so she could lower herself on me. I hissed as her fiery pussy took me in a slow inch at a time. I fought not to thrust up and impale her all at once. Right before she reached the bottom, she swirled her hips. That tore a moan from me.

As soon as I was all the way inside of her, she started to ride me. It wasn't slow and easy. She was riding me hard and fast. My hands gripped her plump ass as I squeezed and pumped my cock in and out of her.

I held her ass until the bounce of her breasts became too much to resist. I leaned up and sucked one into my mouth. She hissed and ground her pelvis into mine. I let go of her ass to find her clit. I rubbed across it as she bucked against me. Her cream was coating my cock and starting to run down my shaft. Her insides were quivering. I knew that meant she was getting close to an orgasm.

I pressed more on her clit and rubbed it in circles as she went back to riding me. As she would descend, I'd thrust up hard. She was panting and tugging on her free nipple. I let go of the one I had in my mouth. As I did, I grabbed her hair and tugged her head back. She arched her back.

"Come, Sloan. Come now," I growled as my balls drew up and got ready to fire off their load. She lifted and lowered herself twice more then she gave a scream as she came. Her hot pussy clasped me tight and milked my release out of me. I roared as I filled her full of my cum. We didn't stop moving until both of us were done coming. She collapsed on my chest.

"T-that was amazing," she panted.

I rubbed up and down her back as I caught my breath. I nuzzled her ear with my mouth. "It was," I said.

Once we caught our breath, she got up and went to the bathroom. I heard the water running and assumed she was cleaning herself up. When she came back, I knew I was right. She had a washcloth that she used to clean my cock. Even after that orgasm, the touch of her hand made my cock stir. When she was done washing me, she leaned down and placed a soft kiss on the head. She laughed when he tried to lift himself up. She put the washcloth back in the bathroom and came back to bed.

I pulled her into my arms and kissed her. We kissed for a minute or two before she pulled away. I saw the look in her eye. She was starting to think about what tomorrow could bring. I didn't want to think about it yet, so I rolled her underneath me and kissed my way down her body. I wanted to feel alive and far from here as long as possible.

✟✟✟✟✟✟

After another round of lovemaking, we gave in to the inevitable. We got down to talking about the next day and what we were going to do at the Legions' compound. I wasn't too happy about the thought of her going off yet with the other women. I didn't trust them not to be as bad as the men. Though Curly and Jester had remained very quiet while we were there.

I didn't sleep much and was up more than once to check to see if our guards were still there. They were. More times than not, she woke up with me. By morning, I was tired and just wanted to get this show on the road. At eight, we left the hotel to get breakfast. We acted like we didn't know the truck was there, even when it followed us to the diner down the road.

Once we were done eating, we took a ride. That made it harder to follow us without being seen, so they stopped trying. I still pretended like I didn't see them and we rode around the area, acting like we were just out for a ride.

Around ten thirty, we headed toward the Legions' clubhouse. The truck fell in behind us. When we got to the gate, a prospect was there to let us in without waiting this time. Inside, I parked in the same spot as I had last time. Sloan hopped off and started to take off her helmet. The two guys in the truck got out and came over to us. They were Hook, the enforcer, and Sig.

I saw both of them checking out Sloan with a hungry look in their eyes. I stood up off my bike and leaned closer. "You keep eye fucking my old lady and we're gonna have a problem," I growled.

They both froze for a second or two then Hook replied, "Can't help it. She's fucking sexy as hell. Do you threaten everyone who looks at her?"

"You're damn right I do. Lucky is mine and I don't share or let others take what's mine. You'd better remember that. Now, are we here to fight or do some talking?"

They looked at each other and after a moment, they moved away from the two of us. She slipped her arm through my left one and we headed for the door. She walked like she was a fucking princess. Her head was held high and she swayed her ass. I wanted to spank her for waving her perfect ass at them. They were right behind us when we entered.

Dax and the others were all waiting and drinking. Hook went right to him and leaned down to whisper in his ear.

"Morning," was all I said. Dax looked up and narrowed his eyes. I saw him looking at Sloan but trying not to make it obvious.

He stood up. "Morning. Why don't you two join us and we'll have a drink?"

We took seats at the table where he was sitting. The idiot had his back unprotected. I sat us down, so we had our backs to the wall. She sat down on my left. A prospect brought us each a bottle of beer. I opened them and took a swallow. Sloan took one too.

"How did you sleep last night?" Dax asked.

"Like a baby, well, for some of it anyway," I said with a smile as I looked at her. No one could miss what I was insinuating. I heard them chuckle. She sat there looking totally unfazed by their laughter. She smiled at me.

"I can imagine. Well, we're glad you came back today. Grumble has been working and so far, he's liking what he's found, but you understand that he has more to do," Dax warned us.

"I imagine it will take a while. The Locos never took anyone without checking either. It's better to be safe than sorry. I doubt any of you want to spend time in jail. I know I don't."

"Fuck that, I'm not ever going back," Roman chimed in from his chair. I saw the scowl on his face. A few of the others were muttering. It looked like most of them had done some time at one point or another.

"Did you by any chance get to talk to Serpent? He can help vouch for me," I said, relaxed and unconcerned. I saw them again stiffen and look at each other, but I pretended not to notice.

"Nah, we didn't. Serpent is out dealing with some shit. We didn't think we needed to call him. Grumble can tell us if we should listen to your proposal or not," Dax said with a growl.

I shrugged. "Whatever works for you. I just thought he might be able to help. If not him, Loon, Chubbs or Tires were there too. Anyway, what did you have in mind for today? We can't talk about business, so what are we doing?"

"We thought we'd have a little party and get to know each other better. A few of the ladies will be here later to bring the food. I thought we'd relax and see how the day goes," Dax answered.

I knew from the way he said it, he was hoping for more. I wasn't sure if he thought he'd get me to let down my guard and talk or maybe see if he could get anything out of Sloan. I nodded like I didn't have a care in the world.

"That works for us. So, tell me about yourselves. You know my story, what about you guys? Have you been with the Legion long? Dax, you and Roman have to have been, you're the leaders. I know that takes time."

They looked at each other and smirked. "Not that long. We came in at the right time. The club had a bunch of old farts who were no longer interested in the club like they used to be. We came in and not long after, most of them left except for Jester, Curly, Frost and Nox," Dax said as he lifted his chin toward them. Those four didn't say anything, just sat there with closed expressions on their faces. *Ah, maybe they weren't as enamored of the new regime as I first thought.*

"None of you were interested in being the leaders after the old guard left?" I asked them.

Jester was the one to answer. He looked at Dax and then at me. "Nah, we decided to leave it to the new bucks," was all he said. I judged him to be in his forties as well as Curly. Frost and Nox looked more like they were in their thirties like me.

"Are you and Curly the only ones with old ladies or will we be meeting more of them later?"

"We're the only ones with old ladies," Curly volunteered.

"Well, if they need any help with food, let Slo know. She's a mean-ass cook."

All of them looked at her. She was relaxed beside me drinking her beer. She nodded. "I'd be happy to help. If it's just the two of them, that's a lot of work. How many guys are in this chapter?"

"There are the ten of us members and then the three prospects," Roman answered. He gestured to the one behind the bar. "That's Mattie, and Vic was at the gate. Luke is around here somewhere."

"Oh, then they sure could use the help," I said.

"They should be fine. We have our bitches help with that kind of shit," Dax said with a laugh.

I pretended to look at them in shock. "You let bitches handle your food? Damn, they must be a lot nicer than the ones we had with the Locos. No way I'd let them near my fucking food," I growled.

They looked a little surprised, but they didn't say anything. We kept talking for the next hour about this and that, nothing important. I was about to suggest we walk around when the door opened and in came Carla and Jane along with the three bunnies from last night. I saw Erica giving me the eye. Sloan had her eyes narrowed on her. The old ladies came over to the table. They were carrying dishes.

"Good news, Slo here can cook. Why don't you take her into the kitchen and get hot on that food? We're hungry," Dax ordered. None of the women said a word, they just nodded. Curly and Jester didn't look happy to hear their president ordering around their old ladies, but they didn't say a word.

I stood up. I brought Sloan to her feet. "Go ahead, help them out, baby. Make sure you come back and give me some sugar every once in a while, Lucky," I told her with a slight suggestive sound in my voice. She smiled before she got on her toes and kissed me. She didn't make it a peck either. She made sure to take her time. When she was done, the guys were hooting. She walked off with the others toward what I assumed was the kitchen. I made a show of watching her until she was out of sight, then I sat back down. Time for more of the game to begin.

Sloan: Chapter 14

I went with the women into the kitchen, but I really wanted to stay with Mark in the other room. I hated to be out of his sight. Not that I thought I couldn't take care of myself or him take care of himself, it just felt safer to be together.

I could feel Erica and the other two bunnies staring holes into me. I ignored them like Carla and Jane were doing. I clapped my hands. "Tell me what you need done. Is there a lot we still need to do? What's on the menu?"

"We made the potato salad already and the meat is marinating in the fridge. The guys wanted steak and chicken. There should be things in here to make some baked beans and whatever else we might want to make. If not, we can see if we can go get it at the store," Carla said. She went to a door and opened it. Inside, I saw it was a pantry. I moved over closer and gestured to it.

"Do you mind if I look?" She and Jane shook their heads no. I walked in. I was surprised that it was as well stocked as it was. After getting an idea of what was in there, I went to the fridge and opened it. It was mostly beer though I did see the meat they'd talked about. In one drawer, I found onions and garlic. I closed the door.

Now, I could have been a haughty bitch, but I wanted to see if I could get them to talk. In order to hopefully make that happen, I wanted to get on the old ladies' good side. "I can make some desserts if we have enough time."

Jane smiled. "That would be great. Why don't you work on that and we'll do the baked beans and some pasta salad?" I nodded and went back to the pantry. In no time, I was using canned fruit off the shelf to make a few pies. Those were easy. I was flouring the counter to make the crust when Jane started talking.

"How long have you and Undertaker been together?"

I didn't know if she was asking to have something to say, or if they'd been ordered to pump me for information. Either way, I told her the lie we'd concocted before we came. "We've been together almost two months, maybe a little longer."

"How did you meet?" Carla asked.

I could see the three bunnies were listening. They were sitting at the counter, not helping a bit. I bet Dax and them had no idea they didn't lift a hand. "It was in a bar, actually. I went there to have a drink. My friends were too busy to go out with me and I thought, what the hell, I'll go on my own. Imagine my surprise when the hot biker I saw across the bar came over to me." I laughed. Both of them chuckled.

"Why would you be surprised? You're gorgeous and he'd have to be nuts not to notice you," Jane said.

"Thank you. I don't know, I guess I thought he

wouldn't like me compared to some of the others in there. They seemed more like the biker type, you know, a one-night stand. Until I met him, I never had been one to just go to a hotel with a guy. Of course, he turned on the charm and the next thing I knew, we were naked and in bed," I told them with what I hoped was a surprised laugh.

I saw out of the corner of my eye, Erica sneered then she popped off, "What, did you think you were better than the other women?"

"I don't know if I'd call it better, or that I was more discerning when it came to who I let in my bed. I could never understand women who spread their legs for every guy who gave them the eye." I knew they'd take it the wrong way. I wanted them to. After last night and the way the old ladies had reacted to them and the way they ignored them today, I knew there was no love lost. It might help me get the old ladies to trust me.

Erica jumped to her feet. She looked at the other two who looked like I'd slapped them. "Do you believe the shit she's saying? She thinks she's better than us, Rissa and Lola." She nodded to each as she said their names. Now I knew who they were. They didn't look happy, but they didn't say anything. I stopped rolling out the dough.

"I never said I was better, but if that's how you want to take it, then go for it. I know what your role is around here. If that's what you wanna do, that's your business. I just don't see the attraction. I mean, letting anyone with a cock inside your pussy isn't my thing."

"Bitch, you're just jealous we can have any man,"

Erica cried.

I laughed. "Yeah, because you have a hole they can stick it in. I want a man who wants me and no one else, like Undertaker. He knows how to treat a woman."

All three of them scowled, though Erica was the only one to say anything back. "Oh really. I bet if I got him away from you, I could have him fucking me in no time. He says a lot of shit when you're there but get a guy alone and their tune changes."

I shook my head. "Better women than you have tried shit when I was there and when I wasn't. He hasn't taken them up on it. He knows who has all the lovin' he needs. I can and do fulfill all his needs. He doesn't need to go to tramps to get anything," I told her spitefully.

She gave a shriek and flew across the counter at me. I heard Jane and Carla gasp. I was prepared for her. As she got within striking distance, with her claws up, I didn't waste time. I pulled back my arm and let my fist fly. It connected with her nose. She screamed after I connected. She stopped dead in her tracks and grabbed her nose. I watched as blood started to stream out.

A thunder of feet came racing into the kitchen. At the head of the pack was Undertaker. He took in the scene with one look and then came over to me. He wrapped an arm around my shoulders. "What's going on here, Lucky?"

I pointed to a crying Erica. "She got pissed when I said she couldn't get you to sleep with her whether I was around or not. She came at me and I stopped her."

I could tell he was trying not to laugh. Carla and

Jane were smothering their smiles. Dax looked from Erica to me. "What the hell? Don't you have better control of your woman, Undertaker?"

Undertaker drew himself up and looked at Dax with a cold expression in his eyes. "My woman did just fine. I don't control her when she's dealing with shit like this. Why was your bitch taunting her about getting with me? I told all of you last night, I'm not sleeping around on my Lucky. That right there will bring me nothing but bad luck and trouble. I thought she'd be okay in here with your old ladies, Curly and Jester. I guess I was wrong. Babe, do you wanna come back out to the bar?"

I shook my head and smiled. "Nope, I'm fine. Just making sure we understand each other. I'm helping Jane and Carla with the food. These three don't seem to be of any help. Maybe they can go do something else. It's crowded in here for this many people if they're not all working."

Dax was frowning and I knew he wanted to say something else, but he didn't want to piss off Undertaker. He gestured to the three bunnies. "Get your asses out of here. We'll see you later."

Erica looked at him in shock. She was crying as she pointed at me. "Are you gonna let her get away with this?"

He shrugged. "Why would I care what you and the other women do? I don't have time for bitch drama. Go clean yourself up and keep your mouth shut, Erica," He growled at her. She gave him a scared-mixed-with-pissed look. She huffed out of the kitchen with Lola and

Rissa right behind her.

I looked back at Undertaker. "Baby, I thought I'd make you guys some pies for dessert. I know how much you love them."

I did know that he did because I'd made them for him at home. He grinned before he kissed me. "That sounds perfect." He turned to Dax and the others who were watching us. "You guys are in for a treat. My Lucky can bake. Let's leave them to it and we can get back to talking." He patted my ass before he left the kitchen. The others slowly followed.

Once the kitchen was clear of men, Jane started to laugh. "I wish I'd had my phone and recorded that. Erica is such a bitch. She thinks she can have any man, even those who have old ladies."

"Does she pull shit like that with your old men?" Both of them nodded. "Well, I hope they don't ever fall for it. I'd hate to think where her nasty ass has been." I pretended to shudder. I saw them exchange looks. I wondered if that meant Curly and Jester did cheat on their women. I hoped not. I'd seen enough of that shit growing up.

I went back to my dough. For the next few minutes, we worked in silence. I was putting the dough into the pans when Jane broke the silence. "The bunnies around here used to be more respectful of the men who were married. Not to say if the men wanted sex, they wouldn't do it, but they didn't try to get their attention. In the last two years, that changed. We lost some and then Erica and those two showed up."

"Listen, I didn't mean to bring up bad memories.

What you and your old man do is between you. I'm just saying that when Undertaker brought up being his old lady, I had to make it clear what I wanted. I didn't want to share him and I told him that. He knows that the one sure way to lose me is to touch another woman. Lucky for me, he seems to realize it and sees me as the one who fulfills all his needs. Hopefully, we'll be together for years to come. How long have you been with your old men?"

"Jester and I have been together eight years," Carla answered after a moment or so.

"I've been with Curly for six years."

"Do you have any kids?" I asked. Both of them shook their heads no. "What about the others? Does anyone have kids?"

"Well, there might be some running around somewhere, but as far as here, no, they don't have any. The ones who did have kids all seemed to want to leave," Carla said, then she looked like she said something wrong. I pretended not to notice.

"I can see it being hard for some to have kids and be in the life. Undertaker told me what I should expect."

"You weren't in the life before you met him?"

I shook my head. "No, I'd seen clubs and wondered about them, but I'd never gone for a biker before."

"I'm surprised. You seem to be able to take care of yourself," Jane said.

"I can. I grew up around a lot of guys. They taught me how to defend myself. There weren't a lot of girls in our neighborhood." They nodded and smiled. We worked in silence as we hurried to get things ready. I didn't think Dax and his guys would be all that patient. Over the next hour, while the pies baked and they got the beans cooking, they let tiny bits of information drop. Nothing about the club's business but about the people in it. All of it would come in handy when the time came.

I learned that other than Jester and Curly, only Frost and Nox were from the old Legion. Both of them had been with the club for four years. Everyone else was voted in after Dax and Roman came just over two years ago. It was a good bet they were either more Soldiers of Corruption or just like them.

The afternoon passed in a haze of feeding the men, watching them get drunker and drunker and the music getting louder. I spent equal time with the old ladies and Undertaker. While he seemed to be steadily pounding the drinks, he wasn't as wasted as the others. I knew he was making it look good. I had a slight buzz going but nothing more.

When it got later, the three bunnies came back to the clubhouse. Erica was staring daggers at me, but I ignored her. Hook had her on his lap while Dax had Lola on his. Rissa seemed to be floating around.

I was hoping to get out of there before things got down and dirty, but no such luck. I was talking to Jane when she shook her head and was looking behind me. I looked over my shoulder to find Hook had Erica up on the table with his pants down and her spread out with her pants off. He was plowing into her.

Shit, this reminded me too much of some of the shit I saw growing up. I looked over to Undertaker. He was pretending not to notice and was talking to Grumble, while Dax was sucking on Lola's breasts. Rissa was now on Cage's lap grinding on him. I got up and went over to Undertaker. He wrapped a hand around my waist and kept talking. I waited patiently for him to finish, then I leaned down to whisper, "Are you ready to go?"

He nodded and stood up. "I think Lucky and I will be going. Looks like you're all busy and I need to take care of her." He smirked as he ran his hand up to my ass. Dax stopped sucking Lola's breasts and looked at him.

"Don't let us stop you two. Go right ahead."

Undertaker shook his head. "I told you, I don't fuck my old lady where others can watch. This body is for my eyes only. No offense, carry on."

"Why don't you stay the night?" Roman added from his spot next to Dax. He'd been avidly watching Dax and Lola. I could see he was sporting an erection of his own. I expected any minute for him to be dropping his pants. Before Undertaker could say anything, we heard Hook grunt and then groan as he came.

Though I hated to look, I did. He pulled out and slapped her on the ass then looked up to holler, "Next." I watched as he stuck his still-wet cock back in his pants. God, he didn't even put a damn condom on! I saw both Jane and Carla wrinkle up their noses. Erica lay on the table with a smile on her face. Roman stood up and went over to her. I heard his zipper being lowered.

Undertaker must have felt me tense, because he shook his head. "Not tonight. We have plans and it doesn't include any of you horny bastards listening outside the door." Instead of pissing them off, they laughed.

Dax nodded. "Okay, we'll see you tomorrow. Why don't you plan to be here around one? We should be awake by then."

"Sure thing. Have fun," he told them as he headed for the door. I waved at the old ladies and they waved back. Outside, I took a deep breath. I'd been worried they'd insist we stay. As we got on the bike, I felt eyes watching us. I didn't turn around. I relaxed after we pulled out of the gate and headed back to town. It was a short ride and then we were back in our room. Mark took up a spot next to the window, pushing back the curtain just a smidge.

I sat down and took off my boots. We didn't say a word. After maybe five minutes or so, he stepped back. He looked at me. "You ready for bed, baby?" he asked as he opened the small case he'd hidden in his bags on the bike. He turned it on and walked around the room with it.

"I'm tired. Yeah, I think I am. Why don't I get the shower rolling while you get undressed?"

"Sounds good. Be there in a minute."

I went to the bathroom and turned on the shower as loud as it would go. I knew he was checking to see if the Legion was sophisticated enough to use bugs. We had no idea how far they went or what tech they might have. If we were dealing with the Punishers or their friends, I would say it was a given. However, Grumble didn't strike me as being as tech savvy as those guys.

A couple of minutes later, Mark came into the room. He shook his head as he closed the door. "The room is clear. I guess they aren't that techie or they didn't get a chance to send someone to do it. We'll have to check every time we leave, babe."

"I wondered if they were or not. Do we have company?"

"Our sitters are out there again. I guess Dax and the gang aren't trusting us yet." I watched as he stripped. Seeing him reveal all that muscle and ink got me to feeling other things than worry over the Legion.

His lips smirked when he looked at me. My nipples were hard and I could feel the beginning of wetness between my thighs. He stalked over to me and gave me a soul-scorching kiss. When he was done, I was short of breath and my pussy was soaked.

"Is my baby needing something?" he whispered as he kissed along my shoulder.

I reached between us and grasped his hard cock. "Yeah, your baby needs this. I need it now and I don't want it to be slow and easy," I panted.

Suddenly, I was picked up and carried into the shower and under the hot spray. Mark hoisted me up higher, so I had to wrap my legs around his waist and I grabbed his shoulders so I wouldn't fall. My back hit the chilly wall and then he was pushing into me full steam ahead. I moaned as he filled me.

As soon as he was fully inside of me, he got down to driving me to a screaming orgasm. He pounded in and out as he sucked on my nipples. I was trying to breathe as the roar of a huge orgasm built up inside of me. I knew I wouldn't last long. The head of his cock was rubbing across that special spot inside me every time he thrust.

I was getting closer and by the sounds of his breathing, so was he, when he took a hand off my ass and slid it between us. He grazed it across my clit a couple of times and then he started to tease it. I lost the battle and detonated. I clenched down on him and cried out as my whole body shook. He kept thrusting a few more times then he slammed into me and held still. A long tortuous groan came out of him and I felt him jerking inside of me as he came.

I have no idea how long we were like that before I could think and he lowered me to my feet. I felt like a wrung-out washcloth. "God, I just need to sleep, Mark."

He laughed. "We will as soon as we wash. Come here." He ended up washing the both of us because I was too weak to do it. Once we were clean and dried, he carried me into the bed and tucked me in. Before he joined me, he checked the window again and then crawled under the covers.

"I assume they're still there," I said. He nodded as he pulled his laptop to him. Seeing him getting ready to work, I sat up.

"Babe, relax. I'm just going to check if there's a message or not. I wonder if they tripped the flags on my background. If they're doing a check like they said, they should be."

I watched as he logged into the special encrypted site and read. He smiled. "They're setting off alerts all over the place. So far, nothing has alerted in my real file according to Gabe. He asks if we're doing okay."

"Tell him yeah, but I can't wait to get the hell out of here. These people are disgusting."

"Did you find out anything from the old ladies?"

"Not much other than they don't seem to like Dax and the gang all that much. It seems like Jester, Curly, Frost and Nox are the ones who are from the old club. Nox and Frost were with them a couple of years before the changeover. Curly and Jester have been with them for twelve years. They were friends that joined together. Anyone else that was part of it left but they didn't say much about why. I could tell they were uncomfortable talking about it. The bunnies they have now are not the ones they had then and the old ladies hate them. I know that's not much and not a lot of help."

I watched as he typed away on the laptop. A couple of minutes went by before he was done and closing it. He looked over at me. "I know this is nerve-racking, babe. I wish I hadn't brought you, but anything you find out helps. Just make sure you don't ask too many questions."

"I won't. A lot of it they let out when we get to talking and I ask an innocent question or make an observation. I can tell that Carla and Jane feel lost in this new club and they don't like to be there, but I guess Jester and Curly insist they stay. After the show tonight, I can't say I blame them."

He slid closer and took me in his arms. "What about you? I know that show wasn't to your liking either."

"I guess I never got the attraction of letting others watch you have sex. I mean, hey, if all parties are into it, go for it, but I never was that kind. I was just happy not to see Curly and Jester having sex with their old ladies or God forbid, the bunnies."

"I don't think those two are into the whole open sex thing. I saw them trying to look anywhere but there and they had their old ladies' attention. Jane and Carla weren't looking either. I think those two might just have a few qualms about what the club does. Is it enough to want to be free of them, I don't know?"

"Do you think the club will let you talk business when we go back tomorrow?"

"It depends on if they like what they found so far. I hope so but be prepared they might make us hang around longer. This could become a battle of wits and waiting. Are you prepared? If you want, I can still get you out of this. I can say your momma got sick or something and you had to leave."

I could tell he wanted me to take the out he was giving me, but there was no way I was going to leave him alone to do this. He needed someone to watch his back. They might think they had the upper hand, but they had no idea who they'd let into their midst. I shook my head no. "No, I'm not ready to leave. Not until you are. I can do this. So far, they don't seem to pay much attention to me. They think I'm your fluffy piece of candy, I think. They have no idea I could kill any one of them in a heartbeat."

He laughed as he kissed me. "That's their stupidity. I'll keep my secret weapon to myself. Just don't let your guard down, Sloan. I couldn't stand it if anything happened to you."

I kissed him before I whispered back, "The same for you. Don't let them win and stay safe, Mark." He smiled before he kissed me. I lay back and got lost in the love that my man was giving and forgot to worry for the moment about the Legion and its snakes, the Soldiers of Corruption.

Undertaker: Chapter 15:

I was right. The Legion didn't give us an answer on Sunday. It was now Tuesday and they were still hemming and hawing around. I decided being nice had to come to an end. They wanted to play. I could play.

"Sloan, pack up our shit. We're going to be leaving today," I told her. She gave me a shocked look then grabbed our bags.

"Really? Won't they get pissed that we're leaving?"

"I expect they will and if that doesn't get them to talk with me, we'll have to figure something else out. I'm done waiting. They hit every one of my files and know the damn backstory. They either believe me or not. Time for them to face the Undertaker. Make sure you're packing that gun. We might need it."

As she quickly stuffed more of our stuff in the two bags we'd brought, I peeked out the door. There was the ever-present truck. God, they were dumb, using the same vehicle every day to spy on us. I couldn't help but shake my head.

The last few days we'd spent a lot of time at their compound and when we weren't, we would take long rides. I pretended not to see their inept tailing abilities.

Every night at their clubhouse, they'd try to get us to stay, but I insisted on us going back to the hotel. It was more of the same. They'd get drunk and then start having sex with the bunnies. I did notice that when we got up to leave, Curly and Jester would do the same. I guess that was the cue to have the couples leave.

Honestly, they either were doing work at night after we left, or they mostly sat around on their asses. Not too sure how that brought in money for the club. Ten minutes later, we had everything ready to go. I gave her a kiss. "Ready?"

"Ready," she said with that smile that made me want to smile. We walked out of the room and over to where my bike was sitting. We made sure to make it obvious we were putting away a couple of bags. I heard the guys get out of the truck but acted like I didn't know they were there. I didn't look up until they got close to us and cleared their throats. When I looked up, I made sure I had my best Undertaker face on—the one that told you that I wasn't about to mess around.

"Where're you going?" Cage asked. He had Nox with him.

"Home. I wasted enough time here. Need to get back and set up the other club I wanted to talk to. You tell Dax it's been real. Maybe I'll see you guys sometime."

"Wait a minute, I thought you wanted to deal with us," Nox hurried to say. I could see that he was feeling nervous.

"I did, but it's obvious your club isn't interested. I'm not gonna sit here, cooling my fucking heels, waiting for them to figure shit out. I got shit to do and I know the next club will be interested in talking business. Good luck." I swung on my bike and helped Sloan to settle behind me. Before I could fire it up, Cage got in front of my bike.

"Whoa, wait, wait, we wanna talk. Let me call Dax and then we'll go over to the clubhouse."

"I'm not wasting another day at the fucking clubhouse, watching you all get drunk and fuck. You might not wanna make money, but I do," I growled. Nox was on his phone. He was talking fast and I could see the frown on his face. This should push them one way or the other.

"We wanna make money, we just need to check you out, man," Cage protested.

I shook my head.

"You had two days. That's what Grumble said he needed. We're starting on day four. I don't have time to waste it here." I turned on my bike and revved the engine. Cage looked like he was going to shit himself.

Nox ran over, waving his hands. "Hey, I just talked to Dax. He said to come to the clubhouse and we'll talk. Don't leave."

I sat there like I was considering whether to do it or not. Sloan didn't say a word. After a tense few minutes, I shrugged. "Fine, we'll come over, but if it's more of the same shit as last time, we're outta here. Understand," I growled. Both of them nodded. Slowly, Cage backed away from the front of my bike and headed to the truck they'd been sitting in. Nox was right behind him.

I squeezed Sloan's thigh. "Here we go, baby." She responded by kissing my neck. I pulled out of the hotel parking lot and followed the truck out to the Legion's clubhouse. This would end one of two ways. I was praying it would go the way I hoped.

When we got there, Dax was waiting out front with the rest of the club. I pulled in and killed the engine. I sat there staring back at him. He had a slightly pissed look on his face but I didn't care. Enough playing the nice Undertaker. It was time to show them why I'd been the enforcer for the Locos.

"Are we gonna fucking deal or not? Because if we're gonna pussyfoot around some more, I'm the fuck outta here. I got other places I can be, Dax. You've had enough time to check me out. I know you have and you know that I'm not feeding you some bullshit story. I was really with the Tres Locos and I lucked the fuck out when they all went down. I don't know if it was just this lucky charm or what, but I did. Are we talking about business or not?"

He took a big breath then waved at us. "Come on in. We'll talk. I'm not gonna talk shit out here in the open. She's gonna have to go somewhere while we do." He pointed to Sloan.

I helped her off the bike then I got off. I wrapped an arm around her waist as we walked over to him. "She stays close. You gotta church we can talk in? If so, she'll stay in the common room while we do. I want this to be done today."

"Fine, she can stay in the common room while we hash this out. It may take a while. Come on." He turned to go inside. I waved to the others to go ahead of us. I didn't want them at our back. I wasn't sure that this was going to go well.

Inside, Vic, one of the other prospects, was at the bar. We'd seen that Luke was at the gate. I wondered where they had Mattie. There were no old ladies here today. That instantly put me on alert.

"Isn't Carla and Jane around today? Maybe they could keep Slo company. In fact, if they wanted, they could help her fix us some food. You don't mind fixin' something, do you, babe?"

She shook her head. "No, I can cook up something for you guys. It would be nice if the ladies were here, at least for company."

Dax shrugged and looked at Curly and Jester. "Call them and tell them to get their asses over here. We could do with something to eat."

Neither man looked like he was thrilled with Dax's demand, but they took out their phones and sent off texts. As soon as they were done, Dax pointed to the bar. "Grab a beer and then we can get started. Sweetheart, you know where the kitchen is. Go get to cooking. If you need something, let Vic know and he or Mattie can go get it."

Sloan didn't do more than nod. She turned and gave me a big kiss. It was one with lots of tongue. I grabbed her ass and squeezed her close. When she pulled away, I whispered so only she could hear, "Stay alert."

She smiled and nodded then sashayed her way

into the kitchen. Now it was time to get down to the dirty work. I prayed they'd share some of their business setup with me. I grabbed a beer along with the rest of them and followed them down the hall and into a small room. As far as churches went, it was pathetic.

It was a cramped, dusty room with a film of God knows what on the table. I'd noticed that keeping their clubhouse clean wasn't a priority with this bunch. They took no pride in the patch they rode for. Maybe it was because it wasn't their real club, or maybe they were a bunch of dirty slobs. Shaking away those wayward thoughts, I took a seat close to the head of the table, with my back to the wall. I wasn't sure who usually sat here and I didn't give a damn. I leaned back and nodded to Dax. "Tell me what you still have questions about that took this long to get us down to talking business?"

"Your story checked out. Grumble said he found the police report that showed where you were when your club went down. Still can't believe how fucking lucky you were. If you still have contacts in the various pipelines, we'd like to talk about setting something up and meeting with them."

"Well before we do that, I need to find out what kind of supply you have. I need to know if you can meet the demand. These guys are used to moving a lot of products. They deal in all kinds of things. From what Serpent said, you align with the kinds of things we dealt with, but I need to be sure," I told them.

Dax looked at Roman for a moment. I waited to see if he'd tell me. Finally, he looked back at me. "Our main products out of here are the weed and meth, plus when we can get them, guns. Of course, that doesn't include the ladies. We have a nice little business going with those. The demand is high and we're always recruiting. Sometimes it's hard to find the right ladies, but we get it done."

I read between the lines. They were doing the prostitution but not all the ladies were there of their own free will. It made my stomach knot, thinking about it. "Is there anything else you deal with besides those three things? I need to know so I can hook you up with the right guys."

"We occasionally have a chance to help with some fire placement, if you know what I mean, and making sure people pay when they're supposed to," Roman said with a snicker.

"So, arson and extortion, you mean. Anything else?"

They all shook their heads. I wondered about the legit businesses that the club had initially had. "What about legit businesses? You said you had those as well and it helps cover what you do on the other side of things. What kind of business are those?"

"We have a trucking company, a garage and a bar in town." Dax answered this time. I thought about those. They were perfect for hiding the others. You could use the bar for drugs and prostitution and the trucking company and garage for the drugs and guns.

"Are most of the employees in on what goes on behind the scenes?" I asked. They gave me a confused look and didn't say anything. I sighed. "Do the regular employees at the garage, bar and trucking company know that there's illegal shit being run through those places?"

"Hell no, they have no idea. Only a couple at each place does. At the bar it's the manager and the full-time bartender. At the trucking company, it's only the supervisor who assigns the trucks and a couple of the guys who load them. The drivers have no clue what they're hauling. As for the garage, that's only us. We put the stuff in the hidden compartments in the vehicles after the others go home at night."

"Okay, that narrows the number of people who can talk. Do you assign one of you to oversee a certain part of the chain? For example, is there one of you overseeing the trucking company? In the Locos, we were assigned to oversee certain aspects and it was our responsibility to make sure nothing went wrong."

Dax squirmed in his chair for a moment then answered. I wondered why. "We do have it broken out between us. The garage is Roman's baby. I oversee the bar and Hook makes sure that the trucking stuff goes off without a hitch."

"What about the others, what do they do?" I gestured to Grumble and the other men in the room.

"They do whatever we tell them. They fill in if we need help, but the real work is done by us," Dax growled. I saw a few looks thrown his way. Ah, so he didn't share the wealth I bet, and it caused some hard feelings. Though, in the case of Curly and Jester, that might not be the case. They were looking more uncomfortable than angry.

"Sounds like we have a lot of work to do. Ready to get started?" I asked them.

"What do you mean a lot? We have the trucks, our routes and the product. What more do we need?" Dax asked, sounding a little upset.

"We need to know the routes of those trucks, how often they move merchandise. How many times do cars go out with products and how do you reclaim it? How far can you make a run? How many girls do you have working and how many can they service a night? Is there room for more to be brought in without bringing us to the notice of the local pigs? Then we need to know for whom and how often do you light things up or go strong arm someone," I explained.

"Why the fuck do you need to know all that?" Roman popped off.

I gave him a bored and slightly condescending look. I could see the anger in his eyes when I did. "Because dumbass, we need to know where to hook into your lines to make them longer, add routes, be able to set up points to get the product and move it along a longer pipeline to get to the end distributors. You've been working in your little area of the woods. I can take this shit to where it's running all over the US. In order to do that, I need to know the ins-and-outs and where to add more people. For example, do you have any of the local law in your pocket? Are you paying them or anyone else to look the other way? We may need to up the output of cash in order to pull this off."

"Jesus Christ, you expect us to tell you everything about our business? We might as well patch you in and be done with it," Hook muttered as he looked at Dax and Roman.

I shrugged. "If it comes to it, I might be willing to consider it, if this club has what it takes. Listen, I was used to bringing in a certain amount every month. I enjoyed that, and I'd like to get back to that level of comfort, if you know what I mean. I'm looking for a place to do that and I'm willing to bring the means for myself and others to be bringing in five figures or more a month. I just need to know I have the right place to do it. If for some reason we decide you're not the ones, I'll promise to leave you at least a little better than I found you. I'm trading my knowledge and contacts for the chance to be a part of the Legion of Renegades. I'm looking for a home."

They squirmed in their seats for a few moments then Dax spoke up. "Listen, everything checks out for your story so far. We just have to be sure that you can deliver what you say you can. We can't bring someone we don't know and trust into the middle of our operation. We need a demonstration. Something that shows you're not just blowing smoke up our asses."

"Okay, what did you have in mind?" I knew they would be asking for something like this. Sean and the guys were ready with the feds to help me pull it off.

"We have a shipment going out in a couple of days. Why don't you tell us where this one can go along the line and we'll see if it gets us further than we usually get?"

"You tell me when, where and what the shipment is, and I'll get you to a bigger buyer further along the line. How many days and how much are we talking?"

"It's in three days, going out with a truck headed

for Kentucky. We have ten kilos going to a distributor there."

"I'm assuming we're talking meth." They nodded. "Let me make a few calls. I think if you divert that haul to Virginia and can double that, I can have a buyer for you. Can you get me that much?"

Roman, Dax and Hook all put their heads together. Again, I thought it was telling that they left the others out of it. Made me wonder what their involvement was and if they saw any of the profit. I saw Curly, Jester, Frost, and Nox all looking like they wanted to be somewhere else. They were the old Legion members. Cage, Sig, and Grumble just looked like they didn't have a care in the world. Were they that oblivious, or were they getting a piece of the action?

Finally, they stopped talking and looked back at me. "We can get that much, but we have to make a few calls. Why don't we get those two things set and we'll see how it goes? If everything works out like we hope, then we can talk about doing more business," Dax told me.

"We can do that, but I have some demands of my own to add. If I show that I'm for real, I don't want to be a goddamn prospect. I've been there and done that and I don't need to do it again. When I hold up my end, I want to be brought in as a damn member and to be involved in the whole operation. I know I can expand this beyond your dreams. I can easily have you making millions," I boasted. Their eyes lit up. I knew pushing not to be a prospect would be something they wouldn't like, but I didn't care. I needed to get in and get the information as fast as I could. Last time around, I had nothing to bring to the Locos. This time, I had plenty I could use to force my way into the middle of their operation.

"We'd have to talk to someone about that. We run this club, but our real charter president, I guess you'd call him, will need to approve it. We need to talk to Slither," Dax cautioned. I tried not to react to hearing Slither's name. He was the head of the proverbial snake I was after. I wanted to take him and Ogre out. After I'd heard what Cheyenne's life was like, I knew I wouldn't rest until those two were no longer a threat to her or anyone else.

"You mean Serpent's old man. Sure, talk to him. Serpent said he was the boss of everything," I said casually. I saw them do a double take.

"Serpent mentioned his old man, did he?" Roman asked a little cautiously.

"Yep, he told me all about him being the head of all operations. We were kind of out of it, so I don't recall if he said where he was located."

"He heads up our main club here in Ohio. I'll get in touch with him. Why don't you see if you can get a hold of your contacts for taking a bigger load in Virginia?"

"I can do that. Hey, question, does the club own the trucking company or is there a chance we need to get it by an owner or something?"

"No, Curly here runs the trucking company with Hook's oversight. He brought it to the club. Jester oversees the bar with my help and Nox runs the garage with Roman's help," Dax said proudly. I saw the blank expression on the old guards' faces. Ah, it was becoming clearer why they had stayed when others had left. They had the key businesses that allowed the club to run their illegal shit out of. I wondered if they had been threatened to stay or did it on their own. Something told me it was likely the former reason.

"Good, don't want anyone mucking up the waters. Okay, let me step outside and make some calls while you do the same. By then, hopefully the old ladies will have gotten us something to eat."

I stood up and strolled out of the room. I couldn't wait to get free of them. I passed through the common room and went outside. I walked as far away as possible to make my call. I didn't trust them not to have someone or something listening, so the phone I had was encrypted though you wouldn't be able to tell it by glancing at it. I placed a call to the number I'd set up with the guys and the feds. After two rings, Sean answered, "What's up Undertaker? Long time no hear. We thought you went down with the others."

"No, Poe, I didn't. I got lucky. Hey, I'm looking to hook up with another club. Thought you might be interested in moving more product since we're no longer providing it from our club. Motherfucking feds ruined that shit," I bitched.

"Sure, what are you thinking and when?"

"In three days, I can have a truck bringing you a sample of twenty kilos. It'll be coming out of Ohio. You got a place where we can make a delivery and get rid of it? I assume you're still looking for as much product as you can find."

"Where in Ohio?"

"Cleveland area and it'll be an ongoing run I believe. I still have to get more details and check out the quality of the product."

"Give me a few hours and I'll have you something. Might need to rearrange some things but we should be able to do it. You find out how much we can expect and how often and make sure it's some good shit."

"Not a problem. I'm with our possible new suppliers right now. Just need to show them that we have the demand if they have the supply. I'll wait for your call."

"Sure thing. Talk to you in a bit." Sean hung up.

I came strolling back into the clubhouse. Dax and the others were sitting around a table still talking. When they saw me, they got quiet. I retook my seat. "My contact is reworking a few things. He'll get back to me in a few hours. He doesn't think it should be a problem. He's interested in knowing how much you can send and how often. Before we make this happen, I promised that I'd check into the quality of what you're selling. Can't have subpar shit out there. That'll sink their business and ours fast. How about while we wait, you let me see the stuff?"

Dax and Roman exchanged looks. It was Dax who answered me. "We can do that. Why don't we take you to see what we have stored here and you can see for yourself we have the good shit? Then we'll come back and grab a bite to eat and wait for your buddy to call you."

I didn't like the idea of leaving Sloan alone at the

clubhouse, but there was no getting around that. I stood up and nodded. "Let's go. Give me a sec to tell Slo I'm leaving and then I'll be good." I headed for the kitchen.

"You gotta tell her everything you do?" Hook asked with a roll of his eyes.

"No, I don't, but I'm not just going to leave her here without a word when she doesn't know you all that well. That's one way to make sure you don't get any pussy for a while." I smirked. They all laughed.

In the kitchen, she looked up from what she was making and smiled. I went right over to her and gave her a kiss. As soon as I was done, I said, "Babe, me and the guys are going to check something out. You stay here and work on the food. I expect Curly and Jester's old ladies will be here soon to help."

"Okay, honey, I'll be here when you get back." She didn't miss a beat. I wished there were some way to have a private chat, but I knew that would seem suspicious. I smacked her on the ass and turned around to leave.

When we got outside, they didn't go toward their bikes. Instead, they led me further into the compound. I looked around with interest. They hadn't given us much of a tour the last few days—just the clubhouse and the immediate area outside. In the back, I saw the grounds were what I would expect from them. Junk cars and other shit were sitting around the property. The grass was overgrown and weeds were everywhere. The whole place had an air of neglect. What self-respecting club would let their place look like this? Hell, even the Locos had taken more pride than this in their compound.

We walked back and into the woods. I tried not

to tense up. This was one good spot for them to take me out, if they had any suspicion that I wasn't who I said I was. I knew if they did that, they'd go after Sloan in a heartbeat. She'd never stand a chance against all of them. After walking for about ten minutes, we came to a small clearing. Sitting in the middle of it was an old barn. They headed over to it.

Inside, they took me to a back stall and kicked the musty hay on the floor out of the way. When they did, I saw there was a trap door in the floor. Cage pulled it open and went down a set of stairs. When he came back up, he was holding a package. Shit, they kept their stash right here and it wasn't that well hidden. How had someone not come in here and either busted their asses or taken it from them? I had to work hard not to ask them how they could be that stupid.

Cage opened the package and using his knife took out a small sample. Now for the hard part. I didn't want to ingest any of that shit, but if I didn't, they might suspect me. I'd tried it in the past as part of my cover with the Locos. I examined the sample closely. It was pure white and odorless. I wet the tip of my little finger and dipped it in the white powder. I stuck it in my mouth. To anyone watching, it would look like I was tasting it. However, I didn't let any of it touch my tongue. As I removed my finger from my mouth, I was quick to drop it. They were so busy watching my expression, they didn't pay any attention to my finger. I let my finger graze my pants, wiping it off.

"Tastes fine. Let's see how it feels," I told them with a smile. They grinned at me and laughed as if I'd told a joke. I'd seen enough people use the stuff to know how they'd react. I didn't wait long before I was grinning at them. "Yeah, that's the shit. Whew, is all of it the same quality? Do you have one person who makes this for you or more than one? If it's more than one, we'll need to be sure they're all up to this quality. Whew, this shit will sell and have them clambering for more," I said with a grin.

"No worries, we have one guy who makes all of our shit, man. Everything he makes is that quality. Come on, let's head back to the clubhouse," Dax said. Cage put the package back in their hidey-hole.

As we walked back, I verbalized my worry. "Listen, I need to ask. Aren't you worried that some cop will come in here one day and find that shit? They'd tear this place apart to find your stuff if they ever get the chance."

"The locals have no damn clue what we do here. To them, we're just a harmless legit club who likes to ride bikes. The Renegades were a bunch of pansies that didn't know what the hell they were missing," Roman jokes. I saw the looks Nox, Frost, Jester, and Curly exchanged. They weren't looking happy to hear their old club being described like that. Hmm, yeah, the longer we were here, the more convinced I was becoming that they were less than enamored with the Soldiers who had infiltrated their club. Was it enough that I could rely on them for help? That was to be seen.

When we got back to the clubhouse, it was to find that Carla and Jane were there. They were helping Sloan in the kitchen. While we'd been gone, the bunnies had shown up as well. I sat down and took the new beer Grumble handed to me. I'd barely opened it when arms came around me. I stiffened as I realized it wasn't Sloan. The scent of overpowering perfume tickled my nose. I knew immediately it was Erica.

"Undertaker, why don't you let me show you a good time? Your old lady is busy in the kitchen. I bet I can make you feel better than she ever has," she whispered.

I looked over at Dax. He was watching us with an expectant look on his face. Had he told her to try this? Probably. They were testing my faithfulness to Sloan. I raised an eyebrow at Dax. "You wanna call off your skank or do you want me to do it?" He lifted his chin to me. I pulled away from Erica and gave her one of my best death looks.

"I didn't give you permission to fucking touch me, did I?" I growled low.

She backed up a couple of steps. She was no longer smirking. She now had a fearful look on her face. "I-I'm sorry. I just thought you might—"

"Might wanna fuck around on my old lady. Yeah, I got that. But what you don't know about me, is once I make a fucking commitment, I keep it. I wouldn't have taken an old lady if I couldn't keep my cock to only her. Slo is the only damn woman I want. I suggest you keep your damn hands to yourself, or we're gonna have issues."

"Too late," I heard hissed. I looked up to see Sloan coming out of the kitchen. She had a pissed look on her face. She came running across the room. Erica shrieked as she tried to duck behind Cage. He grinned as he stepped aside. The next couple of seconds were a blur as

Sloan grabbed her by the hair and hauled her out from behind him.

As Erica screamed and tried to slap her, Sloan got to the point. She punched Erica in the face, then she rained down a few more blows as she told her off. "You keep your goddamn filthy hands off him! He's mine and I'll beat any bitch who thinks she can take him away from me. He didn't ask for your skanky ass, did he? No, he didn't."

"Dax, help," Erica cried out. She was no match for my Sloan. I let my pleasure in watching the exchange show on my face. With a curl of her upper lip, Sloan threw Erica to the ground. She wiped her hands on her jeans and gave a satisfied smirk. As soon as she saw that the bunny wasn't getting up, she sashayed over to me. She made a production of looking me over and then kissing me. It wasn't a quick kiss either. It was one filled with passion. I growled as I squeezed her ass and thrust my aching cock into her stomach.

Eventually the catcalls and whistles had us breaking apart. I saw the Soldiers watching us with avid attention. More than one was sporting a hard-on. I saw Roman cupping himself. "That was hot as hell. Sure you don't want an audience?" He leered.

"Fuck no, I don't want an audience. If we're done with the bullshit, can we get back to work?" I snapped. This got them to settle down. The other bunnies helped Erica to her feet and they went to the other side of the common room to glare at us. God, wasn't this shit day over with yet?

Sloan: Chapter 16

I kept an eye on the bunnies. I knew that Erica would like nothing more than to hurt me. I was on high alert. When I'd heard what was happening in the common room from the kitchen door, I hadn't hesitated to go defend my man. No way was I letting one of those whores touch him. It had been satisfying to hit her.

Now that the excitement had died down, I sat with Undertaker. I was hoping that the others would talk in front of me. Besides, there wasn't anything else to do in the kitchen. The food was almost done cooking. Seeing that I wasn't coming back to the kitchen, Jane and Carla came out and took a seat close to their men. I was happy to see Curly and Jester take their hands and give them a squeeze.

While we'd been in the kitchen, they'd let a little slip. They'd talked about some of the old members who were no longer with the club. I could tell they missed them. When I'd asked them if they ever saw them anymore, they'd looked upset and shook their heads no. From what I could get out of them, they weren't in contact with anyone outside of those in the club. Once again, I wondered if they were only here because of threats to them and their men.

It wasn't long after that, we announced the food was ready. The guys had descended on the food like hungry locusts. I watched as they ate like pigs. The bunnies had begrudgingly gotten a plate of food and went back to their corner. After everyone finished eating a while later, the men had the women leave them alone again. I knew it was so they could talk business. There was no way they'd let me stay for that. I took myself off outside with the two old ladies.

"Carla, if you don't mind me saying it, I don't get the feeling that you're all that comfortable here at the clubhouse. Is it because of those bunnies? I know they can be a pain in the ass. I can't stand Erica. If she keeps going after Undertaker, I'll do more than punch her next time."

She hesitated and looked at Jane as if to see what she might say. Jane shrugged. "Slo, it's not just the bunnies, though they're enough. I know your man is here to work with the club. We don't get involved in club business. That's one thing the guys don't allow. Just know that the club isn't what it used to be. Before, it was a much more family friendly place."

"You mean before Dax and them came or even before that?"

"Since Dax and them came. They brought in a new vibe to the place. A lot of people left."

"If you dislike it so much, why did you stay?"

"We had to, that's all. Listen, don't mind us. We just miss some of our old friends. I'm sure that you and Undertaker will get along with the club just fine. I mean, it sounds like they're going to be doing business with each other. Hopefully, we'll get to see the two of you around here for a while," Carla said with a tiny smile.

"If they can iron out the logistics, we should be around for a while, I think. Though who knows, Undertaker doesn't tell me club business. All I know is he's really looking for a new club to call home. Losing his place with the Tres Locos hit him hard. I'm thankful as hell he was with me the night it all happened. I can't imagine never having met him."

"Anyone can see the two of you are great together. He treats you like a man should his old lady. That's what those whores out there can't stand. They don't have any man who wants to treat them like that, though they think they might be able to snag one," Jane said with a roll of her eyes.

"I was clear from the start that if he wanted us to be together, that I wouldn't just be one of the masses. Undertaker is a handsome, sexy man that most women would love to be with. I know that and there's nothing I can do except roll with it. But when they do shit like Erica did, I'm not going to ignore it."

"And you shouldn't. Her and the others have tried shit with Curly and Jester. They told them they're not interested, but they still try shit. Dax and the others don't understand why they don't fuck them like the other guys do. It's caused a few disagreements. I, for one, won't stay with Curly if he ever sleeps with another woman. He knows that," Jane added.

"Okay, enough of that. Why don't you tell me

about yourselves? Did you grow up around here?"

From there, I listened as they told me about where they were from and their families. Apparently, they didn't have any real support outside of their husbands. I felt terrible for them. They were really tied to the club. As time passed, I wondered what the guys were talking about. I was anxious to get this day over with and back to the motel. The hours dragged by as we let the men discuss their business. When it got dark, we were called back into the common room to join them. I saw they were well onto their way of being drunk like all the nights before. Well, all of them except for Jester and Curly. They seemed to at least stay partly sober.

Though he gave a good impression of being drunk, Undertaker wasn't. It was close to midnight when he called the evening to a halt. The others were busy having sex with the bunnies. I tried to ignore the image of Rissa taking on both Cage and Hook. Though they tried to convince us we should stay the night, just like they'd done every night before, they didn't press as hard as they usually did. In no time, we were speeding down the road to the motel.

When we got in the room, Undertaker held up his finger and took out the equipment he'd brought in from the bike. He ran it all over the room and bathroom. Once he was done and assured that there were no bugs, he pulled out his phone and made a call.

"Hey, I know it's late, but we just left the compound. Yeah, they're going for it. I found out where they keep their meth. It's in a damn barn on the property. It's not even hidden that well. They have a trapdoor in the floor of the barn. There's one guy who does all the cooking for them. His name is Lobo. They're going to take me to meet him tomorrow."

He listened to whoever he was talking to. "Yeah, they use their garage, trucking company and the bar as fronts for the illegal shit. I'll send you all the information. They haven't told me who they get the guns off of yet or where they keep the women they prostitute out. I'm getting the idea this operation isn't as big as some, but they certainly need to be shut the hell down."

He didn't say anything else for a while longer, just a few "yeahs." He continued, "She's hanging in there. I wish like hell she wasn't near any of this. I'll know more after tomorrow. We're supposed to check out the gun situation then as well. My hope is they'll tell me enough that we won't have to stay around here for long. Just looking at them makes me sick. Okay, talk to you later."

When he hung up, he spent a few minutes typing out on the laptop. I knew he was sending the information he'd promised. We weren't worried about anyone else seeing it. They had a very encrypted system in place. Plus, they'd had more help from a guy named Smoke, from the Warriors' club.

As soon as he got done, he put the laptop aside and rolled over in bed to face me. "Baby, how're you doing?"

"I'm doing fine, Mark. Don't worry about me. I'm more worried about you and where they'll be taking you tomorrow. You know they won't let me come along."

"They won't, but I want you to stay behind and see if you can get a chance to either talk more to the old ladies or if it's safe, to have a look around. But only if it's safe," he warned me.

"I think I can get them to talk. They made it more than obvious that they don't like Dax and the others. They told me how the club has changed over the last few years. All their old friends seem to have left the club."

"Yeah, they did. Not sure if they all left or if some might have been killed. I think the reason they kept Curly, Jester, Frost and Nox around is because of their businesses. They're the ones who own the three legit businesses that they're using as fronts to move this stuff. It would have looked too suspicious to have them all sell out to the club and leave."

"Jane and Carla told me that they own them though they now basically have all their profit going to the club. They called it their dues of all things. Why would they have let some of the others go? Wouldn't they be afraid they might tell someone what was going on?"

He shrugged. "It could be they had enough to threaten them with so they didn't need to or they didn't tell them enough for them to be much of a threat. I figure they hold the old ladies over Jester and Curly at least. Maybe they have more family too. As for Nox and Frost, who knows. Maybe they liked the idea of more money and didn't give a damn where it comes from."

I sighed. I was finding I liked the two women, and I hated to think of them having a threat hanging over their heads. "Please be careful tomorrow. I don't like the fact you'll be alone with them. I don't trust them."

"Baby, I promise, I'll be careful. You have to do the same. If you think for a second, they might tell the guys, don't ask them anything too pointed about the club. And keep your eye on those damn bunnies."

"Oh, you don't need to warn me about those bunny bitches. I swear, before we're done, I'm going to knock Erica's teeth down her damn throat. She needs to keep her mitts off you," I growled, remembering her propositioning him. I found that when it came to him, I was possessive, something I'd never been with a guy before.

He grinned and then asked, "So, you don't like some other woman messing with your man?"

"Damn right I don't. You're mine."

"Think how I feel. Having all those bastards watching you with lust in their eyes. They'd give anything to be with you. Whatever you do, don't let yourself ever be alone with them, Sloan. I have no doubt they'd try to take by force what you won't give freely."

I could see the worry written on his face.

I caressed his whisker-rough face. "I won't," I whispered, then I kissed him. It was a slow exploration of his mouth that soon became a desperate one. As we nipped and thrust our tongues, I grew wet and aroused. Before I got too lost in the moment, he pulled away from me.

"Let's go take a shower. I need to wash that place off me. Then I'll see about making love to my beautiful woman."

I didn't argue. I eagerly got off the bed and

followed him into the bathroom. He turned on the shower as I stripped. When I was done, I watched as he shed his clothes. I never got tired of seeing him. His body with those tats was a masterpiece. I couldn't help but to reach out and touch his sculpted ass. He groaned.

"Shit, don't do that yet. I'm on a hair trigger as it is, babe. I've been dreaming about making love to you all damn day," he said before he turned around to look at me. He was as hard as steel and I could see drops of cum on the tip. I licked my lips. I wasn't sure I'd be able to keep my hands to myself. My pussy was flooding my inner thighs with cream as I imagined him inside of me.

He didn't give me a chance to do anything. He grabbed me and hauled me into the warm shower. Then he grabbed the body wash and started to lather his hands. Soon he was running those slick hands all over my body. I couldn't hold back the moans that were coming from my mouth. I tried to return the favor, by washing him, but he kept pushing my hands away.

"Honey, please, I need to touch you too," I pleaded.

"Not yet. Right now, this is all about you. While I'd like nothing more than to take you in this shower, it's too damn small for that. I want us to be comfortable for what comes next. Give me a couple of minutes."

He rinsed me off and then I stood back and watched as he quickly washed himself. I wanted those hands touching his body to be mine, or my tongue. It didn't take us long to dry off and then he lifted me up and over his shoulder. I laughed as he carried me into the bedroom and dropped me gently on the bed.

As soon as I hit it, he started to kiss me. We spent

I don't know how long kissing and running our hands up and down each other. I was lost in a haze of desire. My body felt like it was on fire. When his hands cupped my breasts and then he tweaked my nipples with his fingers, I cried out. I came shuddering just from that.

"Fuck, you're so damn sensitive, babe. I wonder how many times I can get you off without ever touching that sweet pussy?"

"Don't. I won't be able to stand it. Mark, please, I need you," I pleaded with him.

I watched as he sat up on his heels and looked me over from head to toe. The burning lust in his eyes only served to push me closer to another orgasm, even though I'd just had one. His hand gripped his cock and he stroked up and down a couple of times. His fist smeared the cum down over the head. Suddenly, he moved and came to the head of the bed. He straddled my chest then lightly tapped my lips with the head of his cock, smearing precum on my lips. I licked them clean and hummed.

"Open up," he muttered. I smirked at him as I ever so slowly opened my mouth enough to thrust the tip of my tongue out. I licked it across his slit, taking more of his precum inside of my mouth. His salty musk hit my taste buds. I couldn't help but moan as he groaned. His hips flexed and he pressed his cock harder against my mouth.

"Open that mouth and suck my cock, Sloan," he growled. I lifted my hand and gripped the base to guide him to me. I took my time. I didn't immediately swallow him down like I knew he wanted. I knew how to ratchet up his desire. Mark was dominant in bed, but that didn't mean he wouldn't let me have my fun too. Sometimes, he was more dominant than others. I'd soon see if tonight was going to be one of those nights or not. Either way, I knew I was going to be a very satisfied woman when we were done.

"Do you want me to take more?" I teased as I barely let the head of his cock into my mouth. I flicked it with my tongue.

"Woman, if you don't suck my cock like you mean it, I'm going to paddle that ass."

"That's hardly a threat. You know I love it when you smack my ass."

As I finished teasing him yet again, he grabbed my lower jaw and applied pressure. It didn't hurt me, but it did make me open wider. Mark thrust his cock into my mouth and then to the back of my throat. I gagged. He pulled back then thrust again. Teasing over with, I worked to take him as deep as I could while applying the suction I knew that he loved.

I made sure that I gripped the base of his cock tightly and tugged up and down. He groaned and sped up. I couldn't help but want to smile as I worked him. He had his head thrown back and his eyes were closed with a look of intense pleasure on his face. His cock swelled even bigger, causing my jaws to ache even more. He was a mouthful.

Next thing I knew, he had a hand twisted in my hair. He pulled my head back farther and thrust deeper. I gagged but this time he didn't pull back. He kept sliding deeper. He was now looking down at me. I could see that through the tears in my eyes. I knew if I indicated that I didn't want him to go that deep, he'd back off. He'd never done anything I wasn't fully into him doing.

"Can you take it?" he whispered. I nodded as much as I could. If I could, I would take him all the way. I wanted, no, I needed to give him the same intense pleasure as he always gave me. Seeing my consent, he moaned and then thrust faster. It was all I could do to breathe in quickly when he drew back and then hold my breath. I pumped his base even faster and tightened my hold on him.

"God, babe, here it comes," he roared right before he stiffened and then started to jerk on my tongue. His cum flooded my mouth. I had to fight to swallow it fast enough for it not to leak out of the sides of my mouth. Eventually, he softened and drew back. I held onto him until I was finished cleaning him all over with my tongue. He caressed my face and hair as I did it.

As soon as I was done, he moved away and then slammed his mouth down on mine. His eager tongue thrust inside to taste what was still there. Unlike a lot of guys, he didn't seem to care if he tasted his own cum or not. When he finally pulled away so we could both take a breath, I asked him about it.

"Don't you hate the taste of your cum?"

"I don't mind it. Or at least I don't mind it when it's you. I love the way we taste together, baby. I'll admit, before you, I never even tasted it. I never had the desire. What about you? You let me come in your mouth. Do you hate the taste? You know you don't have to swallow if you don't want to."

"No, I don't hate the taste. It's all a part of you, Mark. I love anything that's part of you," I admitted. He got a soft look on his face then he moved away and was pushing my thighs apart. I was wet as hell from sucking him off. His eyes ate up the sight of my pussy.

"Now it's my turn. And before you ask, I love your taste, Sloan," he told me right before he dove between my legs. I couldn't hold back my cry of pleasure as he honed in on my clit and then licked me from clit to ass and back. Mark was a master at eating pussy. He obviously enjoyed it and took pride in making it as enjoyable as possible for me. He didn't rush it to just get to the sex. He made it his goal to get me off at least once or twice before the main event.

Tonight, he must have had other ideas. Since he'd already come, he worked me with his tongue, teeth, and fingers until he'd wrung two orgasms out of me in quick succession. His fingers would twist when he pulled out of my pussy, so he'd scrape them across that magical spot inside of me. I got so lost in how he was making me feel, that I barely noticed when he eased a finger into my ass. It burned, but that only added to my pleasure.

We hadn't talked about anal sex. I didn't know if it was something he was interested in or not. I'd tried it once in the past and it had been less than pleasurable. I knew if it was something he liked, I'd try my best to see if the second time was better than that one disastrous attempt. I wanted to be able to give him everything he wanted in and out of bed.

When I came down after the second orgasm, he

sat up on his heels. His face was slick with my cream and flushed. His eyes were burning. He reached down and tugged on his cock. He was hard again and the head was a deep purple color. I guess he did love going down on me. His hands grabbed my hips and tugged my ass up onto his thighs. He spread my legs even further apart and never looking away from my eyes, he thrust into me in one hard thrust.

I screamed as he parted those swollen, sensitive tissues inside of me. He felt too big for my pussy. I reached up and dug my short nails into his chest. He hissed and bucked. I moaned as he hit my cervix.

His strong hands gripped my hips and he used them to jerk me onto his cock as he thrust inside of me. In and out he worked his cock, hammering it into me. The head blissfully scraped across my G-spot over and over again. I sobbed as I felt my next orgasm quickly approaching. I could tell this was going to be spectacular. "Harder," I cried out to him.

He sped up and took me even deeper and harder. It took less than a minute of him doing that for me to explode. I sobbed as the orgasm tore up from my feet and through my body. I barely registered it when he pulled out and flipped me over onto my hands and knees. I could barely hold myself up as he hammered back inside of me.

The wet sound of our fucking and the scent of sex filled the air. I could feel and hear his balls smacking into my pussy, sending jolts through me. It was too much. "God, Mark, you have to stop. It's too much," I cried out. I felt like I was going to fall into pieces.

"You can take it, baby. I'm gonna fill that pussy so full of my cum, you'll be dripping for days. When we get done with this assignment, you're going to marry me and let me give you a baby. I want a family with you, Sloan. And I want it soon," he shouted.

His words shocked the hell out of me. I knew that I loved him. I knew we'd said we love each other. But for him to want to get married and have kids? He blew me away with that. I briefly wondered if that was just the heat of the moment talking. A huge wave of ecstasy washed over and through me. I screamed as I clamped down on him and I came. I came so hard that I felt myself squirt. Something I'd never done before. He powered into me a couple more times then stilled as he shouted out, "Fuck," and came. We jerked and shuddered together as we came down from the high.

Suddenly, he flipped so I was on top of him. Somehow, he kept his cock from sliding out. He wrapped his arms around me and held me close as he tenderly kissed my forehead.

"Oh my God, that was amazing, Mark," I croaked. I was trying to slow down my breathing. My whole body felt like it was boneless and I could sleep for a week.

"For me too, baby, me too. I meant what I said. I know this isn't the most romantic way to ask, but you know I love you. I want to spend the rest of my life with you. And I want to have a family with you. What do you think of that? Is that something you want?" I could hear the trepidation in his voice.

I raised up so I could see his face. "Honey, I love you too. I'll admit, you surprised me. I didn't know you were thinking along those lines, but I know there's nothing I'd love more than to be your wife."

"What about kids? Do you want some? If not, as long as I have you, I'll be happy," he hurried to tell me.

I ran my hand down his face and touched his lips with my fingers. He opened up to lick my fingertips. "Mark, I'd love to have kids. I'm not sure what kind of mother I'll be. I was starting to think that I might never get a chance to find out. As for having them soon, I think I'd like that too. As soon as we're done with this, let's talk again. There are so many logistical things to figure out."

"Logistical? If you mean your place, you rent, don't you?" I nodded yes. "Then we can let your place go and either you move in with me or we can get a new place, if you want."

"I love your house. I don't want to leave it. Yes, those are some of the main things. Other things are what will this mean for the office? I still want to work, Mark. I can't stay at home all the time. It would drive me mad. I'm too much like Cassidy to do that, though maybe working part time would be okay," I mused.

"We have time. Until then, all I want to do is keep making love to you and working to get this damn assignment over with. Come on, let's get cleaned up so we can get some sleep. Morning will be here before you know it."

I groaned as I rolled off him. A quick cleanup in the bathroom and then we were back in bed. I laughed as he threw a towel over the spot I'd soaked in the bed. I snuggled into his arms and that was the last thing I

CIARA ST JAMES

remembered.

Undertaker: Chapter 17

I had to fight not to let the smile I was feeling show on my face. We were on our way back to the Renegades compound. Last night, Sloan had made me a very happy man by accepting my off-the-cuff proposal. It wasn't anything I'd been planning to do then, but when the time came, I knew I had to tell her how I felt. Nothing would make me happier than to have her as my wife and mother of my children.

After seeing Cassidy and Sean with Noah, I'd been fighting the envy I had for them. I realized that I wanted what they had, a family. I'd never really thought about having one until I saw them. Even then, I figured it was a pipe dream until I met Sloan. One time with her and I knew what I wanted. I'd been biding my time until it was right to ask. However, last night was too much for me. I needed her to know how I felt and what I wanted.

A part of me wondered if it was because of this assignment. Nothing was guaranteed. We could find ourselves at the wrong end of a gun or worse, if they realized we were there to take them down. I was trying my hardest not to make them suspicious. Luckily so far, they didn't seem to be the smartest guys I'd ever met. I could only hope they continued to be like that until we took them down.

While I was working on them, the rest of the team was getting as much information as they could on the other clubs the Soldiers had infiltrated and taken over in the last few years. It would mean little if we couldn't take down the rest of them. I wanted us to be able to bring Slither and Ogre to justice. I knew that was what Reaper wanted for Cheyenne. I could understand him not wanting that threat hanging out there, especially with her being pregnant.

As expected, when we left the motel room, two of them were waiting in a truck outside. This time it was Sig and Frost. I didn't bother anymore to act like I didn't see them. I threw up a hand at them as we got on my bike. We went to have breakfast first then headed for their place. I was anxious to see what I might find out today.

Pulling into the compound, the first thing I saw was all of their bikes weren't there. That was different from the other days we'd been there. I tried not to let it worry me. After I parked, we went inside with our two shadows on our tails. In the common room, I found Dax, Hook, Grumble and Cage. There was no sign of the others. Another thing was I didn't see any of the bunnies or the old ladies.

I led Sloan over to a table and sat down. Mattie came from behind the bar and brought us over drinks. Mine was my usual beer and hers was a soda. She tended not to drink much. I only drank enough to keep them from getting suspicious. Dax plopped down at the table along with the other five.

"Hey, how's it going?" I asked him as I took a

drink.

"It's going. Are you ready to go make that run today?" Dax asked. I noticed he couldn't seem to keep his eyes off Sloan. For her part, she was sitting there, looking slightly bored and like she wasn't paying any attention to us.

"Sure. Where's the rest of the crew? I assume Slo will be staying here. Will she be alone or are the old ladies coming over?"

"Roman and the others went ahead to make sure everything is in order. Yeah, your old lady needs to stay here. No bitches today. I'll make sure Carla and Jane get their asses over here to keep her company. They should be here soon. While we're gone, they can work on fixing us something to eat," Dax said with a smile. He had no idea what a chauvinistic ass he was. Or maybe he just didn't care. In his mind, women were here for two things, sex and food. Though you couldn't see it on her face, I knew Sloan would like nothing more than to shove those words down his throat.

We sat there chatting about bikes and what our favorite guns were while we waited. A half an hour later, the door opened and in came Carla and Jane. Neither of them looked thrilled to be there, though their faces did light up a little when they saw Sloan. She smiled and got up to go over to greet them. As soon as she did, Dax leaned over to me.

"As soon as I get the all clear from Roman, we'll be heading out. I can't wait for you to see what all we can offer. Did you talk to your friends last night?"

"Good. Yeah, I did. They're ready to go. You heard

Poe yesterday when he called back. They can take the drugs in a couple of days. Do you know how you're gonna get those to him?"

"We'll talk about that today after we meet Lobo. After we're done with him, I want to take you to see the garage and the trucking company. Those are our two main distribution points. The bar is more for washing some of our money and the whores."

"Do all the whores work out of there? Doesn't that make it hard to get enough business?"

"Most of them do, but we've got a small motel outside of town where we have an understanding. No one pays attention to who comes or goes there. That's where they take the johns."

I didn't push for more, I just filed that piece of information away. As soon as I finished my beer, he stood up. He looked over at the women who'd sat down at a table in the corner. "We'll be back later. Make sure you have some food ready when we get back. We'll be starved."

"Do you know when you'll be back?" Jane asked him timidly.

"I have no fucking idea, just do it," He growled. She didn't say another word. I saw her and Carla exchange nervous glances. Sloan stood up and came over to me. I wrapped her in my arms.

"I'll be back later, babe. Why don't you see if you can help out Jane and Carla? I figure this'll take a little while."

"I will, baby. You guys be careful," she said before

she kissed me. We made sure that it was an intense one. When we were done, the guys were making their usual crude comments. Sloan just smiled and walked off. I made a show of adjusting myself in my pants then followed the six of them out to our bikes.

As we sped away, I sent up a prayer that today would go well. I was ready to get this shit over with, so we could move on with our lives. If nothing else, this assignment taught me that I wouldn't be willing to give up years of my life again. Not unless there was absolutely no other way around it in order to keep my family protected. If the feds wanted more help in the future, they needed to find it elsewhere. I had plans.

Dax didn't go into town. He stayed out in the country. After taking several back roads, we came up on a run-down house out in the middle of nowhere. I'd call it more of a shack than a house. The place was so old and falling apart, I had to wonder what was keeping it from falling in. The six of them pulled into the overgrown front yard and stopped. I parked alongside them and shut off my bike. I could see the others were already here.

Following them up to the door, I took a look around. It wouldn't do for me to walk into a trap. I was a little concerned that the others hadn't been at the clubhouse when we got there. Were they really just making sure everything was set for the visit or was it more? Did they suspect we were working for the feds or maybe the cops?

Stepping into the shack, I saw the inside wasn't any nicer than the outside. Scattered around the small living room was a couple of ratty couches and a few milk crates being used for tables. Trash was thrown all over the floor. Off to the left was a small open kitchen with dirty dishes piled in the sink and on the counters and table. There was an overwhelming smell of garbage in the air. I could barely keep from gagging.

At least it looked like Roman, and the others had enough sense not to sit on the furniture. Hell, if you did, you'd probably need a tetanus shot at the least. A scruffy guy who had the obvious meth mouth bounded up off the couch and came hurrying over to Dax. He had a smile on his face. As I stared at him, I noticed the glazed look in his eyes. He was high as a kite.

"Hey, Dax, how're you? The guys said you were bringing someone today. Is he a new member? Hi, my name is Lobo." He held out his hand. I didn't take it.

"Lobo, leave the man alone. This is Undertaker. He's here to look at your work. If he likes what he sees, we might be able to increase our business, which I know you'll love."

"Oh, that would be great! Yeah, I could get me that new TV I want," he said excitedly. I looked around. He had to be making money. Where the hell did he spend it? Was it all put back in the business or in his body? I could see the track marks scarring both arms.

Like that, Lobo took off. He led us out a backdoor off the kitchen and then into the woods. We walked for a mile or more. I was about to ask how much farther it was when he veered to the right. At first all I saw was a bunch of brush and vines, then I looked harder. Hidden behind all that was a door. He opened it and went inside. I followed Roman and Dax while the others stayed outside.

I found myself in another old shack. However, this one was set up to produce the meth. I could see the Bunsen burner and other equipment scattered around the kitchen. Sitting out in the open on a small table was packaging materials. I listened as Lobo went into detail on what he was working on. When he paused long enough to take a breath, I jumped in with my question.

"Are you the only one who does the work or do you at least have someone who helps you with the packaging and stuff?"

"Oh, my woman, Lulu, helps me do all that. She's not here right now. She had to go to town. She'll be back later."

I gave Dax a worried look. At the amount I was hinting at moving, how in the hell would one guy and his woman keep up with the demand? I gestured to him to step outside. He took the hint. "Hey, Lobo, we'll be back in a minute. Stay here." Lobo didn't object. He happily stood there as we went outside. As soon as we were clear of that pit, I launched into my objections.

"Jesus Christ, Dax, how in the hell can he keep up with the demand? I'm not talking about moving a little bit of shit every six months here. The guys I work with will want monthly shipments and not in tiny amounts. I wanna make this work, but I'm not feeling too confident in your guy in there. Maybe this was a mistake."

"No, no, he can do it! If needed, we know where we can get him some help," Dax hurried to assure me.

"Yeah, but will the help be able to keep their mouths shut? I assume Lobo and his woman do. You can't be too careful who you tell shit like this. One wrong word and they'll have the law down on you."

"Listen, Undertaker, Slither has resources. If we find that Lobo can't do his fucking job, we'll get someone who can. It's not a problem. You tell us what you need and we'll get it for you." Roman was the one to add that.

I walked off and paced around, making it look like I was thinking. I didn't want them to get too confident. They had to work to show me they could meet my demands. After a couple of tense minutes, I came back to them and nodded.

"Okay, if you're sure, I'll take your word for it. But I want to see the rest of your operations. Drugs are one thing, but I have to be sure that you can deliver on everything, the guns and women included. Is there more to see here or can we go?"

Dax gave a chin lift to Roman. He went back inside. A couple of minutes later, he came back with Lobo in tow. We retraced our steps back to his house and left him there. I wasn't sad to see that place in my mirror. Now, me and the whole club headed back the way we came. We eventually arrived back in town and outside of a garage. Since it was a workday, the place was open and I could see guys were in there working on cars.

Jester took the lead here and showed me his place. I could see the pride in his eyes as he showed me around. It was easy to see that he ran a good garage. He didn't bother to introduce me to the mechanics who were throwing us looks. After he'd shown me around, we went out back where it was quiet.

I didn't waste time. "What do you use the garage for?"

"We smuggle out some of the drugs and if it's a small load, some guns. We come in after the day is done and hide them in the cars that are done and to be picked up the next day," Jester told me. I could tell by the look on his face, he didn't like that at all.

"How do you get them back once they're clear of here?"

"We have guys go out and pick them up. We make sure we pick ones that will sit outside. It's not that hard to get the stuff back. Once we do, it's passed along to the buyer," Roman told me.

"You can't move a whole lot that way. What about when you have a big shipment, like what I'll be bringing you?"

"That's what we have the trucking company for. We have false bottoms in the trucks which we can use to haul guns or drugs. They go out all over the state and beyond, so it's not a problem to tweak the weight numbers of the cargo and get it out," Dax explained.

"Can I see the trucking company?"

From there it was a repeat of the garage. They took me to see their location and showed me one of the trucks and the false compartments they had. It wasn't anything I hadn't seen before and I had to wonder how they hadn't gotten caught. The feds and cops were usually better at finding shit like this.

Once we finished there, they drove me over to a motel on the edge of town. It wasn't busy since it was the middle of the day. However, I did get to see some of the women. It killed me to see the dead or desperate look in their eyes. If I had to guess, I would say not even half of them were here because they'd made the choice. The motel was seedy as well.

It was there that I found they had a couple of guys they hadn't mentioned. They weren't members or prospects. They were hired muscle. I doubted they were here to protect the girls. They were here to make sure they worked, gave up the money, and didn't run off. They were introduced as Alvin and Rhys. Both were muscular guys with a glint of cruelty in their eyes. They wouldn't show the women any sympathy.

By the time we were done there, I didn't have the stomach to see their bar. That could wait. Besides, it wasn't where they did the bulk of their illegal activity. They did point it out as we passed the place on our way back to their clubhouse.

It was early evening by the time we made it back. We'd been gone longer than I'd expected. I'll admit I was anxious to see Sloan. I'd been worried about her. After we parked our rides, we went inside. I wasn't surprised to see that the bunnies were there. They seemed to have a knack for showing up at the right time.

I didn't waste time. I went over to my woman and hauled her up out of her chair. After seeing what I had today, I needed to have something to take the bad taste out of my mouth. I kissed her. She moaned as she kissed me back. I didn't miss the sneer on Erica's face when we parted. I gave her a smirk.

"How did your day go, babe?" I asked her softly.

"You know, about as you'd expect. I'm glad you're back. We've got dinner ready if you guys are hungry." She made sure to say the last part loud enough for the guys to hear. They all cheered and headed for the kitchen. As soon as we finished eating, they sat down to drink. The women were expected to clean up the mess.

As the evening wore on, the bunnies got louder and things got more out of control. The music was turned up super loud, and the bunnies got up to dance. It didn't take long before they were being told to strip. That didn't take long since they had barely anything on to begin with. I could see Carla and Jane were trying to ignore them along with their men. I had Sloan sitting on my lap.

I knew this wasn't anything that she hadn't seen while she was growing up in an MC, but I hated for her to have to watch it. She didn't give away that it affected her one way or the other, but I could feel the thread of tension running through her. I whispered in her ear, "Babe, we can leave if you're ready."

"No, they won't let us out of here this early. You know how they are. I'm alright. I can handle it even if all I want to do is bust all their heads together. Jesus, they have zero respect for women. I shouldn't be surprised," she whispered back.

She was right. They wouldn't be likely to let us leave this early. I ground my teeth and looked on, projecting a look of boredom. Eventually, Roman noticed.

"Hey, why don't you get up there and dance, Slo? I bet your man would love to see what you can do. I know I would." He leered at her.

I glared at him. "If you think my old lady is going to get up there and take off her clothes, you're nuts. I told you. I'm the only one who sees her naked," I growled.

He held up his hands in surrender. "No problem. I wasn't saying she had to take anything off. I just wanted to see if she had moves like the bunnies do. We know that Carla and Jane don't. However, if you don't want to dance, they need to." He laughed as he threw them a smirk. Both women looked very uncomfortable. I guess they'd been made to dance for this bunch of fuckers before.

"Don't react," Sloan whispered and then she stood up. She gave Roman and the others a smile. "I can dance. I love to dance." I watched as she sashayed herself into the middle of the floor. Dax and his guys sat forward in eager anticipation.

I had to clench my fists under the table. I watched as Sloan closed her eyes and got into the beat of the music. Whereas the other women were busy grinding and bending over to show their asses and pussies to us, Sloan's movements were all sensual and seductive. I couldn't look away as she danced. I felt myself go hard, and I had no doubt the other men were the same. Even Curly and Jester were watching her.

She danced three songs before she came to sit down again. The bunnies had stomped off to the side halfway through the first song and stood there looking pissed off. No one paid them an ounce of attention. As soon as Sloan sat down on my lap, she wiggled. She could feel my cock pressing into her.

"That was fucking hot. Jesus, man, no wonder you want her all to yourself. If you ever change your mind, let me know," Dax said as he licked his lips. His eyes were devouring her.

"I won't," was all I said. It was all I could trust myself to say. On top of being horny as hell, I was pissed at the way they couldn't keep their dirty looks to themselves. Sloan half turned and kissed me. I lost myself in that kiss. When we came up for air, I stood up. I'd had enough of this shit.

"We're leaving. We've got things to do. I'll see you tomorrow."

They laughed and gave us knowing looks, but they didn't try to persuade us to stay. I raced her out the door and onto my bike. I had to work not to break the speed limit too much on the way back to our motel. I barely got the door closed and locked before I had her shoved up against the wall. "What the fuck was that for?"

"Baby, calm down. I had to do it or they were going to make Jane and Carla get up there. They can't handle that shit. I can."

"I don't want them focusing on you more than they already do," I snapped as I tore off her cut and top. She reached behind her to undo her bra. I didn't wait for it to fall before I was tugging down her jeans and panties. It took a couple of seconds to get her out of her boots and the rest of her clothes. As soon as she was, I ripped open my jeans and shoved them to my knees.

Seeing her like that, watching her dance, knowing how she affected every man in the room, had me wild. I wanted to mark her so no one would be in doubt she was mine. If I'd been a different kind of man, I would have fucked her right in front of them to show it. However, I would never do that to her.

She gasped as I felt between her legs. She was wet and ready. I didn't wait. I lifted her ass up and as she wrapped those sexy legs around my waist, I pounded into her. I used the wall to give me a hard surface to fuck her into. I knew this wasn't going to last long. I was close to the edge already.

"This body is mine. Mine, you hear me? Anyone else ever tries to touch you, I'll kill them with my bare hands, Sloan," I growled as I hammered into her tight, wet pussy.

She moaned and nodded. "I'm yours, Mark. That was for you, honey. You're the only one I saw. Oh God, oh God," she cried as she clamped down on me. I grunted and rutted as I came right behind her. She sagged in my arms as she came down from her release. I slid out of her but I wasn't done. I turned her to face the wall.

Even though I'd just come, I was still hard. I rubbed her pussy and got my fingers covered in our combined cum. Once I had enough, I found her asshole. She tensed then relaxed as I worked first one finger then another inside. My other hand was busy playing with her clit. When I had three fingers inside of her, I nipped her ear with my teeth.

"Baby, have you ever had a man in this ass?"

She slowly nodded.

"Did you like it?" I grew excited, thinking of being in her ass.

"No, it hurts like hell, Mark."

I bit back my groan of disappointment. "I'm sorry, babe." I went to remove my fingers, but she clenched down on them.

"Don't. Give me a minute."

"Sloan, honey, you don't need to be uncomfortable. You should have told me you didn't like this."

"I do like what you're doing right now. It hurts but only a little. It feels more pleasurable than painful."

"Do you like it enough to maybe one day let me try?"

She was quiet for a long minute then she nodded. "Yes, I'd be willing to let you try. Just go slow. He was in too much of a rush, I think."

I groaned. "I promise, I'll take it slow and easy. If you don't find you like it, I'll stop. I never want to hurt you."

"Okay, go ahead."

"Babe, I didn't mean right now. I want to work on getting you better prepared. There are things we can do. Ways to get you used to having something in your ass."

All she did was moan and press back into me. I couldn't keep this conversation up or I'd be in that ass tonight. I pulled my fingers out and then notched my cock back at the entrance of her pussy. I pushed back inside. The second round took a little longer than the first, but not much. She had me so damn hot for her, I couldn't hold back. This time when we came, my legs went weak and I sank to the floor with her.

We lay there until we could get our legs to move. Once that happened, I helped her up and I got undressed. We took a quick shower together and then crawled into bed. As she snuggled into my chest, she asked me, "How did your day go? Did you get what you wanted?"

"I got most of it, I think. They took me to see their meth producer. Jesus Christ, he was a mess and that place a hellhole. I have no idea how they can think he can keep up with demand. They assured me if he can't, they have people. They mentioned Slither."

"What about the garage, trucking company and the bar? Did you get to see those?" I nodded yes. "What did you think of them?" she added.

"The garage looks like it's a very good one. Jester has a lot of pride in that place. I could tell he hates the fact they use it for drugs and guns. They hide shit in the cars and trucks and then go get it later when they need them. As for the trucking company, there are some of the trucks with false bottoms they smuggle stuff out in. I've seen those before. Not very imaginative on their part, but they seem to be getting away with it. We didn't go into the bar. By then I couldn't stand to see more. I did see some of the women they use for prostitution at a motel they use. God, they looked like they were in hell. There are two guys who stand guard over the place.

They're not there for their protection. God, that killed me, Sloan."

She hugged me tightly. "Baby, I know it did. I don't even have to see it to feel for those women. We'll help them, I promise. When we bring this bunch of bastards down, they'll be free."

"I hope so. I know some are there because they don't think they have anywhere else to be. But I know there's help out there. I pray to God, they let us get them out of this life once they're free of these men. Okay, enough about my day, how did yours go with the old ladies?"

"It went really well. They're relaxing with me. Told me more about how the club used to be before Dax and the others took over. It sounds like it was a good club, Mark. They had friends and kids. I asked why the others left and all they said is they didn't like how the club changed. When I asked them why they didn't go, they more or less confirmed that they couldn't. The club needs those businesses that Jester and Curly have the most. They're the money makers. Even though most of the money now goes to the club, they're owned by those two men. I have no doubt they've been threatened to stay. I tried to get a chance to look around the clubhouse, but they stuck to me the whole time and then those bunnies showed up. Hopefully, I'll get a chance later."

"Don't worry about that. It was only a suggestion. Now, let me send off what we found really quick and then we need to get some sleep. Tomorrow is going to be just as exhausting as today, I figure." I took out my laptop and sent off my report on what I'd seen and found out to Sean and the guys. By the time I was done, Sloan had fallen asleep. I curled myself around her and hugged her tight. It was an exhausted though satisfied sleep that I fell into after that.

Sloan: Chapter 18

The last couple of days had been exhausting for us. The club wasn't fast about showing Mark anymore about their operations. All they did was sit around and drink and talk shit. I knew Mark was about to go off. He wanted this to be over with. Tonight was the night he was going to pass off the drugs to his buyer. We'd hoped to be able to do more than that, but at this point, we still didn't know all the players or had a chance to meet Slither. Mark wanted to meet him and maybe get his foot in the door with him. After all, he was the head of this whole operation. We had to find a way to take him down, not just this one club.

We pulled into the Renegades' compound already feeling disappointed, another day of hanging with this bunch of miscreants. Thank goodness I at least had Carla and Jane to talk to. They were both sweet women who I felt nothing but pity for. They were in an impossible situation with their men.

Today, we came out of the motel to find there wasn't anyone watching us. Mark had looked at me in surprise. Was this an indication they were finally trusting us? Or did it mean they had other things to do? I could feel on the ride over, he felt tenser than usual.

As I swung off the bike, the door to the clubhouse opened and out came Jane and Carla. Both of them looked excited. They hurried over to us.

"We're so glad you're here, Slo. We're going to go to town and do some shopping. Do you want to come with us?" Jane asked.

I looked at Mark. I didn't know if he'd want us to be separated. He took a couple of moments to consider before he nodded. "You should go, babe. You've been cooped up with all of us for days. It'll be nice to get out with the ladies." He looked at them. "Any idea how long you'll be gone?"

"Probably only a couple of hours. We need to hit the grocery store and then maybe another store. The guys want to have a party later and we need to get supplies," Carla told him nervously.

"Okay, are you leaving right now?" he asked and they both nodded. He pulled out his wallet and handed me a handful of cash. "Take this, babe. Grab whatever you think we need or you want. I'll see you later. Be careful," he said. I took the money and tucked it into my jeans' pocket. He tugged me into his arms and kissed me. When he was done, he patted me on the ass. I followed the other two to a car. We got inside and they took off.

On the way to town, I listened to them chat about what they wanted to get at the store. I tried to seem like I was present, but I was really worrying about Mark. What would happen now that he was alone with them? Was this just a way to get me out of the way?

At the grocery store, I grabbed the cart and pushed it around as we walked the aisles. It looked like they were going to do some grilling. As we walked around, I decided I'd see if I could get them to talk more about the club.

"So, did you do a lot of parties like this in the old days? I mean, it seems the guys expect to be fed and drink like it's a party every night that we've been here. Is that just because of us?"

Both of them looked at each other before Carla answered, "No, they didn't do this. We'd have parties, but usually on the weekends, since everyone was busy working during the week. And when we did, the ladies would cook. We had more ladies to help then. Since Dax and the guys took over, it's been just us and you saw the bunnies. No way they'd get their hands dirty, though they have no problem eating what we make."

"I hope you don't mind me saying this, but how in the world do they make any money? I don't see any of them working. I know you have a garage, a trucking company and a bar. Do they all have managers who run them for you?"

"Usually, Curly and Jester work during the week at the trucking company and the garage, but since you and Undertaker have been here, Dax has wanted them at the clubhouse. Nox is the same. He usually oversees the bar. As for the rest, no, they don't really work," Jane said with a slight sneer on her face.

"I can't imagine that. Even though I haven't known Undertaker long, I know he believes in working. He used to work at his old club before they were disbanded. He's looking for some place he'd be able to do that again. He doesn't believe in just taking and not giving back in return."

"He does seem to be different, more like our guys. How do you feel about the things they do? I know we're supposed to be in the dark about what goes on, but we're not stupid. Since the change, the club has gone a different route and we're now into things we never thought we'd be in," Carla said.

"A part of me wishes he wasn't into what he is. I won't lie. I worry that he'll get caught and go down like his old club, but I love him. I couldn't walk away from him even if I wanted to. He assures me that we can have a life and a family. That's what we both want. If I have to put up with that in order to be with him, then I'll do it gladly. I still worry and don't want him to fall in with the wrong group."

"We feel the same. Jester and Curly never wanted to be doing what they are now. It's not what the old club did to make money. All of their businesses were legal. It worries the two of them to death that their businesses are used the way they are now," Jane added.

"You mean to run the drugs and guns?" They both nodded. This was the first time they acknowledged what the club used their old men's businesses for. By now, we were checked out and loading the car with all the groceries we'd bought. No one was around to hear what we were saying.

"Yes, and that they use the bar as a place for men to pick up those prostitutes. They don't know we know that. Or that they use that junkie, Lobo, to cook their damn meth. He's been around here for years. My skin crawls even thinking about him. I wish like hell we'd never taken Dax, Roman, and Hook on. If we hadn't, we wouldn't be in this mess," Carla added with a sigh.

"So, they were the ones who brought that idea to the club. I wonder why they went along with it, if you weren't into that before. Did they just want to make more money? I know there's a lot more money to be made from these kinds of things, but there's also a lot of risk too. I tried to talk Undertaker into working with another kind of club, but he said he needed to go with what he knew."

"The club didn't want anything to do with that stuff when Dax and those other two brought it up. Our old president told them there was no way that was ever going to happen," Jane said with a frown.

"So, how did it happen if he said no? I thought whatever the president said, goes."

"The club as a whole has to vote on those things. So, even if the president isn't for it, the club might vote to do it. In this case, several of the original club members didn't disagree with the president. Or at least no one but Dax, Hook and Roman did. They were all for doing the illegal stuff. As soon as that happened, things around here started to change," Jane added.

"Changed how?" I asked. We were now parked outside of a department store. We were sitting in the car. Both women who were in the front seat turned around to face me. I could see the strain on their faces.

"Sloan, we could get into a lot of trouble for telling you this. However, we think we can trust you.

You remind us a lot of our friends who left. At first, we saw that some of the guys just decided that they weren't going to go along with the change. Those guys up and quit the club. That killed Jester and Curly. New guys were brought in like Sig, Cage and Grumble. They eventually took over the spots of the men who left. Once they left, we had no communication with them or their old ladies. We tried, but they wouldn't respond, so we eventually knew to leave them alone," Carla said quietly.

"Did you guys and your men ever think of leaving?"

"Yeah, we did, but when they tried, they couldn't leave. Our old president had died. He was ran off the road on his bike and was killed. Dax was voted in as the new president. Although Jester and Curly didn't say it, we think they were threatened to stay," Jane told me with a sad look on her face.

"Why do you think they were threatened?"

"Because right after they said they wanted to leave, they became increasingly paranoid about safety. They had alarm systems put in at our houses and we weren't to go anywhere alone. They had us start to carry guns and made sure we knew how to use them. We were told not to go to the clubhouse unless they were there and to never be alone with the other members. They didn't need to tell us the last part. We no longer felt safe there anyway. The way Dax and most of the others treat women is disgusting." Carla shuddered.

I wanted to keep them talking, but I didn't want it to seem like I was pumping them for information. I indicated we should get out of the car. Once we got in the store, we started to look around. I think they just wanted to kill some time before going back to the clubhouse. The cold stuff was in coolers in the trunk. We looked through the clothes. As we did, I got back to talking.

"I never thought I'd be with a biker. I'd never even talked to one until the night I met Undertaker. When he came up to talk to me, I admit, I fell hard. He was so sexy and just came across as so strong. Of course, I didn't know at that point he was in a club. However, it wasn't until I'd spent the next day with him that I found out that part. Seeing his old club had been taken down while he'd been in jail, was a shock. If he'd been with them, he would have gone down with them. I admit when he confessed that to me, I thought about running. I'd heard things about how a lot of MCs were like. I didn't know what was true and what was false. However, I just couldn't do it. I swear it was love at first sight for me. I think it was the same for him. He didn't want to let me out of his sight after that first day. From there, the rest is history."

"Didn't your family have objections?" Jane asked me.

"I don't have any family. I grew up in foster care. I had a few friends, but we weren't that close. I knew that being with Undertaker would mean leaving my shitty job and moving on, but I didn't care. I packed up a little of my stuff and we hit the road. I'll admit, it'll be nice to have a place to settle. That's what we're hoping comes with this move. Listen, with the three of us, I think we can work to make some changes around the clubhouse. For one, knocking those bunnies down several notches.

I know they serve a purpose, but they don't have to be up in our faces or trying to get our men all the time. They have plenty of others they can sleep with."

"Wouldn't that be nice? I hate those bitches. They always try to get Curly and Jester to take them up on their offers. No matter how many times they tell them no, they keep trying. I admit I was happy when Undertaker came and they put their sights on him. I'm sorry. It's just it gave us a break," Jane apologized.

"No need to apologize. I understand. Those bunnies will be learning a lesson. How do you think Sig, Cage and Grumble like the club as it is right now?"

"They don't say a whole lot, so it's hard to say. Although we've seen them get these looks on their faces sometimes when Dax and the other two are talking about certain things. I don't think they're as in love with the whole direction of the club. They came in after the change and haven't been patched for more than a year. They do what they're told, but I don't think they're happy. Honestly, when they were prospects, I expected them to leave, but that never happened. We wondered if they were somehow forced to stay." Carla was the one to answer me.

"You mean they might have been threatened like your men?"

They both nodded. From there, they got quiet. I decided not to push them for more information. I'd gotten confirmation of why their men had stayed and the news that at least three of the men might not be as behind the president as we'd thought. I couldn't wait to tell Mark what I'd learned.

We didn't spend long in the store, but when we left, each of us had a new outfit. In no time it seemed, we were back at the clubhouse. As soon as we stopped the car, the door opened and out came the men.

"What the hell took so long?" Dax asked angrily.

"We had to make another stop. We told you we wouldn't be back for a few hours," Jane told him. I opened the trunk. I was surprised when most of the men stepped up to help get out the groceries. Of course, Dax, Roman and Hook didn't. They all stood there glaring at us.

"We're fucking starved. Get your asses busy. We want to eat before we head out later," Dax growled.

Mark stepped in. He faced off with Dax. "No one tells my old lady what the fuck to do, unless it's me. She'll help them get the sides done. In the meantime, we can get the grills going and work on the meat. Why don't you tell those damn bunnies to get out here and help too? I don't know about you, but where I came from, the bunnies were expected to do other shit to earn their keep when they weren't spreading their legs."

"Oh really, like what?" Roman said with a sneer on his face.

"They cleaned the clubhouse along with the prospects and would help whenever we had parties or meals to get shit ready. It didn't all fall to the old ladies, especially when there were less of them than us. I happen to be a mean grill master. Anyone wanna see if they're better?"

The way he said it, made it a challenge, which he

knew these men wouldn't be able to resist. In no time, they had the groceries inside and unpacked. They yelled at the bunnies, who were lounging around the common room, to get in the kitchen and help us. Mark and a few of the others went out to fire up the grills. In short order, they were back and working on seasoning some of the steak and chicken we'd brought from the store.

I couldn't say that Dax, Hook and Roman did much. They more or less stood there watching the rest of us work, but Jester, Sig, Curly, Grumble and Cage all pitched in. We soon had a laughing group, working together on the food. The other three were watching us with looks of consternation on their faces. They rarely took their eyes off Undertaker. I hope that didn't mean they were going to have problems with him. He'd kind of stepped on Dax's toes as the president.

The bunnies weren't a lot of help, but they did do some. By the time we were all ready to eat, it was late afternoon. The alcohol was rolling. I noticed that Dax, Roman and Hook seemed to be the ones imbibing the most while the others only drank sparingly. Mark was one of the ones who drank the least. I knew he was worrying about the run later tonight.

We were sitting with the others when Mark stood up abruptly and pulled me to my feet. "I need a few minutes with my old lady."

"I'll bet you do. Feel free to use any of the rooms," Dax said with a smirk on his face. Mark grinned at him and took me off to the clubhouse. Only when we got inside, we didn't stay there. He took me out a side door. It put us on the opposite side of the building where all the partying was happening. He pushed me up against the wall. As he attacked my neck with his lips, he whispered, "Are you alright?"

I made sure to make it look like we were whispering sweet nothings to each other, in case anyone came around the building. "I'm fine. Just worrying about later. I talked to the ladies. I'll tell you what they said later. Are you sure Dax and them don't know anything?"

He grasped my breasts and kneaded them through my top. "I don't think they do. While you were gone, he went into more detail on the run tonight. We'll be leaving around nine to go meet with Lobo and get the product. Then we'll be loading it into a truck which will be met at the location I gave them. They'll switch it over to another truck there and that should be it."

"God, be careful, Mark. I hate that you'll have no one to back you up in case something goes wrong. I think that Jester and Curly might be trustworthy, but there's no guarantee that they are." I nipped his ear and was kissing slowly down his neck.

Even though we were doing this as a cover for our conversation, we were both getting turned on. There was no way I could have him touch me and not. I could feel his erection pressing into my stomach. I reached down and squeezed him through his jeans. He groaned. "Fuck, baby, don't do that. I want you even if we're in the middle of this shitstorm. I wish like hell we could get a few minutes to be truly alone."

Suddenly, I knew that I couldn't let him do this tonight without having him. *What if this was the last time*? Ran through my head. I pushed that negative thought away. "Do it. I don't care if they see us. I need you too," I told him.

He pulled away from me so he could see my face. He must have seen that I was serious. He looked around and then took my hand and started off into the trees that were on this side of the clubhouse. Once we got into them far enough not to see the clubhouse, he stopped. Within moments he had my top and bra off and my jeans pulled down. I stepped out of my boots and let him take off my pants. As soon as he had me undressed, I got to work on his clothes. We were both desperate for each other.

He dropped to his knees and parted my legs. His hungry mouth attacked my pussy. I couldn't help but moan as he licked my slit and teased my clit with his talented tongue. I leaned back against the tree behind me. He thrust his fingers into me. I couldn't help the small yell.

"Fuck, baby, you have the sweetest pussy I've ever tasted. I'm addicted to it. The smell of you, drives me wild. Come on, give me some more of that cream. I want to walk around with you on me for the rest of the fucking night."

Hearing him say that, only caused me to gush more. The wet sounds of his licking and fingers seemed to surround us. It didn't take much more for him to tip me over the edge. I bit into one of my hands to muffle my scream as I came. When I was done, I was weak in the knees and he was helping me to stand up.

Before I'd fully recovered, he stood up and wiped his face. As I watched, he licked his hand clean of my juices. There was something sexy as hell about seeing him do that. The look on his face said he was savoring it. As soon as he was done, he kissed me. I could taste myself on his lips and smell my scent all over him. While he was busy kissing me like he was starving, he hoisted my legs in the air. I automatically wrapped them around his waist and my arms around his shoulders. His cock probed my entrance.

"Sloan, I need you too much to go slow baby. I'm sorry." As soon as he said that and before I could respond, he slammed himself into me in one big stroke. I cried out at the feeling of him filling me so damn full. He stretched me like he does every time, only this time it felt like he was even bigger than usual.

He was the biggest guy I'd ever been with. He always stretched me, no matter how many times we had sex. There was a bite of pain this time, but I didn't mind. It made me feel even more pleasure. He didn't wait to start his thrusts. He hadn't been kidding, he wasn't going slow. He pounded away at me. I could feel the bark scraping my back, but I didn't care. All I cared about was his cock inside of me. I wanted to come and make him come too.

"I wish like hell you weren't on anything. I want to fill your belly with my baby. I can't wait until we can get married and start a family," he panted.

The image of me heavy with his baby made me want to cry. There was nothing I wanted more than to be married to him and starting a family together. "Me too, Mark. I want so much to have a family with you too. Please, you have to be careful tonight," I pleaded.

He didn't say anything for a minute or so as he hammered in and out of me. All of a sudden, I felt myself getting to the edge. Things were starting to tighten. I was about to come. Sensing this, he slid one hand around to the front and teased my clit. That sent me over the edge and into one of the best orgasms of my life. I tried not to yell and to muffle it, but I don't know how successful I was. As I came, he stroked a few more times in and out then stilled and shuddered as he came. I could feel his warm cum filling me.

He leaned in and kissed me. Our mouths couldn't seem to get enough of each other. Eventually, we had to take a breath. He looked me deep in the eyes. "I'll do everything in my power to come back to you, Sloan. I love you and I meant what I said. I want to marry you and start our family. You need to be careful tonight too. I don't know if they're sending everyone with us or if some are staying here. I want you to be on your guard at all times, no matter who is here. I don't trust any of them."

"I promise, I'll stay on guard. God, I wish we could just stay here, but I think we should get back to them," I said with a sigh. He pulled out and helped me to get cleaned up and redressed. My panties had to be sacrificed to clean me up, but I didn't mind. He made me laugh when he tucked them into his pocket. We walked hand in hand back into the clubhouse and then back out the front door.

There were a lot of knowing looks and several crude remarks, but we didn't say anything. We just smiled. When we went to sit back down, Mark made sure I was sitting on his lap. As evening came, and things got dark, I saw the guys get restless. I knew it was almost time for them to leave. It wasn't too long before they were all standing up and going to get on their bikes.

I saw Curly and Jester take a moment to kiss their old ladies. Mark did the same to me. I couldn't help but to hold on to him a tad longer. He whispered to me that he'd be back. I fought not to cry as they left the compound. The only ones who were left with us ladies and the bunnies were the three prospects. Ignoring them, I went inside. We were all going to wait for their return together. I sat down with Carla and Jane. The bunnies went off in a corner to talk and give us shitty looks. I couldn't care less.

"Everything is going to be alright," Carla told me as she grasped my hand and squeezed it. I squeezed it back but didn't say anything. All I could do was pray that this went off without a hitch and he'd walk through that door later.

Undertaker: Chapter 19

As I rode off with the Renegades, I couldn't help but hate that I was leaving Sloan alone. Yeah, she was there with a bunch of women, but they weren't the ones I was the most worried about. It was the prospects we'd left behind. They hadn't been involved in much of our discussions the last few days. I had no idea what kind of men they were. Would they try something while we weren't there? Was I leaving her with more dangerous enemies than we knew?

I had to shake off those thoughts and get my head in the game. This was too important for me to screw it up. This was the first step in taking down this chapter and hopefully, getting enough soon to move on the others. I still didn't have anything to tie Slither and Ogre into this, other than Dax's word that Slither was his main contact. He never hinted that Slither was part of another club called the Soldiers of Corruption. I needed to get him to let me in front of Slither.

Our first stop was at Lobo's place which wasn't a surprise. He was there waiting with a beat-up truck that looked like it was mostly rust. I had no idea how the hell it could even still run. I looked around but didn't see the woman he said was his, Lulu. When we stopped, Dax got off his bike and went over to talk to him. I wasn't close enough to hear what was said, but Lobo was busy nodding his head. A couple of minutes later, Dax was back on his bike and we were heading off.

It didn't take us long to get to the trucking company. The lot was dark and I didn't see anyone around. It was well past regular business hours. We pulled around back and parked. I saw a truck sitting there with its doors open. They quickly got the drugs out of Lobo's truck and loaded them into the false bottom of the other truck. They didn't come close to filling up the available space, but it was only to be the first run, a trial to see if my people liked the product and wanted more. I kept watch with Curly at Dax's insistence.

In no time, they had it loaded and the floor back in place. If anyone opened it, it would look like an empty truck coming back from making a delivery. As soon as they were done, Dax came over to me.

"Now it's up to your people. Are you sure they're set to do this?"

"They're ready. I told you where to meet them. They'll be there waiting. Now that I know the truck's license plate and what it looks like, I'll send them a message so they know which one to expect. Who's going to be the driver? Is it one of your club or someone else?"

"One of our regular drivers, Monte, will be here in a minute. He knows the score and will get it there. If this goes off, you can bet we'll be doing a whole lot more with those contacts of yours. I talked to Slither earlier. He said if you come through with this and the guns, he's willing to talk to you about expanding the business even more. We're in with other clubs that can provide more than this one."

This was the kind of news I was hoping for. I wanted to make it attractive enough to get the real president interested enough to see me. If I could do that, I'd be able to hopefully lead the team to his club. From what I knew, they were no longer at their original chapter in Blue Creek. They'd left there and no one knew where to find them. If they did, Reaper would have already taken Slither and Ogre's asses out. I wanted to be able to give him that gift.

"It'll go off without a hitch. My guys are really good. You can tell Slither that I can bring a lot more of this to him. When do you want us to do a gun run? I can get that set up in a couple of days if that works for you."

"Let's get this over with then we can talk."

I had to let it go. About five minutes later, a man came walking out of the dark. They greeted him and introduced him to me as Monte. I shook his hand. I explained to him exactly where he needed to go. He said he knew the spot. After that, he got up in the cab and waved at us as he took off. I wish like hell we could follow him, but that would attract unwanted attention. While we waited to hear from him, which wouldn't be for a couple of hours, Dax suggested we go to their bar and have a few drinks. I'd rather go back to Sloan, but I knew I couldn't pass this up. I agreed, so we set off for the bar.

It only took us a few minutes to get there. It was just a little after ten. Inside, I saw that it was a little on the run-down side. They obviously didn't believe in putting money back into their business, which was a shame. If they did, they could attract a lot more customers and of a more diverse variety. We had a seat at an open table. The place was half full. I could tell this wasn't the place to attract higher-end customers. Mostly they were people you'd expect in a dive bar—drunks, bikers, people out to score to go home with someone for the night and truckers for the most part. I sat back and watched. A waitress came hurrying over to ask for our drink orders then scrambled back to the bar. I wondered if the bartender she was talking to was the one in on the real business. I knew the manager and the full-time bartender were in on it from Dax.

I didn't have long to wait to find out. After he got her order together, the bartender left one of the others behind the bar and came over to our table. Dax and the others shook his hand. He looked at me with interest in his eyes.

"Laurent, this is Undertaker. He's here checking out our club. He's looking for a new club," Dax told him. Then he looked at me. "Undertaker, this is Laurent. He's the bartender I was telling you about the other day. He and Tyson, our manager, keep things running here for us."

Laurent held out his hand and I took it. He tried to squeeze the hell out of mine, but I just applied pressure back. He was the one to let go first. I was satisfied to see him wiggling his fingers when I let go. "Good to meet you, Undertaker. You look like you've ridden with a club before. Mind if I ask which one?"

"Yes, I've ridden with a club before. Which one is

between me and the Renegades. Let's just say I know what MC life is about and I can help this club out in more ways than one."

I could tell my response didn't satisfy him, however, Dax broke in at that moment. "Yeah, Undertaker definitely knows the life. We're just here to relax for a bit. Keep the drinks coming. Is Tyson here tonight? I wanted to introduce him to Undertaker too."

Laurent gave me another piercing look then answered Dax's question, "Yeah, he's in the back. Give me a minute and I'll go get him. Let me know if there's anything else I can get you." The guys gave him chin lifts, so he left and went toward a hallway. When he came back a few minutes later, he was followed by another man. This one took me by surprise. He looked more like an accountant, than someone who managed a bar. Introductions were made. Tyson didn't ask any probing questions. When they were done with him, he seemed happy to hurry back to the office.

"Funny guy," I said.

"Tyson is quiet, but he does his job. We brought him on to help with the books about six months ago. Hook knew his old man. He's solid," Dax offered as an explanation.

"Hey, as long as you can trust him, who cares," was my only response back to him. After our drinks came to the table, I got back to watching the bar. It wasn't hard to figure out which of the women in here were most likely the prostitutes the club had working for them. Something in their faces seemed to give it away. I saw more than one leave with a man only to be replaced not much later by a new woman entering the bar.

The chatter from my group was light and mainly about bikes and making comments about the women around us. I was trying not to stare at my watch. We'd be hearing soon if the run went as planned.

An hour and a half later, I was ready to call it quits and head back to the clubhouse. I was just about to suggest we do that, when Roman waved a woman over to the table. As she approached, I knew she had to be one of their whores. She made sure to plaster a smile on her face, but it didn't reach her eyes.

Roman pulled her down on his lap and slid his hand up her thigh, under the short mini skirt she was wearing. "Poppy, how's it going tonight?" he asked her.

"Things are going alright. It could be busier, but for a weeknight, this isn't too bad," she said softly. I caught her looking at me with a questioning look on her face. Roman pushed his hand up under her skirt farther. I knew he had to be touching her pussy by now. He didn't seem to care who saw him. Poppy had a resigned look on her face.

"Poppy, this is Undertaker, a friend of ours from out of town. Why don't you take him to the hotel and show him a good time?" Dax said with a smirk on his face.

"Hello, Poppy," I said before I turned to Dax. "You know I have an old lady. I won't be going anywhere with anyone."

"Come on, I know you say that at the clubhouse. I

get it, you have to, with her around, but she's not here. No one's gonna tell her," he offered with a grin.

"I don't just say it because she's there. Thanks for the offer, but I'm gonna have to say no." As he looked unbelievingly at me, I waved over our waitress. "Can we have another round and, Poppy, can we get you something?"

She looked surprised that I'd offered. "Sure, I'll take a cranberry and vodka, please."

We sat there in silence as we waited for our drinks. Roman didn't stop his fondling of her and she suffered in silence. As soon as our drinks were served, Roman growled at her. "Drink up then I want your ass out back."

I knew he was planning to fuck her behind the bar. I wanted to say something to save her from having to go with one more man she obviously didn't want, but there was nothing I could say. As soon as she finished her drink, he dragged her out of the bar. Dax leaned over to me.

"I don't know how you do it. No way would I give up all the pussy out there for just one. You missed out. Poppy is tight as hell." He rubbed his crotch, and I hid my disgust.

"Until you meet the one who's perfect for you, you can't understand. I never understood how guys could settle for just one woman until I met Lucky. She understands me and lets me be who I am without trying to change me. This life isn't for everyone, but she's taken to it like she's lived in it all her life."

"Well, I guess you're a lucky man. She's beautiful and I bet she's something else in bed." I could tell he was hinting at wanting to hear how she was in bed, but I didn't say a word. I just nodded. Seeing that I wasn't going to discuss sex with my old lady, he pointed across the room. He pointed to various women.

"See those women? They all work for us," he said with satisfaction.

"How many do you have working for you between here and the motel you showed me? Is it a decent amount of business or just a small sideline profit?"

"We have fifteen who work for us."

"Do they only work here in town or are they in the surrounding towns as well? How do you find all of them?"

"They only work here at the moment. We want to expand. We find them all over the place. Some take a little persuasion, but in the end, they see things our way," he said with a grin on his face. I wanted to punch him in the mouth. He was confirming what I already suspected. Not all of these women were here of their own free will. I swallowed my anger and grinned back at him.

"Good. If you're serious about expanding, I can definitely help you with that as well. You want to be careful not to take women all from the same place. That can attract too much unwanted attention. If you bring them in from other places, it helps. My contacts have unlimited resources for that."

I saw his eyes as well as Hook's gleaming with

greed. Curly, Nox, Frost, and Jester looked like they wanted to be anywhere but here. As for Cage, Sig, and Grumble, they didn't look that interested. I had to wonder where they fell in the mix.

"Great. Let's talk about that after we get this done and the guns," Dax said. Before I could say anything else, Roman came sauntering back in with a smirk on his face. He was still zipping up his pants. Poppy wasn't far behind him. She looked like she was limping. I could tell she was hurting. God knows what he did to her. I fought the bile at the back of my throat. It was just like old times with the Locos. I thought I'd left that world behind.

Roman sat back down and yelled for another beer. I glanced at my watch. It had been over two hours. We should have heard something by now. Had something gone wrong? I tried not to let any worry show on my face. I took another drink of my beer.

"What the hell is taking so long?" Hook growled as he looked at me.

I shrugged. "These things take time. He could have run into a delay. Give it just a little longer then I'll call. I don't want to interrupt them at the wrong time. They need to be on alert, not talking to us on the damn phone."

He rolled his eyes but didn't say anything else. Ten minutes later, my phone rang. I saw it was the number I was waiting on. I answered it quickly. "Talk to me."

It was Gabe on the other end. "Undertaker, everything went as planned. We have our merchandise.

It's some good shit. Tell your friends, we'll be wanting more of that. How about we say in two weeks? That'll give them time to get the amount we want. We need four times that amount. Talk to you later." He hung up. He'd said exactly what I'd told him to say.

I looked up at the expectant looks of Dax and his guys. "It went off without a hitch. Let's go back to the clubhouse, where we can talk." I glanced around the bar. They didn't bother to argue. We got up and left the bar. The ride back to their clubhouse was quick. I couldn't help but wonder what had gone on with Sloan while I was gone.

As we backed into parking spots at the clubhouse, the door opened and out came the old ladies followed by the bunnies and the prospects. Sloan came straight over to me. I shut off my bike before I pulled her into my arms and I kissed her. I needed a taste of her to get the bitterness of this night out of mine. She kissed me back just as eagerly. We took our time before we parted and I got off my bike. The others were standing there staring at us.

I didn't say a word, I just shrugged and grinned. We walked inside. We took seats at one of the tables. Dax yelled at the prospect, Vic, "Bring us some fucking beers, Prospect. What're you waiting for?" Vic jumped to attention and grabbed an armload of beers. He almost tripped over his own feet, bringing them to the table. His gaze showed hero worship for Dax. As soon as he sat them down, Dax looked at the women.

"Bitches need to get lost. We have business to talk about."

"Where do you want us to go?" Jane asked him. He thought about it for a minute then he sighed.

"Never mind, we'll go into church. Don't bother us. We have shit to do." He stood up. I got up to follow them into church. I squeezed Sloan's hand before I left. It was time for me to sell this some more.

"Okay, we're here and away from prying ears. Tell us what your man said," Dax ordered.

"They got the stuff without a problem and liked the product. He said they want more. Four times as much and they want it in two weeks. Can you get that much from Lobo?"

I saw Dax exchange a worried look with Roman and Hook.

"Listen, if you can't, I need you to tell me now. You said it wouldn't be a problem, but if it is, I need to know. These aren't the kind of men you want to piss off. They're dead serious about business. They don't mess around. I put my reputation on the line for you guys. Now I need you to be able to deliver," I growled as I glared at them.

"Hold on, we didn't say we couldn't deliver. Lobo isn't going to be able to get all that together in just two weeks. However, we have other resources. Let's call Slither and see what he has in mind. I know he has other resources we can use."

His guys nodded. I waited with my heart pounding. Were they going to make the call with me in the room? I hoped they did. Earlier, I'd gotten a chance to pick up Dax's phone when he wasn't looking. He'd left it lying on the table. I'd hidden a tiny recording device in it. Sean and the guys would be able to trace any calls he made. I'd done that before we left for the drop. It was while he and his club had been in the food line in the kitchen.

I held my breath as he took out his phone and dialed. He pressed a button and laid it in the middle of the table. After a couple of rings, it was picked up. A gruff voice asked, "How did it go?"

"Hey, Slither, it went perfectly. I have you on speaker and we have Undertaker with us. We want to talk about the next steps," Dax told him.

I heard nothing for a couple of moments then Slither answered him, "You know I hate to be on speaker, Dax. However, in this case, I'll allow it. Welcome, Undertaker. Dax and the guys tell me you have a lot to offer us. I'm really hoping that's the case. If not, you and I will have a problem." I knew he was insinuating he'd have to kill me.

"Slither, I don't believe in blowing smoke up anyone's ass. Just like I don't believe in letting others blow it up mine. I'm here to do business with like-minded people. I'm looking for a new home. I was told that this club was where I could find that. Is that the case, or should I take my business elsewhere? Serpent assured me I would find that here. Have you talked to him? I'd like to talk to him."

I saw the uneasy looks go around the table. I wanted to laugh. Slither cleared his throat. "Glad to hear we're on the same page. As for Serpent, he's not available for you to talk to right now. Tell me about tonight."

"It went off without a problem. The exchange happened and my people liked the quality of the product. They liked it so much, they're asking for another shipment in two weeks. Only they want four times as much this time. I know the amount needed will only increase after that. Dax seemed to think Lobo can't come up with that much that quickly. Also, he said you'd have other resources who could."

"I've got the resources, that's not a problem. I just need to get things coordinated to get the stuff to you in time for the next shipment. What about our guns and women? Are you going to be able to help with that?"

"I can help with all those and more. You know who I used to ride with. There are more things out there you can tap into than you can probably imagine. As the enforcer, I was involved in a lot. I asked Dax if he wanted to set up a gun delivery in the next few days. I want to show you I can keep up my end of the deal."

"Tell you what. Why don't we meet in person? I'd rather not talk about business over the phone. I'll set something up and let Dax know when and where. In the meantime, kick back and enjoy the club."

I hated that he wanted to wait a few days, but I was happy to hear I'd be able to meet him in person. If he brought Ogre, that would be a prime opportunity to get the two of them. With them and the guys here, we should be able to get all the dirt we needed to go after the other four clubs they'd infiltrated. The end of this assignment might just be within sight.

"Sure, that sounds good. I look forward to

meeting you."

Slither didn't waste time talking to Dax. He told them he'd talk to him later and hung up. Dax gave me a relieved look. "Things are looking good, man. Let's go celebrate." I got up and followed them back to the common room. When we got there, I saw the old ladies huddled at one table and the bunnies at another. Vic and Mattie were sitting at the bar talking. When they saw us, they jumped to attention. Roman yelled at them to bring us more beers.

As we sat down, Sloan and the other ladies came over and sat down on our laps. I watched as the bunnies sat down on whichever guy's lap who grabbed them. I nuzzled Sloan's ear. I could feel she was tense. "Relax, it went fine. I'll tell you as soon as we get out of here," I whispered in her ear. She turned her head and kissed me.

I let myself get lost in kissing her. The others carried on conversations around us. I ignored them. All I wanted to do was go back to our motel and get lost in her. She was the one good thing in the middle of this whole thing. After a half hour of watching the others getting drunk and starting to get naked, I called it a night. I stood up.

"It's been a good one, but I need to get my old lady back to our room. See you tomorrow. Enjoy yourselves," I said as I winked at them. They all laughed and hollered at us not to do anything they wouldn't do. I held onto Sloan's hand as I led her out of the clubhouse. I needed to call the guys and tell them what I'd discovered then I needed to make love to my woman. I didn't waste any time driving us back.

Sloan: Chapter 20

I could tell Mark had a lot on his mind as we rode back to our motel. His body was tense, and he kept clutching at my hands that were around his waist. He didn't waste any time hustling me into our room. I watched silently as he checked the room for hidden bugs, like he did every time we came back. I didn't blame him for being paranoid about it. This could mean the difference between life and death for the both of us.

Once he was satisfied nothing had been implanted, he pulled me over to the bed and we sat down. He opened up his computer and brought up the secure program we used to communicate with our team. It wasn't long before we were seeing Sean, Gabe, and Griffin on the screen.

Sean was the first one to say anything. "How did it go? Are they all good to do another run in a couple of weeks?"

That was news to me. I sat there quietly listening. Mark nodded his head. "Yeah, they were happy with the news. I told them we needed four times as much, just like Gabe said. They can't get that much that quickly from their contact here, Lobo, which I knew was going to be the issue. However, they assured me they could get it and they called Slither while I was in their church with them."

I saw the guys perk up. "Oh really, and how did that go? Gabe asked.

"He wasn't thrilled that they had him on speaker, but he's confident he can get us the product we need. He's going to work on getting it together and moving over here, so we can send it out. Also, he wants to meet with me face-to-face to discuss the other aspects of the business. I offered to do a gun run in a few days if he wants to see what I can do. He's waiting on that until after we talk. Did you trace that call Dax made?"

"We did and we have the location. Can't tell you yet if it's just where he is at the moment, or if that's where the whole Soldiers of Corruption are now holed up. We'll be able to tell once we get some eyes out there. We don't want to spook them, so we'll wait until the day of your meeting with them. Once we know they're the one and same, we'll be able to move in if you give us the signal. Do you think they suspect anything?" Griffin asked this time.

"It's hard to tell for sure, but I don't think so. They seem to be taking me at face value. I have to be honest, I expected it would take me longer to know as much as I do about them and their operation. It's like they're so damn greedy, they can't think of anyone taking advantage of them. Slither sounded a little more cautious, but even he wanted to meet. As soon as I know when and where, I'll let you know. How's things on your end?"

"Well, we've not fed much back to the feds yet.

We're keeping Reaper in the loop. I know he's hoping he'll be the one to end Slither and Ogre. Can't say that I blame him after what they've put Cheyenne through. Don't let your guard down around them. You're not out of the woods yet," Sean warned us.

"I hear ya and we won't. They have fifteen women working for them as prostitutes. Dax more or less confirmed that they're not all here of their own will. They snatch them up. I assured him we had resources and more places we could get them women, if they needed them. Also, I suggested they think about expanding outside of this town. Right now, they seem to concentrate all their business here."

"Shit, we were hoping they at least weren't forced to do it. I knew that was a pipe dream. Okay, we'll get things in place to help them out once we take this shit show down for good. It's late and I know you have to be tired. We're gonna let you go. Call us or send a message if you need anything. Stay safe. Cassidy sends her love," Sean added.

We said goodbye to all three of them then signed off. When Mark put down the laptop, I crawled onto his lap and wrapped my arms around him. He buried his head in the crook between my neck and shoulder. "Jesus, babe, it's the same shit. I hate this. I never wanted to be in this type of situation again and here I am. Only this time I dragged you into it."

"Honey, you didn't drag me into anything. I volunteered, remember. I know how much you hate this. Hang in there. We're gonna take this whole damn dirty club down. They'll pay for what they've been doing."

He didn't say anything. All he did was tug up my shirt until he could see my bra-covered breasts. His eyes met mine. I could see the desire burning in them. I knew exactly what he wanted and how to make him forget for a little while. I leaned away from him and pulled my top off. Once it was off, I undid my bra. He laid back and watched. I shimmied around so I could kick off my boots and socks then get my jeans and panties off.

As soon as I was naked, he pounced. He pushed me onto my back and yanked my legs apart. His face dove between my legs and he attacked my pussy with his tongue, lips and fingers. In no time, he had me wet and writhing on the bed as he pushed me toward an orgasm.

As I climbed higher, he increased the thrusting speed of his fingers, making sure he teased over my special spot. His lips sucked on my clit, making me see stars. I grabbed his hair and tugged. He chuckled which only made me wetter. He lifted his head. "Does my baby need something?"

"Yeah, she needs you to get me there. I'm so damn close, Mark. I want to come all over your face."

He growled and lowered his head again. He increased his attack and within a minute or less, I was thrown over the edge into a beautiful orgasm. He worked to make it last as long as he could, before I became too sensitive. As soon as I told him I couldn't take any more, he got up off the bed.

I watched as he stripped for me. I couldn't help but lick my lips at the incredible body he revealed. I thought about it every time, but it never got old looking at all those muscles and his tats. His huge cock was hard and red with cum leaking from the slit. He got back on the bed and straddled my chest. Mark tapped my lips with the head of his cock. "Open up, I need that mouth," he growled.

I slowly opened and sneaked my tongue out to tease his slit. He moaned then pressed against my lips. I let him inside. I could taste the saltiness of his cum. I quickly swallowed him deeper. I knew what he liked. He loved to have me deepthroat him and play with his balls at the same time.

I sucked him deeper and used one hand to tease his balls and the other to grab his ass and hold him to me. He thrust in and out, groaning as he hit the back of my throat and I gagged. He didn't stop pushing and I didn't want him to. As he powered in and out of my mouth, I fought not to let the aching in my jaw stop me from getting him off.

His breathing picked up, and I knew he was getting there as his balls drew up tighter. Before I could get him to come, he pulled out of my mouth. His breathing was ragged. He moved off me and slapped my hip.

"I want you on your knees with that ass in the air. God, baby, tell me you're ready."

"Ready for what?"

"Ready for me to fuck you until you can't walk."

The look on his face and the tone of his voice made me wetter. I was always weak in the knees after Mark made love to me. It didn't matter if it was slow and easy or hard and fast. He always makes sure that I get the utmost satisfaction and multiple orgasms out of our encounters.

While I'm thinking that, he took me by surprise when his hand landed on my right ass cheek with a crack. Heat and slight pain coursed through me. He quickly did the same to the opposite cheek. As I whimpered, he got into the drawer beside his side of the bed. He brought out two things, a bottle of lube and a small butt plug. He'd shown me those a couple of days ago. Apparently, he had them hidden in his bag that he brought his clothes in for this trip. He'd informed me it was just in case I wanted to play.

After our discussion about anal sex, he'd been using his fingers to prepare me for more to come. This would be the first time he was going to use the butt plug. I admit, I was nervous. My one experience with anything bigger than a finger hadn't gone over well. However, I had faith that Mark would take it easy and wouldn't just shove it in there.

I guess he saw the worry in my eyes, because he sat down and caressed my cheek. "Baby, I promise, I'll go slow. If you don't like it or it hurts too much, tell me and I'll stop. This isn't going to be good for me if it's not good for you. Do you want to try it, or forget about it?"

I reached out and took his cock in my hand. He groaned as I stroked up and down. I smeared the cum across the head then licked my finger. "I want you to show me what this can be like, Mark. I trust you. I won't lie. I'm a little nervous, but I know you won't intentionally hurt me."

He gave me an intense kiss. When he pulled away, he said, "How did I ever get so lucky to find you? Push that pretty ass in the air and try to relax. When I press in, you press out."

I laid my head down on the pillows and thrust my ass up. He spread my ass cheeks, and I felt him probe my asshole with a lube covered finger. I was able to relax and let him insert the lube. He worked it around until I was gelled up to his satisfaction. When he removed his finger, I tried not to tense when he pressed the lube covered butt plug to my hole.

It was a lot bigger around even at the tip than one of his fingers. It burned as he pushed it in and past that first sphincter ring then the second one. There was a sensation of giving when he got it past the second one. He stopped and let me get used to the feeling before he started to advance it more. Mark murmured soothing words to me as he worked it into me. It took several minutes of back-and-forth action before he stopped.

"Are you alright, babe?"

"I'm fine, Mark. Are you almost all the way in?"

"I'm there. Now, it's all about your pleasure from here on out."

I glanced at him in surprise over my shoulder. He smiled at me and then pulled the plug back and then pushed it back inside. Though it was still burning a little, the pleasure it shot through my nerves was greater. I couldn't help the tiny moan that escaped my mouth.

I got lost in the sensations he was creating in me

as he worked that plug in and out. I was soon climbing the hill toward another orgasm. This one felt like it was building deeper in me than any of the others I'd had.

Suddenly, as he pushed it back into the hilt, I felt his cock probe the entrance to my pussy. I threw back my head as he sank into me. The tightness of having both my holes filled made me cry out. He groaned as if he was in pain.

"Jesus, that feels fucking spectacular, baby. You're so damn tight, I can barely move. Hold on and let me take you to heaven."

I curled my fists into the sheet as he pulled back and then slammed back into me. I not only felt it in my pussy but in my ass since he was doing the same with the plug at the same time. Electricity ran through me. I couldn't help but cry out. Not hearing me telling him to stop, he kept going. Soon I was having to hold on to the headboard of the bed, so he wasn't pushing me against it. He was hammering into me and I could do nothing but sob and let the wetness run down my thighs.

In a matter of minutes, I lost it and I came. I clenched down on him and he swore as I did. He never stopped thrusting as I came and came. When I finally was able to ease up and came back to my senses, he asked, "Do you like that feeling in your ass, Sloan? Does it feel good?"

"Oh my God, it feels so good, Mark."

"Good," he said and then he pulled out. I felt him take the plug out of my ass too. Before I could ask what he was doing, he pressed back into my ass, only this time it was with something softer, his cock. I couldn't help but buck and push back against him as he slid into my ass. After using the plug, he went in without too much pain. The feel of his velvet covered cock was so much better.

"You feel amazing, baby. God, I can't go slow. I've gotta come," he groaned then he sped up his thrusts even more. He was going deep and the sensations he was triggering with his movements had pleasure flowing through my whole body. As crazy as it sounded, he had me headed for another orgasm and I could tell it was going to be better than the last one.

A couple of minutes of sweaty, heart pounding thrusting saw me coming again. As I screamed, "God," and came in a blinding flash of light and clenched down on him, Mark came a few seconds behind me.

"Son of a bitch!" he yelled as he jerked.

I lost track of what was happening after that. I think I might have blacked out or something, because I found myself flat on the bed with my eyes closed. I couldn't feel Mark inside of me any longer. He was rubbing my back and telling me, "It's alright, baby." I noticed I had tears on my face.

I rolled my head to the side so I could look at him. "What happened?"

"You sort of collapsed on me. I thought you had fainted for a second, but you were just moaning and shaking. You scared me for a second."

"That was unbelievable. I never expected anything like that. It was so different from the last time I tried this."

"I hope that means you liked it."

"Oh, you can bet your ass I liked it. Though if you're going to make me faint every time we do that, make sure I'm always on the bed."

He laughed as he snuggled me into his chest. "Did you enjoy it?" I asked him.

"Babe, I enjoyed it so damn much I saw stars and thought my heart stopped for a second. I can guarantee you, if you enjoyed it, we'll be doing that again. I've got a question for you."

"Sure, what?"

"Can you walk?"

I moved my legs. They felt weak as hell. "I'm not sure if I can or not. They feel awfully weak."

He smirked then nodded. "Good, that means I kept my promise. I said you wouldn't be able to walk."

I rolled my eyes at him but didn't disagree. He was right. He had promised me that. After we laid there for a while, he got me up and into the bathroom, so we could take a bath. As soon as we were clean and dry, we went back to bed. As we laid back down, I knew it was time to discuss what the next part of the plan was.

"What are we doing tomorrow?"

"Hell if I know. It's a waiting game now as we wait to see Slither in a few days. Right now, he doesn't seem too keen on having me set up a gun run. He wants to meet and talk about what else I can do for his club as a whole."

"If that happens, will that be when the feds and the others take him down? Or will they wait until you have time to get them even more information on the club?"

"I'm hoping they'll make their move. I'm not going to let it become the clusterfuck it was when I was with the Locos. They kept telling me to wait and to gather more information. As much as I want to take them down for good, the real goal here is to get Reaper his chance at Slither and Ogre. If he takes them out, the rest of the club should fold pretty easily. This time my hands aren't tied like they were last time."

"What do you mean, they're not tied like last time?"

"Last time, Dark Patriots had been hired to help with the investigation. Even after I got my memory back, we were technically in their employ. This time, we agreed to feed them what information we find, but we're not working for them. We're helping out a friend, Reaper. This gives us a lot of leeway in how we chose to help. The feds can push and insist all they want, but I won't let them back us into a corner. We can get our hands dirty if we have to in order to get the information we need and to bring about the outcome we want."

"You mean you can torture them, if you have to."

"That's exactly what I mean. Reaper doesn't give a damn about anything other than making Cheyenne safe. I don't blame him. If that was you, I'd do the same thing. Before we left, Sean told me he spoke to Anderson. He's given us the green light to do whatever it takes to take the leaders down. He knows things like this have a way of getting out of hand. His niece, Zara, is part of the Archangel's Warriors MC. He'll turn a blind eye to our methods. As long as it's not used against someone innocent."

"That's good to know. I did have a little luck getting some information out of Carla and Jane while you were gone. They finally came out and admitted that the only reason they and their men are still part of the club is because of threats. They were told they'd lose their businesses and that it would be a shame if someone got hurt over a business deal gone bad."

"Did they say why they were telling you that?"

"They said they didn't want to see me get into something I couldn't get out of. They know we haven't been together that long. I think they wanted to make me reconsider if I should stay with you. I told them I would keep what they said in mind and I'd keep it to myself. Mark, I really hope there's a way to get them free of Dax and his guys. I don't think they had a choice when it came to this. They were scared and felt like there was no way out for them."

"Babe, I know. I feel the same. If there's any way at all to protect them, I will. However, I have to be sure they were led against their will into this, not a part of it. That might be the hard part."

"As long as you try, that's all I can ask."

We both got quiet after that. It took us a while to fall asleep. I know we were both thinking about what the next few days would bring. I was praying it would be the end of this whole assignment. I spent time praying to God to keep Mark and I safe. I didn't want us to go through this, just to end up losing him. If I did, I don't think I'd ever be able to recover.

Undertaker: Chapter 21

It took three days, but we were finally on our way to meet with Slither. I couldn't help but be excited and nervous at the same time. I was excited at the thought that this might be the end of this assignment, or damn near it. I was nervous that something might go wrong. If it did, I wasn't the only one who might lose their life. Sloan would be dead too.

When the call came in from Slither, setting up this meeting, I tried to have Sloan stay behind at the motel or the Renegades clubhouse. I knew she wasn't happy with it, but it would give me one less person to worry about. If something went wrong, I only had myself to worry about getting out of the mess. However, Dax shot that suggestion down. He told me that Slither wanted to meet me and my old lady, something about welcoming us to the family.

I would have felt a little better about it, if Jane and Carla were going too, but they were staying home. The Renegades and us were the ones invited plus the bunnies. I'd seen Jane and Carla exchange worried looks when they heard the news. I steeled myself for the worst while I prayed for the best.

Last night, back at the hotel, Sloan and I called the

guys and went through our final setup for today. They had a tracker that was hidden on my bike. It wasn't turned on, in case someone would sweep my bike for a bug. It was unlikely, but just in case. As soon as I felt it was safe, I could activate it. This would tell them where we were. On top of that, I had an emergency signal built into my watch. If I pressed the correct button, it would send out an alert and the cavalry would come rushing to the rescue. I was hoping the latter wouldn't be needed. Sloan had a similar alert button built into the necklace she wore. It looked like a metal silver cross with studs on it.

After we'd gone through the plan and discussed contingencies, we'd hung up and made love until we both couldn't do it again. If this was the last time I ever got to be with her, I wanted to remember it in my dying moment. All I could pray is she'd get away even if I didn't.

The weather was cold when we got on the road this morning. I wasn't told exactly where we were going, only that we wouldn't be leaving Ohio and it was about a two-and-a-half-hour ride. I made sure Sloan was bundled up. Luckily, there wasn't any snow or ice to worry about. That stuff is treacherous on a bike.

Dax, Roman, Hook, and Nox were in the lead. Sloan and I rode in the middle with Cage. Behind us were Grumble, Frost, Sig, Jester and Curly. The three bunnies rode up behind Frost, Sig, and Cage.

Around noon, we passed through a town called Pataskala, near Columbus Ohio. On the outskirts of town, we came up on what looked like an old mill of some kind. It was enclosed in fencing and had a gate across a crumbling driveway. I saw Dax signal and we turned into the driveway. A prospect came to the gate and let us inside. As I passed him, I noticed he had a cut on which said *Soldiers of Corruption*. Bingo, we were in the right place.

We rode up to the mill and parked our bikes alongside several other bikes. I took my time getting off my bike and helping Sloan out of her helmet. Dax was standing there, waiting impatiently for us to finish. When I thought I'd pushed it far enough, I took her hand and walked up to him.

"Let's go," he said as he turned to the door. Roman opened it and waved the rest of us through it. Inside, I found we were in what was a crudely furnished bar area. The air was thick with smoke and the odor of oil. I wasn't sure what kind of mill this had been. The inside was hazy and the floor looked dirty. Ratty chairs and tables sat around the room. Along one wall there was a pool table. Along another was what looked like their actual bar. I could see stools under it and bottles of alcohol lined up against the wall.

As we entered, the room got quiet and everyone turned to look at us. I took quick notice that other than a bunch of men, the only women in there were dressed like bunnies. If they were old ladies, they sure as hell didn't dress like any I'd seen. I held onto Sloan even tighter. I made sure my face showed only mild interest, no fear.

Dax wound his way over to a table and up to a man who was sitting there, drinking a beer and smoking a cigarette. The man was in his fifties if I had to guess. His hair was long and greasy. His beard was wild and unkept. When he looked up at us, I noticed his eyes were small, beady and cold. A quick glance at his chest showed this was Slither. He looked me up and down before he looked at Sloan. I saw heat and interest enter his eyes when he saw her. I wanted to gouge out his eyes for even looking at her.

"Hey, Pres, this is Undertaker and his old lady, Slo," Dax told him eagerly.

Slither took his time before he answered him. Finally, he gave me a chin lift. "Undertaker. Welcome. I'm glad you got here alright."

"Thanks. It's good to be here. I've never been to this part of Ohio."

"Yeah, it's not home, but it'll do. This is Ogre, he's my VP." He gestured to another older man who had come up beside us. So, this was Cheyenne's dad. He didn't look much better than Slither. His hair wasn't greasy, but that was all there was to recommend him. He stood around six foot maybe a tad shorter. He was heavy set and his hair was mostly gray. Slither's was a dirty blond with streaks of silver in it.

Ogre held out his hand to me. I shook it. He tried to crush my hand, but I didn't take that shit. I applied pressure back, and he was the one to flinch and let go first. Next, Slither held out his hand. In his case, he didn't try to get into a pissing contest with me. I fought not to wipe my hand on my jeans after touching them.

"And you said this beauty is Undertaker's old lady. Hello, darlin', I'm Slither. I'm the charter president," Slither said with a smile. His yellow crooked teeth showed. Sloan didn't bat an eyelash. She smiled and held out her hand.

"Hello, nice to meet you. You said you're the charter president?" He nodded. She frowned. "Maybe I missed something. Forgive me, I'm new to this whole MC thing. I thought you all would be in the same club, but your cut reads Soldiers of Corruption on it and Dax's reads Legion of Renegades."

Slither, Ogre, and Dax exchanged looks. Slither smiled. "Yeah, they do. We've recently expanded and decided to keep the old club names. It helps to not confuse people. They're used to seeing a certain club in their area, so we like to stay the same. Why don't you two have a seat and we'll get you a drink? I want to get to know you."

I pulled out a chair for Sloan and she took a seat. I sat down next to her. Slither waved and two beers appeared in front of us. The guy carrying them had *Prospect* on his cut. We'd barely taken a drink when Slither started the interrogation.

"Undertaker, tell me about yourself. You seem to be one lucky man. You escaped the takedown of Tres Locos and the law isn't after you. How in the hell is that possible?"

"Well, Slither, it's all because of this beauty right here. Like I told Dax, I lucked out the night the feds raided the compound. I was out of town at a bar. I met Slo and things got a little heated with another guy who made a move on her. We got into it and the next thing I knew, I was sitting in jail. I admit, I wasn't happy about that. The next morning, to my surprise, I was bailed out by Slo. Apparently, I'd made an impression." I sent her a sexy smile. She smiled back at me.

"Anyway, after I made bail, we headed to a hotel. I spent a while there with her. I was about to head back home, when she happened to turn on the television and we saw the news about the Locos. I'll admit, I was stunned and pissed off. Who in the hell had slipped up and told the feds about what we were doing? That was the first thing to come to mind. Then I got to wondering if we had a mole and didn't know it. I knew that I couldn't go back there. That kind of decided things for me and I stayed with Slo."

"Sounds like you were lucky. Too lucky if you ask me," Ogre chimed in with a fierce glare on his face.

"I know it sounds crazy, doesn't it? That's why I call her my lucky charm. I knew right then I wasn't going to let her out of my sight. If I hadn't been in that jail, I'd have been scooped up with the rest of them. I tried to get into contact with our pres, but there was no way to do that without getting caught myself. I heard they're all going down for life. Unfortunately, Tres Locos is no more and I have to figure out where to spend the rest of my life. That led me to go looking for like-minded clubs."

"Dax said you spoke to Serpent, my son. That's odd, because he didn't mention anything to me," Slither said.

"Man, I have no idea why, unless he was too drunk to remember. But I bet he's remembered me now. He was quite taken with a woman I was with. I thought we were going to have a fight over who had her first." I figured Serpent had to be the kind of guy to go after any woman he wanted, even if she was already taken.

Slither chuckled. "Yeah, I can see him being like that. He loves pussy. I'll admit, I'm intrigued with the opportunities Dax says you can bring to the club. That run the other night was just the start. How about we relax for a bit and we can talk business later? After all, we don't want to bore Slo with all those details." He gave her a leer.

"I'll gladly party with you. However, until I know you better, she stays with me. No offense, but I need to know I can trust you in more ways than one. I have a lot I can bring to the table. I need to be sure this club is the one to fit my needs as well."

This caught him off guard. Yeah, asshole, you're being auditioned just like you're doing to me. After that exchange, we spent the next couple of hours talking about random things like bikes and places we've been. Luckily, I knew Rex Reed's background inside and out. No matter what they asked, they couldn't trip me up. They asked Sloan a few questions, but she was unflappable and was able to answer them without a problem.

Things were starting to heat up even though it was only early afternoon. The women we saw, who I assumed earlier were bunnies, was a correct assumption. Some of the guys were hooking up with them right out in front of us. No one batted an eye, or treated them with an ounce of respect. I fought not to take Sloan away from it, but she acted like she wasn't affected by it, though I knew she was. It reminded me too much of what the Locos had been like. I didn't necessarily care that they were doing stuff in front of me. It was how badly they treated the women.

After they got their rocks off, they started to get serious. Slither and Ogre came back over to us. They had gone off in the corner and chatted for a while. I knew they were talking about us. I hoped that they believed what I'd told them. While I wished I could take them down today, I doubted that was going to happen. I needed to get something concrete on them before I called in the troops.

"Are you ready to talk? You can leave your old lady here. No one will bother her," Slither told me.

I wasn't crazy about the idea. Nothing about this bunch made me feel like it was safe to leave her with them. More than one guy had been giving her looks. Sloan smiled at me. "Don't worry about me, babe, I'll be fine. Why don't you go talk about your boring business with Slither and his guys? I'll hang out here."

"Is it only going to be a few of us, or is it the whole club who'll be talking? I would like to get started with things. My guys are anxious to see what all you can bring," I asked Slither.

"We'll have church with the guys. Come on," Slither yelled. He stood up.

I got up and leaned down to give Sloan a kiss. When I did, I whispered, "Be alert."

"I will, you too," she whispered back to me.

I followed Dax's group along with ten others into a room that was down the hall from the common room. The only ones left with Sloan were the bunnies and the six prospects. I took the seat that Ogre indicated to me.

The room settled down as Slither called everyone to order.

"All of you have met Undertaker. As you know, he was a Tres Locos, and he's looking for a new home. He approached us because he heard we're his kind of club."

Several of them exchanged smirks and a couple laughed. I gave them a smile and nod. Slither continued, "What most of you don't know is he set up a buy the other night for some of Lobo's product. It went well and his buyers want even more in less than two weeks. Plus, he has those who want to get their hands on guns and can help us expand our whores. This could mean a lot of money for us. Undertaker, what can we do to make this all happen?"

"Well, first, I want to thank Dax and his guys for welcoming me and giving me a chance to do this. Yes, I was a Tres Locos, and if they hadn't had the terrible misfortune to go down, I'd still be one. I was with them for five years and had worked my way up to enforcer. With them gone, I know there's a need out there with our old buyers. I want to be able to fulfill that. We all want to make money and this is the best way I know how to do it. Fuck the working at boring jobs trying to make a buck. You'll go old and gray trying to earn a living that way. I can help you all earn in a year what would take years the other way."

"So you say, but how the hell do we know that you're not just jerking us around? Or worse, that you're not trying to set us up? I think it's awfully suspicious that your whole club went down and you seem to have avoided going down with them," a guy named Shaft said with a big frown on his face.

"I don't blame you. I'd be suspicious too. However, I think I've demonstrated that I am on the up-and-up. Ask Dax. I came to you because one of your own, Serpent, told me about your club. I'm sure if you've talk to him, he'd vouch for me. I'm only sorry that I wasn't able to bring this to you sooner. I had to lie low for a little while after the whole bust."

I saw a number of them exchange looks when I mentioned Serpent. It was time to push to speak to him. I looked at Slither. "I'd like to speak to Serpent. You're not the only one who has to worry about this situation. I only have his word about you guys. I want to find a home and I'm hoping it's with you guys. When can I talk to him?"

"That's the problem, we can't ask Serpent about you, Undertaker," Slither answered.

"Why the hell not?"

"He's disappeared. You said you met him in Tennessee, right? Well, he was working on something for us down around there and in Virginia. He and the other three with him have gone missing. You assure us that he mentioned us, but we can't know if that's true or not. In fact, how do we know you didn't have something to do with their disappearances?"

I let a look of astonishment come over my face. I needed to convince them I didn't have anything to do with that, or Sloan and I were dead. "What the hell do you mean, they disappeared? How can that be? Someone has to know something about them. Four guys don't just up and go poof. I have contacts. I can have them look into it, if you want. Does it have anything to do with that club they were going to check out?"

Slither and Ogre leaned into the table. Both gave me a searching look. "What do you know about the club they were going to meet?" Ogre growled.

I shrugged. "Not a lot, just that they were going to meet a club somewhere down there. It was one that they thought they could get to join with your club. Serpent seemed eager for it to happen. He mentioned something about getting back something that belonged to him. He said after he was done there, he would talk to you about me and the Locos. Shit, I'm sorry. That blows. Listen, I can see that this isn't the right time for us to discuss business. You need to find out what happened to him and the others. Also, you need to know you can trust that I'm not setting you up. I get it. Why don't we set up another deal and I can show you I'm for real?"

All of them started to murmur and discuss what I said. I was the most interested in what Slither and Ogre had to say. They were the leaders of this band of degenerates. After several minutes of this, Slither yelled for them to get quiet.

"Shut the hell up. Okay, Undertaker, let's make a deal. You set up a gun deal for us with your guys. However, this time, you go along. And as insurance that you're on the up-and-up, we'll keep your old lady here with us. Anything happens to my men or those guns, and we'll make sure you both pay." Slither gave me an evil smile.

My heart almost stopped. My worst nightmare was coming true. Sloan was going to be left at the mercy of these animals. What could I do? There's no way I could say no and there's no way I could get her away from them. I was backed into a corner with no way out. I took a deep breath and took the plunge.

"I'll prove you have nothing to worry about. Give me a couple of days to set it up. However, when I get back and I will be back, if one hair on her head has been harmed, I'll fucking kill every one of you. Don't forget, if you fuck with me, you fuck with all my associates. I have way more than you could ever have. They won't hesitate to take this whole fucking club out," I warned them with my most deadly stare. More than one squirmed in his chair.

"You keep your end of the deal and I promise not a hair will be touched on Slo. Okay, why don't we let you get to work on setting up the deal? If this goes off without a hitch, we'll talk about our associates. And while you're setting it up, you and Slo will be our guests."

I silently cursed but acted like his threat didn't worry me. I nodded and stood up. "If that's all, mind showing me and Slo to our room? I'll get started on my calls."

Slither shook his head. "No, I want you to call them and set up the details with us here. Just in case, you know."

I sat back down and took out my phone. I dialed the number for the guys. I wondered which one of them would answer. A couple of rings later and Griffin gruffly answered, "I see you've finally gotten around to me. What can I get you, Undertaker? I heard you've brought some new business our way. I expect you're calling to send us some more."

"Hey, Dirk. Yeah, I've got some business for you. I'm here with our new friends. How soon can you get ready for us to have a shipment ready for you? We'd like it as soon as possible. They're eager to see what we can do."

I used the code word friends. That would tell Griffin that I wasn't alone, and that I was under suspicion. He didn't miss a beat.

"Hell, yeah, I can stand some new stuff. You tell me when and where and I'll get things set up. I have a buyer right now who'll take everything we can get. He's across the border doing some shit, I heard. What kind of stuff are we talking about?"

I gestured to Slither. He answered Griff, "This is Slither. I'm the president of the club Undertaker wants to join. He assures us that you guys can be trusted and can take whatever we have. We have an assortment of small caliber handguns as well as rifles and even a few bigger items. We can get you a couple of dozen of each to start and then we'll see. Think of it as a trial run."

"Well, Slither, I usually don't mess around with anything that small, but since Undertaker is vouching for you and I can understand needing to verify he's not selling you a bunch of bullshit, I'll do it. Where do you want to do this? I can have my guys anywhere in three days. Two if you're in the Midwest."

"Good. Why don't we set this up for two days from now? It'll be in Cambridge, Ohio. I'll have Undertaker send you the address, right before the meet."

"Done. If you need anything before then, just let me know. I'm looking forward to a lucrative business. We miss the one we had with our old friends. Undertaker, I'll see you Monday night." Griff didn't bother to say goodbye. I knew as soon as he hung up, he'd be hot on trying to check to see where I was. I haven't activated the tracker on my bike. Something told me, they would be looking it over to see if I had one.

As soon as the call was over, Slither and Ogre got to their feet. "Let's go back to the common room. If you don't mind, I'll take your phone." Slither held out his hand. I reluctantly handed it to him. He wasn't taking any chances that I'd contact anyone. When we got outside of church, I saw him say something to one of the guys and he hurried off.

I found Sloan sitting where I'd left her. She was surrounded by a bunch of the bunnies. A couple of the prospects were watching them with interest. When I got close to her, I could hear what she was saying. "I'm not here to take anyone away from you. I'm not a bunny. I'm Undertaker's old lady. He's the only man I'm interested in. Now, if you don't mind, get the hell out of my face before I put you out of it."

I swooped in before things could get out of hand. I shoved my way between a couple of the women. "Hey, babe, are you ready to go lie down or do you wanna hang out here for a while longer? We're gonna be staying with the guys for a few days. We're all going to be setting up this new friendship."

I had to give it to her, she didn't show an ounce of concern. "Whatever you wanna do, honey. That's great news about you guys. I know how much you're looking for a new family."

"Don't go yet. We want you to stay and have another drink with us. Something to celebrate this new, hopefully profitable, venture," Slither said. He waved to one of the prospects who came hurrying over with more beers. I couldn't say no. I sat down and made sure to have Sloan sit on my lap. An uneasy half hour crawled by. We didn't speak about anything significant.

After I thought we'd stayed long enough, I asked him again to show us to our room. This time, he had one of the prospects come to get us. Before we went with him, I told them, "We need to get our stuff off my bike. Good thing we brought stuff in case we stayed." Sloan and I went outside. The prospect went with us. I got our stuff out of my bags. As I did, I saw that things had been moved around a little. They'd searched my bike, just like I'd thought they would. Back inside, we told everyone goodnight and let the prospect show us to a room down the hall.

As soon as he closed the door, I kissed Sloan. I didn't trust them not to have the room bugged. I didn't want to chance her saying the wrong thing. When I got done, I said, "Babe, why don't you get undressed and we'll take a shower? It's been a long day."

"Sure, honey, let me get the water started." She walked off to the bathroom. While she was in there, I hurried to search the room. I checked the obvious places. I wish like hell I had my equipment with me, but I'd left it back at the hotel. It was hidden. Not finding anything, I didn't linger. I joined her in the bathroom. She was already naked. Even with the danger we were in, I couldn't help but get turned on seeing her. I quickly stripped off my clothes and grabbed her. I dragged her into the shower.

"Fuck, babe, you look so damn sexy."

"Thank you, honey. You don't look bad yourself," she said with a smile, then she pulled my head down so she could kiss me.

I hurried to whisper, "They're holding us here. May have a bug or camera in here."

She didn't miss a beat. She started to moan and grind herself against me. Despite the situation, I couldn't resist. I sucked her nipple into my mouth and kneaded the other breast. If the bastards were watching us or listening, I'd give them something to see and hear. I hoisted Sloan in the air. She wrapped her legs around my waist. I pushed her into the tile wall for leverage and sank into her. She was tight and wet like always. I didn't bother to take things slow. I needed to feel that we were both alive. I pounded away. I made sure she came twice before I let go and came. She clung to me as we came down from our high. As we did, I prayed that we'd get out of this in one piece. I couldn't lose her. When the water began to run cold, we roused ourselves and got out. A quick dry and then we went to bed. I'd find a way to fill her in on the details without taking a chance on prying eyes or ears tomorrow. Right now, I need to rest.

Sloan: Chapter 22

It had been two days since we'd come to meet the Soldiers of Corruption. It had been a very uncomfortable two days. After the meeting the other night, we'd been under a microscope. Mark and I had searched our room and found they had a microphone in it. There was no sign of a hidden camera. We made sure that our conversations weren't anything that could be taken the wrong way.

I'd noticed when we got our stuff that first night, my phone was missing from the bags. I'd left it out there at Mark's suggestion. I found out the next day, they had taken his too. We were in this deep. They didn't trust us and if this gun deal didn't go as planned, we'd both be dead. We got enough time walking around the compound for him to tell me that much. Our prospect guard had trailed behind us far enough that he could tell me.

As for Slither, Dax, and the rest of the men, they had been partying for the last couple of days. All they seemed to like to do was drink and fuck. I was tired of seeing them bending a bunny over the nearest pool table, chair, or couch, and pounding away at her. One night, I saw them pull a train on one of the women. When they were done, she couldn't even walk. It turned my stomach. They'd been like animals as they took her. Undertaker was asked to join them over and over, but he patiently explained that he had an old lady.

I was nervously waiting for this evening. Tonight was the night the guns would be exchanged. They'd been in church a couple of times these past two days. During those sessions, they let Mark use his phone to contact Sean and the guys about the weapons. They still hadn't told them exactly where in Cambridge they were going to make the drop.

I couldn't blame them for being cautious. They had no way of knowing whether Mark was setting them up or not. I kept praying that this would go well, and they'd believe he was on the up-and-up after this.

I knew Mark was worried about leaving me alone while he went on the run. I would be at the mill with bunnies and prospects, as well as possibly some of Slither's men. I had confidence in my ability to protect myself, but not against several attackers at a time. Luckily, they hadn't searched me for some reason. I had my guns on me and my knife. They wouldn't touch me without the fight of their lives on their hands.

I tried to not let him know that I was worried about what they might do to me when he was gone. I knew he was worrying enough about it on his own, as well as cursing the fact he let me talk him into letting me come along on this assignment. It was obvious in the way he watched me and made love to me every night. There was desperation in his touch. I knew he could feel the same in mine.

It was late afternoon when Slither and the others

called for one last meeting before they left. I sat out in the common area. They were behind closed doors for more than an hour. When they came out, they sat down to have a drink. That was what they seemed to do all the time. I didn't notice any of them leaving to do a regular job. Mark took me aside.

"We're going to be leaving in a few hours. You'll stay here with some of the others. I'll be back as soon as I can. Once I am, we can celebrate." He couldn't say much else since we had an audience.

"Honey, I know you have work to do. I'll be fine. You go do what you need to do. I'll hang here and get to know the others. I'll be ready to celebrate when you get back," I told him before I kissed him.

"Hey, enough of that. Come have a drink, Undertaker," Slither yelled. We both took a seat. It was seven o'clock when they got up to leave. I watched as Slither spoke to a couple of the prospects. I figured they were getting their orders to keep an eye on me.

Mark came over and kissed me. "Be careful, baby. I love you," he whispered.

"I will. You be careful too. I love you."

I went outside to watch them get on their bikes and for a couple to get into the cab of a truck. They pulled out, and I went back inside. As soon as I did, the bunnies, who were there, descended. Erica was one of them. She sneered at me. "What're you gonna do now that your man isn't here to protect you?"

I laughed at her. "I don't need my man to protect me from the likes of you, Erica. Didn't you learn your lesson before? Why don't you go somewhere and bug someone else? I'm not interested."

She huffed and said a few derogatory things to me, but she didn't do anything. It was hard not to pace as I waited to find out what was happening. I hated to be left out of the loop. As time dragged by, I watched the others. The prospects were hitting on me, but I just ignored them. So far, that has been all I had to do. The other bunnies, who hadn't come with us, watched me with puzzled looks on their faces. They didn't know what to think of me.

Cambridge was about an hour away from Pataskala. I was figuring an hour there, maybe an hour to do the deed, and then an hour back. That meant they should be coming through the door around ten o'clock or a little after.

When ten o'clock came and went, I got more nervous. None of the prospects seemed to be worried, but maybe they knew more than I did about what was planned. Had they discovered we were undercover? Was Mark already dead and they would be killing me next? If so, was there any way I could make it out of here alive?

I couldn't stand it. I got up and headed down the hall. One of the prospects stopped me. "Where are you going?"

"I'm going to my room. I'm tired and I want to rest. Tell Undertaker when he gets back, I went to bed."

"You should stay out here."

"I don't think so. I was told I had to stay here. I wasn't told I couldn't go to my room," I told him as I walked off. He didn't try to stop me. Back in our room, I lay down and tried to rest. I knew I might need my strength soon. As I waited, I prayed harder than I'd ever prayed before.

Undertaker:

The ride out to the drop off was nerve-racking. It was right before we left that I found out we were going somewhere outside of Cambridge Ohio. I was riding in the middle of the pack. I had no idea how in the hell they thought almost two dozen bikes wouldn't be noticed, but what the hell did I know about this area? Maybe people were used to seeing a bunch of them out riding.

I tried to keep my mind on what I was doing and not worry about what was happening back at their clubhouse. It had almost killed me to leave Sloan there alone with those people. I tried not to think, what if this was the last time I saw her?

I followed them through Cambridge and outside of town several miles. We came up on what had to have been an old farm. There wasn't anyone around or a house, just an old run-down barn. We pulled in behind it. Ten minutes before, we'd stopped and they let me call Griff and tell him where to meet us. They didn't want to take any chances that they would be able to set up a takedown, if I was undercover.

I got off my bike and leaned against it like I didn't have a worry in the world. I stared at Slither and Ogre. What I wouldn't do to be able to kill the two of them right now, but that would have to wait. My phone rang. I answered it as they eagerly gathered around me as I put it on speaker phone.

"We're about twenty minutes out. Tell your guys that we want to be loaded and off within fifteen minutes. I don't know this area and I don't want to attract too much attention," Griffin barked. As usual, he hung up without waiting for me to respond.

"You heard him. Be ready. These guys don't like to be kept waiting," I told them. Dax came over to stand beside me.

"Listen, Undertaker, I know you're not digging this, but it's for all our sakes."

"Dax, you're right, I don't like it, but I understand. Let's get this done. I hope once I show you that I'm on the up-and-up, you'll relax. I'm not here to fuck you over. I want a family. I hope it can be you and your clubs, but if not, I'll try my luck elsewhere."

Slither came over to us. "If this goes well, you don't need to worry about finding another family. We'll be that family. Trust has to be earned."

"You're right, on both sides."

He gave me a surprised look but didn't say anything else. The spot between my shoulder blades itched. I hated to have any of them at my back, but there was no way I could keep all of them in front of me. Almost twenty minutes on the dot, I heard the sound of a couple of vehicles. I watched as an SUV and a small panel truck pulled into the farm. I went over to the SUV and greeted Griffin as he got out of the SUV. I was happy to see Sean and Gabe were with him, acting as his bodyguards.

As his men got to work with the Soldiers unloading boxes, I introduced him to Slither and Ogre. They shook hands. Griff looked them up and down. "Let me see the guns." I led him over to our truck. He expertly checked them out. Griff asked a few questions and then nodded to his men. They got started, moving them to their truck and hiding them in a hidden section under the floor.

"These look good. If I'm not mistaken, this looks like it's all military stuff. As long as our buyer is satisfied with them, I think you can expect a lot more business to come your way. We have a lot of people who like what we can get them. Is that going to be a problem?"

"Not a problem. We have a contact who can get us military-grade stuff any time we need it. Just give us a heads-up, so he has time to get what we need. This stuff was easy. He had it in storage, but other things can take a while depending on what you want," Ogre told him.

"Excellent. I think this is the beginning of a beautiful relationship. Undertaker, can't thank you enough. I was wondering what we were going to do to replace the merchandise you and the Locos were supplying us with. I'm happy to see you figured out a new supplier. Now, all we need to do is make sure the fucking feds don't mess with any of us again. The bastards have been trying to take down my ass for years. Payment is in the account we agreed on." He chuckled darkly.

"I hear ya. I'll be in contact soon," I told him as

I shook his hand. He nodded to Slither and the others then got back in his SUV. A few minutes later, the transfer was complete, and they left. I held in a sigh of relief.

Dax came over and clapped me on the shoulder. "That's what we're talking about." I watched as Slither and his treasurer looked at something on his phone. I knew they were making sure the money was deposited. I saw them both give a nod. After that, we got back on our bikes and headed back to Pataskala. In all, it had been an anticlimactic experience. All that worry for nothing. I only hoped this would put me in a good place with them. I needed them to trust me, so I could get the details on all their businesses and their contacts. I was ready to take them down and get on with my life with Sloan.

I could barely wait to shut off my bike and put down the kickstand before I was bounding inside to see Sloan. When I got into the common room, I didn't see her anywhere. Before I could demand to know where she was, one of the prospects hurried over to me. "Your woman went to your room. She said she was tired."

"Thanks." I turned to Slither, Ogre and Dax. I could tell by the expressions on their faces, they expected me to stay out there with them and have a drink. I stamped down on my impatience. "Let me just tell Slo I'm back. Then, why don't we have a drink to celebrate? You made a nice little profit tonight."

"Go ahead, let her know. Once you're back, we'll relax and then tomorrow, we'll talk more business," Slither said with a smile. I forced myself to grin back and went down the hall to our temporary room. The door was locked. I knocked on it.

"Babe, it's me. Open up."

It took only a few seconds for the door to fly open and Sloan was in my arms. I backed her into the room and shut the door behind us. I kissed her. She kissed me back with a desperation in her touch. I took my time kissing her. When she had to finally take a breath, I spoke, "Hey, babe, that's the kind of greeting I like. Did you miss me? How did things go with the prospects and the bunnies?"

She was busy looking me over as if to see if I was hurt. "Things went fine. You know, a little smack talk from Erica, but she hasn't forgiven me for warning her off you. I was tired, so I thought I would wait for you here. I assume everything went well?"

"It went great. I'm gonna have a drink with the guys. Do you wanna join us, or stay here?" I shook my head to let her know I wanted her to stay in the room.

"If it's alright, I think I'll stay here. I'm gonna take a shower and relax. See you in a bit. Go have fun with the guys." I couldn't help but hug her tight and give her one more kiss before I left. I was happy to hear her lock the door behind me.

Back out in the common room, I saw the party was getting started. Guys were drinking, and the bunnies were already getting naked. I took a seat beside Slither. A prospect brought me a beer. I held it up and gestured to the guys around the table. "Here's to a successful night. Cheers."

"Cheers," rang out. I took a healthy swig.

Slither swallowed his drink and spoke, "It was a good night. That's two great deals. What I'd like to do next is see what we can do about the whores. I want to expand that business and Dax says you have ways to get us into more areas, not just the towns we're in right now."

"I do. No offense, but you're missing out. It's one thing to have them in a bar and a run-down motel. That attracts only a certain type of clientele. What I have in mind will get you in the door with the more high-end clients. In order to do that, we need to get the right kind of women and the right kind of place for them to enjoy the women. Your higher-end customers don't want just an hour and then done. They sometimes will want a whole night. They ask for an escort that can be seen on their arm when they go out with friends and business associates."

"You're talking about call girls," Ogre exclaimed.

"I am. That's where the real money is. Now, no offense, I haven't seen all the women you have, but from the ones I've seen, you need to attract some high-quality bitches. I can help you with that. I have contacts that can get us the kind of women I'm talking about. Ones who've been trained to do this kind of work and won't cause trouble, if you know what I mean."

I saw the excitement enter their eyes. Ogre rubbed his hands together. "That sounds perfect, don't you think, Slither?"

"It does. Let's wait until we get together in the morning and we'll talk to all the guys. Right now, they're too busy to listen." He chuckled as he nodded toward the guys getting drunk and fucking the bunnies. "Let's say eleven. Undertaker, thanks for tonight. I expect you have some celebrating of your own to do."

I grinned at him and winked. "I sure as hell do. No offense, but my woman is way better looking than you fuckers. I'll be off to bed." I stood up to their hoots and hollers to fuck her right. I waved as I walked off. I kept the grin on my face until I got her to open our door. As soon as I was in, it dropped. Aware that we still had ears on us, I didn't say anything other than, "Take off your clothes."

Sloan raised her eyebrows, but she didn't argue. She slipped off her nightclothes. I kicked off my boots and hurried to strip off the rest of my clothes. I needed to be lost inside of her. Talking about that shit made me want to forget the scummy bastard I had to play. I fisted my hard cock and stroked up and down.

Her nipples were hard, and she was watching me. "Lie on the bed and spread those legs." She scrambled to do what I asked. As soon as she was on the bed, I crawled onto it and laid down between her thighs. I could see she was getting wet. I swiped my tongue from her entrance to her clit and then back, so I could rim her asshole. Her unique taste exploded on my tongue. I nipped her lips with my teeth. She moaned.

I wanted her to be crazy with lust. I knew she loved it when I talked dirty. It turned her on even more. I nuzzled my nose into her wet slit and sucked on her clit. Her ass came up off the bed. "That's it. Give me all that cream, baby. Fuck, you're wet and taste so damn good. I wanna see how many times I can get you off before I get off. Why don't you play with those pretty nipples for me?"

She latched onto her breasts with both hands. I watched from my spot between her thighs, as she worked them with her fingers. She tweaked them hard and pulled on them. I knew she was enjoying it, by the amount of juices that were flooding my mouth. "Do it harder," I told her as I lapped at her pussy. I pushed my fingers into her and teased her G-spot. She wailed as she tightened down on me and came. I prolonged her release as long as I could with my fingers and mouth. Eventually, she shook her head, and I knew that meant she was too sensitive.

I reluctantly left my feast. I loved to eat her pussy and if she'd let me, I could do it for hours. Seeing that she was too sensitive at the moment, I moved up to her breasts and went to town on them. She was into breast play and could get off by me just playing with them. I sucked, bit, and squeezed them until she was panting. Her hand came down, and she wrapped it around my cock. I couldn't help the groan that came out of me.

Her eyes were blazing as she whispered, "Baby, I want you to fuck my breasts."

I shuddered. She hadn't ever asked me to do that. Her breasts were big enough that I could make a snug tunnel for my cock. I looked around. I had no idea what we'd use for lube. She took care of that for me. She dipped her hand between her legs and then smeared her juices between her breasts. I watched, entranced as she did it and then went back for more. The second time, she applied it to the length of my cock.

When both of them were slick, she reached up

and pressed them together. I scooted up and slid between them. I groaned at the sensation. I slid in and out between her plump breasts. I couldn't help but tweak her nipples as I did. She moaned and pressed her breasts tighter around me.

"Fuck, baby, that's hot. Why don't you open that pretty mouth and suck my cock?"

Her tongue snuck out, and she swiped it across the head of my cock, as I slid up and out the top of her breasts. On the next thrust, she sucked the head into her mouth and applied the perfect amount of suction. In no time, I was thrusting harder and faster. I could feel my balls tightening and her breath had become a pant.

Before I could explode, she did. She cried out as she writhed on the bed. The vibration of her cry had me almost coming, but I gripped my balls tightly and held it back. As much as I wanted to come all over her chest and rub my cum into her breasts, I wanted to come inside of her pussy more. I needed to feel that tightness around me.

I tugged and twisted her nipples as she kept coming. When she started to settle down, and the tension started to leave her body, I moved off her. "Get on your knees and lay your head on the pillow. Ass in the air," I ordered. She slowly rolled over and got to her knees. I could tell she was still shaky. Good. She spreads her ass cheeks with her hands.

I didn't give her time to prepare for me. I grabbed her hips and slid into her in one long, hard stroke. She was tight and slick from her orgasm. She moaned as I parted that tender flesh. My balls slapped off her pussy as I bottomed out.

"Ahh, that's it. You feel so damn good, babe. This pussy is the best in the world. I wish I could stay here all the time. Hold on. I need it hard and fast tonight."

Her fingers stroked my hard length between her legs as I pulled back. "Do it. I want it hard and fast. Make me feel you tomorrow, honey. Fuck me raw," she cried out. The image that put in my mind made me forget where I was. I attacked her pussy like a man who'd been denied sex for years. I pounded in and out of her. The air filled with the scent of sex and the sound of our bodies coming together. My balls bounced off her wet pussy as I sank every inch of myself into her.

Grunts, moans and groans filled the air too. I don't know how long that lasted before she began to beg me. "Please, oh God, please, come. I need you to fill me. I want to drip your cum all day tomorrow. Give it to me harder."

I grabbed her long hair and pulled her head back. Her neck and back arched, and it changed the angle of my penetration. I lifted her until her back was flush to my chest. I thrust up into her hard. She was breathing hard. I felt her start to tighten. I wanted us to come together. I wrapped my hand around her throat and squeezed a tiny bit. She clawed at my arm as she screamed and she gushed down my legs. I kept thrusting until my balls tightened and the fire raced through me to my cock. I roared as I came. I filled her with jet after jet of my cum.

"That's it. Take it all," I hissed. She shook and shook in my arms as she milked me dry. When we both collapsed to the bed, it was all I could do not to fall on top of her. I fell to the side and wrapped her in my arms. I was still inside of her and tiny tremors kept shaking both of us.

Sometime later, when we could move, I kissed her tenderly. We took our time kissing and caressing each other. I didn't say a word. It wasn't necessary. I saw the love in her eyes and I knew she could see it in mine. My cock had softened, and I'd fallen out of her. I got up and grabbed a washcloth. I cleaned myself up and then her before I crawled back in bed and tugged her back into my arms. I kissed her. By the time I was done, she was already asleep. "I love you," I whispered before I closed my eyes.

Undertaker: Chapter 23

We stayed with the Soldiers in Pataskala for two more days. I wanted to head out the day after the gun sale, but Slither had other plans. He wanted to talk about the various businesses. It was like a cork had been removed. He shared most of the ins-and-outs of the prostitution business they ran in the various towns. I was able to confirm the other four clubs they had infiltrated. He bragged about how they had been stupid and never saw it coming. I noticed that Curly, Jester, Nox, and Frost didn't look pleased when he said that.

The more I saw, the less I thought the four of them were with the Soldiers because they wanted to be. I hoped when this was over, I could save any of the good men who'd been forced into working with these bastards.

On top of sharing their prostitution business, he told me more about where he could get us more drugs to supplement what Lobo was making. He had a couple of places. I made sure to remember what he told me. Also, he told me where his contact was who supplied him with his weapons. He was a guy who'd been in the military and still had active-duty contacts. I'd gladly take that fucker and his friends down.

On day three, we said our goodbyes and headed back to the Renegades' compound. I was happy to see it, only because it meant Sloan and I would be able to get some peace and stay at the motel. Or at least I hoped we would. It wasn't long after we got back that I let Dax and the others know we were going to head back to our motel. He tried to convince us to stay, but I told him I needed to get our stuff at the motel and make sure they hadn't given our room away. He agreed only after I promised we'd move over to the compound the next day. Things were about to get crazy. I had so much to tell Sean, Griffin, and Gabe.

As soon as we got settled back in our room, I did a sweep to be sure no one had bugged our room while we were gone. It was clean. We sat down on the bed and I called the guys. I now had my phone back and it had been checked for bugs and was clear. I hadn't wanted to chance a call while I was with Slither and them. It was answered on the second ring by Sean.

"Where the fuck have you been? We've been going crazy worrying about you," he barked.

"Hey, calm down. I couldn't call. We had to stay with Slither and the rest of the bastards. We just got back to Cleveland and our motel room. I'm sorry you were worried, but we couldn't risk our cover. I have a crap load to tell you."

"Sorry. It's been tense as hell here. Cassidy has been worried out of her mind. Griffin, Gabe, and I haven't known what to tell her. We kept hoping since neither of you pressed your emergency alert buttons that you were both okay."

"We're fine. It's been tense for us too. Listen, I won't bore you with all the details. I just need you to check out some things. Slither and the guys told me a lot about how they run things and who some of their top contacts are. I need you to carefully check into them and see if you can verify if what he told me is true. If it is, I think we should have enough to take them down and clean up the other clubs they took over."

"Shit, that was quick. Okay, do you wanna tell me over the phone or send it to me on the secure site?"

"I'll send it all in writing as soon as we get off here. I need you to get this verified as fast as you can. I don't wanna stay here a moment longer than I have to."

"Absolutely. How's Sloan doing?"

"I'm fine, Sean. Tell Cassidy that we're doing okay. Mark is right. We want to get these dirtbags behind bars as fast as we can."

"I'll get started tonight. I can't wait until you guys get home. Reaper will be overjoyed to hear the news. Do you want me to tell him, Mark?"

"Hold off for now. I don't want to get his hopes up, just in case we have to stay longer than we think. As soon as we have this lot taken care of, I'll personally call him and Cheyenne. Is anyone else there with you?"

"Cassidy is with Noah, trying to get him to sleep," Sean said. At that moment, I heard two other voices join him.

"Hey, man, we're here. It's so good to hear your voice. We'll get to work on this as well. I admit, when we met that bunch the other night, they made us want to take a shower afterward. I don't know how you and Sloan can stand to be around them," Gabe added.

"It's an effort. I still think that some of the old guard isn't doing it because they want to. I believe they're being threatened. Something they're old ladies said to Sloan made it seem like it. If that's the case, I'm hoping we can help them instead of taking them down with this bunch too. It might not be possible, but I'd like to try."

We chatted for a few more minutes. It was enough time for Cassidy to join and I got to hear her cry. I hated that I was causing her so much worry after what she'd already been through. As soon as she settled, we told them goodbye. Sloan sat beside me as I typed up the information for the team. She added a few comments here and there. It took me over an hour to get all the pertinent information down. Once it was, I sent it off and put away my laptop. I looked at her. God, she was so damn beautiful. If anything happened to her, I'd never forgive myself.

"Don't, Mark. I can see what you're thinking. You didn't drag me into this. I came willingly. If I had to do it all over again, I wouldn't change a thing. There is no way I could stay away while you had to deal with this."

"Sloan, things are heating up. While I hope we can take them down soon, it could get messy. I don't want to have you here when that happens. I can make up an excuse for why you had to leave. A sick mother or grandmother would do it. Let me get you out of here," I pleaded.

She shook her head. "I can't and won't do it. You're

not going to be left to deal with this alone. We're in this together, no matter what. Besides, my backstory is I grew up in foster care and have no family."

I got up off the bed and paced around the small room. I wanted to hit something or better yet someone.

"Do you know what it'll do to me if something happens to you? Do you? It will kill me, Sloan. I fucking love you more than anything. I'm not the sort of man who lets his woman be in danger. It's not how I'm made."

"I know that. And I'm not the kind of woman who lets her man put himself in danger and not be there to help him anyway I can. We're so close, I can feel it. Let's not rock the boat. Sending me away, no matter what excuse you give, could make them suspicious. We can do this."

I sighed then sank back down on the bed. I pulled her into my arms and held her tight. She wrapped her arms around me. We didn't say another word. We just held each other. We fell asleep, holding each other.

It was a restless night for both of us. The next morning, I woke up exhausted. She had circles under her eyes. Reluctantly, we got up and took a shower then got ready to head back to the Renegades' clubhouse. We had work to do.

When we got there, she greeted Jane and Carla, who were in the common room. Both of them hugged her. Seeing that made me hope again that I could save a few of them from prosecution. Dax and Roman were behind closed doors when I went looking for them. The rest of the club seemed to be sleeping off the night before or back to drinking already—all except for Nox, Frost, Curly, and Jester. The four of them were huddled in the corner, whispering softly. When I went over to them, they abruptly stopped talking.

"Mind if I join you guys?"

"No go ahead," Curly said as he glanced at the others. I could tell they weren't excited to have me there. I sat down. Sloan was over talking to the ladies.

"What do you think of this new business I'm bringing to the club?" I asked them suddenly. It took them by surprise and they weren't able to mask their distaste fast enough.

"It's the direction Dax and the officers think we should go. We'll do what's good for the club," Jester hastily said.

"I can understand not trusting it. It's a lot to take on, but I promise, it'll all be worth it. Hey, I've been curious. You guys were here with the old guard. What was it like? I mean, I know you all were legit and shit, but did you like it?"

They hesitated then Curly was the one to answer me. "It was legit, but we enjoyed running our businesses. We had a good reputation around town and we did a lot for our community. Our wives spent a lot of time here, even if we weren't. It was just different. There were more old ladies then and some kids."

"It can be like that again. Do you guys want kids? Slo and I do. I'm hoping we might get started on the first one as soon as things get settled here." I was trying to let them see that I wasn't as bad as I might seem. I wanted so badly to ask them to trust me, but I couldn't risk blowing my cover.

Curly and Jester looked surprised at my admission. "You want kids?" Jester asked. I nodded. "Well, I can't say that Carla and I haven't talked about having some. It just doesn't seem that the club would welcome it. I want my kids to grow up safe and protected, you know what I mean?"

"I do. I want the same thing. A brotherhood is what I want. One that protects each other. I think there's a place for your businesses in all of this. Not just as fronts for the other stuff. I saw when we toured them how much work and pride you take in them. I don't see that disappearing. Nor would I want it to."

I didn't say any more. I'd let them think about what I said. We sat there talking about their businesses for a bit until they had to go. When they left, I went over to the ladies. I flung my arm around Sloan's shoulders and kissed her temple. "Hey, babe, you doing alright?"

"I'm fine, Undertaker. The ladies and I were going to start working on something for dinner later. Are you still waiting to talk to Dax and Roman?"

"Yeah. They should be done soon. Don't let me stop you ladies. I can't wait to see what you prepare." I smiled at the other ladies then took myself off. With Roman and Dax otherwise busy and the others into their own thing, I took a chance and wandered around the small compound. Everyone lived either at the clubhouse or off the compound like Jester and Curly. I knew from Sloan that they had houses in town.

I took note of the defenses, which other than a

flimsy chain link fence, wasn't anything. They didn't have cameras or anything I could see that would tell them if someone was coming. That was good to know. I'd been out there for maybe an hour when Vic came looking for me. He was flushed and out of breath.

"Dax wants to see you. He's been wondering where you were."

"Just getting more familiar with the club. I like to know all there is about my new home," was all I told him. I followed him back to the clubhouse. When I got there, Dax and Roman were waiting at the door. Neither of them looked pleased. I ignored their looks and smiled as I greeted them.

"Good afternoon. It's a great day, isn't it?"

"Where have you been?" Dax asked tersely.

"Exploring. I thought I'd see what all the compound had to offer. If you don't mind me saying, I have a few ideas about what we could do to beef up security around here. You can never be too careful." My response seemed to take them by surprise. I kept going as we walked into the clubhouse.

"Are you ready to meet and go over the next steps? I'd like to meet and talk to some of the whores. It'll give me a better idea if any of them can be brought up to snuff for the higher-end clients. Once I know that, we can start working on getting more from my contacts."

Talking about business was the right approach. They relaxed, and we sat down to talk. It was a slow afternoon. They didn't want to go today. They said we'd go tomorrow. I tried not to show that I was anxious.

However, I knew I had to give Sean and the guys time to check out what I'd sent them. They wouldn't be able to move right away on anything.

The ladies fed all of us an excellent dinner. Sloan and I stayed until the bunnies and the guys started to hook up, then we excused ourselves for the night. We wouldn't be going back to the motel anymore. Dax was insisting we stay here. That made it impossible for me to talk to the guys, though I did check my phone to see if I had any messages from them. When it was a go, they'd promised to text me a message that would just say, *looking forward to doing more business soon.*

The next day, I went to the motel with the club. Alvin was watching them today. I sat through several interviews with the women. It was heartbreaking to see them. I could tell out of the dozen I spoke to, maybe three of them were there because they chose to be. And even those three seemed like they didn't think they had any other choice but to sell themselves.

When we were done, we stopped by to check on the bar. It was the middle of the day, so business was slow. Tyson was behind the bar. I wondered if the man ever took time off. We sat down and he came over to chat with us. I noticed the club seemed to be relaxing around me and they weren't watching what they said. I got some more information just from listening to them. How in the hell they hadn't been taken down before this, I don't know?

That night, I made slow gentle love to Sloan. I wanted to show her how much I loved her. While I liked sex usually hard and fast, with her I could do it slow and easy. Every time with her was the best I'd ever had.

It wasn't until the weekend that things changed. Early Saturday morning I got the text I'd been waiting for from the guys. I had no idea what time to expect them, but it would be today. I quickly warned Sloan to stay close to me. We both made sure our weapons were loaded and easily accessible. I sent up a prayer that we'd get out of this in one piece.

We were sitting with most of the club, having a drink, when Mattie came running into the clubhouse. He was pale and sweating. He came straight over to Dax. "T-there's several dark SUVs coming down the road. It looks like trouble. What should I do?"

Dax jumped to his feet and yelled for the others to hide the guns and anything else they had that would attract unwanted attention. I watched as they took up boards in the floor and stashed the incriminating stuff. Sloan and I hurried around, helping where we could. I saw Roman giving us questioning looks. He was suspicious.

We'd barely gotten the boards back in place when the door came crashing open and in marched a load of other men I didn't know. I knew they had to be the ATF guys. An agent stepped forward and called out a couple of names. When Dax, Roman, and Hook answered them, they approached them and said they were under arrest. From there, it was pandemonium. The others tried to run, or at least Grumble, Sig and Cage did. Jester, Curly, Frost and Nox seemed to be resigned to their fate. They didn't put up a fight.

Carla and Jane cried, but they went peacefully. The bunnies, on the other hand, went crazy and were fighting the agents. One guy got a good scratch to his face from Erica. Sloan and I put up a fight. We didn't want to blow our cover. She screamed at the agents and was shoved to the floor. I'd be talking to that agent when we were done. There was no need for him to be that rough. I resisted the two trying to put cuffs on me. They hit me in the face and took me to the ground because I let them.

More agents poured in and started to search the place. I'd have to clue them into the floors later. We were marched out to waiting vehicles and started to get inside. That's when it happened. I heard a yell and turned to see Vic had gotten away from the agent who'd had a hold of him outside. Somehow, he'd gotten his hands on a gun and was pointing it in my direction.

"I knew it. You're a goddamn narc," he screamed. In slow motion, I saw his finger squeeze the trigger. I heard Sloan scream from a distance then agony blossomed through my chest. I hit the ground. I couldn't catch my breath. Chaos reigned around me, but all I could do was look at Sloan. She was bent over me, crying. Her hands were pressing on my chest even though they were cuffed. I could feel myself slipping away.

"Please, please, hang on, Mark," she pleaded.

I lifted my hand and wiped the tears away. "I love you," I whispered. It hurt to talk.

"I know, I love you too. You can't let go. Please, we have a whole life ahead of us."

I tried to answer her, to reassure her I wasn't going to give up, but nothing would come out. As I stared at her, my eyes got hazy and then everything went black.

Undertaker: Epilogue
Two months later

Annoying beeping caused me to pry my eyes open. I looked around in confusion. Where was I? The last thing I recalled was being shot and then everything going black as Sloan cried beside me. As I glanced around, I realized I was in a hospital room. The beeping was from the machines I seemed to be hooked up to.

I shifted my weight and groaned at the pain that went through my chest. I noticed Sloan sleeping in a chair beside the bed. She jerked awake. Her eyes met mine and widened as she took in the fact that I was awake. She bounded to her feet and hurried to me. Tears were already streaming down her face.

"Oh my God, you're awake. Mark, I've been so worried," she sobbed. She laid her head down on the bed.

I lifted my hand and caressed her hair. "Baby, it's alright. You know it takes more than a gunshot to kill me. Tell me, did they get everyone yesterday? Where are Sean and the guys?"

She lifted her head and gave me a concerned look. "We need to let the doctors know you're awake.

They'll want to examine you." Before I could protest, she pushed the call light.

"How may I help you?" the voice on the other end said.

"He's awake. Will you please tell his doctor?"

"Of course, we'll be right there."

"Babe, forget about the doctor. I want to know what happened. What time is it?" I looked around to see if I could find a clock.

She fussed but didn't answer me. I was about to ask her again when a couple of doctors and a nurse entered my room. They jumped straight to asking me a million questions. I answered several until I had had enough. "What the fuck is your problem? Why all the damn questions about my head and what I remember? I was shot in the damn chest. Though it doesn't feel too bad now, so it must've not been as bad as it felt at first. I want to talk to my woman and see my friends," I growled. The one that I assumed was the head doctor frowned at me.

"Mr. O'Rourke, we're trying to assess your mental state. Yes, you were shot in the chest, but it was a very traumatic wound. We lost you more than once and had to bring you back. You've been in a coma."

I jerked in surprise. I looked at Sloan to see if he was telling me the truth. She nodded her head. "How long have I been out?" I asked hoarsely.

She sniffed. "Two months. We didn't know if you were ever going to wake up." Her voice broke, and she sat down in the chair, sobbing her heart out. I wanted to get up and get to her. I needed to hold her and reassure her. The fact that I'd been in a coma for two months didn't seem to be real. No wonder my chest didn't hurt much.

Over the next several hours, I was rushed from one test to another. I tried not to lose my temper with all the stuff they seemed to think they needed to do. Each time I came back to my room, she was there waiting for me. I drank in the sight of her. Finally, after they'd poked and prodded me to death, they left me in my room with her. I opened my arms even though it hurt my chest. "Come here, baby."

She came over to me and crawled up on the bed. She curled up against my good side. "God, Mark, I thought you'd never wake up. The guys and Cassidy will be here soon. I told them they needed to wait until the doctors were done with all your tests. They're so excited to see you."

"How're you doing?"

"Me? I'm fine now that you're okay."

"Babe, look at me. I'm sorry that I put you through this. I never wanted to have you worry about me. I want to know what happened with the clubs, but first I need to know how you're really doing. You've lost weight and you're pale. Have you been staying here with me the whole time?"

Before she could do more than nod, the door to my room opened and in came Cassidy, Sean, Gabe, and Griffin. I was greeted by their hellos and Cassidy's tears. She hugged me carefully. Sloan tried to get up off the bed, but I wouldn't let her.

Once they settled down, I asked them, "Tell me what happened. Did they get everyone? Tell me that Slither and Ogre went down with the rest of them. What happened with Jester, Frost, Nox, and Curly? Are they going to get the same charges as Dax and the others? Did you find all their contacts?"

Sean laughed. "Hold on, one question at a time. I don't think you should be worrying about this right now. Everything was taken care of. You need to worry about healing and getting your ass out of here."

"I will as soon as I know they're all behind bars. Is there any chance they might come after me or Sloan?"

Gabe shook his head. "No, you don't need to worry about that. As far as they know, you were killed and Sloan was arrested. Yes, we think we got all of them. You'll be happy to know, they're never going to see daylight again. We got all their contacts."

"What about Reaper? Is he disappointed that he didn't get to take out Slither and Ogre?"

Griffin exchanged a look with the guys then looked at me. "He didn't get his chance, that's true, but he did get his revenge. It seems that someone on the inside of the prison had a grudge against Slither and Ogre. The feds don't know why. He's not talking. He's a lifer who was in there for more than one count of murder. He killed both of them."

I couldn't help but smile. I bet that lifer had a connection to the Iron Punishers or at least one of their friends. "Were you able to help those women?"

"We were. Most of them were being forced to

work as whores like you suspected. A few thought they couldn't do anything else. For their testimony, they're getting immunity and a chance to start new lives. As for Curly, Jester, Nox and Frost, they're going to serve time, but not like the others. They're also turning over evidence on Dax and the others. They were threatened into helping the club or they would kill their families."

I sagged in relief. That was one of my main concerns. I hated that they would see time, but it was better than the rest. "So, it's over. We can get on with our lives. As soon as I get out of here, we're getting married," I told Sloan.

"Did you tell him?" Cassidy asked Sloan. I saw a funny look come over her and she shook her head no.

"Tell me what?"

"We'll leave you two alone. We'll be back tomorrow. We're so glad to see you awake, man," Sean said. He and the guys all gave me fist bumps. Cassidy protested as she gave me a kiss and let Sean pull her out of the room. As soon as they were gone, I looked at Sloan. She was avoiding my stare. She tried to get off the bed again, but I held her tightly.

"Look at me. Tell me what Cassidy meant. What aren't you telling me?" I was afraid she was going to tell me she'd changed her mind and no longer wanted to marry me. If she didn't, I'd do everything in my power to convince her to change her mind. I couldn't live without her.

"Mark, I didn't know. I swear I didn't. I want you to know that."

"You didn't know what? Come on, talk to me. You're scaring the hell out of me. What's wrong? Don't you want to marry me anymore?"

Her eyes flew up to look at mine. I could see the love in them. "Of course, I want to marry you. I love you. I'm just not sure you're still going to want to marry me."

"Why wouldn't I want to marry you?"

"I don't want you to feel trapped. I didn't do it on purpose. It was an accident."

I impatiently asked her, "What was an accident?" If she didn't tell me in the next few seconds, I was going to lose my cool.

She took my hand and slid it down her chest and then rested it on her belly. It took a few seconds for the significance of what she was doing to sink in. When it did, my heart accelerated and I couldn't catch my breath. Was she telling me what I thought she was?

"Are you pregnant?" I whispered. She nodded. I crushed my mouth to hers and I kissed her with all the love and joy I felt. We got lost in that kiss and didn't break it until she pushed me away.

"You're happy about it?"

"Of course, I'm happy. I love you and there's nothing I want more than to start a family with you. Aren't you happy?"

"I'm beyond happy. I just worried it was too soon. We've barely known each other for three months."

"It doesn't matter how long we've known each other. All I care about is that you and the baby are healthy. Are you? You look pale and you've lost weight," I asked with concern.

"I'm fine. Just some morning sickness which is easing up. The doctor told me that weight loss isn't unusual."

"You should be home resting, not sleeping in a damn chair next to my bed," I growled.

"I couldn't rest. I needed to be here."

I rubbed my hand gently over her still flat stomach. "How far along are you? Do you know when it happened?"

"I do. The doctor did an ultrasound. It looks like my birth control shot ran out and I forgot it was time to renew with everything going on. He said I got pregnant almost immediately. The baby is due October thirtieth. I'm fourteen-and-a-half weeks along."

Her answer blew me away. She was already a third of the way through the pregnancy. I'd missed so much. "Jesus, we have so much to do. We need to get married, set up the nursery, buy stuff for the baby. Do you know what it is yet?"

"Slow down. We have plenty of time to do all that. As for the sex, we'll have to wait a few more weeks to find out. Do you have a preference?"

"No, I just want a healthy you and baby. I need to get my ass out of this bed."

She spent the better part of an hour getting me to see that I couldn't get up and leave. In the end, I had to stay another week in the hospital. The one good thing about the coma was my gunshot wound was mostly healed when I woke up. I impatiently waited to get out. I had a life to live and a woman to marry.

Sloan: Epilogue One month later

The last month has been a crazy haze. Mark got out of the hospital and a week later, we were married in a small ceremony with just his closest friends, Sean, Gabe, Griffin, and Cassidy in attendance. We were having a reception later with all the staff at the Dark Patriots. We didn't want to wait and have a big production wedding. That wasn't us.

We'd been getting the work done on the nursery. He wasn't up to doing it himself, so the guys were doing it for us. I tried to tell him I could paint it, but he refused to let me smell the fumes. He'd been treating me like I was fragile. I tried to tell him I was fine and pregnancy didn't make me sick. He didn't listen. Finally, I gave up trying.

Today, we were in my doctor's office. He'd just finished my exam, and the tech was getting me prepped for the ultrasound. I know I had a tiny belly showing. I was eighteen and a half weeks along. We were hoping the baby would cooperate and let us see what we were having. I was hoping for a boy. I thought that would be the perfect way to start a family—a son to look out for his younger siblings. I knew that we both wanted more than one child.

Mark was holding onto my hand as the tech put the gel on my stomach and moved the wand around my stomach. We both smiled as we heard the whoosh of a heartbeat. It sounded strong and fast. The doctor was watching the screen with her. After a couple of intense minutes, he smiled and looked at us.

"Everything looks good. The baby is growing and right on track for where I'd expect you to be. You're gaining weight, which is good. Are you ready to find out what you're having?"

"You can see what it is?" Mark asked with an excited look on his face. My doctor nodded. "Yes, please, we want to know."

"Congratulations, you're going to have a baby boy," he announced. I saw Mark freeze for a second then he was kissing me. As he did, the doctor and his tech left the room. When he was done kissing me breathless, he closed his eyes.

"Thank you. Thank you for loving me and giving me a family. This is one of the happiest days of my life."

"I should be thanking you for loving me. I never imagined my life would turn out like this. I can't believe we're having a son."

"Baby, I promise you, no matter what, I won't be taking any more assignments like those last two. I'm here to stay. Undertaker might have been resurrected, but only so he could assume the real life he's supposed to have. Let's get out of here and share the news with our family."

He helped me get cleaned up. I couldn't help but

smile as we left the doctor's office to share our joy. Mark held onto my hand the whole way home. As we pulled into the driveway, I saw there were pink and blue balloons tied to the porch and our family was waiting with smiles on their faces. The best decision of my life was to take a job with the Dark Patriots and say yes to the assignment with Mark. I'd found my happily ever after and I wasn't going to ever let it go.

The End Until TBD Book 2 Dark Patriots

Printed in Great Britain
by Amazon